The Lethean Gentlemen

Also by Dominick Pratico

non-fiction

Eisenhower and Social Security: The Origins of the Disability Program

fiction

The Enemy Within

The Lethean Gentlemen

A Novel

Dominick Pratico

iUniverse, Inc.
Bloomington

The Lethean Gentlemen

iUniverse books may be ordered through booksellers or by contacting:

iUniverse
1663 Liberty Drive
Bloomington, IN 47403
www.iuniverse.com
1-800-Authors (1-800-288-4677)

ISBN: 978-1-4759-0778-0 (sc)
ISBN: 978-1-4759-0777-3 (e)

Printed in the United States of America

iUniverse rev. date: 4/19/2012

For Chrissy, the love of my life

The history of the Interstellar Web was written and taught as if the Union of Worlds was inevitable, and that the prosperity it brought a birthright. Web citizens tended to think of themselves, the residents of The Great Elliptical Galaxy, as one homogenious group. In fact, nothing was further from the truth.

In the beginning, worlds were isolated and inter-global communication and commerce was minimal. Ethnic, economic and religious concerns varied greatly from world to world and quadrant to quadrant. Compounded by social stratification, these divisions became even more distinct. What brought these disparate groups together was wealth. Revisionists have long tried to disguise this fundamental truth. The simple fact is that there has never been complete agreement on government, religion or ideology, but the want for a system that generated personal wealth—and the comforts that came with it—cut across all cultural lines.

All innovation and progress had its root in improving commerce. Simple conquest and then the Interstellar Corporations bound worlds together.

Not ideology.

Not religion.

Not politics.

All of the things that gave them pause, the divisions along racial, sectional and ethnic lines, simmered under the surface as all chased what they felt was owed to them, and the power it brought. This ethos could not sustain itself forever, and tensions had begun to boil over. Social and political unrest had pushed The Web to the brink.

And then came the Vaengel.

The War Against The Enemy brought true unity to The Interstellar Web. Sectional and racial divisions were discarded as all of society came together to repel, and then finally defeat, The Enemy Threat. The Post War Era became a time of unparalleled prosperity.

And fear.

Fear of the random and persistent acts of Enemy terrorism, and the emotional and material destruction it wrought. Employment opportunities created by the need to rebuild and secure dozens of shattered, frightened worlds fueled the economic boom. Many corporations profited from this enormous investment in the infrastructure of The Web, both large and small. With the specter of anti-matter holocausts now a daily part of life, the necessities of this constant state of prepardness brought advances in all disciplines– science, engineering, medicine and munitions, among others, and these advances benefited no corporation more than Abernathé Stoneworks.

Based on the virtually lawless world of Lethe, the syndicate that would become AbStone flourished for generations as a power limited to the Outer Haven star system. Lorenzo de Abernathé created a financial empire based on corruption and greed, and maintained it through thievery, extortion and thuggery. As time passed, his only son, Lorenzo II, founded Abernathé Stoneworks and used it to expand his family's influence beyond the solar system and over the entire Quadrant. Under his deftly ruthless direction, the organization haltingly altered its business practices and gained some acceptance in the realm of legitimate enterprises.

At the start, AbStone dealt only in precious stones as both a wholesaler and retailer. Under the guidance of Lorenzo III, AbStone's interests expanded in the Post War Era to include other raw materials, and the procurement and refining of various ores, metal and glass, key components to the rebuilding effort.

Even with all this success, Lorenzo III remained unsatisfied to thrive only as a local figure, for AbStone to remain a mere regional power. He sought to build AbStone into a Web wide juggernaut and to have the Abernathé name, *his name,* revered across the entire galaxy just as it was on Lethe. To accomplish this he would have to tear down the reigning corporate superpowers, particularly the Cathedral Corporation and NYSAAC. And then after a chance meeting with the mysterious Mr. Ecks, when the secret of a staggering fortune in precious stones fell into his lap, it was all suddenly within his grasp.

The business and political climate of the Post War Era served as the perfect veil for AbStone to complete its transformation from a motley criminal organization into a fully legitimate business enterprise. Lorenzo III carefully and quietly accomplished this move into the mainstream, much to the chagrin of his father, who at a relatively young age was forced to yield more and more authority to his son due to a string of devastating illnesses. Over time Lorenzo II became consumed with maintaining his health, to the exclusion of all else. He eventually dropped out of sight altogether, leading many to speculate that he had gone mad in his pursuit of immortality. AbStone and the Abernathé family refuted such rumors, of course, and after a time, refused to acknowledge them at all.

Chapter 1
Ven Ashram

On this quiet antebellum morning, eight years before The War Against The Enemy, the sun shone brightly over the City of Ven Ashram. The barest wisp of a spring breeze whistled gently through the ancient man made canyons of the Ricezza Nova peninsula, and the sky breathed as clear and clean as a cold glass jar. Grand spires towered over a pristine ocean shoreline, where the ornate windows reflected the light that sparkled on the blue waters below.

A single aircar cruised over the old charm of the Sothemax section in the early dawn. It glided easily away from the peninsula, along the coastline, headed north.

Rocco Sicuro wearily steered the car safely away from the skyport and gladly put the old skyscrapers behind him. It had been a long trip, but finally, at last, they were almost home. He glanced into the rear view mirror where his wife, Saffron, sat comfortably in the back seat. Bathed in the warm sunlight, she gazed down into the infant seat next to her. She smiled and adjusted a colorful plastic mobile. As the infant seat faced the back of the car, Rocco could only hear Pierce's contented, sleepy breathing.

Saffron caught his eye in the mirror.

"Oh, Rocky, you should see him," she smiled. "He's such a good baby."

She touched the baby's nose gently and he cooed softly, raising a tiny hand to grasp her finger.

"Not for long if you don't let him alone," he said gruffly.

"Oh, he's fine," she beamed. "He sleeps so well."

"Yeah. Kid's been quiet since we hit orbit."

A smile cracked Rocco's sullen visage. He scratched at the stubble on his chin and ran his knuckles thoughtfully along the edge of his rounded jaw line.

It had been three weeks since they left the starport orbiting the Rim world of Dalton Five. The adoption people had kept them waiting for hours that day. All day, really. Instantly cross at the memory, a dark scowl settled easily on his large face.

He sourly recalled those offices, with the glass walls, the cushioned fabric furniture and cold marble tables. Everything so clean and neat. Everyone in the place with ties and suits. Rocco didn't even own a shirt with a collar.

Those people thought they could push him around because he didn't have an expensive haircut or a thin waist. The rooms were perfect, the people perfect, and it made the hours they waited seem like days, and Saffron, poor Saffy, hid her tears in his arms the whole time, convinced that something had gone wrong. They had said it would only be a few minutes, but instead it dragged on for hours.

Long hours.

And those people told them *nothing.*

Through it all, Rocco remained strong. He was always strong. He enveloped her in his big, thick arms and held her so closely that she all but disappeared in his embrace. With only her golden hair visible below his shoulder, he held her upright for the entire day. He wouldn't give those people the satisfaction of putting her in one of those chairs.

Even now, well past his prime, Rocco hardly felt her mass at all. He'd been hauling all kinds of burdens his entire life, all of them much heavier than his precious Saffron, but none of greater weight. His wife had always been thin, waif-like, and when the sun caressed her back, she seemed almost transparent, her golden blonde hair blending in with the light.

And that corporate holding pen had plenty of light.

The longer he held her and the more she cried, the angrier he became. He comforted her with a gentleness that belied his calloused hands and unrefined appearance. He swore to himself that the next twerp in a tie that wandered in to ask if they wanted more coffee and doughnuts was going to get hurt. No one pained his wife like this, disappointed her so cruelly, not without answering to him.

By this time, he'd started to wonder if they'd made some mistake in the process, or if something in their background check had suddenly made them unfit. What could it be? They hid nothing. He was very candid about his Marine service in The Canite War, his job with the sanitation department at the starport, that they lived on Gran Nexus, that Saffy never finished college, that he never went...was that it? They weren't educated enough? Or that they already had three boys of their own? He earned a good living, they lived good lives. They said they were good people.

Rocco snarled at the memory of that moment. He inadvertently mumbled something out loud and covered it with a loud cough. He cleared his throat self-consciously and readjusted himself in his seat. He glanced quickly at Saffy in the mirror. She seemed not to notice.

Rocco covered his frowning mouth with the back of his hand like he always did, and again pondered that moment. A set of wooden doors in the next room over suddenly flew open and through the glass walls, Rocco saw him. He gently turned Saffron around. A nurse stood primly in that doorway, in a starched white uniform, trimmed in red. She cradled a blue swaddle.

Saffron wiped at her nose and dried her eyes. Annoyed, she pushed hard against Rocco to free herself from his powerful, suffocating embrace. She stepped cautiously away from him. Another woman in business attire appeared, followed by a man in a charcoal suit. The business woman opened the glass doors for the nurse. Rocco recognized her as one of the adoption chicken necks they had met earlier in the day. The man was unrecognizable and walked with an ebony cane. Just looking at him gave Rocco a chill, and was glad when the man remained in the other room to watch through the glass.

The nurse entered. The business woman followed.

Saffron hesitated.

"Is it...?"

The nurse smiled.

"Yes. He—"

The business woman interjected.

"His name is Pierce."

"Oh," Saffron sighed affectionately. "Oh, Rocky...a little boy."

Rocco glared at the woman, just for spite.

"Unless you decide to change it," she said quickly.

"Pierce is a lovely name," Saffron breathed. "Can I...?"

"He's all yours," the nurse said, carefully handing over the sleeping baby. "He's just two standard months old—"

"Yes," said the business woman. She handed Rocco a silver disc. "Here is all of the baby's biographical and medical data. He's in perfect health."

He snatched the disc and then put himself between Saffy and these other people. He purposely turned his back on them and put his thick arm around his wife and new son.

"Is there anything else," he asked over his shoulder.

"No. You can leave whenever you're ready."

And they left.

Rocco picked up the carrier from the floor and led Saffron, rocking Pierce gently in her arms, out the glass doors, out the wooden doors, out of the building, and off that planet.

Fast forward three weeks later, and here they all were, two hundred meters over Ven Ashram, almost home. Rocco angled the aircar due north, following the forested sections that still existed within the city limits. He stayed safely above the trees so the intakes wouldn't get clogged with leaves. He spied the steeple of Peroxide di Doloret e Sophrire, and the adjacent parking lot, and angled his descent.

Almost there.

Rocco gazed down at the old church and smiled a bit, in spite of himself. This all started right down there, three years ago.

The church stood proudly on the common border of three neighborhoods, Doloret, Sophrire and Piacevole. Doloret and Sophrire presided as the older communities, with histories going back thousands of years. Fifty years ago, Piacevole had been carved out of some undeveloped park land and neglected sections of Doloret and Sophrire. The government made these lots available to those unable to afford homes in Sothemax. Affordable lots within the city limits of Ven Ashram, especially this close to the Ricezza Nova, were scarce. The legal resistance on the part of their future neighbors was fierce, but ultimately futile.

Piacevole, where the Sicuro's lived, boasted a much larger population than Doloret and Sophrire, and some tension existed between the three communities. The older families of Doloret and Sophrire turned their noses up at the working class that comprised Piacevole. While nurturing their dislike for one another, these three neighborhoods did agree on the issue of religion. The Church of Peroxide, honoring one of the demi-gods that served Clorox, became a focal point for all three communities.

Rocco had little use for religion. While raised in the traditions of the Clorox Pantheon, their hold on him as a child had been weak. His military service left the remainder of his faith badly shaken. He could not reconcile a belief in a benevolent, higher power after what he had seen on The Rim. Had he not married Saffron immediately upon his discharge, he would never have set foot in a church again. She insisted that they go to services together, and he couldn't disappoint her. They had long ago stopped arguing over the subject but once Dante, their oldest, was born, she constantly warned him against setting a poor example.

Three years ago, during the winter High Holy Days.

The whitest of the whitenecks, the now infamous Father Foco Sfiatatoio, stood at the pulpit that night. He had been hissing and spitting his own unique brand of fanaticism for what seemed like forever, while Rocco dozed on and off. The guys were old enough to behave themselves by then, for five minute stretches at least, and Saffron nudged him in the ribs when he started to snore.

Little Alex had been out of diapers for awhile, and Dante and Antonino were in school all day. Saffron had been listless for months, then all of a sudden restless or overly emotional. Rocco took her to the picture shows, to dinner, or took the guys out of the house for long afternoon stretches, but nothing seemed to make her happy. She finally confessed that she wanted another baby. No one had forgotten how difficult Alex's delivery had been, and how she'd nearly died. The thought of putting her life at risk again sent Rocco through the roof. He vehemently refused. She insisted that they take it up with a priest, but he steered her toward their doctor instead, and the doctor sided with Rocco.

She tried to put on a happy face, for his sake, but he knew that deep down she was lost and very sad. Her unhappiness pained him, but he didn't know what else to do. That's when Father Frick Face got his hooks into her.

Father Sfiatatoio liked to think of himself as the cutting edge, modern holy man. Rocco didn't like it that politics colored his preaching. His favorite topics spanned the ruination of The Rim to the plight of the brave colonists crushed by the evil corporations, the same evil corporations who ran wild, unchecked by the military or the government.

Rocco had been there, to The Rim. Sfiatatoio had not. Sfiatatoio abused his standing in the community to make himself a false authority on a subject of which he had no first hand knowledge. He merely parroted the prevailing opinions offered by the media. His posturing eventually attracted the attention of powerful people and he got into trouble over fundraising. He was defrocked for his efforts. Rumors now had him out at Pomellego working with mutant children, but the cynics, like Rocco, believed he was really in prison.

Three years ago.

Rocco had only a vague recollection of exactly what Sfiatatoio said that night. It was all about orphaned children, and how they were being sold into prostitution and slavery on The Rim. Of course, Rocco knew the truth. It wasn't just orphans, but parents selling off their own offspring for profit as well. And somehow, through his own snoring and their three boys pinching and slapping each other, Father Sfiatatoio got through to Saffron. From that moment on, their adoption of one of these lost children of The Rim was inevitable. Rocco hoped to put her off until she got over this premature empty nest syndrome, but he never had a chance. A few days later, after her refusal to let the matter drop, he angered her when he said that adopting a Rim child was like buying a used aircar, just inheriting someone else's defective merchandise.

She slapped him in the face for that.

Hard.

And he took it, but not because he was wrong. After a very pregnant pause, she challenged him to dispute what Father Sfiatatoio had said about how children were treated on The Rim. He remembered the exchange like it happened yesterday.

"Not every kid—"

"Tell me it doesn't happen."

"Even in the Inner Web—"

"Tell me it's better out there than here."

Irritated beyond reason, he screamed at her.

"Saffy, you don't understand! What that part of space does to people, it screws them up! Turns them into...into *animals!* That's why colonists are on a one way ticket! That's why they can't come back!"

"Tell me here is not better! Tell me *we* are not better!"

They went around in circles for hours, but he couldn't change her mind. Father Frick Face had given her the holy high ground. They sparred for a few more weeks before he finally relented. There would be no living with her if he didn't do this. And maybe, just maybe, they would get lucky that whatever kid they rescued from a nightmare of a life didn't turn theirs into one instead.

Rocco still had some old friends, a few connections in the Marines. Ron Burke was still in, a Lieutenant now, posted out at Quagmar. Yaza piloted bulk freighters for Cathedral Corp, near Ursus. Roulon had a security gig for AbStone on Lethe.

He ultimately made some headway through Roulon, which made sense as his old pal had a reputation as an operator when they were "in". Rocco had always liked Roulon, and was sorry to learn that his wife had left him rather than follow him out to Lethe. Roulon got them an interview with the adoption agency and offered an endorsement using an AbStone masthead.

Then came the interviews. Background checks. Visits by the executives to their house. Interviewing their kids. Interviewing their neighbors, his bosses, his old CO from the service. Finance checks. Everything but cavity searches. And then the fees. There were always fees. It went on for years. Three long, draining, expensive years.

He looked again in the rearview mirror. Saffron smiled beautifully in the morning sun, and a tiny hand reached up and grasped her finger, then slipped away. The little hand appeared again and this time got a firm grip, with all six little fingers. Rocco yawned wearily.

And he would do it all over again.

In a second.

All for his beautiful wife.

The ground flattened out below them and the trees gave way to the suburban sprawl of clapboard houses and townhouses that comprised Piacevole. He merged into the main artery of air traffic that moved swiftly over the snarl of ground vehicles that clogged the central avenue below. He circled over their block, a corner known locally as Serenity Mission, where they'd lived for the last eleven years. He landed the aircar on the small landing port on top of their garage. He powered down the car and the dashboard went dark.

Everything was quiet.

He looked back at Saffron, who already had Pierce in her arms. They smiled at one another and she took his hand, moving forward so he could see the baby.

Pierce had his whole fist in his mouth.

"This kid's a circus act," Rocco grunted. He pulled the tiny fist away by tugging at the corner of Pierce's elbow. Pierce put his fist right back into his mouth. "Won't quit, either."

"We should go in," Saffron said. "The boys will be happy to see us."

"It's early. They're probably not up yet. Today a school day?"

Saffron nodded.

"We should enjoy the quiet for another minute, then."

The back door suddenly flew open, and their three boys burst through the doorway. Antonino led the charge and threw his arms up in the air, shouting at the top of his lungs.

"THEY'RE HOME!!! THEY'RE BACK!!! THEY'RE BACK!!! DANTE!! DANTE!! DANTE!! ALEX, C'MON!!!"

Bounding across the small yard, the boys barrelled toward the garage. They roughly tackled and pushed one another to reach the steps first. Nino surged ahead, jumping and waving.

"I TOLD YOU THEY'D BE BACK BEFORE MY BIRTHDAY," he shouted. "DADDAY! MOMMAY!"

Saffron smiled and Rocco rolled his eyes. He wearily got out of the car, then helped out his wife and new child. She smiled brightly as she held the baby close to her. A gentle breeze and the warm sun…it all seemed to radiate from her. She stood on her toes and kissed her husband on the cheek.

"Thank you, Rocky," she whispered.

"DADDAY!"

He embraced Saffy against his broad chest, kissed her forehead, and held them both tightly.

All three of the boys were yelling now.

"DADDAY! MOMMAY!"

Rocco lumbered down the steps.

"Who're you animals barkin' at down here?"

They pounced on him at once, and he gathered them up in his burly arms. Dante, now ten, was big for his age and strong enough now to knock him over all by himself. Rocco tumbled backward onto the bottom steps as his three boys bumped, elbowed and fussed for his attention. They all talked at once, trying to tell him everything that had happened since they'd gone.

"Nino said you were going to let him get a tattoo for his birthday, just like yours," Alex pouted. "If he does, I want one, too."

"What?"

"You said when I was old enough, and eight is plenty old," Nino said, slapping his brother's shoulder. "Big mouth!"

"You get one when you can pay for one," Rocco said.

"Cool," Dante said, pumping his fist. "I'm gettin' one like a race car!"

"No," Alex said. "It's got to be a knife, like Dad's!"

"No—"

"Dad," Nino said, "can I come to work with you at the starport, to get some money?"

"Guys, guys, guys" Rocco shouted over them, nuzzling all of their heads at once. "We'll talk about tattoos another day. There's someone I want you to meet."

They all stood up as Saffron came down the stairs, cradling the baby in her arms.

"Boys," Rocco said, "this is your new brother."

The children gathered around Saffron to get a closer look at Pierce.

She smiled at them all.

"I trust you were good boys while we were gone?"

"Yes," they all droned at once.

"Is that what Mrs. Vicinotta is going to tell me?"

The boys glanced at each other nervously, then nodded hesitantly in meek solidarity.

Rocco looked right at Alex.

"What's broken, young man?"

"It was Dante, Dad! Not me! He knocked over the lamp in the hall, I tried to fix it, but—"

"You jerk," Dante said. "Dad, he always does this—!"

"Enough," Rocco said, tapping the side of Dante's head gently with the back of his hand. "Later."

The baby yawned loudly, commanding everyone's attention.

"Is it a boy," Nino asked. "What's his name?"

"This is Pierce," Saffron smiled. "Your new brother."

"And what about his real Mom and Dad," Dante asked. "Where are they?"

Rocco felt the disc in his pocket.

"They're dead, son."

"They died in the bad place? Where you fought the war?"

"Yeah. On The Rim."

Nino leaned in closer.

"And you and Mommy went back out there, to rescue him?"

"We did."

"Did you get shot at?"

Rocco laughed.

"No, Nino, we didn't. It wasn't like that where we were."

"Can I touch him," Alex asked.

"Sure, honey, go ahead," Saffron said, and crouched a bit so the small boy could reach.

Alex reached out with a shaky finger and Pierce grabbed it tightly.

Alex smiled.

"He's so warm. Hey! He's got too many fingers! Cool!"

The boys chattered excitedly and looked closer.

"Only on that one hand," Saffron explained.

"That's just weird," Dante commented, wrinkling his nose.

"Oh, don't say that, dear," Saffron scolded gently, standing up straighter. "It's just another reason that he's special."

Dante smiled.

"Does he have six toes, too?"

"All right, that's enough," Rocco admonished, nuzzling his head. "You nut."

"If you boys will all excuse me," Saffron said. "Pierce and I need to go inside and get settled, and I want to talk to Mrs. Vicinotta."

The boys started to follow their mother across the lawn, chattering loudly, hopping and shoving.

Rocco called them back.

"Hey, you apes! Get over here!"

The boys stopped and turned back, round shouldered.

"Wha-a-a-at?"

"There's a whole car full of your mother's stuff that needs to be brought into the house. Get busy, all of you!"

They trudged back up the stairs and Rocco followed, chuckling softly to himself. He opened the trunk to the car and then paused.

"Hang on a minute, guys. We need to talk."

He got down on one knee as his sons gathered around him.

"I know we talked about this before we left, but I want to make sure you understand the way it's going to be around here from now on."

He looked at each one of them, pointing a finger as he spoke.

"Pierce is your brother now. He's one of us. He's a Sicuro. And he's just a little guy. That means we've got to help him. And protect him."

"How are we supposed to do that, Dad," Alex asked.

Rocco smiled at him.

"It wasn't so long ago that you were just like that. It's gonna be your job to teach him how to walk, okay?"

"I can do that, Dad," he said, suddenly beaming. "What about running, and jumping? I can teach him how to throw a ball, too!"

"All good ideas."

"What about me, Dad," Nino asked. "What's my job?"

"Mommy's going to need help at meal times. You can help feed Pierce, get his food ready. Can you handle that?"

"Yeah, but Dad—," he whined.

"And," Rocco said, talking over him. "You can paint his crib and table, and help me put together some of his toys."

"Yeah," he said pumping his fist.

"Now you two get started bringing this stuff into the house."

Nino and Alex yanked a pair of heavy bags out of the trunk and started hauling them toward the stairs, dragging them roughly across the pavement.

"Pick up those bags, dammit," Rocco shouted.

The boys obeyed, struggling to hold them off the ground as they walked.

Rocco stood up and put his arm around Dante, leading him a few steps away from the car.

"Dad?"

"I have the most important job for you, son."

Dante nodded.

"You're the biggest, you're the oldest. I don't want anybody hassling Pierce. Ever. You understand?"

"No sweat, Dad. I already do that for Neen, Alex and Mommy. I can handle it."

"Nobody hassles Pierce, not even your brothers."

Dante looked at him strangely.

"Why—"

"Remember when Alex was born?"

"Yeah, Neen used to shake his crib, and—"

"It's gonna be awhile before Pierce can take care of himself. Mommy's not going to be able to pay attention to you dopes as much as you want."

"I know, I know, you said the same thing when Alex was born."

"Yeah, and Nino still dropped all his stuff out the window! Nothing like that will happen this time, understand?"

"Dad—"

"You will protect him. You will keep your brothers in line."

"Dad—"

"—or it's *your* ass!"

"Okay! Okay!"

Rocco took a deep breath.

"He's just a little guy."

"I can handle it, Dad."

Rocco looked down at him. Dante already stood as tall as his shoulder. For a moment, he was awed by his son's size and strength.

"You better."

Dante punched his father playfully in the arm.

"There's nothing you and me can't handle, right Dad?"

Rocco smiled.

"That's right. C'mon, let's get the rest of this stuff. And if I know Mrs. Vicinotta, and I do, she'll want to take a holo."

They took a couple of bags out of the car, then Dante paused and turned to his father.

"Was it really bad there, Dad?"

"Bad where?"

"Where Pierce came from?"

Rocco took another deep breath.

"Yeah. Yeah, it was."

Dante nodded seriously.

"Don't worry, Dad. I'll take care of him just fine."

CHAPTER 2
SUMMA AVARICI

Few places on the planet Lethe weren't hot and humid. As a bastion of the shamelessly rich, only the wealthiest of them could afford to live in the cooler climes. The Abernathé family kept ownership over this whole world, and they chose to live within the reaches of the antarctic circle, residing on the largest of the southern continents. The narrow, angular peaks of the Summa Avarici Mountains ringed the interior of this frigid, regal land mass. The tops of the snow capped peaks disappeared into the rolling, frosty mists.

Nestled into the ridges of the steepest canyons stood the Castel Mons, the home of the Abernathé family. Constructed from stone blocks cut from the surrounding mountains, the castle took fifteen years to build. Masons placed each stone by hand, with great care and precision. All of the details of the construction were overseen by Lorenzo de Abernathé I, and the colossal structure dominated the coastline. The anniversary date of its completion had been celebrated every year for the last one hundred years.

Four massive buildings formed the heart of the structure, each one larger than the next, with smaller and equally magnificent apartments surrounding them. A river surged beneath its powerful walls and a dozen massive towers studded the perimeter at regular intervals. It appeared as a mighty citadel and bustled as a small city unto itself.

Three proud generations of Abernathé's had lived here and Lorenzo de Abernathé III carried himself no differently. At 32 years of age, he was just coming into his own as patriarch of the family. Still young and handsome by any standard, he wore his jet black hair long and kept lean and fit, but had yet to produce any offspring. Both his father and grandfather had already made their marks on the Web by his age, and soon the galaxy would revere his name as well.

As the sun descended into a hazy twilight, Lorenzo sat in his study, which had been his father's and his grandfather's before him. With his clean shaven chin perched on his thumb, he watched the monitor on the desk in front of him intently. After a few minutes, he got up and stood in front of the great window that overlooked the ocean. Through glass eight and a half meters tall, he watched the sun set into the fog that rolled in off the water.

Tiers of bookshelves ringed the square room. Actual books, with actual paper and leather covers, surrounded him on three sides. They had no real purpose as relics from a long dead era, but the rarity of printed literature gave them some modest value.

His reflection shone clearly on the polished glass. His dark suit was unwrinkled and his hair combed neatly, setting about his shoulders just the way he liked. His hands in his pockets, he cast a long, dark shadow over the desk behind him.

Once the sun had set completely and the window became like a mirror, he turned back to his desk. Still standing, he looked at the monitor again without expression. He pressed a button and the console disappeared beneath the marble desk top.

Without looking up, he realized that he was no longer alone. He turned back to the window and saw in the reflection an old man with an ebony cane standing stiffly near the door.

James Cervello had been in his family's employ for over forty years. Cervello worked directly for his father, doing whatever needed to be done, without hesitation. Cervello's loyalty to his father was admirable, but misplaced. His first obligation should be to the family, and that meant him, but some of his actions indicated otherwise, like this habit of entering his study without announcing himself.

Lorenzo didn't trust him.

"Good evening, James," he said. "What are you doing here? You're supposed to be on Dalton Five."

"I arrived yesterday, in the evening. I returned only after the successful completion of your business there."

"What do you want, then?"

"Your father would like to see you, Lorenzo."

Lorenzo nodded.

"And what have told him?"

"Why, nothing, Lorenzo! You delivered your instructions to me very clearly. I have discussed nothing with your father."

"Do not feign indignation with me, James," he sighed. "You wear your deceit like a cellophane mask."

Cervello cleared his throat.

"Your father is waiting, Lorenzo."

"And?"

"The procedure was successful. His body has accepted the new liver and kidneys."

"And the cancer?"

"Gone."

He cursed softly to himself. To mask his anger, he sipped from a glass of cold water on his desk, set on a diamond encrusted marble coaster.

"And his mood today?"

"Much brighter, I think."

Lorenzo turned and walked across the room. Cervello held the large door open for him as he passed through, buttoning his jacket. Lorenzo's footfalls echoed on the marble floor as he walked briskly down the hall. Cervello followed with difficulty, his cane clicking on the floor.

"Does he know what year it is today," Lorenzo asked, not bothering to turn around, his voice echoing off the stone walls. "Is he going to throw things again?"

"One can never tell, Lorenzo," Cervello puffed. "But when I saw him this morning, he had all of his faculties."

Lorenzo stopped in front of the door to his father's bedroom. He straightened his tie, waiting impatiently for Cervello to catch up.

"I don't want to be in there for more than five minutes, James."

Cervello paused to catch his breath. He dabbed at his bald forehead with a white handkerchief.

"You know I don't—"

"I don't care what you don't like," Lorenzo said curtly. "In five minutes, you will enter and announce that there is some urgent stone business I must attend to."

"I work for your father, Lorenzo. We both do."

"I have the business, James. I control the money."

Cervello straightened his jacket and tie and put his handkerchief in his pocket.

"Yes, but your father still runs this family."

Lorenzo turned and looked at the old servant.

"*My* family, James. Mine. Not yours."

Cervello cleared his throat.

"Of course, Lorenzo." He grasped the door handle and pushed open the huge wooden door.

Lorenzo entered his father's bedroom and Cervello followed. Lorenzo stopped and glared at him. With an exaggerated nod of his head, Cervello backed out into the hall and closed the door as he went.

Lorenzo de Abernathé II dozed lazily in a bed of polished snakewood. Big, fluffy pillows enveloped his thin head. His arms rested neatly on top of silk sheets and a puffy down comforter. A variety of tubes protruded from his arms and numerous vital signs monitors on carts hummed with power. Constellations, as seen in the Lethean night sky, decorated the high, domed ceiling. A young nurse sat quietly in a chair at his bedside, checking his vitals, adjusting his pillows. She stepped away when Lorenzo entered. She self consciously fixed her hair and smoothed her white uniform.

"Mr. Abernathé," she said, her eyes shyly failing to meet his. "Good evening. He's been asking for you."

Lorenzo said nothing.

His father, The Finest Lethean Gentleman, was now in his 81st year. He'd been dying for over a decade, but somehow always managed to cheat the black end. Coronary artery disease. Diabetic blindness. Crippling arthritis, first in his hips, then neck. And now a certainly lethal trifecta of cirrhosis, renal failure and lung cancer.

All trifles.

He simply refused to die. His innate stubbornness, when combined with the resources of half a dozen solar systems, made even the ridiculous suddenly plausible.

The Old Man, still with a full head of snow white hair, slept rather grotesquely. With his mouth agape, his tongue draped over his lower teeth and saliva dripped down the side of his face. The nurse dabbed the moisture away with a clean, white towel.

Multi-trillionaire businessman. Founder of Abernathé Stoneworks. A philanthropist when it suited. If they could only see him now.

"What do you want, Pop," Lorenzo asked loudly.

The elder Abernathé awoke with a start.

"Lorenzo?" He squinted in the dim light. "Is that you, son?"

"What do you want?"

"James," he croaked. "James told me that you went ahead and bought out Vangata."

"Yes," Lorenzo replied impatiently. "The transaction was completed yesterday."

"Even after I told you not to?"

"Pop..."

"You waited until I was in surgery," he shouted, "and went behind my back like a coward?!"

"Pop..."

"I said, *a coward!*"

Lorenzo refused to be baited into losing his composure.

"Pop, they were the only local distributor with the drills that could withstand the heat and pressure of the volcanic furnaces on Ustione."

"Lease the damn things, instead, Lorenzo! Fiscal irresponsibility—"

Lorenzo sighed.

"They declined a leasing arrangement. Cathedral is paying them to withhold the equipment from us. I told you before, the

Cathedral Corporation is moving into the stone trade. They want to block NYSAAC from using pestlestones in their prototype fusion ship drives—"

"Oh, nobody uses fusion anymore, Lorenzo," he said, shaking his head angrily. "You need to talk to the Vangats. Talk business. Work out a deal."

Lorenzo shook his head.

"They refused all of our overtures."

"So?"

"Pop, it's not like that anymore."

"Sounds to me like you got scared."

"Pop..."

The Old Man's eyes narrowed and his mouth became like a slit in a money box.

"Afraid to get your hands dirty, Lorenzo?"

"They wouldn't lease, so I bought them out instead. A simple business decision."

"But the overhead of maintaining the equipment, more employees—I've told you again and again, minimize your costs!"

Lorenzo took a deep breath. For all his business acumen, his father simply couldn't grasp the amount of personal wealth the Abernathé family possessed, which was dwarfed by the net worth of Abernathé Stoneworks. Buying Vangata was an annoyance, nothing more. As he stood here, Vangata was being dissolved. The five hundred or so employees had already been fired and the company's assets liquidated. The drilling equipment they needed was already enroute to Ustione. The conditions on Ustione were so harsh that the hardware would most likely be destroyed in the mining process. Any pieces that survived could be reused on other jobs or parted to fix other machines. He projected the profit margin at, minimally, a thousand percent. And all without resorting to thuggery.

"Pop, I run the company now."

"And I will not let you run it into the ground! Don't you ever forget that this is still *my* planet!" He paused for breath. "Did you ever stop to think *why* Cathedral is moving against us?"

"NYSAAC needs our pestlestones—"

"We are not the only source of pestlestones in this galaxy!"

"But we are the most accessible. Pop—"

"If your grandfather could see you now, he'd die all over again from the shame."

Lorenzo glanced at the nurse, who followed their every word. She wilted under his gaze and averted her eyes, pretending to adjust the IV drip.

"If grandpa could see *me* now, Pop? What about you?"

His expression went dark. An angry shadow fell over his craggy face.

"*You* do not judge *me*."

"This...this business with the clones, Pop. It has to stop."

"I don't want to hear—"

"It has to stop," he shouted. "What you're doing is abominable... disgusting and, and..."

Both men fell silent.

"Are you saying I'm disgusting, Lorenzo? Then what about *you?*"

"It's not the same thing."

"Maybe I should send James to check the freezers, then?"

"I said, it's not the same thing."

"Of course it isn't, you hypocrite. Always the moral high ground with you. But me? I wouldn't be here now without those cloned organs. Would you rather I be dead?"

"Pop, they're living beings—"

"They are not!! They're me!! It all comes from me!! They have no free will, they have no souls. They have no legal standing!! They're my property!!"

Lorenzo spoke emphatically.

"It was one thing to create insentient tissue, but whole bodies? Adult bodies? And now you've set them to manufacturing children? *Infants?* Why, Pop?"

"*Because I must live!*"

"You can't live forever."

"But I am not ready to die! So much is unfinished—"

"Pop—"

"I will persist, *I will live,* for as long as I need to," he insisted, jabbing an index finger into the bed. "It is my *right.*"

Lorenzo shook his head in frustration.

"When?! When will you decide that you've lived long enough?"

The Old Man averted his eyes.

"You know that I have periods of fugue, forgetfulness."

"Yes."

"My doctors have a theory about that."

"I know all about it. Pop, you will not raise cloned children to harvest their brains. I won't allow it. It's fantasy—"

"So was my heart transplant! My liver transplant! They said they couldn't be done. The pancreas, too. In spite of all that, it's all starting to slip away, Lorenzo. My mind, my memories...it's so hard simply to think...but it can be fixed."

"No, it can't."

"Yes, it can."

"No!"

"Yes!"

"You've had no success cloning a perfect copy of yourself as an adult. The infants are no different! Some of the defects are horrifying, Pop! It's...it's inhuman!"

Lorenzo glanced at the nurse. She had moved away from the two men, self consciously trying to busy herself with the monitors. His eyes went from the young woman to his father, then back to the woman again.

"Mr. Abernathé, perhaps I should leave," she suggested akwardly.

"That won't be necessary," Lorenzo said, frowning a bit. "My father requires constant medical attention."

"Yes, that's right," the Old Man said. "Certainly, my dear, you don't think I'm some kind of monster, like my son does, do you?"

She blushed shyly.

"O-of course not, sir." She glanced at Lornezo uneasily.

Lorenzo stood up straighter.

"Pop, I'm blowing up the labs and killing the scientists. This all ends now."

"You wouldn't dare."

"Pop, I run the company now. It's me they listen to. *Me.* Not you."

The Old Man frowned and banged his gnarled hands on the bed rails.

"Damn you, Lorenzo! Damn you!" He looked up, tears streaming from his eyes. "There were breakthroughs. Seven, maybe eight of the babies, the worst of the transcription errors were limited to an extra finger. Their minds were free to develop…one of them could save me. I can't believe that you would murder children! Murder me!"

Lorenzo buried his smooth hands in his suit pockets and glanced over his shoulder at the door. He took a cautious step away and glanced everywhere in the room but at his father.

The Old Man watched his son through his tears. For a moment was right again.

Shrewd.

Perceptive.

Intuitive.

He studied Lorenzo's face, the slight tick of his jawbone, the slightly rounded shoulders. He saw through his son in an instant.

The Old Man nodded.

"You've already done it, haven't you?"

Lorenzo's tongue poked into his cheek.

"Yes."

The Old Man's eyes narrowed.

"But you didn't kill the babies, did you?"

"Pop…"

The Old Man smiled cynically.

"I'm not so far gone yet that I can't read my own son!"

"It's over, Pop."

"Not so long as those children live."

"You'll never find them."

"I will."

Lorenzo grit his teeth in a childlike fury.

"Let it go, Pop. We'll find some other way to restore your faculties."

"You think I'm powerless because I'm in this bed, Lorenzo?!! You were always so, so naiive."

"I said to let it go, Pop."

The Old Man's lower lip trembled.

"My son, my only son...has killed me."

There was a knock at the door.

"Go away," the Old Man shouted.

"Come in," Lorenzo shouted over him.

They glared at each other angrily, then watched the door.

It opened without a sound. Cervello entered.

"I said to get out," the Old Man screamed.

"What is it, James," Lorenzo asked calmly.

"Lorenzo, Mr. Venison is requesting to speak with you regarding the Vangata acquisition."

Lorenzo nodded.

"I have business to attend to, Pop. I will check on you later."

The Old Man slumped back angrily into his pillows.

"I need something to drink!"

The nurse sprang back to life and brought a glass of water to his bedside.

Lorenzo paused to confer with Cervello in the doorway.

"Better late than never. Thank you, James."

"This is no ruse, Lorenzo. Mr. Venison is waiting in your study."

Lorenzo flushed with anger. He would deal with Cervello later. He watched as the young nurse held the glass close enough to his father's mouth so he could drink using a straw.

"Kill her," Lorenzo said. "Today. She doesn't leave this house."

"Your father likes her."

"Too bad. She's heard too much."

"I understand."

"For your sake, James, I hope you do."

Lorenzo eyed him severely, then walked purposefully down the hall.

Cervello closed the door behind him softly, then approached his employer of forty years.

"Mr. Abernathé, is there anything else you require?"

"Yes," he said, waving the nurse away. "The infants still live, but Lorenzo has seen fit to disperse them. I want them found. Establish a new facility and bring them there. You must see this through, James, even if I...I...cannot communicate my wishes. I do not trust Lorenzo, but I trust you, my old friend. Am I clear?"

Cervello put his hand on Abernathé's reassuringly.

"Of course, sir."

The Old Man relaxed, visibly relieved of all his worries in the presence of his remaining loyal retainer.

"Now leave me. I need to rest. I'm so tired..."

He was asleep in an instant.

Cervello walked around the bed and took the nurse elegantly by the hand.

"Miss, if you'll please come with me. Mr. Abernathé does not wish to be disturbed. May I offer you some refreshment?"

The young woman smiled.

"Why thank you. That's very nice of you."

He smiled in return and led her out of the room.

Chapter 3
The Timberland Fens

The Sicuro men lived outdoors. They took every opportunity to escape to the woods. A day without killing and skinning a stag was like a day without sunshine. As a right of passage, they learned how to stalk prey, handle weaponry and survive in the elements.

Save one.

Saffron abhorred these frequent hunting trips and refused to allow little nine year old Pierce to participate. It didn't matter to her that the rest of the boys had started hunting at the same age. It didn't matter that Alex and Nino teased him about it. She wanted at least one of her sons to not consider the *Lasers and Bolt Clips* annual as great literature.

To Saffron's relief, Pierce showed little interest in these outings and his young mind accepted it simply as something his brothers did, and not him. Rocco fumed over his indifference and turned uncharacteristically subtle in undermining his wife's mission to sissify the boy. For three weeks, he spoke excitedly of the next hunting trip within Pierce's earshot, but never to him directly. He told the other boys to do the same.

When Rocco announced at dinner one night that the next hunting trip would be that weekend, Pierce was suddenly desperate to come along. His mother flatly refused. Normally a very obedient and agreeable child, especially to his mother, Pierce put up a tantrum like Alex never did, and once his father spoke up in his favor, Saffron relented. As success rarely comes without cost, Rocco spent the night on the couch.

Pierce could barely contain himself for the two hour car ride out to the forest. They left well before dawn. Saffron fussed over them all, saying over and over again that they'd thank her later. She stuffed Pierce into a sweatshirt, then over that a sweater, and topped him off with a fleece coat. She tied Rocco's scarf around his neck extra tight. The other boys stripped everything off once they got in the car, but Pierce kept his on, worried that his mother might find out.

It was still dark when they arrived at their usual spot in the Timberland Fens. Rocco, Alex and Nino took their guns and gear and disappeared into the black, misty trees. Dante led Pierce to a stag blind, where they settled in. Having Dante to himself appealed greatly to Pierce, and he immediately expected something happen. He clutched a small pistol to his chest and looked around eagerly, half expecting a stag to jump right into the blind with them. His mood quickly soured when his older brother sternly told him to sit still and be quiet.

A hush fell over the dense, dark woodland. After two days of steady rain, the air had a cold, dank feel. By the time the sky gradually brightened with the dawn, Pierce had grown bored and irritated. The thrill of the hunt had worn off the second the mossy ground soaked through the seat of his pants. He morosely watched the wet leaves, orange ones, brown ones and some yellow, fall to the ground with dull smacks. He listened to the trees grow. He counted the water droplets condensing on the flat, green paddies.

What was supposed to be fun about this, he had no idea. Thinking back on it, he didn't understand why he even wanted to come in the first place. He pulled absent mindedly at a patch of grass next to his leg and sighed loudly.

Dante's head snapped around and he put a finger over his lips severely. Pierce rolled his eyes.

Even with four kilograms of shirt on, Pierce could still feel the gray cold. He admired Dante for the way he sat perfectly still, his cheeks flushed, white breath puffing in the damp air. Even without a coat, the chill had no effect on him. He sat big and strong, his massive bulk compacted, but ready to move in an instant. All of his brothers were bigger and stronger. No matter how hard Pierce exercised or how much he ate, he remained a skinny, wiry kid.

Dante held a rifle in his hand, a long brown one that fired old style projectiles.

A real gun.

His father wouldn't let him use anything but an old Moon pistol with a filtered clip. It had no kick and wouldn't disturb the dirt at point blank range. Pierce knew better than to ask to handle one of the real guns. It annoyed him when they all treated him like a baby, which they did all the time. He sometimes felt like he had four mothers instead of just one, and the one was more than enough.

Some leaves rustled in the distance.

"Did you hear that," Pierce whispered. "I heard a stag!"

Dante smiled and shook his head.

"No, that's Nino and Alex. And be *quiet.*"

"Are you sure?" Pierce looked around. "I don't see them."

Dante pointed at a big tree some twenty meters away.

"They're over there."

Pierce squinted. He still didn't see them.

Dante pointed to his eyes.

"Don't. Just listen. And smell. Especially with stag. You smell anything?"

Pierce closed his eyes and took a deep breath through his nose. He shook his head. "No, just—" He stopped speaking suddenly, then opened his eyes. He looked away from Dante, embarrassed.

"What?"

"I don't smell anything."

"No?"

"No."

"Pierce..."

The young boy shook his head vociferously.

Dante frowned.

"Alright. No more talking." He flashed a hand signal. "Use the cant."

Pierce didn't like to be teased, especially by Dante, who he admired so much. The truth was that the forest smelled a cold, terrible pewter blue, almost a silver.

Ever since he was a baby, Pierce perceived things differently from other kids, other people. Numbers and letters suggested certain colors, as did music and other sounds, along with odors. His mother became concerned about him as a toddler, when he complained that the letters in his wooden jigsaw puzzles were the wrong color. He insisted that the letter A was blue and not green, that the letter B was red and not yellow, and so on. He would tell his mother that his breakfast smelled orange and tasted pink or that the music coming from Nino and Alex's room sounded purple or red.

Pierce didn't simply read, listen or taste. He savored. He got lost when looking at simple letters, absorbed by whole novellas. Music of the right color captivated him, as did certain scented candles his mother used, and the way the kitchen smelled just before dinner. The world around could be so rich and colorful, full of such vibrance and power, but he had to be careful. Some things that he found disagreeable made him physically ill.

The doctors who examined him identified this condition as synesthesia, and while this initially upset Saffron, she eventually came to accept it. She made every effort to surround him with things that appealed to him, and it was only with her that he felt comfortable describing what he perceived. This was the real reason that Saffron did not want Pierce going into The Timberland Fens. Given the intensity with which he experienced things, she feared what encountering something truly ugly would do to him.

Pierce's brothers kept his synesthesia a closely guarded secret within the family. Stories had begun circulating in the media about kids who had their gene sequences altered while still in the womb. There was a lot of loose talk about it, none of it good. That didn't stop them from teasing him mercilessly about it, as only brothers could. Pierce kept his perceptions and observations largely to himself, and felt that he could only express himself to his mother. For Saffron, the only one who seemed to understand him and could provide some comfort, he always saw as a warm, soft yellow. Unless she was angry. Then she became a dark, dark pink. He didn't like pink.

Dante looked at him and tapped his foot with his own.

"What's this I hear about you and that canite kid, Niqi?"

Pierce responded with a hand signal.

"S'all right. There's nothing around, just whisper."

"He's a jerkface."

Dante nodded.

"So for that, you knocked his front teeth out?"

"He started it. He made fun of me for dropping the ball. I'm the best player in the class and everyone knows it! He's the one that stinks!"

Dante waved at him to lower his voice.

"Shhh. It's just not like you, is all."

"Why? It's what you would've done! You never let anyone push you around—"

"Yeah, but you gotta learn when to ignore people. Especially when they're bigger than you."

"I'm not a wimp!"

"No, but you're not a brawler, either. You got lucky this time, Pierce. If you're going to pick fights, pick them with guys your own size."

Pierce folded his arms angrily and stared in a huff at the ground.

"What do you care, anyway? You're leaving for the Army tomorrow."

Dante nodded.

"*The Marines*, Pierce. Yeah, I have to report tomorrow, but that doesn't mean this continues. I want you to promise me you won't get into anymore fights. You're not that kind of kid."

"Okay," Pierce mumbled. "Fine."

"I mean it! And you know Mom doesn't like it."

"Fine, fine," Pierce said, annoyed, waving him off. "*Fine*."

"And I won't be around to stop Dad from beating your ass."

"I said all right!"

A twig snapped loudly, silencing them both. Dante cautiously peered over the blind and then ducked back down. Pierce looked at him eagerly. Dante nodded.

Pierce signed that he wanted to see it.

Dante indicated for him to go ahead, but be careful.

Pierce stood on his toes to see over the blind. A stag nosed about in the brush, close to a hundred meters away. It was huge, standing about two meters at the shoulder, with a rack of massive black antlers. He ducked back down quickly.

Pierce pointed to his eyes and smiled. He canted, 'What now?'

Dante showed him his gun. Pierce nodded, clutching his own weapon. Together, they leaned over the blind. Dante took careful aim with his rifle and Pierce copied him, holding his laser out straight.

At that moment, the animal's head jerked around. Nino tripped and fell out into the open from behind a tree. Dante and Pierce fired, just as the stag bolted in alarm. The loud register from Dante's rifle echoed in the quiet woods, and he missed his target. The thunder of three more rifle blasts assaulted Pierce's senses and the stag went down in a puff of green leaves. Pierce crouched in the blind and threw his hands over his ears. He winced painfully as tears ran down his cheeks.

Alex came running forward from behind Nino, holding his rifle over his head.

"I got him! I got him," he shouted over and over.

Dante put his hand on Pierce's shoulder.

"You okay?"

Dante's voice was muffled, distant. Pierce wiped his face with his hand and nodded.

"C'mon, then," Dante said, pulling him up. They ran out to join Alex.

"Blazes you did," Nino called after his brother. "I got him!"

"From your knees? No way," Alex said. "I got him!"

Dante was quick enough to head him off.

"Stop right there, Alex," he said quickly, pointing at him. "Don't get too close until we know its dead."

Nino strode confidently toward them.

"Outta my way, Dante. I shot it clean through the head."

Dante stepped in his way.

"No, you're wrong, and that thing'll spear you with its antlers."

Nino hesitated, then twitched his head and shoulders to crack his thick neck.

"I told you, I shot it through the head."

"You're unblieveable," Alex said. "You go by you, you've never missed a shot in your entire life! I tell you, *I* shot it!"

Dante smirked at them both.

"You think so?"

"Yeah," they both said at the same time.

Dante looked at Pierce.

"What do you think?"

His ears still ringing, Pierce responded uneasily.

"I think you all missed."

"What do you know, Pierce," Nino said angrily. "I mean, really?"

Pierce became just as angry.

"I'll bet you the front seat on the way home you all missed!"

Nino blew a raspberry.

"You're on!"

Cautiously, the four brothers approached the fallen stag. Moving the brush aside with their rifles, they found the animal lying on its side, a big chunk of its hind quarters a bloody mess. Blood speckled the surrounding plants and matted the ground red.

Pierce stared wide eyed at the carnage, then clutched at Dante's shirt. Dante put his arm around his little brother and then turned to Nino.

"Through the head, huh?"

"Up yours, Dante."

Dante ignored him and looked upward.

"Nice shot, Dad."

Sitting above the four brothers, in a low hanging tree branch, was their father, his rifle set casually across his lap. He jumped to the ground and joined them.

Rocco looked at them all and grunted.

"Nice shot, my ass."

He looked at Nino.

"Now *I* would've shot it through the head if you could keep your clumsy feet! Keep your hand outta your ass next time!"

Nino flushed a deep red, then nodded.

"Sorry, Dad."

Alex was next.

"Are you desperate to get gored? Like a little girl you were—'I got him! I got him!'?" He imitated Alex running through the woods. Nino laughed and Alex punched him in the arm.

"Shut up!"

Rocco glared at Dante.

"And you. What're you, cockeyed? How could you miss a shot like that?"

Dante shrugged it off.

"One of those things, I guess. Can't get 'em all."

Rocco fumed, then put his hand on Dante's shoulder.

"Son, where you're going, you can't afford to miss targets like that."

"I won't."

"You can't. Listen, some of these guys, they think they're invincible in these armored rigs and omnisuits. The easiest way to score a hit is in the chest, but that part of the body is usually protected. If you just wanna knock a target down, that's the way to go. Otherwise, it's the neck and head, or any joint. The neck is always vulnerable. Good aim, steady hand. *Never panic.* Understand?"

Dante smiled weakly, and Rocco patted his shoulder roughly.

"Anyway, Pierce here is the only one of ya that can shoot," Rocco barked. "He hit it square in the back of the head."

"Lucky shot," Alex said.

"More than once," Rocco shouted, making Alex flinch. "Nothing is lucky if you take the time to prepare yourself. How many times I gotta tell ya?"

"D-Dad," Pierce said, still clutching Dante. "W-what about the stag?"

Rocco cleared his throat and moved around to the head of the wounded animal. He put the barrel of the shotgun against its head. Pierce bolted from Dante's side and ran for several meters, until he couldn't see anyone. He put his hands over his ears and shuddered at the sound of the fateful discharge.

"If any of you meat heads could shoot straight," his father's voice said, "that wouldn't have been necessary."

Pierce huddled close to the damp, cold ground. He wanted nothing more than to go home to the warm yellow embrace of his mother. He caught a glimpse of something moving far ahead of him and the waft of a dirty brown, almost black scent that washed over him. He inhaled the mucous from his nose into his mouth and spit it out furiously, trying to clear the stench from his nostrils. In a moment, it was gone and he shivered, but not because of the cold. In the stillness, the only noise came from the ringing in his ears.

The leaves rustled behind him.

Pierce turned around and Rocco walked toward him.

"What's the matter with you," he asked gruffly.

Pierce relaxed in the presence of his father, but still couldn't shake this sudden chill.

"Dad, why did you..."

"What, shoot the stag?"

Pierce nodded slowly.

"It's why we're out here, isn't it?"

"But it was already shot."

Rocco shook his head.

"It's wrong to let an animal suffer like that."

"But—"

"If this is how you're gonna act, next time you can stay home and wash dishes with your mother! We're not out here to pick flowers, you get me?"

Pierce nodded slowly. His brothers surrounded them now.

Dante put his arm around Pierce and nodded reassuringly. Pierce choked back his tears and casually tried to conceal himself behind his older brother. Rocco looked them over and smiled a bit, then led the way back to the stag.

They all stood around the carcass, Pierce the closest. He stood with his hands on his hips and his skinny chest puffed out.

"This thing must weight a ton," he announced, waving his arms. "How're we supposed to get this outta here?"

"A ton? Are you sure," Rocco asked, amused.

Pierce put his hands back on his hips and inspected the scene more closely.

"At least," he confirmed.

"Everyone grab a leg then," Dante said.

Pierce kicked at one of the hoofs with his foot and wrinkled his nose.

"And drag it all the way back to the car," he almost shouted, throwing his arms wide again. "I'm not touching that thing!"

Nino gently nudged Alex in the ribs.

"Go back to the car and get the hatchet, then. We can carry it back in pieces."

Pierce's eyes grew as wide as saucers. He then abruptly grabbed a leg and started to pull. After a lot of panicked grunting and frustration, he got angry.

"C'mon, you guys! This thing isn't gonna move itself!"

The others smiled and bent over to help.

Less than an hour later, they were tying the stag to the rack on the roof of the car. The boys all tumbled into the backseat while Pierce elbowed his way up front to sit with his father. It wasn't mid-day yet and they were already on their way home.

"I don't have to remind you mooks not to mention any of this to your mother," Rocco said.

"We know, we know," Nino moaned. "We leave everything in the Fens."

"Like what's left of that stag's ass," Alex said.

They all laughed.

The car gently ascended to cruising altitude, then Rocco fired the accelerator.

"So let's hear it for Pierce," he said. "Bagged his first buck, and hauled it in. I'm proud of you, son."

The other boys cheered and patted him on the shoulders from the back seat. Then they each took turns telling about the first time they went stag hunting. After all the shouting and laughing ebbed, Rocco turned on the wireless.

"Let's see if we can get some scores from yesterday's games."

He worked the console, but couldn't find anything about sports. All of the frequencies were abuzz with news about the still developing situation at Ursus.

"...it's been five days since the quarantine alert was last heard and *Cryer's Wheel* went completely dark...holos taken by military vessels from the edges of the solar system show a vast graveyard of ships, obscured by mysterious white clouds...a holocaust of staggering proportions as there is still no indications of life...only a few hours ago, transmissions within system resumed, and *Cryer's Wheel* was once again lit and visible to scopes...the transmissions are of an unknown language and ten to twelve ships, Enemy ships, have entered the system having routed the few military vessels remaining in the area..."

Rocco shut off the wireless. No one said anything.

"No doubt about it, now," Dante said from the back seat.

"There was never any doubt," Rocco replied. "From the minute that system went dark. You knew. Everyone knew. It's why you and everyone else ran to enlist."

Dante nodded.

"What's Ursus like?"

Rocco shook his head.

"Dunno. Never been there. Ten to twelve ships? Only one station of corridors to secure? A month, maybe two and it'll be all over. Real easy. Almost wish I were going."

Exhausted, Pierce dozed for the rest of the ride home. He awoke to an early twilight and the car buzzing at street level. Around another corner, and they came to a stop in front of a drab clapboard house, a few blocks from home. Pierce gazed groggily at the faded siding and the crab grass that grew around piles of junk. Connected to the main house was a smaller building edged by a narrow driveway, which was blocked by two rusting ground cars.

Rocco shut off the engine.

"Nino, Alex, let's go."

"Why us," they whined.

"Because you guys think you're so smart." He looked at Pierce. "Stay in the car."

The three of them got out, leaving Pierce in the front seat and Dante in the back.

"Where are we," Pierce asked.

"Butcher. Dad gives the guy half the meat to clean the stag for us."

The carcass scraped and thumped on the roof as Nino and Alex rather roughly dragged it off the car. Rocco approached the smaller building. Pierce squinted and made out a door, a door recessed and hidden by a dark shadow cast by a frayed awning. Hauling the stag, Nino and Alex followed Rocco through the darkened doorway. The door opened and then slammed closed behind them. A light came on, and a line of bright yellow shone under the closed door.

Dante leaned forward.

"I heard the Atleta drafted some good players this year. Next season could be a good one."

"Will you be back from Ursus by then?"

He smiled.

"There's no guarantee that I'll be sent to Ursus. You heard Dad. This could be over before I get a chance to see any action."

"Then why go?"

"Because it's necessary."

"There's plenty of other guys, let them—"

"Pierce. There's nothing to worry about. I'll be fine." He put his hand reassuringly on his little brother's shoulder. "I'll be fine."

Pierce shrugged the hand off his shoulder, not believing a word of it. Pierce was angry at him for going, for leaving everyone behind. Angry that he would be so foolish to risk his own life when he himself said it really wasn't necessary. It wasn't right, it wasn't fair.

Pierce looked out the window, anywhere but at Dante. His eyes fell on the name on the address box. His face went pale and he suddenly looked around in a panic, then slouched in the seat a bit.

"What," Dante asked.

Pierce looked at him sheepishly and squirmed.

"Remember how the side mirror on the car got busted last month?"

"Yeah. Some guy side-swiped Mom, ran her off the highway. She could've been killed."

"Well, at the block party right after, me an' Nino an' Alex, we overheard Dad talking to Mr. Vicinotta and everyone. They were laughing about Cans McNally, y'know, Murph's mom who still wears the tight jeans and tanktops?"

"Yeah, yeah," Dante said impatiently. "What about her?"

"Well, we heard Dad say that he knew it was Scatto, Tommy Scatto, who hit mom, and that he was no good, always in trouble. Nino said you knew him from school and that he was a jerk, so—"

"So? So?!" Dante rubbed his forehead. "What did you morons do?"

"We, we snuck over here later on, and with some metal stakes we took from the garden, we...we...scratched up Mr. Scatto's car and broke off the side mirror."

"What?!" Dante winced. "Of all the dumb things you guys have ever done, this is the most—!" He looked at the closed door and winced again. "Anyone know about this?"

"We kinda think he saw us running away."

"You think?? Aw, Pierce!" He shook his head, looking anxiously at the closed door. "And you guys had to break the mirror?! Pierce, Dad was so lit that night, he blamed everyone in the neighborhood at one time or another. What were you guys thinking?!"

"But Mom was almost killed!"

"And Tommy didn't do it! That accident was on the BonStrada thirty kilometers from here—no one in Piacevole hit Mom that day!"

They both stared at the closed door tensely, one anxious moment to the next. "Wh-what do you think Dad's gonna do," Pierce wimpered.

"I don't know how you're gonna get outta this one," Dante said quietly.

Foot shadows finally appeared. They danced back and forth across the yellow line of light ominously. The door suddenly flew open and Nino and Alex came out first, round shouldered and staring at their feet. Rocco came out afterward. He walked at a brisk pace and reached the car before the two boys. He got in and slammed the door shut. Nino and Alex tepidly got in the back seat.

Rocco turned angrily on Pierce.

"So the three of you dingbats, it was all three of you who hit Scatto's Roscollo the night of the block party?"

The three of them nodded timidly. Rocco shot an angry look at Dante, who raised his hands innocently and shook his head.

Rocco floored the accelerator and took off, first straight up and then down the street. He turned sharply around the corner and then slowed down, his forehead knotted in anger.

"You idiots just cost us that entire buck," he shouted, his face turning purple. "Dinner for a month! And that sonofabitch was waiting all these weeks for me to wander in there with no idea—!!"

"W-we thought he hurt Mom," Pierce said weakly.

"I TAKE CARE OF YOUR MOTHER," he shouted hoarsely. "ME!!"

"You mean 'we', Dad," Dante said quietly, but firmly. "It's always been 'we'."

Rocco looked at his oldest son and his lip trembled angrily, then he frowned. He steered the car silently until they landed on the port above the garage. As the sound of the engines quieted, Rocco looked at each of his sons in turn, the color of his face returning to normal.

"We came up empty on this trip," he said. Alex, Nino and Pierce exchanged surprised glances. "We leave everything in the Fens." They all nodded quickly. "And remember to tell your mother how pretty she looks today."

Pierce bolted from the car and charged down the concrete steps. Alex and Nino followed, slowly, not sure if their father was done yelling at them.

Once alone, Dante looked at his father, who sat with eyes closed, hands still gripping the wheel.

"Dad—"

"Shaddup!"

"It's not fair of you to come down on them like that—"

"I said shaddup! And get outta here! Just...*go*."

Saffron Sicuro sat demurely on the wide steps that led up to the back door of the house. Hands in her lap, she hummed quietly to herself while enjoying the warmth of the setting sun. As the long shadows crept ever closer across the small yard, she saw the aircar alight atop the garage. She breathed a sigh of relief and sat up straighter. She adjusted the blue ribbons in her hair and waited anxiously.

Pierce came down the steps first and bolted across the lawn. He jumped into her outstretched arms and gave her a big hug.

"My," she exclaimed, sitting him down next to her. "So, tell me. Did you have fun with your father?"

"I did," he said quickly. "It was cold at the start and pretty wet. We did a lot of sneaking around in the bushes." He avoided telling her that they killed anything, because he knew she wouldn't like that, plus his father told him not to.

"Look at you," she said, fussing over him. "Have you been in these wet clothes all day? Inside and change."

"Okay." He gave her another hug, then said, "I like your ribbons today, Mom. They look nice."

"Well, thank you, Pierce. Blue is such a nice color, isn't it?"

He nodded. He liked blue. When he reached the top of the steps, he could smell the kitchen. Winter greens and golden browns...He looked down and watched as Nino and Alex got closer, whispering quietly to each other.

"And what are you two so quiet about," she asked.

They both smiled with false bravado.

"Nothing," they both said in unison, grinning cheesily. They bent over a bit to kiss her as they went by, and up the steps. When they reached Pierce at the top, Nino stopped Alex.

"Let's hear it for the hair," Alex announced. Both he and Nino clapped and wolf whistled. Pierce glared at them angrily.

"Very funny," she said smiling. "Please go inside and get changed for dinner."

Alex and Nino went inside, slamming the screen door behind them. Pierce could hear them in the kitchen, rummaging through the cabinets and refrigerator.

"Be careful, the oven is hot," she called after them, frowning a bit. She wrung her hands worriedly in her apron. "Pierce, go inside and see what they're doing!"

Pierce opened the door, but paused before going inside. His father and Dante were coming across the grass.

Saffron trembled a bit as Dante approached her, and she held him tightly for a long while. Pierce couldn't see her face, but he thought she might be crying. Rocco stood off to the side, uncharacteristically patient. Dante had a hard time prying his mother off him.

He looked over his shoulder at Rocco.

"Dad?"

Dante passed her off to his father and Rocco waved him up the steps. Seeing Pierce, Dante grabbed him and tickled his stomach.

"I heard the news today," Saffron said sadly. "They're saying everyone at Ursus is dead. T-they, they—"

"Oh, come on, Saff," he scoffed. "You don't know what you're listening to. The news is always fulla crap—"

"An entire Navy yard was blown up!" She pounded her fist on his shoulder. "Don't let him go. *Don't you let him go.*"

He wrapped his arms around her even more tightly and glared up at the two boys. Dante quickly scooped up Pierce and hurried into the house.

Pierce slouched on the couch, exhausted. He listened to the muffled commotion in the kitchen and waited for his mother to call everyone to dinner. His father came in and flopped down next to him, dropping a plastic tray of cookies on the coffee table. Without a word, they both sighed deeply and ate one cookie after another, until the tray was empty.

Saffron came into the room and looked at the two of them, hands on her hips. They both stopped chewing. She leaned in close to Pierce

"You're not eating cookies, are you? This close to dinner?"

Mouth still full, Pierce looked at his father. His father, also with his mouth full, shook his head quickly. Pierce then looked back at his mother and also shook his head.

"Go wash up," she said. "And tell your brothers dinner is ready."

Pierce ran from the room and stomped up the stairs.

Rocco swallowed hard, then smiled, his teeth full of chocolate chips.

"See?"

She rolled her tongue in her cheek, then picked up the empty tray and went back into the kitchen. Rocco followed her and a few minutes later, they all sat down to dinner.

Sarcastic applause and more wolf whistles greeted Saffron as she placed the final serving dish on the table. After much laughter, rude noises and bad manners, Nino signaled the end of the meal by belching loudly. Rocco reached out and pinched his ear between a thumb and forefinger until he apologized, still laughing through his pain.

Saffron looked at the boys crossly.

"I hope you don't behave like this out among people."

They all wilted under her gaze.

"No, ma'am," they mumbled in unison.

She got up, and with that, the boys bolted from the table.

"STOP," Rocco shouted, and everyone froze. "Whose turn is it to clean up the table?"

All at once, there was a lot of shouting and finger pointing.

"Forget it," Rocco said, waving his arms. "Alla you apes. C'mon."

"And you, too," Saffron demanded. "And you will not do what you did last time."

She meant not to scoop everything up in the tablecloth and dump it in the dishwasher, and then throw the tablecloth in the washing machine.

Rocco rolled up his sleeves and manned the sink, soon up to his tattooed biceps in suds. Nino, Alex and Pierce cleaned up, shoving everything into the wrong cabinets, in a hurry to run off and be anywhere else.

Saffron sat at the table with Dante, holding her son's hands in hers. He made her laugh, but spoke to her somewhat earnestly at times. The boys stormed out of the kitchen, but Pierce lingered in the doorway. The image of his mother and his brother like that, happy, yet sad...

Rocco grabbed him up in his arms and swung him over his broad shoulders.

"C'mon, buddy, before it gets too late, you gotta do some reading."

Chapter 4
Tabella de Mons

Many traditions governed the behavior of the Abernathé family and none were more strict than in the way they took their evening meals. The dining room itself, with its polished hard wood floors and ornate chandaliers, had blossomed into the stuff of legend. The Abernathé men gathered around the cold, black marble table for repast every night, without fail, at precisely half past seven. No guest had ever been invited to sit at the Tabella de Mons, nor had any woman ever glimpsed the inside of the room.

This evening, Lorenzo de Abernathé II, the Finest Lethean Gentleman, dined with his son and three year old grandson. To his consternation, he sat on the left side of his son, who sat at the head of the table. His grandson, Lorenzo the Fourth, sat across from him. He envied his grandson's precociousness, his energy, his vibrant health, or at least the rumor of it. How he longed to be young again. Yes, he was old, but far from finished. His mind still surged with verve, no matter what his son thought. He glared out of the corner of his eye at him and loathed his perfectly coiffed appearance. Every day, more like a woman, his son, and ran the business like one.

The three year old child sat at the table very properly with his back ramrod straight, dressed identically to his father in a dark business suit and dark red tie. The child appeared ill, his face pale and quivering from the effort to sit properly. His left hand rested on his lap, wrapped in an oversized bandage. The hair on his head was slowly growing back, and would soon be thick enough to hide the thin, white scars in his scalp. With a shaky right hand, the child picked up his pastry fork to eat his salad, and his father did nothing.

"Young man," the Old Man barked. He held up the correct fork for him to use.

"Not at the table," Lorenzo said. "I will take it up with his tutors in the morning."

"Children are like dogs, son. You correct the mistake when it's made, otherwise the lesson is never learned."

"Pop...," Lorenzo sighed.

"If I learned it at his age, so can he."

Young Lorenzo the Fourth cut his salad into small pieces and ate very slowly, careful not to let any food touch his lips or fall back onto his plate. He did not want to upset his grandfather, which in turn always led to an argument with his father.

"Pop, I prefer to take my meals without acrimony. It is a time of solemn contentment, to be savored. Or am I wrong?"

The Old Man hated it when his son quoted him. He grumbled as he wiped his mouth with a linen napkin.

"What in Blazes is wrong with that boy now? Every time I see him, he looks sick to his stomach."

"He's still recovering from the surgery to his hand."

"And how long does that take," the Old Man shouted. "What does his hand have to do with his stomach? Everything I hear from everyone else is that he's a human tornado! I see him, and he looks like he could keel over any second. He's either throwing up or about to throw up! You need to take better care of him, Lorenzo! You need to pay more attention! You are ruining him. Give that child to me. I will raise him, and raise him right. Stay out of my freezers and go out and find a woman and have your own child."

"Enough, Pop! He's *my* son."

"Really," the Old Man said dryly. His eyes glazed over for a moment, then narrowed into thin slits. "And what about this morning?"

"Pop..."

The Old Man banged his dessert plate on the table.

"You thought I forgot? This morning! Solar Major! It's been a year since The War started, and we're still retreating. The military!" He snorted. "Little better than civil servants. The Enemy is now threatening Solar Major! What have you done about our interests there?"

Lorenzo slowly, deliberately, finished chewing. His father, at times, still retained his senses, his savvy. The Old Man believed that he still maintained control of the business operations through Lorenzo, as his proxy. He retained his title, position and some nominal authority, but Lorenzo truly ran things. This façade had its advantages. For one, his father's reputation, obviously, but the liabilities had taken on a life of their own. Liabilities such as moments like this.

"I've seen to it, Pop."

The Old Man glared at him for a long moment.

"I should've known. You've done nothing! How many times do I have to tell you—"

Lorenzo snapped his fork on the table.

"Pop, that part of the company was sold off eight years ago. *Eight years ago.*"

As an agricultural collective, Solar Major had little to offer AbStone. Years ago, Lorenzo shut down all company operations in that star system because the ruling class of anthropods had proven progressively more difficult to deal with. They were also immune to more direct methods, and even AbStone didn't have deep enough pockets to subdue fifteen billion bugs.

Lorenzo swallowed hard.

"Enough business." He looked at his young child. "What lessons did you cover with Ms. Impari today?"

Young Lorenzo beamed, glad for his father's attention.

"The Macropian alphabet, sir. And colors."

Lorenzo nodded a bit.

"Recite them, please."

The Old Man interrupted.

"And what about this hoax business and the Ashpole Hearings? That we destroyed our own ship yard in The Hub? It's all over the news. What are our people saying? Never mind that. Any business with NYSAAC has to be terminated immediately. Were you dumb enough to negotiate any contracts directly with this Chamberlain, this fool of an Admiral? Get out of them now. You also must distance yourself from Senator Blommish. He's up for re-election. His opponent, the bug Hi'icki, is a bit too young and reform minded, but you contact its people and let them know that we're behind it, but on the condition—"

"POP!!"

The Old Man quieted, startled.

"No more business!" Lorenzo glowered at him. His hopes that his father would die soon had been dashed over the last few years. His mental state had stabilized, even improved. While no longer prone to as many violent outbursts, a pattern had emerged where his cognitive deficits grew more pronounced in the evenings. However, Lorenzo had recently learned the reasons for his father's recovery, and evening relapses. This wasn't good news, as it only confirmed his long harbored suspicions. He put his hand on his child's arm.

"Please take the rest of your dinner with Ms. Impari in her rooms. I will join you later."

Young Lorenzo nodded. He folded his napkin neatly and placed it on the table. He hopped off the chair and ran akwardly across the room, slamming the door behind him.

The dinner plates vibrated on the table.

"Dammit, Lorenzo, that boy of *yours*," the Old Man groused. "I told you keeping him in stasis for so long was no good! Always running and slamming things! You had better get control of him, Lorenzo, before it gets worse!"

"There are still some lingering effects from the craniosynostosis correction."

"Stop making excuses! It's because you treat him like an idiot! Talk to him like an adult, treat him like an adult, and he'll become an adult! It's what he wants!"

"And now you can read his mind?"

The Old Man leaned over the table.

"More so than *you*."

Lorenzo sipped his wine.

"It's time you and I had a long overdue conversation, Pop."

"About what?"

"About what you think you've been doing behind my back."

The Old Man smiled wryly and leaned back in his chair.

"Behind *your* back? I need no one's approval, least of all *yours*."

"Do you remember after your last surgery nine years ago? For your lungs?"

The Old Man peered at him quizzically.

"Yes?"

"I shut down that body bank of yours. And we agreed that was the end of it."

"I agreed to nothing."

"Then you set James to the task of rebuilding that effort—"

"Lies!"

Lorenzo sighed.

"I dealt with James this morning."

"T-the audacity! You had no right! James is in my employ—"

"Pop—"

"I run this family! I will not be crossed!" The Old Man pursed his lips and folded his arms angrily, turning his head. "Lorenzo, you continue to disappoint me. Don't force me to cast you out."

"You'll be pleased to know that James located the last of the five cloned infants," Lorenzo said, sipping his wine calmly. "The youngest one, the nine-year old, was the last. He said there was no point in recalling them now as they can't be considered until they've matured." He paused. "Considered for what, Pop?"

The Old Man drummed his bony fingers on the table and continued to cast his gaze to the side.

"As a complete surprise to me," Lorenzo said, "James told me that until a short time ago, four of the remaining adult clones were at large and outside of his control. None of the other captive adult clones were suitable candidates, and that the last one yielded enough fluid for only one more treatment." He glared at his father over his glass. "What could he have meant by that, Pop?"

"I needed that cranial fluid," he shouted. "I needed to keep my wits about me, otherwise you'd have bumbled away our fortune!"

"Still haven't given up on finding that lucky brain, have you? Well, James also related a much larger problem. One of your adult clones became a true renegade. No one understood how or when he divined his true nature, or why he had some affinity for finding other clones, or why he felt compelled to seek them out. Very shrewdly, James left him at large so he could lead them to the other clones."

The Old Man's fingers flat lined on the cold, hard table.

"And?"

"And nothing."

The Old Man smiled sardonically.

Lorenzo dabbed at the corners of his mouth with a napkin.

"But not before you took what you wanted. I've dispatched James, shut down your project for good and resolved all of the loose ends. No one will ever know what you've done."

The Old Man balled his shaking hands into fists and set them on his lap, trembling with rage.

"Who do you *think* you are?! Killing my retainers, interfering with my business?! I want *you* and that child out of here, Lorenzo! Disowned *and* disinherited! I'm calling the lawyers in the morning! I never want to see either of you again! Do you hear me?! *Do you hear me?!*"

He flipped over his salad plate onto the table, toward Lorenzo. The lettuce and white dressing didn't quite reach him, and the silverware clanked on the floor. The Old Man struggled to his feet and stormed out of the room, shouting epithets at the empty halls.

Lorenzo quietly finished his salad. After a few minutes, Cervello entered. He puzzled at the scene before him.

"It is half past the hour, Lorenzo," he said, nervously. "I'm here, as you instructed. I expected your father to be here as well."

Lorenzo took a long moment before speaking.

"My father believes you're dead. He also believes that your project has been terminated."

Cervello wrung his hands together anxiously. He didn't even try to continue any pretense.

"And his reaction, I may ask?"

Lorenzo glanced at the lettuce strewn across the table, then said, "As expected. My inheritance and legacy are now forfeit."

Cervello began to sweat.

"I'm so sorry, Lorenzo."

Lorenzo dismissed it all with a wave of his hand.

"Usually it's just one or the other, rarely both."

"I see."

"I admire your loyalty to my father, James. But I warned you not to ignore me, yet you did anyway. You continued to feed into my father's lurid fantasies of immortality after I told you to stop. This continued travesty with the clones is disgusting, and the only reason you're still here is that I want it cleaned up. I want my family's name protected. I want that self aware monstrosity, Menscher, and the other adult clones found and destroyed. Is that clear?"

Cervello nodded quickly.

"That could be difficult. Menscher is a very cunning adversary. He's gone into hiding, but not before warning the others—"

"No move is to *EVER* be made against the infant clones. Is that clear?"

Cervello continued nodding.

Lorenzo wiped his mouth and set the linen napkin on the table. A canite in a black suit and tie entered the room behind Cervello. Cervello glanced over his shoulder, his face pale.

Lorenzo stood up and approached his father's oldest, and most loyal, retainer.

"You will have no further communication with my father. You will leave Summa Avarici this instant and never return. You will clean up this mess, and then get out of our lives forever."

Lorenzo left the room, leaving Cervello alone with the canite in black.

Chapter 5
Sophrire

At three hours before sunrise, Pierce Sicuro steered his ground car off the main thoroughfare and onto the local streets that comprised the rustic, elegant charm of the Hamlet of Sophrire. He smiled as he looked around at the quiet streets, lit by street lamps and neon window signs. In the passenger seat sat his girlfriend of over a year, Angelica Smart. She leaned in close to him as he put his arm around her, and she dozed lightly.

They were on their way home from a night in Sothemax. He had taken her to an upscale restaurant and a picture show to celebrate their high school graduation some two months ago, and her acceptance to Elysian University on Nostrova, for which she would be leaving the day after tomorrow.

The War had officially ended about six months ago, right before Pierce turned eighteen. He still tasted the bitter disappointment at being turned away by the recruiters. All of his brothers had enlisted and seen action. Dante had served with distinction at Coleo'Ptera and won a medal. While Pierce still harbored some resentment over his exclusion, he took pride in the sacrifices his family had made. Now that everyone was home in one piece, Nino being the last to arrive the previous week, Pierce couldn't imagine his life getting any better than this moment. Everything had turned out perfectly, but not according to plan.

And Pierce always had a plan.

By his fourteenth birthday, his brothers had all become Marines and gone off to war. Desperate to grow up, desperate to enlist and be just like them—a soldier like their father—required some scheming. His first plan involved enlisting while underage. He'd heard stories about guys getting fake ID chips and bribing recruitment screeners, but his parents found out and put an end to that idea. That's when his father got him the job with Wren Customizers out at the starport, where he could keep an eye on him.

WrenCo manufactured small, specialized air and space ships for celebrities and rich corporate types. Once The War started, a fat Navy contract dropped into their laps to build small command level transports and tender ships. The WrenCo techs, all master craftsmen, customized each vessel to specific Naval requirements. Pierce's father worked for the starport's sanitation outfit, mostly disposing of hazardous waste and policing the workspace. His route brought him through WrenCo's hangars three or four times during Pierce's after school shift, and Rocco became fast friends with the shift supervisor.

To his own surprise, Pierce had an affinity for the work and enjoyed the creative process. His new plan became to learn everything about starships, get his pilot's license and become a naval aviator. His apprenticeship would end next year, when he turned nineteen. He already had a class ten license to operate ground vehicles and had just passed the test which earned him the same license for air constructs. Even with his application for a learner's permit for starships still pending, he had already flown everything up to a hull size of six, as the guys let him 'work the board' on shakedown runs.

Now that The War had ended, his latest plan turned on starting his own company, customizing starships. He would continue working as a journeyman for WrenCo the next few years, saving every disc note, until Angelica finished college. After her graduation, he would have enough saved to rent hangar space and lease equipment from WrenCo, then expand from that. Then he would marry Angelica, get a nice house somewhere nearby, maybe Piacevole, and take care of her the same way his father had taken care of his mother.

Pierce didn't like the idea of Angelica going off to college, especially on another planet. She talked about it all the time, and it annoyed him as she seemed a little too eager to go sometimes. He wanted to be near her, to look out for her, to be close in case she needed help. He worried about her being hounded by other guys. Most of all, he would miss her company. What he wouldn't miss was her father.

Mr. Smart was a software engineer for Du'uomo, the local Cathedral subcorp. He kept a sports craft in his two car garage to drive on the weekends, and a boat to put in the water every spring. He kept his daughter and wife at arm's length and his whole life revolved around his son and his expensive toys. He was white hem through and through, everything Rocco Sicuro was not. Mr. Smart had definite ideas about who his daughter should and should not associate with, and Pierce fell into the latter category. He disliked the boy from Piacevole immediately, and, for now, Pierce had to deal with him. However, once Angelica left for school, he could visit her there instead of at her house, and once married, he could ignore the man altogether.

All according to plan.

Pierce and Angelica were an odd pairing, and he liked that. She ran with the posers and cheerleaders while he took pride in being a clique of one. She had won all kinds of academic awards and earned a scholarship to college, while he only showed up for science and math class and skipped the rest, sneaking off to the starport instead. A little more than a year ago, while on his way home from the starport, he spotted her stranded on the side of the road, her ground car sparking and belching steam from under the hood. They knew each other from school, always having the same homeroom, but not well. He fixed her car, and a short time later, they were a couple. He knew he had scored way over his head, and her preference for the finer things irritated him sometimes, but he was prepared to give her everything she ever wanted, as soon as his company got off the ground. He loved Angelica and all he cared about was her happiness.

He turned the last corner and eased the car into her driveway. She stirred as the car came to a stop. She felt warm and red against him. The violet of the car halos reflecting off the garage doors colored her soft, contented smile. He touched her smooth face with his calloused hand and she shook her head irritably.

She yawned as she stretched.

"Pierce?"

He could see a light on in the picture window.

"We're back, Angel. Someone's still up."

"You know it's my father," she sighed, sleep still in her eyes, grabbing her purse. "He always waits up now."

He nodded.

"Tonight was a great night."

"It was," she agreed, smiling.

"Tomorrow's going to be better," he boasted.

"Really," she said, looking at him coyly. "Where are we going?"

"I told you, it's a surprise." There was a moment of silence. "I wish you weren't going so far away to school."

She sighed wearily.

"Pierce, we'll be able to see each other at breaks. Maybe."

"I'll visit."

"Sure," she said vacantly.

"Now that I'm working full time, I can make the trip every month or so."

She became serious.

"Pierce, it's still not too late for you to enroll somewhere for the spring."

Irritated, he said, "You, too, now? I've already got a good job. It paid for tonight! It paid for tomorrow night! It'll pay for everything you and I'll ever want. Once I get my own company going—"

"Your own company," she exclaimed, incredulous. She looked away from him, to hide her amusement. "You? When did you get that idea?"

"I've always had that idea!"

"Well, how would I know? You've been a ghost all summer! Every time I try to find you, you're at work. Work, work, work. That's all you ever do. You wasted my whole summer. All of our senior year. The ball team won the championship, and you could've been on that team, if you'd only tried! Everyone else had so much fun traveling all over Gran Nexus, and instead we were stuck here."

He gripped the steering wheel angrily.

"What's so wrong with here?"

"Oh, Pierce," she sighed. "Don't you want to see other places, other planets?"

"I look at pictures all the time."

She leaned in close to him.

"I don't want to fight with you tonight. I had such a good time. I'm going to miss you."

He kissed her and she put her arm around his neck, pulling him closer.

The yard lights suddenly came on and the front door to the house flew open. Light streamed out onto the sidewalk.

She groaned and got out of the car.

"I love you! I'll see you tomorrow night at...?"

He got out of the car, too.

"C'mon, I'll walk you to the door."

"Pierce, please, not tonight."

He held out his hand.

She folded her arms and stood firm.

"No. It'll only cause trouble."

"Angel, the front door step is not in the house."

She rolled her eyes and took his hand, and they walked to the door together. They stepped over a thick crack in the walk. Angelica's father stood in the doorway.

"Good evening, Mr. Smart," Pierce said, tongue in his cheek. "How're you tonight?" He smirked in spite of himself.

Angelica gave him a quick peck on the cheek and went into the house, ducking under her father's arm.

Pierce and Mr. Smart looked at each other for a moment.

"Have you got some fill and a trowel, Mr. Smart," Pierce asked, pointing to the imperfection in the cement. "I can patch that crack for you, no sweat."

The door slammed in Pierce's face. The door rattled in its moorings and Pierce's hair blew off his forehead. The house and yard went completely dark an instant later.

He smiled foolishly to himself, then suddenly felt cold. Cold as blue steel. In the sultry summer night, in the dim light cast by other porch lights up and down the street, he stood alone, afraid to move. The hair on the back of his neck stood on end, and his very keen senses strained to make sense of the shadows, the far off sounds of The Concourse. A terrible nausea knotted his stomach, with that brown-black syrup trapped in his nostrils again. Growing up, he'd felt like this at odd moments, but for the last couple of years, it seemed to be happening all the time. He somehow sensed that he wasn't alone. The wave of nausea passed quickly this time and he wiped at his nose furiously. He took one last furtive look around before turning back to the car.

He glanced at his timepiece.

"Dammit!"

He jumped into the car and peeled out of the driveway, leaving wicked skid marks on the clean blacktop. Angelica's silhouette looked on from her bedroom window above.

He ignored several traffic devices as he maneuvered through the deserted local streets, and made his way into Piacevole. His tires screeched as he rounded a hard corner and barreled the wrong way down a one way street. He pounded the wheel in frustration and cursed out loud as he fish tailed around a final corner. His tires squealed and left a trail of white smoke in his wake. He approached his house much too fast and skidded loudly to a stop in front, only centimeters from the fender of his mother's ground car.

His father and brothers busied themselves above the garage, packing the aircar. He could see them in the spotlight. He ran down the driveway as fast as he could.

"You smell that," he heard Nino say.

"Yeah," Alex replied. "Combustion exhaust, burning rubber. I didn't think he'd make it."

Pierce ran up the stairs three at a time and paused at the top, barely breathing. They had all just gotten into the car. His father turned over the engine.

"You're late," his father yelled, rolling up the window.

The jets kicked on and the car would be airborne in just a few seconds. The back door flew open and Pierce jumped in just in time, landing hard on Nino and Alex, who could barely fit their knees into the once spacious back seat.

Alex pulled him in by the seat of his pants and closed the door.

"Where've you been," his father demanded. "You can't read a timepiece no more?"

Pierce took a seat in the middle, shoving his brothers to either side.

"I was out, Dad. Y'know, with my friends."

His brothers howled at the obvious lie.

"C'mon," Alex said, elbowing him roughly. "You were out with that girl, weren't you? What's her name again?"

"The *Smart* girl," Nino reminded him.

They all whispered her name reverently.

"Oh yes, the *Smart* girl."

"Her *name* is *Angelica*," Pierce said, annoyed.

"Sawrrry," Nino said sarcastically.

"Now, now, now," Dante admonished. "Wasn't the big date tonight? Where'd you take Angelica, Pierce?"

Pierce folded his arms over his chest and tried to stare out the window.

Alex leaned in close.

"You went to Sothemax, didn't you? Dinner and a picture show, big guy?"

"Shut up," Pierce said, jabbing him hard in the ribs with an elbow.

Alex winced and backed off, all of them laughing.

"Pierce is in looove!"

"You ask that girl to marry you tonight, Pierce," Nino teased. "Did ya?"

"No," Pierce mumbled. He paused akwardly, then blushed. "Tomorrow night."

The three of them stopped laughing all at once.

Rocco laughed uproariously as he steered the car toward the Timberland Fens.

The first rays of sunlight shone through the mists of the dense forest. A trio of stags moved soundlessly through the brush. Two nosed around, nibbling at the tall grass. A third stood tall and resolute.

Pierce sat absolutely still in a copse, down wind of the stags. He wore only a thin t-shirt, impervious to the cold morning dews. He observed the animals carefully. Every twitch, every glance, and inhaled their placid, white scent.

For the last six years, it had just been himself and his father on these trips. In that time, his own skills and strength had improved, but his father's had waned. The dampness in the Fens aggravated the arthritis in his knees. At the start, they stalked and killed their prey in tandem, but those days had long passed. Rocco refused to acknowledge his limitations in any way, so Pierce learned to subtley scare the game in his direction, and never the same way twice, to avoid suspicion. His father had no idea.

It had been just the two of them for so long, he barely remembered ever coming out here with his brothers. He didn't like the way they changed the routine and forced him again to compete for his father's attention. They still treated him like the little kid who cradled a Moon pistol. They relentlessly teased him, made him feel sub-human, because he wasn't a Marine. The initial euphoria over their safe return had passed and now he resented the unique bond they shared with their father as combat veterans. He resented how everyone in the neighborhood made a fuss over them. He wearied of the stories, wearied of the boasting, wearied of everyone calling them heroes. He sometimes wished they'd never come home.

As much as they enjoyed the adulation, Pierce sensed that not everything was well with his brothers. He discovered that he had the ability to terminate conversations just by walking into a room. The three of them shared many hushed conversations and akward silences, and fell into random moments of melancholy. During the day, his brothers exhibited an overly playful, over the top exuberance at organizing neighborhood ball games, as if they were still kids. It belied their skittish paranoia after dark, when they took turns peering out the black windows, behind the curtains. He knew that all three of them slept with weapons under their pillows, when they slept at all.

Pierce focused on the stags. He had worked hard to become a skilled hunter and outdoorsman since Alex enlisted those six long years ago. He learned every trick his father knew, and more. Today, he would show them all that he was every bit of a man as they were, Marine or not.

The fog clung low to the ground and rolled thickly, like cotton, around the trees. Pierce tracked the stags through the scope of his rifle. Carefully, quietly, he closed in on the trio of gray silhouettes, his movement masked by the mists that snaked like smokey tendrils through the brush. Closer, always closer, until he could almost touch them. He clutched his rifle calmly, then held his breath... and waited.

He suddenly jumped to his feet, waving his arms wide. The startled stags scattered. He followed the one with the black snout, rifle in hand. He caught up to it easily and slapped it in the rear end to make it run faster. It gained on him, and he shoved its hind quarters to the side, steering it toward his brothers. The stag was fast, but Pierce was faster, and it could not elude him. Its fear streaked behind it as it thundered through through the woods, Pierce setting the breakneck pace. He shrugged off the sharp branches and the wood that snapped and cracked against his body.

He wished Angelica could see him now, then decided not. Stag hunting did not impress her. It lacked refinement. It wasn't school centric. It wasn't *popular.* She had very specific ideas about how things should be, what he should be, and they had nothing to do with running down game in the bog. She was sometimes subtle, sometimes not, but always adamant. A certain kind of shirt, the right pants, and Mother of Peroxide, the shoes...

He couldn't understate how lucky he felt to be with her. So beautiful and graceful, she could have been with anyone else, but she chose to be with him. Girls like her didn't go around with mutts from Piacevole. They just didn't. He worked hard to avoid upsetting her—it was wrong to upset girls—and he struggled to find ways to placate her without compromising himself. She wanted him to try out for the school ball team. He tried out for the ball team. She wanted to attend only certain parties. They only went to certain parties. She wanted to associate with only a close circle of friends. They associated with a close circle of friends. The socializing didn't bother him, her friends seemed harmless enough, but he drew the line at playing ball.

Truth be told, playing ball bored him. It was all too easy. And he didn't care for the other guys, the way they'd act and talk about other kids, especially the girls, behaving like they were better than everyone else. And the locker rooms always smelled a vile puke green and brown.

'Lay down with mongrels, don't complain when you get fleas,' his father would say. Angelica always pushed him to try out. He made all the teams, but each time let her believe that he got cut for being lazy, as opposed to quitting.

He couldn't think of a bigger waste of time than playing ball. Except maybe school. He enjoyed creating and building, earning money to buy his own things. School got in the way of that.

Pierce smiled once he saw the stag blind and his brothers crouched behind it. He overtook the stag, then put one arm around its neck and threw the animal to the ground. The stag fought him and they tumbled roughly through the brush, a tangle of legs and antlers and broken tree branches. When the leaves settled, Pierce stood up and brushed at the twigs and leaves stuck in his hair and clothes. He held a bloody knife in one hand.

Dante, Nino and Alex emerged slowly from the blind and stared slack jawed at him. Pierce smiled smugly and cleaned the blade on the stag's hind quarters. He heard their father approaching, cursing as he stumbled through the brush. Pierce placed his rifle against the stag's head and fired a laser bolt into the animal's neck, obliterating any evidence of the cut across its throat.

Rocco arrived, breathing deeply. He looked at the stag, then at everyone staring at Pierce, and then the flattened and broken foliage that surrounded them.

"What in Blazes happened?"

The four brothers exchanged akward glances.

"It was like this," Nino finally said, looking his father in the eye. "Me an' Alex and Dante were in the stag blind over there, when outta nowhere this stag came barreling at us through the woods.

I'll be damned if Pierce wasn't running right behind it, tackled it, slit its throat, and then shot it just to be sure."

There was a moment of silence as Rocco locked eyes with his son.

"Get the fuck outta here," he finally said, waving him off and turning his back on him. "Looks to me like you all had too much beer and were lucky you didn't shoot each other. That what they teach you guys in the service these days, how to waste ammo? In my day, we could *shoot*."

Nino rolled his eyes.

"Dad, I'm tellin' ya—"

"Aw, shaddap! Each of you grab a leg. I'll meet you at the car."

Rocco disappeared into the woods.

The brothers looked at each other and shared a good laugh.

"Looks like Pierce is all growed up, now," Dante said, giving him a high five.

Alex whistled softly.

"No joke," he seconded.

Nino rubbed Pierce's shoulders roughly and tousled his hair, and then they all took to the task of dragging the stag back to the car.

Chapter 6
Memstar

Pierce pulled his chair up to the dinner table and rolled up his sleeves. His mother set a dish of vegetables in the center of the table and sat down.

"Let's hear it for the carrots," Pierce announced.

He and his brothers clapped, whistled and cheered sarcastically.

Saffron blushed.

"Very funny, very funny. Everyone sit up straight, now."

Chairs scuffed the floor as they all shuffled in their seats, including Rocco.

She took a deep breath and smiled warmly, taking in the sight of her entire family sitting at the same table. The boys, much bigger now, bumped elbows playfully as they tried to squeeze into their usual places. She tried to imagine them as the rambunctious children they used to be, but too much had changed. Dante, Nino and Alex had gone to war as boys and returned as men. They had been allowed to keep some of their weapons, which Rocco assured her was standard practice, and it worried her that they spent so much time cleaning and maintaining them. The three of them never seemed to stray too far from each other, and often used hand signals to communicate, rather than talking. Last evening, she had gotten up in the middle of the night for a glass of water, and came upon Alex and Nino in the kitchen, sitting in the dark, in silence.

She voiced her concerns to Rocco about all this odd behavior. They were less humorous, always tired, and easily startled. Again, Rocco assured her that everything was fine and that it would take some time for them to readjust to civilian life. He remembered being the same way when he came back from The Rim and he promised to talk to them about being more discreet with the guns. She still worried, but rejoiced in having all her sons together at last. Her eyes met Rocco's and they shared a secret smile across the table.

"Gentlemen," Rocco said, holding his glass. "Listen up."

Everyone settled down.

"It's been almost ten years since we've all sat at this table together. You've been to war, and been returned safe and sound."

"Under the watchful eye of Peroxide," Saffron added.

Rocco cleared his throat.

"Right. And now Pierce has grown into a man, a Sicuro through and through, and is now a high school graduate."

"Just barely," Nino whispered sarcastically.

"Shut up," Pierce said, bumping his brother's shoulder with his own.

"And now what college," Dante asked.

Pierce shook his head.

"Don't need college, Dante. I got a job already."

Dante frowned.

"The one at WrenCo?"

Pierce nodded, shrinking in his chair a bit.

"Pierce and I have discussed it," Rocco said. "Your brother's good with his hands, Dante. Scholarship...school's not his best career path."

"Maybe not for us," Dante said, also indicating Nino and Alex. "Pierce, you need to rethink this."

"At least he's got a job," Rocco said acidly.

"Dad—"

"I'm gonna have my own company one day," Pierce boasted. "I will! And don't any of you losers come to me looking for work!"

"Yeah, okay," Alex scoffed. "When's that gonna happen? Right after you marry the Smart girl?"

Alex and Nino whispered her name over and over reverently.

"The Smart girl...the Smart girl..."

"Why don't you guys go back into the service," Pierce shouted. Then he insulted them all using the Marine cant they used while stag hunting. This set off a furious argument of hand signals that left Saffron sighing in dismay at her end of the table.

"Knock it off, you clowns," Rocco barked. He cleared his throat. "To the Sicuro men!"

"And their mother," Pierce added.

"Here, here," they all repeated in unison, clinking glasses.

"Hey," Nino exclaimed. "Mom made the red potatoes!"

Glasses dropped and spilled. A sudden flurry of forks parried other forks. Grabbing hands got stabbed and battling elbows knocked glasses to the floor, while knives clashed like swords. When it was done, the tipped serving plates were bare and pieces of food and drink stained the white table cloth.

Saffron watched in silent, disapproving exasperation at the appalling behavior of her children. Rocco at first scowled with anger at his sons, then tried to hide his amusement.

"Look," Pierce said. "Dante's got most of the potatoes!" The other three attacked Dante's plate with their forks and hands. He tried to fight them all off at once with his own fork and failing at that, tried to lift his plate away from the table, which then spilled into his lap. The brothers roared with laughter.

"Dammit," Rocco yelled, trying to be angry. "What in Blazes is the matter with you meat heads? If you're gonna take somebody's potatoes, you do it like this!" He then deftly took a number of potatoes from Alex's plate with one sweep of his fork.

"Not so fast, old man," Alex laughed, then came at his father's plate with his own fork.

"Boys," Saffron said softly.

All of the commotion suddenly stopped, and Pierce bumped his elbow into a decanter of water which wobbled precariously near the edge of the table.

They all wilted under her stern and disapproving gaze.

"I hope you all don't behave like this out among people."

They all eyed each other warily for a moment. Then the wobbling decanter next to Pierce fell to the floor with a wet crash.

"Ooooooooooh," his brothers hummed in unison. "Pierce is in trou-*ble*."

She hit him with a dish towel, then handed it to him.

"Oh, Pierce," she moaned, trying not to smile. "Clean it up!"

Muffled snickering continued as they all straightened up the table.

Pierce was in a hurry. He didn't want to be late picking up Angelica. The sun had already set as he ran to his car in the driveway. Dante stood there, waiting for him, his arms crossed purposefully over his broad chest.

"Outta my way, Dante," Pierce said quickly. "I don't wanna be late."

Dante moved in front of the driver's side door. He was still bigger than his younger brother, but not by much.

"We need to talk first."

Pierce rolled his eyes and exhaled dramatically.

"Move it."

"No."

With little effort, Pierce shoved him out of the way with one hand. Surprised at his strength, Dante stumbled a few steps to the side. He recovered quickly and twisted Pierce's wrist behind his back, and pinned him against the car.

"You gonna ask that girl to marry you tonight?"

"What's it to you?"

"Are you?"

"No!"

Dante shoved his free hand into Pierce's jacket pocket and pulled out a velour jewelry box.

"What's this, then," he demanded, holding it to Pierce's face.

"So? Why do you care?"

"Why? *Why?* Why do you want to marry this girl? What makes her so special?"

Pierce struggled against his grip and wriggled free.

"You haven't seen her...she's pretty, Dante. So pretty. And she loves *me!*"

The two of them stared at each other, Dante huffing and puffing.

"She's not the only pretty girl in The Web, Pierce. And she's not the only one who'll ever want to be with you."

Pierce tried to open the car door, but Dante put his hand on it, holding it shut.

"She's leaving for college in the morning, right? And you're worried she'll meet someone else or you'll grow apart. You're worried she's leaving you behind."

"I always get left behind."

Dante's jaw tightened.

"Is that what you think?"

"Go get a life, why don't ya, instead of picking on those of us that do."

"Listen to me," Dante said, shrugging off the barb. "Don't marry this girl out of fear."

"I'm not afraid of anything."

"No?"

"No!"

"All the messages you sent me while I was in the service. How much her father hates you and how much you enjoy ticking him off. It's all fun right now, but marriage, Pierce? It doesn't seem to me the two of you want the same things."

"You don't even know her, Dante!"

"But I know *you,* Pierce. Have you given that girl anything that she wants? You nearly flunk out of school because you spend every spare minute at the starport. Your plan is to stay here, to live here. That girl is leaving this *planet* to get an education. Last I checked, there are still schools on Gran Nexus."

"Her father wants to get her away from me, but he won't win."

"Pierce, Pierce. Do you hear yourself? It isn't a contest—"

"Give me back my ring," Pierce demanded, holding out his hand.

Dante held the ring behind his back.

"Listen to me. There's been some talk since I've been back. Guys've been telling me that you're an incredible athlete. Coach Falcone came by here the other day, wanting to know what you're problem is."

"Yeah, so?"

"He told me he's been after you since your second year, him and all the other coaches, that you still have a chance to write your own ticket to college."

"Bullshit."

"Yeah, I didn't believe it either, not the Pierce I remembered. Then I saw you run down that stag in the woods and break its neck with your bare hands. I wouldn't have believed it if I hadn't seen it with my own two eyes! So I looked into things. Found out you made every team you tried out for, but quit right after. What's going on with you?"

"Ball players are just that. *Ballplayers.* And let me tell you about Coach Falcone. He spent more time flirting with the mothers than running the games, especially Cans McNally."

"Really?" Dante paused, his mouth wrinkling a bit. "She still prowling the ball fields? Yikes." He shook his head to free the image from his mind. "All right, so you don't like hanging with the jocks. Why try out at all, then?"

Pierce didn't answer, and his eyes fell on his shoes.

"Just like I thought," Dante nodded, understanding. "You did it for her. Let me guess. She's Little Miss School Spirit and she pussy whipped you into doing it. Then you lied to her and told her you got cut, right?"

"No," Pierce moped.

"You are such dope. You haven't even asked this girl to marry you yet and already you're living a lie. Look, you don't wanna go to college, you wanna stay here for the rest of your life cutting chairs and tables into cabin cruisers, that's fine. But think hard before asking that girl to do it with you."

"It's not gonna be like that, Dante! I'll have my own company by the time she finishes college."

Dante shook his head.

"She'll be a completely different girl from the one you know now. And you'll be a different guy."

"But she'll still be with *me*."

Dante opened the jewelry box. The ring within sparkled in the dim light.

"Well, well. An Abernathé Diamond. As stupid as you are, at least you're not cheap."

Pierce reached for it and Dante pulled it away. Pierce shoved at him to try and get it back.

"Or what," Dante challenged. "You gonna take it off me?" Dante could see that part of Pierce wanted to try and that he had the strength to do it. Dante sighed. He didn't come out here to fight with Pierce. He gave him the jewelry box.

Pierce opened the door and got in the car.

"You want my advice," Dante shouted over the revving engine.

"No!"

"At least wait until winter!"

Pierce made an obscene gesture and peeled out of the driveway in reverse. Dante watched until the red tail lights disappeared around the corner.

During The War Against The Enemy, anyone going in or out of the grounds at the S'Hax Brennert Memorial Starport endured any number and type of searches, scans or interrogations. Proper credentials had to be displayed at all times and verified at every checkpoint, and then re-verified. No one, or thing, got in or out undetected. Since the end of The War, security at MemStar had grown lax, and Pierce had an instinct for finding the seams

Tonight, he happily pulled his ground car into the darkened, deserted WrenCo Hangar Number Four. Angelica crouched next to him, blindfolded and on the passenger side floor.

"Pierce, where are we? I can't believe I'm letting you do this!"

"Okay, okay. We're here!"

He shut off the engine and got out of the car. With the headlights doused, it was almost completely dark. He helped Angelica out of the car from the passenger side. She reached to take off the blindfold.

"Not yet," he said, holding her hands. His voice echoed in the large building.

"Where are we," she whispered, cringing at her sense of the enormity of the place.

He led her over to an area behind a canvas partition and stopped next to a work bench. With the silhouette of a small Porbeagle class starship only a few meters away, he stood behind her and took off the blindfold.

"What are you doing," she whispered, giggling a bit. "It's so dark here! Where are we?"

He turned on an overhead light.

Angelica gasped. She looked over her shoulder at him, and then back at the starship.

"Is this where...?"

He thrilled at the thought of her finally being here.

"This is where I work," he said. "Well, actually, a little bit behind us, but Mr. Sporgenza, my boss, he lent me this area."

She looked over the neatly organized tool bench and then at the two separate rows of square lidded containers next to it. One row was red, the other green, each emblazoned with different hazard logos.

"What are those," she asked.

"Safe disposal units. Alotta this stuff is inert by itself, but if not disposed of properly, especially if exposed to the vapors of some of the hybrid class fuels, enough of it, and this whole place could go up in a mushroom cloud."

Her face paled.

"Pierce, we shouldn't be here."

He smiled reassuringly.

"Don't worry. I know how to handle this stuff. During the work day, my Dad's team comes and empties them every seventy five minutes. They're empty. There's no danger."

She warily moved closer to the starship and put her hand on the hull. She ran her fingers over the peeling white paint, over every dent and imperfection. She quickly pulled her hand away, looking for something to clean it with.

"It doesn't look like much right now," he said, using a rag to clean her hand. "I didn't have time to strip the old paint and bang out the dents before tonight. Next week, maybe. It passed inspection, though."

She seemed rather unimpressed, and confused.

"Why are we here? I didn't think this is what you had in mind after dinner at Costoso Merda. I-I thought we were going to our usual spot behind the field house."

"Don't worry, we're not going to be here for long," he said, taking a keycard out of his pocket.

"Pierce," she whispered loudly. She ran at him and put both her hands over the keycard, pushing it back into his pocket. "You could get into so much trouble just being here! You can't just take someone's ship for a joy ride! That's stealing!"

"Angel," he deadpanned. "It's okay. It's mine."

"Yours?"

He nodded.

"I built it."

She smiled weakly.

"*You* built this?

He beamed proudly.

"Well, I had to hire one of the engineers to refurbish the engine, but I repaired the hull. I gutted the insides and customized the interior myself."

She seemed curious.

"Can we go inside?"

"Even better, would you like to pop over to EU a day early? The ship has a system certificate."

"You're going to fly us," she asked, hesitant.

"I got my learner's permit and I've already logged five hundred hours, a hundred more than I need." He led her by the hand to the door of the small ship. "Come on, it'll be fine."

"Pierce, *no!*" She yanked her hand away. "You could be arrested!"

"Don't be like this, Angel. C'mon, I know everybody around here. I arranged for clearance. I know a guy on the traffic deck. A quick hour. Fifty minutes, and we'll be back."

She folded her arms and stamped her foot like she always did when angry or annoyed with him.

"I said no! Look, Pierce..."

He approached her and she took a step away.

"Angel, if you're worried about not seeing me while away at school, I've solved that problem. I've already got my air license. I'll have my system license in a month. I can come and see you whenever I want now."

"It's not that," she said, her brow furrowing. She hesitated.

Pierce realized it was exactly that. His voice stuck in his throat as a twinge of nausea wobbled his knees. That dirty, brackish smell flooded his nostrils again and he reeled a bit, unsteady on his feet.

She seemed unaware of his sudden illness, even as she took a step closer.

"Won't you reconsider college?"

"I don't need college," he replied, frustrated, almost gulping for air. "By the time you're done with school, I'll have my own company! I'm gonna get space here in the hangar and—"

"Pierce, you'll never have your own company!" She looked around and wrinkled her nose. "Is this what you want? To hang around here and drink beer and take out the trash?"

"What," he exclaimed, peering at her through squinting, tearing eyes. "You think that's what I do here?" He would have cried had he not felt so ill. "I-I spent all my savings on this ship, on..." He palmed the jewelry box in his coat pocket. "So I...we wouldn't be apart, after you left."

She looked at the ship, then at him.

"This is why you didn't make any of the teams, why you almost didn't graduate?" She threw her hands up in exasperation at the surroundings. *"For this?"*

"Again with the sports! You and everybody else—" He paused, nauseated and frustrated. "You wanna know something, Angel? I made all the teams. *Every single one.*"

"And you *quit?!*"

"Yes," he said, indignant. "And I did it for you. So I could work on this, so we could be together and have a future. Now."

Her face flushed in anger.

"How could you, Pierce," she screamed, her hands on her hips. Her voice reverberated all around them. "You're such an idiot!" She spun on a heel and stormed off toward the car. "Take me home!"

Stung by the ferocity of her anger, his stomach turned violently. He leaned unsteadily on the wing of the small starship and vomited uncontrollably.

Ten hours later, Angelica Smart sat quietly on her back porch, sipping at her morning tea. A slight breeze blew threw the yard and rippled the surface of the water in the inground pool below. The cool morning air hinted at the coming autumn. A small video monitor faced her on the table and *Good Morning, Stelumiere* had just signed off. With everything calm and quiet, she relaxed, contented to take a last look around. She vowed never again to return to such a ridiculously small town as Sophrire.

Every few minutes, she could hear her father going in and out of the front door, packing the aircar with her things. She thought about calling out to him, to tell him to be careful. Those bags were brand new. She wished he would hurry up. She didn't want to miss her early flight out of MemStar.

MemStar.

Pierce.

She still couldn't believe that she wasted her entire senior year and a whole summer on him. Her friends kept saying that he would never grow up, and they were right. She should have listened, but she got such a thrill out of the way everyone constantly talked about them. Once school ended and she drifted from her friends, she lost interest in Pierce as well, especially after his brothers came back from The War and he spent every weekend stag hunting with them. She wearied of trying to get him interested in things at school, to get him interested in more dignified pursuits. She should have realized this early on, when she couldn't get him to wear anything other than t-shirts. What her father and mother said about people from Piacevole, that they lacked sophistication, was so true. It's the only possible explanation for why he turned his back on athletics, and maybe a college scholarship, to pursue something so pedestrian as being a craftsman. And that fantasy about having his own company! He didn't even handle their break-up maturely. He brought her home without saying a word and he had this vacant, yet pained, looked on his face, like he might throw up at any second. Still, he was good for sex and annoying her father, but all of that needed to end. Now she needed her father to pay for school and she didn't want to risk messing that up.

She sighed and lowered the volume on the broadcast as the local Suetonia news feed came on. The image on the screen showed a house that caught fire overnight in Piacevole. How appropriate.

She held her teacup demurely with two fingers and looked absent-mindedly at the row of deciduous trees that ringed the yard. Some of the leaves had already turned. She imagined all the things she could enjoy now, free of Pierce. There would be no more boys in her life. Only men. And of course, she'd have to revamp her wardrobe once she got settled into the dormitory, away from her mother's prying eyes.

The timepiece on her wrist chimed. Time to go. She rummaged through her purse and made sure that she had her ID and ticket disc. She found a holodisc underneath it that she didn't recognize. She turned it on and a hologram of herself and Pierce appeared, an image of them holding hands, yet looking in opposite directions. She didn't remember where or when it was taken, and wondered what happened to the shirt she had on in the image. She shrugged and dropped the holodisc into the trash can near her feet. She finished the last of her tea, took her purse, and went into the house to tell her father to hurry up.

Chapter 7
The Tombs

Pierce awoke slowly.

Painfully.

The weight of the dark was suffocating.

He wheezed with each labored breath.

His chest hurt, his throat raw. His mouth tasted chalky and black. His whole body ached as he rolled gingerly onto his side. He felt, cold hard metal. In the pitch darkness, he could see nothing. He sat up and rubbed his eyes, to his immediate regret. His eyes stung badly. It had to be soot. Soot on his hands.

He had been in a fire. His house was on fire!

Jumping to his feet, he swung his arms all around. Nothing but air. He wasn't home anymore. But where, then?

His mind raced.

What had happened?

He couldn't remember.

He'd had a fight with Angelica and got home very late. He went in through the garage and to his own room behind the kitchen, so he wouldn't have to see anyone, especially Dante. The fluorescent light hummed over the kitchen sink, the dishwasher gurgling quietly. He heard his parents watching a picture show and his father roaring with laughter. Everything seemed normal. He put Angelica's ring in the stone hollow of his bedroom floor, with all his green disc notes and other stuff. Then his mother came in, to ask if everything was okay. Her company at that moment annoyed him. It was like she had radar or a sixth sense or something, always appearing whenever he wanted to be alone.

Then came all that noise, followed by his father shouting from across the house. A round container fell in his lap, and then the air smelled a sweet, golden brown. The rest was hazy. Smoke and fire everywhere, unbearable heat. Everything got so blurry so quickly, but he had to get his mother out. Mom first, everyone else last, Dad always said.

The nausea.

While fighting the heat—again that sudden, overwhelming wave of nausea. That same foulness that had crippled him at MemStar earlier that night. It knocked him to his knees. It worked him over even more severely this time, perhaps because that golden brown scent felt so good. Then someone grabbed him, someone impossibly strong, who set him on his feet and got him moving toward the door. He remembered a white macropian, or was it smoke?

Then nothing.

The dark stuck to him like black ink.

He instinctively touched the back of his head. He grimaced at how tender it was, and at the dried blood that coated the back of his neck.

Where was he now? What happened to his mother, his father?

He panicked and flung himself violently about in the darkness.

"HELP! SOMEBODY HELP ME! CAN ANYONE HEAR ME??!!"

His voice echoed in the emptiness.

"WHERE AM I? HELP ME, SOMEONE!"

He heard a loud hiss. He stood still, listening, straining to see in the dark. The air again smelled that golden brown, but this time much sweeter.

Almost sticky.

He blacked out.

He awoke to the same darkness, but this time bound at the wrist and ankles, his hands behind his back. The cold air and floor chilled his now naked body to the marrow. He felt clean and his head tingled, as if his head had been shaved.

A door opened and a bright white light fell on him. He squinted painfully, looking all around. He was in a metal box, about five meters by five, no furnishings, completely bare. Two black silhouettes, canites as best he could tell, approached him and pounced on him roughly. One held him down while the other pulled out a long silvery-white stiletto.

Pierce struggled and screamed as loudly as he could, but to no avail. The canite held his chin firm and hacked at his ear.

"Hold him still," he demanded of his partner, over Pierce's screaming.

"He's too strong!"

"I can't break the skin! Maybe I can gouge his face!"

Pierce felt his mouth forced open and his screams died stillborn as he gagged on the hairy fingers in his throat. He felt the blade set into the corner of his mouth, and then slice through his cheek to the back of his jaw line.

Pierce coughed on his own blood and sputtered mists of red as he screamed in despair.

"WHY?! W-WHY?! WHO ARE YOU?!!"

The canites stepped back, one cleaning his knife with a white cloth.

"WHAT...WHAT HAVE YOU DONE TO M-MY MOTHER?! WHERE'S MY FATHER?!"

The canites turned without a sound and the door clanged shut behind them.

Pierce let loose a final scream. A primal, feral scream.

"WHAT DO YOU WANT WITH ME?!!"

And then he cried.

In the absolute silence, he cried for his mother. He cried for his father.

He hacked and gagged at the blood and tears pouring into his mouth, streaming down his face. Sputtering and blubbering, he dissolved morosely into confusion and hopelessness.

He drifted in and out of consciousness. The gash in his mouth stung more than it actually hurt, so long as he didn't touch it with his tongue. This didn't surprise him, he had always been a fast healer. He had no way of telling time, but when he got all wet below his waist, he rolled to a dry spot on the cold, hard floor.

For awhile, he thought he might escape. After a struggle, he worked his bound hands to the front of his body. He dragged himself along the floor and explored every inch of the metal walls that he could touch. He felt for the seams in the door, but couldn't find them. He kicked at the walls with his bare feet and pounded on them with his fists. Hunger came and went, and he used one corner of his box for defecation. The horrible smell hit at him like a fist for a time, but he eventually grew accustomed to it.

The silence frightened him the most. Always so maddeningly quiet. He sat still for long periods, always listening for the slightest sound. Water poured in a thin stream from the center of the room periodically. He clawed at the metal floor, but couldn't find the drain.

When he heard the hiss again, when he breathed in that sweet golden brown aroma, part of him hoped he would not wake up.

Pierce started abruptly. No longer hungry or thirsty, he felt somewhat refreshed. Free of restraints, he touched the side of his face. The blood from his cut had been cleaned and stitched, but the wound still throbbed painfully. He was still naked, but no longer smelled his own waste. He sat up, shivered in the suffocating darkness, and cried into his hands.

He wiped his nose with a forearm and laid back down on the cold metal floor. He thought of his mother, his family. Did they get out of the fire? Were they okay? What would his father do in this situation? Certainly not cry. He wondered what Angelica was doing right now. Was she still mad at him? Was she even madder because he didn't see her off to school? He didn't want her to leave mad at him. Had she even realized he was missing yet? And Mr. Sporgenza—he'd be furious that he didn't show up for his shift. How long had it been?

He screamed non-sensically until he ran out of wind. Then he screamed every profane word and phrase that he knew, including things he'd heard his father say that he knew were foul, but had no idea what they meant.

"I'LL CLUB YOUR NUTS LIKE A FAT SKINNY!!"

He had no idea what else to do.

It occurred to him that his brothers used a lot the same phrases as their Dad once they came back from The War.

Dante, Nino and Alex.

Surely they were all searching for him…if they were alive. He thought of them burning, on fire.

He cried again, for a long time.

Then…*sound.* Noise other than himself.

He stifled his tears and listened intently. It was a voice! But from where?

"Will you shut up!"

He scrambled to a wall and crouched, his ear pressed against the metal.

"Who's there," he shouted.

"Henry?"

"Pierce! My name is Pierce!"

No response.

"Who are you?! Where are you?!"

No response.

He pounded on the wall.

"ANSWER ME!!"

No response.

He slumped onto the floor and pounded the wall repetitively, until his palm started to bleed. Then he used his other hand. Then his foot. Then the other foot. And then came the hiss. The hiss followed by the merciful golden brown release.

Pierce awoke in motion, strapped to a gurney. A white sheet covered his naked body, save for his head. Four men in surgical masks wheeled him swiftly down a brightly lit hall.

He couldn't speak. A metal plug filled his mouth that he couldn't remove. The cut side of his face throbbed and the air blowing against it felt like fire. The four men paid no attention to his muffled screaming.

They rounded a corner and proceeded toward a set of double doors. Pierce could hear a fifth set of footfalls rapidly approaching.

"Stop," someone yelled.

The gurney came to an abrupt halt. Through one of the windows in the double doors ahead, a pair of eyes appeared. Macropian eyes. They were as big as green saucers, and they stared at Pierce with an intensity bordering on desperation.

"Mr. Abernathé," one of the men asked.

"There's been a change in plans."

"I don't understand. Mr. Cervello personally sanctioned the procedure. The subject is ready."

"The procedure's been aborted."

Four pairs of eyes shared a confused exchange.

"My instructions are not to abort unless directed personally by Mr. Cervello or Mr. Abernathé." The man cleared his throat. "I mean, your father."

More footfalls surrounded them.

"Escort these men off the premises," the voice said. "And take.. *this*...back to The Tombs."

Chapter 8
Ecks

Above The Barrier Peaks, a luxury aircar cruised over barren, rugged terrain. Shafts of black rock jutted from a thin crust of snow and ice across an empty landscape. A thick mist rolled off the Summa Avarici mountains as the proud spires of Castel Mons loomed into view.

In the back seat of the aircar, behind tinted windows, Lorenzo de Abernathé III stared into a portable monitor. He scrolled with fascination through a gemological report on a trio of diamonds identified as Ecks stones. Another monitor built into the front of the seat beeped.

Without taking his eyes off the portable screen, he said, "On."

The other screen came to life and the picture of twelve year old boy, wearing a school uniform, came into focus.

"Hi, Dad!"

"Hello, son," Lorenzo replied distantly, his eyes still fixed on the portable screen. "Term has ended. Have you received your scores yet?"

"Today, yes."

"And?"

"Top five."

"Top five what," Lorenzo pressed, still distracted.

Young Lorenzo swallowed nervously.

"Percentile."

Lorenzo did not respond immediately.

"Dad?"

"That's unacceptable, Lorenzo."

The boy held up a glass object.

"But Dad, I won the—"

The graphics on the portable monitor faded. In its place appeared the craggy, weather beaten face of an old soldier. Lorenzo scrolled through his bio with interest.

"Awards are clutter," he told his son, still not looking up. "I will see you tomorrow evening for dinner. Have your things ready, Tomasso will be escorting you home at mid-day. Off."

The monitor faded to black.

"Well, well, well," Lorenzo said softly. "Mr. Ecks has a name." The aircar followed the curves of the towering spires and skimmed high above the smaller buildings. He finished reading through the file as the aircar landed at his personal port, adjacent to the largest spire. The driver got out and opened the door for him. As he got out, he put the portable computer in the pocket of his overcoat. A stiff wind blew at his back as he went inside. He meticulously smoothed out his long hair, annoyed that his neat, thin lines had been ruffled by the wind.

Max Siniscolchi waited by the elevator. He was dressed conservatively in his customary non-descript black suit and tie. As his top operative, Siniscolchi had a reputation as a man who knew how to get things done.

"Good morning, Mr. Abernathé."

"Max."

They stepped into the elevator and descended.

"The Cathedrals definitely have an Ecks Stone, Mr. Abernathé. Probably three."

"You're absolutely certain?"

Siniscolchi nodded.

"Yes, sir."

"How?"

"When Ecks was on the run from the authorities, he sold some stones to a high end broker, who in turn sold them to the Cathedrals. I assume you have seen the Ecks file, sir?"

"I have. It's incomplete."

"Yes, sir."

"You still haven't found out where or how he got the stones."

"It's only a matter of time, sir."

Lorenzo sighed.

"Time we do not have. Enough has been wasted already. The Ecks stones belong to AbStone, not Cathedral Corp, do you understand?"

"I do, sir."

"I want them. *All* of them."

"Yes, sir."

"The Cathedrals are coming for me, Max. My father believes that it's about pestlestones, but that's only pretense. Somehow they learned that I also have Ecks Stones and are as eager to learn their secret as I am. I don't have to remind you, Max, that for all my power and influence, I can't hope to stand toe to toe with the Cathedral Corporation. I do not want to fight a war with them, not without control of the stones. Do you understand?"

"Yes, sir."

"It is only with the wealth of the Ecks Stones that I can challenge the Cathedrals."

"Yes, sir."

"Where are we with Ecks?"

"He's proven resistant to babble juice. He has demonstrated an atypically high threshold for pain. We're now pursuing a psychological approach."

"And?"

"Still nothing, sir, but I am very optimistic. The first two subjects he wouldn't even acknowledge, but this last one provoked a verbal response."

Lorenzo looked at him, alarmed.

"*Two?!* Who do you have him speaking with? You recommended he remain completely isolated."

"Yes, sir, I did. But extended periods of isolation have had no effect. Given his tenacity, I reconsidered and pooled resources with a medical project that was also using the cages."

Lorenzo's mind exploded, but his face remained passive.

"Medical project?"

"Yes, sir. Under the direction of James Cervello. I'd worked with him very briefly before, back when Mr. Abernathé the Second was running the company. He assured me that he obtained your consent."

Lorenzo nodded, his brow furrowed.

James.

Siniscolchi appeared confused.

"Mr. Abernathé? Have I done something inappropriate?"

"No, Max. In fact, I must commend you. Excellent work thus far. But I *want* the secret of those stones."

The elevator came to a stop and the doors opened.

"Yes, sir. And you'll have it."

Alone, Lorenzo walked into a conference room and took a seat in front of a large flat screen monitor. The screen displayed a close up of Mr. Ecks, who sat slumped on the floor like a rag doll, his face adorned with a grim, yet vacant expression. A dense, bright light beat down on him from overhead. His brow cast a shadow over his eyes and the top part of his face. The picture widened to show Siniscolchi standing over him, hands in his pockets, inside a drab metal box. The technicians sitting next to him operated a complex board that monitored vital signs, room temperature and numerous other variables.

On the monitor, Siniscolchi took a step closer to Ecks.

"Remember when we renewed our acquaintance in the park on Gran Nexus earlier this year? And how I told you, Mr. Ecks, that there was no place you could hide from me? That there was nothing about you that I would not eventually learn? Your recalcitrance is not serving you well."

Ecks remained still.

"Galvin, Zoeicelli K. Lieutenant Commander, IW Marine Corps, twenty years. Multiple campaign medals for the Canite War. Merit Citation for the Occupation. Recycled into the Navy. Commander, Black Operations, Black Flag, five years. Commanding Officer of the Solonova Pathfinder. Killed in action at *Cryer's Wheel.* Convicted posthumously of breaking the original quarantine at

Ursus and bearing sole responsibility for spreading the chlorid foam throughout The Web, thus paving the way for the Enemy invasion." Siniscolchi clicked his tongue sadly. "My, my. That puts the deaths of billions squarely on your shoulders, doesn't it?"

Still no reaction. Not even the flicker of an eyelash.

"This information, Commander Galvin, was not easy to come by. Commendable work, surrounding your true identity with so much false biographical data. Even as we tracked your movements out to Arietta's Star and back, we still questioned your true name. The encryption that protected the discs you carried proved problematic, but not unsolvable. And now that we have that cipher, we know everything about you and Black Ops. In all that has transpired to this point, what I find truly remarkable, sir, is your posthumous conviction." A wry smile rolled across Siniscolchi's face. "Death offers many freedoms, Commander. Limitless possibilities."

Still nothing.

Siniscolchi squatted on his haunches and lifted Ecks' chin with a finger.

"Yet you threw it all away on that business with Lieutenant Ergaster. You've lost your anonymity, Commander. As a consequence, we now know that MacRaw is still out there, and since we now know his true identity, it won't be long before he's sitting right here next to you. Any thoughts you might be harboring, Commander, of him breaking in here to rescue you are severely misguided."

Ecks held his head up under his own strength for a moment, and his cold, penetrating eyes met those of Siniscolchi. Ecks set his jaw firmly and a chill went down Siniscolchi's spine. Siniscolchi flinched, certain that Ecks was going to strike him. Instead, Ecks again went flaccid and unresponsive.

Siniscolchi stood up.

"Now that we know who and what you are, Commander, it won't be long before we find out through other means the origin of the stones. It will go much better for you, sir, if you just tell me now. Where did you get the diamonds?"

No reaction.

"This is the last time I will ask nicely."

Silence.

Siniscolchi exited without another word.

Lorenzo sat at the head of a large conference table. The cold marble cooled his hands. Siniscolchi and Mr. Sa'am, an albino macropian, sat with him, along with two other men in dark suits.

"So what you're telling me Max," Lorenzo said, "is that you followed this man from one side of The Web to the other, taking his direction to the far reaches of space, but never learned his true identity?"

"That is correct, Mr. Abernathé," Siniscolchi said. He nodded at Sa'am to continue.

The white macropian leaned forward.

"We knew he was military, we knew he was a criminal, otherwise Ergaster and his men wouldn't have been involved. We couldn't betray your interest in Ecks to the authorities or your competitors by probing for additional information. At the time, it didn't matter who he was. It was enough to keep tabs on him, and we believed he'd eventually lead us to the stones. Once it became clear what he and his group had planned for Ergaster at Arietta's Star, we had to apprehend him before he either disappeared or accidentally killed himself. Nothing in his behavior profile suggested Black Ops."

"Is there anything else about him I should know," Lorenzo asked.

Siniscolchi shook his head.

"No, sir. He's unremarkable in every respect. He was recycled from the Marines into the Navy and dumped into Black Ops, probably commanding a decoy unit. According to court records, it was his unit that made first contact with The Enemy at Ursus, and his negligence allowed the contagion to spread throughout The Web. If not for that, the Vaengeli invasion would have stalled there. His unit, Black Flag, was presumed KIA as a result of their own bumbling. According to official records, that man we're holding is dead."

Lorenzo shifted his weight, growing impatient.

"Sa'am, is it possible he got the stones from The Enemy?"

Siniscolchi looked to the macropian.

"Highly improbable, Mr. Abernathé," Sa'am said. "We have no evidence or innuendo linking the Ecks Stones to the Vaengel. After Ursus, Black Flag literally disappeared for nine years before reappearing at one of the abandoned Clorox churches, here on Lethe."

"Yes, yes, yes," Lorenzo said quickly. "I know that part."

The macropian cleared his throat.

"Yes, sir. Sometime between Ursus and your meetings with them at the old church, Ecks acquired the stones. But he also acquired something else. This."

Sa'am placed a silver canister on the table.

"This was taken from Ecks when we apprehended him on Gran Nexus. It contains twenty-six black insects of an unknown genotype encased in solid amberenatol gel."

Lorenzo was unimpressed.

"I'm not interested in insects, Mr. Sa'am."

"Yes, sir, Mr. Abernathé. A critical part of the Ashpole Hearings was the assertion that the chlorid foam could be controlled with insects, and that the Navy had deliberately covered up their existence. Ecks was apprehended outside of Senator Ashpole's offices. We believe he was going to deliver this canister to the Senator."

Lorenzo looked from one to the other, then spread his eyes wide.

"So what?"

Sa'am swallowed nervously.

"The existence of this canister is very bad news for Kane, Abel and S'Gorbissa."

"Not to mention the Navy, if not the entire government," Siniscolchi added.

Lorenzo rested his chin on a thumb and forefinger.

"If I have this right, you're saying it's true that we created the chlorid foam, or at least allowed it to proliferate unchecked, and not The Enemy?"

"That's exactly what I'm saying," Siniscolchi said. "And Ecks can prove it. And is willing to do so."

"Which would make him innocent of the crimes he has been convicted of," Lorenzo mused.

"Yes, sir."

Lorenzo rolled his eyes.

"This is all very fascinating," he sighed. He leaned back in his chair and crossed his legs. "But I'm not interested in toppling governments or weakening the forces that protect them. It's bad for business. Nor do I care about drumhead court martials. This still tells us nothing about the stones."

"Not directly, sir," Siniscolchi said. "But it all comes back to this nine year stretch. Ecks was carrying a number of data discs along with this canister. The discs were compromised and unreadable, all save one. From this one disc, we know his unit was charged with pursuing and apprehending another rogue unit. It's unknown to us if they ever completed that mission. Wherever Black Flag was during that time span, they acquired the stones, the discs and this canister. The stones are unknown to modern geology the same as these bugs are unknown to modern entomology. There is a high probability that they came from the same place. The more we learn about Ecks, the easier it becomes to recreate his movements. There is no data on him for this particular nine year gap as Black Ops was purged before The War ended and its records destroyed. Outside of Admiral Kane, there is no one left alive that has any true knowledge of Black Ops."

"So you have no leads."

Siniscolchi barely repressed a smile.

"It's a challenge, sir, but not impossible."

"Where does this leave us?"

"I made some progress with Ecks today, sir, as you saw on the screens. Isolation suits him, but even the most solitary of men are compelled eventually to reach out, to connect with someone or something. We all have a need for companionship on some basic level, no matter how hard we try to deny it, which is why he's finally given in and spoken to the boy. I was able to cater to that instinct by referring to people that he knows. Notice his reaction to my simply speaking the name of his Lieutenant Commander, Tug MacRaw. I provoked an overly emotional response by merely *suggesting* the remote fantasy of rescue."

Lorenzo scoffed.

"He lifted his head. You call that emotional?" He shrugged. "Go on."

"We know MacRaw died on Arietta's Reckoning," Sa'am continued. "And so does Ecks. But now he thinks he knows something we don't. Now that he's feeling the undeniable urge to communicate, his overconfidence will let something slip."

Lorenzo arched his eyebrows.

"You think he *wants* to tell us where the stones are?"

"It's not as ridiculous as it sounds, Mr. Abernathé," Siniscolchi said. "He certainly wants to tell somebody."

"What have he and these boys discussed," Lorenzo asked.

"There have been no exchanges between Ecks and any of the boys," Sa'am explained. "Until this latest one."

"And?"

"Ecks asked his name," Sa'am said.

"*His name? That's it?*"

Siniscolchi nodded.

"Aren't they in the cages?"

Siniscolchi nodded again.

"The steel ones. In The Tombs."

"He asked this boy his name. Through a steel wall. In the dark. *That's it?*"

Siniscolchi cleared his throat.

"Considering that Ecks hasn't uttered a sound the entire time he's been our guest, sir, it is *very* significant. With your permission, I'd like to move both Ecks and the boy from the steel cages to the clear ones."

"The plastic steel boxes are already in place," Sa'am explained. "We're ready to proceed with your authorization."

"In The Tombs?" Lorenzo rubbed his forehead with the corner of his palm. "Max, I certainly hope you know what you're doing, because it doesn't sound like it."

Siniscolchi and the macropian made eye contact nervously.

"Mr. Abernathé—"

Lorenzo pointed a finger at them.

"Resources are not unlimited! I have the Cathedrals to worry about! I want no more excursions like Argulski's Star, am I clear?"

"Yes, sir," Siniscolchi said.

"Have you thought about Kane," Lorenzo asked.

"Yes, sir, I have. Blackmailing the Admiral for his knowledge of Black Ops would be risky. Again, it would draw attention to yourself and increase the likelihood of a leak that could reveal the existence of the stones. And there's still no guarantee that Kane knows anything relevant."

Lorenzo pounded a fist on an armrest in frustration.

"And there's not one other person in this whole damned galaxy who has *any* information?"

"That appears to be correct, sir," Siniscolchi answered. "Admiral Chamberlain, Kane's superior when he was running Black Ops, died in prison. All of the Black teams were murdered by political officers. What little bureaucracy there was running Black Ops has vanished, also probably murdered by the PO's. As we know from the good Senator Ashpole, Kane's aide, Vice-Admiral Panya, presided over the destruction of all of the Black Ops data. She's dead, too. The data we took from Ecks is insightful but useless, and he's not talking. Kane is all that remains."

Lorenzo had no interest in bringing down the government. He thought a long moment.

"What about that former political officer you recruited? The one who worked directly for Amos Emmett? Surely he must have access to information exclusive to the PO's."

Siniscolchi paused.

"What is it," Lorenzo insisted. "And don't tell me he's not willing betray old allegiences. It's why I hired him, Max."

"Cosbie's dead, Mr. Abernathé."

Lorenzo's face contorted in anger. Political officers simply didn't turn to private employment. It was part of their psychotic devotion to whatever paranoid fantasies they believed in.

"What," he shouted, standing bolt upright. "I invested a fortune in him at your urging! How?!"

"The Cervello Project, sir. Mr. Cervello let us use his detainees, so I loaned him some of my personnel for a minor field op. Mistakes were made, none of which are traceable back to you, sir, but Cosbie was injured and died enroute to a medical facility."

"A rogue political officer, working for *me,* and you let him get killed," Lorenzo fumed, his hands on his hips. He shut his eyes and tilted his head to the ceiling. "What mistakes?"

"A simple stealth op, sir. Live target retrieval on Gran Nexus, for this latest boy. Trained military personnel were unexpectedly present in the targeted residence. There was resistance, but the target was retrieved. The location was burned to maintain your anonymity, sir."

"*My anonymity,*" Lorenzo shouted.

Siniscolchi nodded weakly, as if he had resigned himself to this moment sometime ago.

"The team was driven from the residence and it was burned only as a last resort."

"You burned them alive?"

"If you wish to view it that way, sir. To be precise, the surviving occupants would have been overcome by smoke inhalation long before the flames reached them."

Lorenzo's jaw clenched in exasperation.

"And you're sure no one survived this fiasco?"

"Not according to the report filed by Mr. Sa'am, the team leader."

"And none of this is traceable back to AbStone?"

"No, sir."

Lorenzo pounded his fist on the table.

Siniscolchi sensed Lorenzo's mounting anger.

"We can overcome this, sir."

Lorenzo's response died in his throat as Cervello entered the room, followed closely by a large plasmoid. Cervello was much thinner than he remembered and looked well for his age. Cervello appeared calm, either unaware of how much danger he was in at the moment, or simply didn't care.

Lorenzo smoothed the lines of his suit and wiped at the sweat forming on his forehead. He took a long moment to regain his composure. He buried his frustration over the stones, buried the rage he felt at seeing this man again. Only upon the restoration of a calm, controlling veneer did he dare speak.

"Max, your people are dismissed."

Sa'am nodded, then led the other two men and the plasmoid out. Only Siniscolchi remained.

"Hello, Lorenzo," James said. "You seem well."

"I said I never wanted to see you again."

"Yes, you did. I did everything I could to ensure that."

"Very cunning of you to hide in plain sight," Lorenzo said, trying his best to sound agreeable. "In spite of my instructions, Max here tells me that you've made some progress."

Cervello's expression brightened a bit.

"Yes, Lorenzo. The boy we have in custody now is the last of the infant clones. They can hardly be called infants anymore, at eighteen years of age. The cranial material we harvested from them was of little help to your father."

"And this last one?"

"He was harder to locate and, unlike the others, had to be separated from an adoptive family. Mr. Siniscolchi's personnel were very helpful in this effort."

Lorenzo glanced severely at Siniscolchi.

"Yes, so I've been told."

"There are some...unique aspects to this one's genome, and there is reason to be optimistic."

"Unique?"

"His sensory perception is atypical, some enhanced physical characteristics, but I am assured his tissue is suitable."

"Where is he now?"

"He's being prepped for harvesting."

"And Menscher?"

"Still at large, I'm afraid."

Lorenzo nodded.

"Might I ask," Cervello said hesitantly. "How is your father, Lorenzo?"

"His mind is rot," he responded angrily. "But his body is strong, much too healthy for his own good. He doesn't know me, nor can he remember his own name. He wanders aimlessly down hallways that he doesn't recall one moment from the next. He should have died years ago, but now he won't because of what he—you—have done. You robbed him of his dignity. Paradise forgive me for not killing you a long time ago, James."

Cervello trembled at the force of Lorenzo's words.

"I'm terribly sorry, Lorenzo. I-I was only doing what your father wanted. But this last infant, h-he's different, h-he just might—"

"Might what," Lorenzo shouted.

"W-w-we've come so f-far," Cervello stammered. "T-this one, the s-synapse strength is eighty percent above mean!"

Lorenzo stepped aside as Siniscolchi came up behind Cervello. He took the old man by the back of the neck and violently bent him down on top of the table. Siniscolchi looked up at Lorenzo.

"Lorenzo," Cervello pleaded, his face pressed hard against the cold marble. "Y-your father would not want this."

"It's not about what he wants, anymore, James."

Lorenzo nodded. Siniscolchi took a laser from inside his jacket and shot Cervello through the back of the head. Blood and tissue splattered across the table.

"Get someone in here to clean this up," Lorenzo said, then opened the door and walked out.

The door closed softly behind Lorenzo. He stood alone in the deserted hallway. Angry, he walked purposefully toward The Tombs, his fists pumping with each stride.

Why should he intervene? Let the surgeons finish this boy off and end this ugly chapter of his family's history. He could then have Max send that young macropian, Mr. Sa'am, after Menscher full time. Sa'am had some promising attributes and Max thought highly of him, but Max also thought highly of Cosbie.

Cosbie.

An incalculably valuable and unique asset. A potential path to the Ecks Stones.

Simply erased.

Because of James.

And this boy.

The boy.

Ecks had spoken to him. Why him and not any of the others? What is it about this boy that appealed to Ecks? Max considered this a sign that Ecks was starting to break. And if Ecks wouldn't reveal the location of the stones to Max, perhaps he'd be willing to tell this boy. He took his comm from his pocket and signaled for Max.

"Yes, Mr. Abernathé," his voice said.

Lorenzo thought about sending him to intercept the surgical team, but then reconsidered. This clone business had been mishandled through delegation. The time had come to take care of this business personally.

"Make sure all of the people working on Cervello's medical project are escorted off the premises immediately." He put the device back in his pocket.

Lorenzo doubled his pace, then started to run. He didn't stop until he rounded a corner beyond the cages. Four men in scrubs wheeled a gurney toward some double doors at the end of the hall.

"Stop," he yelled.

The four men halted.

"Mr. Abernathé?"

"There's been a change in plans."

Chapter 9
The Eternal Hour

Pierce awoke gradually from a profound blackness. He sat up slowly and everything spun out of control. It took several minutes for his senses to clear. He was someplace bright now, too bright. An overhead light weighed on him, made his limbs heavy, and pushed him back to the floor.

It smelled green, almost minty.

Clean, but sterile.

He had been washed again and put into turquoise surgical scrubs, like a doctor. He felt his face gingerly and his wound had been cleaned and the stitches removed. That side of his face hurt very badly, as if he had been hit repetitively without mercy.

His foggy vision cleared. This other place, it had transparent walls. That voice called it The Tombs. The light poured with a harsh brightness from above and outside the rather large box. Darkness surrounded him on all sides.

But one.

His container shared a common wall with another, identical to his own. It even had an occupant. On the other side of the barrier, a man, also in surgical scrubs, sat slumped on the floor, against the far wall. A shadow fell across the entire front of his body, obscuring his features. He looked more like a discarded marionette than a human being.

"Hey," Pierce called out. "Can you hear me?"

He wearily separated himself from the floor and pounded on the transparent wall with his fists.

"HEY!! CAN YOU HEAR ME?!"

No reaction.

What was the point of all this now? To see each other, but not be able to communicate?

Pierce turned away from the man and sat down cross legged in the center of his box. The cube measured four meters by four, and about two and half meters high. A very small toilet and wash basin occupied the far corner. He gaped at the starkness of his surroundings, the hopelessness of it all, and couldn't make any sense of it. Overwhelmed, he felt another wave of hysteria building, but this time he resisted, and took deep, long breaths to keep from hyperventilating.

No more crying. His father wouldn't cry. Dante wouldn't cry. Neither would Pennsylvania Smith, his favorite hero from the picture shows.

Think.

His father always said that The Enemy's greatest weapon was fear. Don't be afraid, or at least don't let it show.

He took a moment to gather his thoughts. Somebody called Cervello wanted to operate on him, and another guy, Abernathé, had stopped it. This Abernathé's father wanted the operation to happen. What kind of operation? The only Abernathés he knew of were the ones who owned the jewelry stores. How common a name was Abernathé, anyway?

And what had changed? What made this Abernathé intercede on his behalf? Did he arrange for this light, instead of darkness, and the cell mate? Why attack his family? Was this Cervello responsible?

He shook his head in confusion. His father always said to be aware of your surroundings, no matter where you were. He peered into the darkness outside. He could see nothing. He got up and ran his fingers along the walls. They weren't entirely smooth, a bit rough to the touch. He recognized the feel of plastic steel. He marveled at the construct—he didn't know it could be manufactured as transparent at this size. Spacesuit helmets, starship windows, sure, but in three by four sheets? That made this cell, this tomb, as Abernathé called it, very, very expensive.

The seams and the corners had no imperfections. He could detect no door, no method of entry. The plumbing for the toilet and sink was not exposed. The fixtures were stainless steel instead of ceramic.

He still had no idea if he could be heard outside the walls. He stepped up to the wall separating him from the other man. He pounded on the plastic steel with all his strength.

"MISTER," he shouted. "HEY!!"

Still no response.

Frustrated, he thought maybe the guy was deaf. He instinctively signaled in the Marine cant that he used when hunting with his father and brothers, and then stopped abruptly. It had no similarities to Websign.

He sighed deeply and shut his eyes, leaning with both hands against the wall. He could feel the air circulating just a bit, but heard no sound. That minty, sterile air. No hum of a motor, no hum of power lines. Just the air moving. How? His anger again mounted. Who in Blazes were these people? What did they want with him? He pounded his fists again on the wall and opened his eyes.

And the other man's face, not a meter away from his own, glared at him with a cold ferocity.

Startled, Pierce let out a frightened yelp and fell onto his backside. The man, a grizzled old man, didn't move. He just stood there, his balance precarious, watching him with a forceful, penetrating stare.

Pierce looked him over carefully. A bushy gray beard coated a craggy face, his jaw rounded and sagging. Deep scars cut into his face and neck, and his long hair thinned at the top. He stood at over two meters tall, but was sickeningly thin. One leg looked shorter than the other, which threw him off balance. He wobbled a bit, then sat down roughly. He pressed his face close to the transparent wall. Dull, vacant blue eyes stared back at Pierce, unblinking.

Pierce sat upright.

"What in Blazes, hah?"

The man's face sagged from a straight line into a frown. He spoke with great difficulty, as if it pained him to do so.

"Are you the one?"

"The one what?"

"I called you Henry."

Pierce flushed in embarrassment. Then, astonished, he excitedly moved in closer.

"Yes! Through the wall! Was that here?"

The man shook his head.

"We're someplace else. Now."

"Who are you?"

"Call me Ecks."

"Why—?"

"I know why," he interjected curtly. "I know *why* I'm here. What about *you?*"

"I have no idea! One minute, I'm talking to my mother in my house, the next we were attacked! They cut my face—"

"Here? Or in your house?"

"Here."

Ecks nodded.

"Two other boys, before you. Nick Wright. Henry Mason. Those names. They mean anything to you?"

"No. Where are they now?"

"No idea." Ecks looked around with deliberate calm. "Be careful. What you say and what you do. Always listening, always watching. *Give them nothing.*"

"Who's watching?"

Ecks eyed him warily.

"Pierce, right?"

"Yeah. Pierce Sicuro. From Gran Nexus. Are we on a different planet now? What's going on? What do these people want with me?"

Ecks' flabby jaw set squarely and Pierce could hear his grinding teeth.

"What do they want with us," Pierce pressed. "Why are we here?"

Ecks groaned as he stood up, using the wall for support.

"It'll come to you. Eventually."

He turned his back on Pierce and slowly shuffled his way back to the far wall.

"How," Pierce shouted.

Ecks slumped heavily to the floor.

"In time. Plenty of it."

Ecks said 'They' were always watching. Whoever 'They' were, Pierce never saw them. They gassed him at regular intervals to wash him, change his clothes, provide food and clean the cell. He tried to hold out against the gas a few times, without success. He discovered the source of the gas at the base of the wash basin, and he tried everything he could think of to separate the fixtures from their moorings. Time lost all meaning and he measured the days by the number of times they knocked him out.

Through an agonizing stretch where the weeks melted into months, Ecks did not utter a sound. He just sat there, perfectly still, the whites of his eyes following his every move. At first, Pierce found it infuriating, but soon grew accustomed to it. He screamed all his frustrations at Ecks, insulting him everyway possible for his silence. Then he ignored Ecks, figuring two could play at the same game, and concentrated on finding a way to escape. Giving up on that, he finally just lay down on the floor, near their shared wall, and spent endless days giving excruciatingly detailed instructions for retro-fitting cabin cruiser interiors.

Then Pierce hit on the topic of stag hunting.

"We'd go out to The Timberland Fens once a month. My Dad taught us to hunt the same way they did in—"

"I don't wanna hear about no fucking stag hunting."

Pierce sat bolt upright and looked at Ecks.

"What did you say?"

"You're weak. Typical Inny Trash."

It a took a minute for Pierce to find his voice.

"R-right back at ya, pal. That all you got to say, or are you having too good a time eyeing me like some fag canite?"

"You're gonna die here," Ecks growled. "Me much sooner than you."

Pierce stood up, as if threatened in some way.

"How can you know that?"

Ecks crawled closer to Pierce, dragging his body using only his arms.

"These people. They don't make mistakes."

Pierce's lower lip trembled.

"Don't cry," Ecks barked. "It can't be changed."

Pierce nodded slowly.

Ecks bent his knees, groaning from the effort.

"I know why you're here."

"How?! You said before you had no idea!" Pierce shook his head in frustration. "Just tell me!"

Ecks took a long pause.

"That's the last time you yell at me. Understand?"

Pierce swallowed hard and nodded.

Ecks pressed up against the wall that separated them.

"It's also the last time you speak. You will not speak again. Ever."

"I don't—"

"Ever."

Pierce nodded quickly. The way this man spoke, the way he moved—his words had power.

Ecks studied him closely. For the first time, his eyes resonated.

Bright and perceptive.

Penetrating.

Ecks tilted his head to the side a bit and then nodded imperceptibly. His left eye half-winced as he pressed both hands against the transparent retaining wall, his index fingers curled into his palms. He leaned heavily on the wall as he got to his feet, his fingers a dark pink from the effort. His balance was precarious, but he managed to walk back to the far wall of his cell. He sat heavily on the floor and assumed his familiar, sodden shape.

Infuriated, Pierce slammed his fist on the plastic steel and opened his mouth to shout, but the storm died in his throat. He raged in silence at Ecks and pounded repeatedly on the unforgiving transparent wall. He kicked at the wall and fell to the floor in agony, thinking for sure he'd broken something. He rolled about clutching his throbbing foot, all the while not making a sound. When the pain ebbed, he stood up again and paced the length of the wall, his eyes burning into the passive Ecks. With his front ensconced in shadow, Pierce could very clearly see the whites of his eyes, those ice blue orbs following his every move.

He stopped pacing and leaned on the glassteel with both hands, his index fingers curled into his palms. He locked eyes with Ecks and grit his teeth for spite.

And then those eyes went dark.

Pierce angrily pushed off the wall and retreated to the far side of his own container, as far away from Ecks as he could get. He sat down and waited.

He would wait a long time.

Time ceased to have any meaning. Pierce's hair and beard grew long and stringy, only for it to be shaven off, only for it all to grow back again. Threadbare clothing vanished, his fingernails stayed nicely trimmed. His surroundings never changed, the routine never varied. A prisoner not only of space but also of time, he heeded the enigmatic demand of this stranger, Ecks, and did not speak.

In the interim, Ecks slowly came to life. He started with arm exercises, then built up strength in his legs. Pierce mirrored his every move, matched his every inflection. Through it all, Ecks said nothing, never looked Pierce in the eye, never acknowledged his presence. This game of shadows went on until Ecks had enough strength to shadow spar with Pierce through the transparent wall. Then Ecks demanded Pierce's full attention, which at first Pierce found withering.

This routine of vigorous, strenuous exercise continued unaltered throughout the length of this eternal now. These two imaginary combatants, so intent on outdoing one another, grappled with each other endlessly through the wall. As the sessions wore on, both Pierce and Ecks grew stronger, until the moment came when Ecks finally, inevitably, ebbed. A single misstep, an errant gesture, and Ecks was done. He simply stopped in mid stride, turned and sat against the far wall, his entire front doused once again in shadow.

Ecks never moved again.

How long Pierce waited for him to rise, he didn't know. His patience worked against him. He eventually blacked out from exhaustion. When he awoke, Ecks was gone. No surprise registered with Pierce at all. He resumed his exercises in silence.

Alone.

Time.

More time passed. Pierce's captors gassed him less frequently. His container wreaked of his own waste, his hair and beard growing long and scraggly again. They stopped bathing him and fed him irregularly. He tasted the dark brown tinge of waste in the spigot water.

Pierce endured in silence.

He continued to exercise until he no longer had the stamina, his body gradually failing under the conditions. He sat down against the far wall of his cell and let the shadows fall across the front of his body.

In the howling silence, he waited.

He brushed the hair away from his brow and rolled onto his back. Through bloodshot and blurry encrusted eyes, he looked up into the black. The darkness that surrounded him on all sides... unforgiving, unchanging.

Then...movement. Something moved on the top of his cell. No, not something.

Someone.

Pierce scrambled to his feet. He quickly looked in all directions, then back up again. A figure covered head to toe in a skin tight, jet black body suit melted out of the darkness and descended toward him.

It had three arms and legs.

The plasmoid soon stood face to face with Pierce. He could see the clear, plastic steel cable in its grasp.

"Do not speak," the plasmoid hissed. "Nod if you want out."

Pierce nodded vigorously and accepted one of the plasmoid's outstretched hands. The cable retracted without a sound, lifting them both up and out of the container, and into the stygian blackness.

The plasmoid shoved him off the cable and onto what felt like scaffolding. Pierce's eyes adjusted quickly to the darkness. He crouched on a narrow catwalk, one of a dozen spokes that stretched out over the two brightly lit cells below. Light fixtures mounted on the railings flooded the cells with an impenetrable wall of light. An army of people could have been walking around up here at any time and he wouldn't have known.

Without a sound, the plasmoid led him toward a smooth rock wall where it inserted a plastic card into a metal slot. A hidden door slid open and they passed through into a dimly lit space.

The plasmoid thinned its body shape and squirted out of the body suit. It handed Pierce a ball of clothing.

"Change into this."

Pierce obeyed. The plasmoid sprayed Pierce's head with a small aerosol can. Then three padded hands ran over his face and head, stripping away all of his hair.

Pierce stared at clumps of hair in his hands and before he could say anything, another man joined them from out of nowhere. Thin and gaunt, he also had no head or facial hair, and wore the same clothing as Pierce.

The man looked Pierce up and down and nodded his approval.

"Are you okay," the man asked.

"W-where are we," Pierce asked, his eyes flitting nervously between the two.

"Listen," he said quickly, leaning in close. "This place is called The Tombs, and it's where the Abernathés store all of their old stone lathes and other equipment that they've never patented, see?"

Pierce nodded dumbly.

The lights suddenly went out and even dimmer emergency lights clicked on.

The man continued, but with less urgency.

"It's all worth a fortune, alright? But they can't do anything with it because—"

"We're in a network of caves," the plasmoid interrupted. "Deep within the Summa Avarici mountains, but connected by one heavily guarded tunnel to Castel Mons. We're close enough to The Barrier Peaks to get you out of here."

None of this made any sense to Pierce.

"I mean, what planet?"

The human and the plasmoid looked at each other in stunned amazement, then back at Pierce.

"Lethe," the man said. "You've heard of it, right?"

"Who are you?"

"The good guys."

"Why are we just standing here? Surely they realize I'm gone already!"

"Don't count on it," the plasmoid said, glancing purposefully at his timepiece. "We still have a few minutes. The animate containers aren't watched as closely these days. They still watch the drills and all the other hardware like perverts ogling street walkers, of course."

"You ready," his companion asked.

"Yes."

The trio moved stealthily into a warehouse. They brushed against row after row of magnetically sealed crates, each placed neatly on steel gray shelves and marked with four digit serial numbers.

"If this stuff is so valuable," Pierce asked, "what about security?"

"We are the security here. We've got maybe another fifty seconds before the defenses come back online."

The plasmoid halted abruptly.

"7011...7010. Right here," it said.

The plasmoid and the human each took one end of the crate and lowered it to the floor. Using a keypad on the top, the plasmoid punched in a series of numbers and the lid slid off without a sound. The plasmoid lifted a very large drilling apparatus from the box and slung it over its broad shoulders. The man returned the crate to the shelf.

The trio moved with haste down the last few rows of shelves. The man pulled Pierce along, who stumbled in bewilderment at the events and his surroundings. Even with its heavy burden, the plasmoid kept up, clearly conditioned for this kind of strenuous exercise.

The darkened exit doors loomed ominously in front of them. The trio burst through these doors and the human shoved them closed, just as the lights clicked back on and the magnetic locks reengaged.

They hustled down a wide corridor hewn from the black rock. They passed under one concrete arch after another, until the plasmoid indicated they stop.

"I counted 26."

The man nodded in agreement.

The plasmoid flipped the drill off its shoulders and held it balanced on the floor with one hand. With its two free hands, it put on a pair of gloves and then set about priming the tool, handling it like an expert. At the same time, its entire body expanded, growing a meter wider and taller.

"Stand back," the man said to Pierce.

The drill now seemed like a toy in the hand of the plasmoid. It pressed the tool against the rock wall and with a dull hum, huge sections of rock melted to the floor in a fine, black powder. It wasn't long before a large enough space had been hollowed out that could accommodate all three of them.

The plasmoid turned off the drill.

"Let's go."

It stepped inside the hole and the man shoved in Pierce after. The plasmoid recalibrated the drill, and a thin laser cut chunks of rock from the ceiling. They fell with one loud crash after another. Before Pierce could react, the entrance had collapsed, trapping them in utter blackness, and separating them from the human.

Pierce coughed and wheezed, tasting the sandy, black grit of rock dust in his mouth. He could feel the plasmoid next to him, and see the drill in his three hands glowing in the dark.

"I can't breath," Pierce rasped.

"Imagine how I feel," the plasmoid replied impatiently, fiddling with something behind his back.

"How will your friend escape," Pierce coughed.

"He's not my friend. And I told you, we're part of the security here."

Pierce's eyes burned.

"We're buried alive!"

The plasmoid flicked on a battery light and handed it to Pierce.

"Only for a moment."

In the confined space, the plasmoid had shrunken from the bulk it had put on in the hallway, to the point where it measured just as big as the drill.

The plasmoid adjusted another setting on the bulky tool and set to work again. Pierce held the light over its shoulder. Again, the humming drill ground the rock down to a fine powder.

The dust coated Pierce's sweaty face like a black paste. After a dozen or so meters of progress, he could feel dampness on the rocks.

He tapped the plasmoid's shoulder vigorously, who only looked about, and then nodded.

"We're under a river, kid. When I break through, this space will fill with water quickly. Hold your breath. Wait until it fills up, then swim out into the current, and up to the surface. The river is only three to four meters deep here, but the current is strong. Let the current take you out of the mountain, then swim to shore. Do you understand?"

"The mud and silt from the riverbed will choke us to death! Don't—"

The plasmoid hefted the drill.

"This'll take care of it. The water will be hot at first, but it won't last. And don't panic. Swim easy, broad strokes. Got it?"

Pierce swallowed hard.

"Okay."

The plasmoid again adjusted the settings, and resumed drilling. Now instead of dust, the rock liquefied and Pierce gasped deeply in the brackish green humidity. He could see the plasmoid working at cutting a space with a wide circumference. There would be plenty of room to swim through.

"Get behind me! Get behind me," the plasmoid suddenly shouted. Pierce did as told, leaning against one of the walls. The rock in front of him suddenly melted away to be replaced by the rushing sting of hot water. The plasmoid disappeared in the violent surge and everything went dark. Pierce braced himself against an outcropping as the water pounded against his body. In sheer terror, he found it impossible to take a deep breath. Then the water turned shockingly cold, making it impossible to breathe at all. The small space filled almost instantly and the pressure against his body eased considerably.

Already desperate to draw another breath, Pierce began to swim. He kicked and swung his arms wildly in the pitch black water. He didn't feel like he was making any progress, but then he remembered what the plasmoid had said.

Swim easy.

He forced himself to relax and he pushed off the rock wall, kicking and spreading his arms in rhythm. A strong current bent and pulled him up at the same time. He rushed forward as if he were flying, terrified at the thought of blindly plowing face first into the rocks.

With considerable effort, he propelled himself upward, moving with the torrent of rushing water. Lungs bursting, he broke through the surface and gasped loudly in the open air. The sound of his labored breathing echoed off the stone walls. In random spots, a glowing, soft blue lichen coated the rocks, and the patches of light whizzed by like a strobe. He could barely keep himself above the surface of the icy cold waters. He struggled as the river carried him further and still further downward, deeper into the mountain. The deafening crush of the surging waves pounded his ears in the confined space. He didn't know for how much longer he could survive this.

After a sudden drop, Pierce poked his head up above the surface just in time to be flung high above the water. Suddenly, free falling through the cold air, he grasped in panic at the open space under him, unable to see. He hit the water again, hard. Stunned by the impact, he slowly made it to the surface. The water here flowed calmer and the current didn't pull at him as hard. Treading water, he breathed deeply and looked around.

The night sky.

Stars!

A dark forest on each river side, coniferous and birch trees.

The outside!

He tried to wipe the water from his face with a wet hand, then swam to shore. He pulled himself up on the rocks, then dragged his wet, exhausted body closer to the trees. Panting, he lay on his back, suddenly giddy with laughter.

The wind blew on him and his breath hung in the air like a frozen, white vapor. It was cold. Very cold. He needed to find shelter, get out of these wet clothes.

And the plasmoid.

Where was it? And why?

He scrambled to his feet and clawed his way up the rock line. He only got a few steps into the forest before being struck hard in the face and knocked backwards, back down the rocky embankment. Before he could pick himself up, the plasmoid jumped on him and hit him again.

Pierce lay on his back, half conscious, blood dripping from his nose. The plasmoid stood next to him, pushing buttons on its forearm.

"Wha—," Pierce stammered. "What...*why?*"

"You're important to the Abernathés," the plasmoid replied. "That makes you valuable to us."

"I-I'm not going anywhere. W-with you."

"I'm not giving you a choice."

A small aircar approached from down river, skimming over the water. The plasmoid pushed another button on its forearm and the car landed quietly next to them. A door opened, and the plasmoid used oversized hands to scoop up Pierce and toss him effortlessly into the empty car.

Three more aircars appeared in the dark sky, approaching from the opposite direction, from over the mountainside. Probing searchlights slashed the night in repetitive patterns.

The plasmoid got in the car, only to be ejected by Pierce's foot. He climbed out of the car and stood over the stunned plasmoid.

"No more cages!"

"You damned fool," the plasmoid shouted. "Those aircars'll be on us in seconds!"

Pierce picked up the plasmoid by an arm and a leg and flung it into the aircar. It struggled to get up.

"They'll kill us both!"

Pierce jammed the throttle to the floor and backed away from the car.

"No. Only *you*."

The aircar blasted upward in a cloud of dust, spinning slowly, higher and higher. The aircar fell immediately into the searchlights of the other three. Pierce scrambled up the rocks and paused at the tree line. A salvo of rockets whooshed through the air, leaving white vapor trails in the night sky. In an instant, the aircar carrying the plasmoid exploded in a fiery conflagration. Flaming bits of metal and plastic splashed into the river, and the smoldering debris washed further downstream. Pierce ducked into the woods, disappearing in a whispering puff of pine needles.

The three aircars flew low along the water, searching the shoreline, floodlights flitting this way and that with practiced precision. A few minutes later, the aircars abruptly ascended and disappeared back over the mountainside.

Some fifteen minutes later, the sun came up over the horizon. As the shadows of the trees fell across the river, the water flowed clean and clear downstream, and it was as if no one had ever been there before.

Chapter 10
Siniscolchi

A month had passed since the Sicuro boy's escape and Max Siniscolchi's hair was falling out in clumps. With his black tie loose about his neck and his white shirtsleeves rolled up to his elbows, he wearily crossed his arms over his chest to hide his shaking hands. The team under his command filled the conference room, two operating the consoles and the other eight seated around the large table. Soiled styrofoam coffee cups lay strewn about and ashtrays spilled over with cigarette butts. Candy wrappers ringed the overflowing trash bins.

The conference room had the stench of a locker room with no one having been in or out in over a week. Around the clock since the Sicuro boy had escaped, they poured over the video and audio feeds of his ten year captivity, minute by minute, second by second. They watched the images on the screen in manic stillness and scratched notes furiously on e-pads.

It all looked the same.

Sleep, exercise, eat and repeat.

Every damn day for ten years.

They were nowhere closer to finding the answers to the questions that Mr. Abernathé would surely ask, and he was due to call at any moment.

Siniscolchi sat quietly at the table. His bleary, bloodshot eyes stared blankly at the large flat screen monitor on the wall. His top lieutenants had been screaming at each other from opposite ends of the table for most of the day, Stick Breufogle in his left ear and Mr. Sa'am in his right. The shouting had ceased, for the moment, but a thick sense of anger and hostility still hung in the air.

Siniscolchi pinched the bridge of his nose with two nicotine stained fingers and shut his eyes tightly. They teared at the corners from the strain and he sighed loudly.

"Breufogle?"

The unusually lean man sitting to his left shook his head.

"I got nothing."

"Sa'am?"

The albino macropian sat on his right, his thick white mane matted flat to his head. He smelled worse than all of them put together. He wore headphones, his eyes shut.

Siniscolchi nudged him, thinking he was asleep.

Annoyed, Sa'am opened one eye and glared at him. He shook his head.

"Nothing Max." Then he muttered under his breath. "This is a waste of *fucking* time."

Breufogle leaned across Siniscolchi and shouted, "*Then why did Ecks suddenly sit and not get up?!*"

Sa'am hopped to his feet and slammed the headphones on the table.

"Because he stroked out, dammit! There's no sound! You know why there isn't any sound, Stick? *Because there isn't any sound.* They were communicating non-verbally!"

Breufogle pointed angrily at the screen.

"No they weren't, Sa'am. Look! There's no indication—"

"The boy tried using Websign—"

"And then stopped because Ecks wasn't deaf," Breufogle shouted. "And that wasn't Websign! And no hand movements remote to Websign were ever used again!"

"Then we're missing it!"

"Oh, we're certainly missing something," Siniscolchi sighed.

They were all exhausted and frustrated. Sa'am and Breufogle had strongly differing opinions on how to interpret the data and with everyone's nerves frayed, it had become personal. Only Sa'am had developed a theory, and Breufogle grew more steadfast in his attempts to discredit it. They were competing for Siniscolchi's approval, and while he normally encouraged competition among his subordinates, right now, it only gave him a headache. His head pounded from their bickering.

"This routine they had was seamless from day one," Siniscolchi said. "Somehow it was mapped out and agreed upon."

"Yeah, yeah, yeah," Sa'am said quickly. "I'm telling you, it wasn't verbal, Max. The answers are in the *images*, not the *sound*."

Breufogle tossed his e-pad on the table and his stylus bounced across the marble surface.

"There is no material deviation in their body language!"

"By what standard, Stick?! You cling to these arbitrary guidelines—"

"Sa'am, you're wrong, you're wrong! *You are wrong!*"

Siniscolchi sighed again and stood up. He walked away from his squabbling lieutenants as they continued to argue behind his back. It was the same argument they'd been having for years, ever since he brought in Breufogle after Sa'am botched the Sicuro field op.

Every day since that night ten years ago, when they took the boy from his home, they examined the daily footage of Ecks and Sicuro, formulating theories, investigating what seemed plausible, and then rethinking it all over again.

And coming up with nothing.

Always nothing.

Since the death of Ecks, followed a month later by the escape of the boy, they had gone back to the beginning. They studied all of the footage over again, going more than a little crazy, at each other's throats, frustrated, running out of patience...and still *nothing.*

Siniscolchi had been in the employ of the Abernathé family for the last fifteen years, the last twelve for Lorenzo III directly. Never in all that time had he been more infuriated than right now. Lorenzo's obsession with Ecks and these diamonds colored everything, and over time it had evolved into his only assignment.

He wanted nothing more than to be done with it. There were greater issues facing AbStone that he felt better suited to deal with. This was a problem for the geologists and businessmen in procurement, not an ex-starhound like himself.

Like half the Web, Maxwell Siniscolchi had enlisted right after Ursus. Recruited directly by Naval Intelligence, he served as a special agent assigned to a unit that gathered data in advance of the approaching forces. It was dangerous work with a high mortality rate, but he excelled at it and moved up through the ranks quickly, eventually becoming the commanding officer of his unit.

After five years and surviving dozens of sorties virtually unscathed, he inhaled a large dose of phosgene gas and suffered a potentially crippling neck injury. Scar tissue on his lungs reduced his breathing capacity by twenty percent. His spine at the base of his skull had been weakened. While in no immediate danger, another severe blow to his neck area could leave him paralyzed, or dead. It ended his career with the Navy.

Not long afterward, he found work as a low level operative for AbStone. After three years, Lorenzo III hand picked him to gather intelligence on his rivals, both personal and corporate. Siniscolchi recruited a team from the only pool of talent that he trusted, that of his fellow Naval Intelligence officers, which constituted all of the people in the room at the moment, save for Mr. Sa'am. Siniscolchi had earned the trust and loyalty of Lorenzo III, especially after apprehending Ecks some ten years ago.

The credit for his success he attributed to the excellent people working for him, of whom Mr. Sa'am stood above the rest. After the fiasco in which Sa'am apprehended the Sicuro boy, which was preceded by being outsmarted by that Ergaster clown at Arietta's Squire, Siniscolchi thought it better if Sa'am focused more on logistics, his true strength, and left the field work to someone else. The War had just ended, and NIO's were being discharged by the dozens. Stick Breufogle was the best of the lot and Sa'am saw him as a rival.

Siniscolchi was paid to do what Mr. Abernathé wanted, but this search for the Ecks Stones had become a fool's errand a long time ago. He knew it, and his people knew it. No solution to this puzzle existed in The Tombs. They were as much captives here as Ecks and the Sicuro boy. Sa'am and Breufogle had differing opinions on how to proceed and the other members of his team had chosen sides. With Ecks gone and the boy at large, the circumstances now required resolution with a much different, and still greater, sense of urgency.

"...ten years, Sa'am, of half leads," Breufogle said, "of wasted ventures. We've searched every star system worth looking at with ties to Ursus. The only thing out there is that pus world, Aevoz! We've already determined that the stones could not have come from that part of space."

"You can't possibly know that for sure, Stick. After you've eliminated everything that appears reasonable, whatever is left, no matter how improbable, must be the truth."

"Here you go again with the dwarf and binary systems."

"A simple flyby, Stick, is all it will take."

"Great! We'll cruise all the wasted space from here to Arietta."

"I was thinking Aphelion would be a good place to start."

"Said the guy who took a ride all the way out to Argulski's Star," Breufogle said sarcastically. "Mr. Abernathé wants facts. Results. Not fishing expeditions."

"Aphelion is not as far out as Argulski, Stick."

Breufogle shook his head.

"For ten years we've been looking at these images and learned nothing! Why? Because there's nothing to learn. Ecks tells Sicuro to shut up, they trade insults, they declare their hatred for one another, then never speak again. Then Ecks just sits there and doesn't move for weeks out of spite. There's no hidden meaning here. His whole life, this guy Ecks has had an affinity for anti-social behavior and isolation. He has no need for interaction."

"No, Stick! No. You're wrong. It's been proven that on some basic level, every sentient being has a fundamental need to emotionally connect with something, someone. To be so devoid of emotion is to be a machine or—or—clinically insane."

"Alright. By your own logic, then, Ecks must be clinically insane. Phew! Glad we straightened that out."

"Stick—"

"Enough, Sa'am! You still you refuse to accept that you're wrong, even when the evidence is right in front of you."

"Then why does Ecks decide to get up and exercise, when it must have been incredibly painful for him to do so?"

"Boredom? Self-loathing? I have no idea."

"Because, Stick, he's communicating with the boy, that's why!"

"There's no audio, Sa'am. They're not speaking. Not even a grunt. You said so yourself. They never spoke to each other again. It's not like they could pass notes to each other. Communication between the two of them, without our knowledge, was impossible."

"Okay, so why does Ecks suddenly stop," Sa'am asked.

"Maybe it's like you said, he stroked out. Or maybe because he can't take it anymore."

"After ten years? C'mon, Stick, it's what he wanted us to think! We're meant to believe the boy mimics him just to annoy him, but it's all a ruse. They're communicating, and Ecks only stops because he's finished with what he has to say."

"Again with the sign language. And what kind of message takes ten years to convey? Who in the name of Clorox would have that kind of patience?"

"Ecks, apparently."

"Very funny."

"The only thing not identical in their movements is their hands," Sa'am insisted. "It's very clear, very distinct, day after day. An errant gesture here, a finger there. It's obvious."

"To *you*, maybe," Breufogle said, crossing his arms. "I'm not the only one who doesn't see it."

"I'm not the only one who does."

"Sa'am, the somatic linguistic software still hasn't found a detectable pattern that constitutes language. You can tweak the programming all you like, but you'll never find what isn't there. Ecks stopped exercising because he stroked out. The effort finally killed him. End of story."

Sa'am's eyes bulged out of his furry, angular head.

"And yet the boy shows no overt distress or even remote concern at Ecks' sudden decline and then absence," he yelled. "Certainly this change in routine should matter to him, at least pique his curiosity! It's because Ecks told him of his declining health and they had no further need to communicate—"

"WE HAVE NO IDEA what the boy could possibly be thinking," Breufogle shouted, slamming his hand on the table. "What would ten years of confinement do to *you?!*"

The door sliding open silenced them both. One of Lorenzo's anthropod secretaries stood in the doorway.

"Mr. Siniscolchi," it clicked. "Mr. Abernathé will see you now."

Siniscolchi turned around. He rolled down his sleeves and buttoned his coffee stained cuffs. He straightened his tie. He put on his jacket. He brushed aside some ash trays and coffee cups on the table and uncovered a disc in a plastic case. He glared disapprovingly first at Breufogle, then at Sa'am, and then at the disc. The secretary stood to the side as Siniscolchi walked out.

The secretary opened the large ornate doors to Lorenzo's study. Siniscolchi walked in and the door shut quietly behind him. He glanced quickly over both shoulders to see if anyone stood behind him, then made sure he wasn't standing on plastic. Lorenzo sat behind his desk, preoccupied. He didn't look up from his work.

Siniscolchi approached the desk and stopped at the accustomed spot, but did not sit. He waited. Each second that passed seemed longer than the last, and Lorenzo made him wait much longer than usual.

"Where are my stones," Lorenzo finally asked, still not looking up.

"I can't answer that yet, Mr. Abernathé."

Lorenzo finally looked up, visibly annoyed.

"Still? But I'll bet you can find your bank account at the end of every month."

Siniscolchi pursed his lips.

"Yes, sir, I can."

"You must have some new information, considering recent events."

Siniscolchi cleared his throat.

"We're still analyzing the data, sir."

Abernathé sighed in exasperation.

"Surely you're joking."

"Your interests, Mr. Abernathé, are best served by an honest exchange. My evaluation of our lack of progress is that this problem is not immediately solvable. We simply do not have enough information. Yet."

Lorenzo's eyes burned into him for a long, tense moment.

"Max, I respect your candor. Please sit."

Siniscolchi sat down slowly. Lorenzo locked his hands together and held them up against his chin.

"So you're sure the Sicuro boy was not killed trying to escape?"

Siniscolchi nodded.

"Yes, sir. Without a doubt, he survived."

Lorenzo nodded.

"And you and I are the only ones who know this?"

"We are."

"And this boy knows where to find the Ecks Stones?"

"Yes, he does."

"And how did he learn this?"

"That matter is still pending resolution."

"Then you had better resolve it. It's what I pay you for, in case you've forgotten."

"Mr. Abernathé," Siniscolchi paused, leveling his gaze. "I need more time."

Lorenzo was calm for a moment, then slowly began to shake.

"Time? *Time?!* You have the *temerity* to come here and ask for more *time?!*" Lorenzo leapt to his feet and leaned across the desk, on his fists. "How many more decades, exactly, do you need?! You don't just *work* for me, Max. I *own* you. Like I own this house, like I own this *planet*."

The color drained from Siniscolchi's face. His stomach knotted. A wave of hopeless despair and frustration washed over him, and all he wanted was to scream, to just abandon this impossibly infuriating puzzle, the same as a child tosses aside an incomprehensible toy.

"The Ecks Stones are my legacy," Lorenzo shouted. "They are the capital that will make AbStone a Webwide power! The master of both Cathedral and NYSAAC! No more will the influence and power of the Abernathés be limited to just this quadrant!"

Lorenzo pushed off the desk, his chest heavy with rage.

"But now the Cathedrals have learned of the stones as well, and they're coming for *them* as well as *me*. This problem has escalated to the point of armed conflict. My resources are under a severe strain, Max. I need those stones to fight off the Cathedrals. And if the Cathedrals find them first...it would be the end of my family. It will be the end of *me*. As it stands now, I am seriously contemplating blackmailing the government for assistance. *The government.* Do you understand my predicament, Max?"

"I do, sir. But I believe the time has come to consider a more immediate alternative, one that does not involve the Ecks Stones, to advance the interests of the company."

"Alternatives," Lorenzo sputtered. *"Atlernatives?!* You mean failure, don't you, Max?"

"Mr. Abernathé—"

"I've left this matter for these last years in your supposedly capable hands. You assured me of success. And now you sit here humbled by a cripple and a boy? *A boy?!* It seems my direct involvement is now warranted." He nodded angrily. "I now need to know everything you know."

Siniscolchi expected this. He calmly took a portable disc player from his jacket and placed it on Lorenzo's desk. He inserted a disc. As he spoke, images and data filled the space above the great marble desk to illustrate his narration.

"This is an Ecks Stone, designation ES-3. The ES-3 diamond is representative of the typical make up of all six known Ecks Stones. What makes them distinctive is the way in which the carbon atoms form the lattice and the extraordinary variations in bandgap. Without exception, they are eye clean with no internal imperfections. They are easily identified by the unique pattern of octagonal rainbows they cast when held up as a prism. Facet ranges vary, the smallest at 250, the largest 300. At first glance, density ranges give the indication that they are artificial constructs, but further examination at the nanocrystalline level determined this to be a false assumption. The enigma surrounding these diamonds is that the location containing the pressurized environmental conditions required for their natural formation has yet to be discovered. To control this location, and by extension control over the distribution of the diamonds themselves, would be worth inestimable trillions.

"Of the six known stones, AbStone has three. Cathedral Corp the rest. Cathedral obtained theirs from a diamond broker on Arietta's Squire, who got them from Ecks himself. Before we could apprehend this broker, he was taken into custody by the authorities who were in pursuit of Ecks for his war crimes.

"This is Pierce Sicuro, cloned as an infant from you father's DNA. Note the scar on the side of his face. This was done so he would not be mistaken for a true member of your family. He was one of a litter of infant clones. Your father planned to harvest cranial material from this brood in a desperate bid to stave off dementia. James Cervello was put in charge of this effort. You disbanded this project shortly after its inception, and the surviving eight infants were put out for adoption.

"Pierce was adopted by Rocco and Saffron Sicuro of Center Web, where he lived a normal adolescence. In that time, James Cervello continued to do your father's bidding, in spite of your direct order to cease. He tracked and monitored the infants as they grew, and abducted them in turn to try and help your father. None of the cranial material procured proved suitable. At what point is not clear, a rogue adult clone from one of your father's previous projects became self aware and took the name Eiger Menscher. Menscher sought out his fellow clones to try and protect them from Cervello. He was not successful, but has thus far eluded capture, although we have not been searching for him since Cervello's termination.

"Sicuro's apprehension by Cervello was marred by the presence of trained military personnel in his household. These were his brothers, Dante, Nino and Alex Sicuro. All were recently discharged veterans of The War Against The Enemy. They were able to offer resistance, which resulted in the death of a former PO in your employ, John Cosbie. To conceal AbStone's involvement, the Sicuro residence was burned to the ground. None of the

Sicuros were reported to have survived, but my sources are reporting that the Cathedrals have been making inquiries about the official record. I'll have more on this in the next twenty hours.

"Your direct intervention spared Pierce from the knife, but while he was held in the metal boxes in The Tombs, Ecks responded to his ranting. We don't know what triggered a response from Ecks, but it gave us a glimmer of hope of cracking his veneer. They were put in the clear containers together, hoping that Ecks might try to pass on information about the stones.

"This is Zoeicelli K Galvin, the man we know as Ecks. Ex-Marine. Ex-Navy. Ex-Black Ops. The man whose name lives in infamy for spreading the chlorid foam throughout the Web, among other things. We know he is innocent of these crimes. We know little about his Naval career, but his Marine record shows that he served with distinction on The Rim during the Canite War and the occupation. What little we have discovered is that Ecks was at Ursus when the chlorid foam took out that system, which is now accepted as the start of The War. He was there searching for a rogue Black Ops unit. He and his crew disappeared for nine years immediately thereafter, and we have no clue as to where they could have been, or what they were doing, but at some point during this vanishing act they acquired the six known stones.

"When they resurfaced, after nearly being apprehended by the authorities at *Gateway*, they came into contact with you, where they sold you the stones currently in your possession. We protected Ecks and his crew from the authorities long enough to follow what turned out to be a false lead to Argulski's Star. We then picked up his trail again by piggy-backing the officer leading the official search, one Lieutenant Archibald Ergaster. Again, we prevented Ecks' capture, but could not save the lives of his fellows, and ultimately took him into custody on Gran Nexus, thwarting his intention to bring down the government.

"We put him in the metal boxes and worked on him for almost a year. He proved extraordinarily resilient to all manner of torture and coercion, and utterly unresponsive to external stimuli. With one exception. The Sicuro boy.

"Pierce ranted for days on end when put in the box, the same way all the others did before him. Ecks reacted only to Pierce. We still aren't sure why.

"But a reaction was a reaction, so we put them together in the clear containers in The Tombs. They interacted verbally for a short period, then spent their time performing mirrored exercises in a mute, monotonous, repetitive ritual that lasted for years. We monitored their vitals around the clock, all the standard procedures. Ecks' vitals remained steady throughout. This was clearly a man who had extraordinary control of his mind and body. Despite his severe physical infirmities, he willed himself through these daily exercises in what could only have been extraordinary pain, a sheer torture worse than any we could have inflicted."

Lorenzo crossed his arms over his chest.

"You sound like you admire him."

"Don't you?"

Lorenzo scoffed and wrinkled his mouth.

"As for the boy," Siniscolchi continued, "in the beginning, he was constantly agitated for a span of months, while appearing outwardly calm. Gradually, he became just like Ecks, almost as if he had been made over in the same image. A startling transformation."

"Osmosis?"

Siniscolchi smirked in spite of himself.

"I'm not willing to rule out anything at this point, sir. Ecks stopped the exercise regimen after ten years. According to the docs, he most likely suffered a severe stroke when a blood clot shot from his left leg directly into his brain. After that, he simply sat back down, like nothing ever happened, and died a few days later."

"And the boy's reaction?"

"Not a flicker of emotion, his vitals steady, blood pressure low. He continued the exercise regimen. Alone. He didn't even react after Ecks' body was removed."

"And his escape?"

"Cathedral, as expected. Given the escalation of our conflict with that corporation, I took it upon myself to re-vet all of the personnel in The Tombs. Several individuals came under immediate suspicion.

"Pierce had a number of handlers. He was an extraordinary physical specimen, with skin as pliable as yours and mine, but dense, like brick. His vision, his hearing, all of his senses are razor sharp, on par with any number of apex predators. His reflexes measured at two standard deviations above mean. His strength and stamina also registered beyond normal. He heals quickly and his cellular structure decays at a third of the rate of a normal person."

"You mean he doesn't age," Lorenzo asked incredulously.

"That's not what I said. He will grow old, but a much slower rate."

"So my father inadvertently created a superman."

Siniscolchi nodded.

"A miracle on many levels, considering the quality of the people and science behind his creation."

Lorenzo became lost in thought.

Siniscolchi continued.

"The only way we could clean him or feed him was to gas him. He proved highly susceptible to an aerosolized tri-opioid. When he was in far from peak physical condition, he held his breath for eleven minutes in an attempt to not breathe in the gas."

"And Ecks observed all of this?"

"Yes. We had no need to render him unconscious to enter the containers. After Ecks died, I lightened the security around The Tombs. I created the impression that Pierce wasn't so important anymore without Ecks. Your reluctance to continue to finance Breufogle's fieldwork also served to frustrate the Cathedral teams that were shadowing him, hoping to leap frog him once he learned something about the stones. With one source of information shut off, I opened another. I expected that the operatives Cathedral had working in The Tombs would take the opportunity to move on Pierce. They did, and we were ready for them."

"How did they get away?"

"They used one of the old Trivello class of drills to burrow under the riverbed and reached the Barrier Peaks on the far side of Summa Avarici. Ingenious. It caught us by surprise. There were two of them. The official report is that we caught one in The Tombs, and that the other was in the aircar with Pierce when it was shot down."

"That car was vaporized," Lorenzo recalled.

"Yes, it was. But Pierce was not in the car."

"You're absolutely sure of this?"

"Yes, sir. A microchip was inserted into the back of his neck after Ecks died. It's still transmitting."

Lorenzo was silent for a moment.

"The manner in which you allowed the boy to escape was very risky. He could have been easily killed at a number of junctures."

"It was a necessary risk, Mr. Abernathé. I told no one of this plan because I wanted the responses of our personnel to be genuine. I didn't want to tip off the Cathedrals, or Sicuro, that he was being permitted to leave. After the fact, I wanted my team to analyze the available data with the proper intensity and resourcefulness, without the knowledge that there was still another option to gather information."

"So what makes you think the boy knows the location of the stones?"

"My gut."

Lorenzo shook his head in slow disapproval.

"And yet you let him get away."

"In no way has he eluded us, Mr. Abernathé. His every movement is being tracked and monitored. I thought we were in agreement on this, sir. He was of no use to us imprisoned. It also forced the Cathedral agents to expose themselves. And as I said, one is in our custody. He is not nearly as resistant to our methods as Ecks. We'll find out what he knows."

Lorenzo still eyed him suspiciously.

"What else do you think this boy knows, Max?"

"I think he knows everything, Mr. Abernathé."

"*How, then? How* did they communicate?"

Siniscolchi squirmed a bit.

"As I said earlier, we're still working on that."

"The question now," Lorenzo said, "is where will he go? What will he do? If he believes he got away cleanly, he could lead us to the stones."

Siniscolchi nodded patiently.

"Yes, that's the plan."

"But he will also lead the Cathedrals."

Siniscolchi sighed.

"Everyone believes Sicuro is dead."

"Nothing in this galaxy remains a secret for very long."

"I will deal with the Cathedrals when the time comes. The chip gives us an edge, but it's not a guarantee. I plan to deploy both Breufogle and Sa'am to the field. Breufogle will be the decoy, to lead the Cathedrals astray. Sa'am will have the dual task of keeping tabs on Pierce and also identifying whatever he covets, so we can use it against him, to control him, and learn what he knows. My expectation is that Pierce's next movements will be emotional rather than logical."

"Hmmmm. The boy wasn't too bright when he was apprehended, and he didn't get any smarter in our custody."

"Supposedly. Yes."

"And your fallback, if this doesn't work?"

"Wait. Eventually he will lead us to the stones."

"Wait! Wait! Wait," Lorenzo exclaimed. "I don't have the luxury of time, Max!"

"Mr. Abernathé," Siniscolchi said patiently. "It is not in the best interests of Cathedral to eliminate AbStone until the secret of the Ecks Stones is discovered. They will try to pressure you into making foolish, hasty decisions that they can exploit to get the upper hand on you."

"You sound so certain."

"It's what I would do."

A moment of silence passed between them.

"Right now," Siniscolchi said, "the advantage is all yours. What you do next will have long term implications. You should be thinking in incremental terms. Time, Mr. Abernathé, is not your enemy."

"But the longer that monstrosity is out there, the greater the chance of it being discovered what my father and James were up to. The integrity of my family's name is equally as important as securing the Ecks Stones. Am I clear on that as well, Max?"

"Yes, sir."

"You had better not lose control of this."

"Me, sir? Mr. Abernathé, I've already made arrangements to turn this project over to Mr. Sa'am—"

"*You* had better not lose control of this," he repeated.

Siniscolchi's heart sank.

"I won't."

"Good! I want to be informed of your progress every ten hours."

"Yes, sir."

"Now get out." Lorenzo turned his back to stare out the enormous plate glass window. Siniscolchi nodded and reached for the projector.

"Leave it," Lorenzo snapped, without turning around.

Siniscolchi pulled his hand back and exited without a sound.

The daylight faded.

An overcast sky muted the horizon and the churning mists melted into the ocean waves, white capped and unsettled. Lorenzo stood quietly in the darkening room. He studied his brooding reflection in the polished glass as it grew more and more distinct with the approaching night.

He pondered Siniscolchi. His loyalty was beyond reproach and his competence and dedication to task made him a valuable asset. Yelling at him or laying down threats seemed pointless. A man like that wasn't motivated by fear, negative reinforcement or false appeals to his ego. His lack of success wasn't due to lack of effort, but Lorenzo needed results.

Badly.

Perhaps he should replace Siniscolchi outright, give him a new assignment, get a fresh perspective on all this. But replace him with who? This Mr. Sa'am had potential, more so than this newcomer Breufogle.

No.

Lorenzo wasn't interested in potential. He needed someone who could step in and take over without allowing time for a learning curve. And with anyone else, there would always be an issue of trust. Even though Siniscolchi's skills were much better suited to directing operations in the coming conflict with Cathedral, there was no one to replace him in the search for the Ecks Stones. Besides, he already had other people in place to deal with Cathedral.

The Ecks Stones remained a riddle unto themselves. He couldn't do anything with the ones he had now. Who in all of The Web could he sell them to? A private interest? There wasn't anyone wealthy enough. Another of the big corporations? That would just put him in another set of crosshairs. The enormous value of the Ecks Stones made the few he possessed practically worthless. The key was finding and controlling their source, controlling the market and distribution. Monopolizing the revenue stream. Damn that Sicuro boy and damn Ecks himself.

Ecks.

There was some value in the other information that infuriating man possessed. The level of intrigue inherent in the data that Ecks wanted to deliver to Senator Ashpole, that proved the government's complicity in The Enemy Hoax, was very compelling, and very damning, indeed. A strategy had already been formulated to use this proof to align the government against Cathedral in the coming conflict. For all it was worth, it would only amount to a stalling tactic, a single bullet. He would save it for a prescient opportunity.

A knock at the door interrupted his chain of thought. In the reflection of the window, his personal secretary entered.

"Mr. Abernathé," the anthropod announced. "You asked to be advised of the hour."

Lorenzo glanced at his timepiece and sighed. He turned and waved the anthropod out. He opened a desk drawer and picked up a box wrapped in gleaming, silver paper with an amethyst encrusted bow. He walked purposefully out of his office and down the grand hall to his father's room.

Balloons and streamers adorned the walls and ceiling, and a festive banner spelled out 'HAPPY BIRTHDAY'. A mountain of gifts were stacked precisely on a table in the corner. His father lay unconscious in a hospital bed and his canite nurse sat next to him, reading a book on a portable reader. The autodocs showed that his father's vital signs were strong and in no immediate distress.

The nurse wearily stood up and put the reader to the side.

"Gevenin', Mist' Abbanathay. He's been askin' f'yoo awl day."

Lorenzo briefly cast one eye in her direction, then checked the log and reviewed the entries made by the day nurse. His father had his daily walk, then his exercise. He ate within his prescribed diet, moved his bowels. His father stirred, so he shut off the display.

"Pop! Happy Birthday, Pop!"

"I'm a 109, dammit, not deaf!" He squinted as he looked Lorenzo's way. "You...," he growled.

"Happy birthday, Pop."

"I saw the news, Lorenzo! She tried to hide it from me, you know...she thinks I can't think! The Cathedrals, Lorenzo?! You damned fool..." He waved his arms about maniacally. He dozed off, then came awake. "We don't have the resources for a prolonged conflict. You should never have attracted their attention to begin with. It's not smart business!"

"Pop—"

"I want James! Where *is* he?"

"Pop, Happy—"

"Get bent!" He looked at Lorenzo blankly for a moment. "You've got a hair out of place," he said, pointing. "About halfway up on your right side. You always were a slob."

Then he rolled over and fell asleep. The nurse fussed over his covers.

"Pay him no attention, Mist' Abbanathay."

Lorenzo ignored her and put his gift on the table with all the rest. He reached out for his father's shoulder, then thought better of it. He stood quietly for a few minutes, until the beeping of the vital signs monitor started to annoy him. He slammed the door on his way out.

Chapter 11
Serenity Now

It was just before dawn on this most miserable of mornings in Piacevole. Bruised and glowering storm clouds morosely weighted down the light of day. Two half walls of white brick marked the entrance to Serenity Mission, one stationed on each side of the street. A black shape moved swiftly in the brightening murk, darting across the sidewalks and careful to avoid the bright glows cast by the occasional porchlight. The shape stopped at a conspicuously vacant lot amidst the dense, but neat, rows of houses. A porchlight at the next house hissed and came to life. The shape silently waded deep into the charred remains of wood, mortar and concrete, far away from the light.

Carl Vicinotta came out of his house and closed the door behind him. He tucked a metal lunch pail under his arm and put on a yellow hardhat, which covered his thinning gray hair. The morning stayed quiet, save for the constant hum of far off traffic. As the night muted into a dull gray day, he walked past the rubble strewn lot on his way to the metro. The sound of stone scraping on stone caught his ear and he stopped, peering into the low pile of rocks and wood. A black shape arose from the broken brick and ashes.

"Hey," Vicinotta called out. "You! That's private property! Get away from there!"

The shape seemed to glide toward him, like a ghost.

"I'm sorry," a voice said. A very tall man with broad shoulders came of the shadows and onto the sidewalk. He wore dark clothing and a black raincoat. He carried a black duffel bag over his shoulder, like the kind used in The Navy.

Vicinotta reached into the pocket of his orange vest and wrapped his hand around the pommel of a blackjack. He studied this man carefully. His face was hard to see, covered by a thick, black beard and ringed with long, straggly hair. A wicked, white scar snaked from the corner of his mouth back to behind his ear.

"Who are you," Vicinotta demanded. "What were you doing over there?"

"I apologize if I startled you," the man said. "I think I might be lost. I'm looking for the Sicuro house."

Vicinotta eyed him suspiciously.

"You're not from around here, are ya?"

The stranger's eyes darted this way and that, looking in all directions at the same time.

"I've been away a long time." He smiled insincerely. "The Navy, you see. Dante Sicuro is who I'm looking for. Do you know him?"

"You got a name, pal?"

"Perso. Petty Officer John Perso."

"Vicinotta." He reached out and shook his hand. "You don't look Navy to me, Petty Officer Perso."

"I've come from The Rim, wandered my way here over the last couple of months. I knew Dante during The War."

"Except Dante was a Marine." Vicinotta stood a bit taller, and pounded his thumb into his broad chest. "Like me. And his father."

"Yeah, but I forgave him for that." He wrinkled his mouth akwardly. "My ship got detailed to Var Fleet. We landed his unit at Coleo'Ptera." He shrugged his shoulders. "We got to know each other during the long layover before the op."

"You seem a bit young to've been at Coleo'Ptera."

Perso smiled weakly.

"I get that a lot."

Vicinotta frowned.

"So now you're out, looking up an old pal. In the middle of the night."

"Yeah. I just landed at MemStar. I don't have a place to stay, and he said his door was always open. He was like that, always so generous. This was the address I had for him, but..."

Vicinotta gestured at the ruins.

"You've got the right place, Petty Officer. Dante used to live here with his parents, and his brothers."

"Alex, Nino and Pierce?"

Vicinotta glanced at him.

"You knew his family?"

"No, but he spoke of them often. Alex and Nino were Marines, too, as I recall." He shrugged. "Nobody's perfect."

"Well, what happened was there was a fire here, about ten years ago. I'm sorry to tell you that Dante was killed. Damn shame, to have made it through that meat grinder at Solar Major only to..." Tears welled up in the older man's eyes.

Perso nodded gravely.

"No one survived?"

Vicinotta shook his head, wiping at his eyes, embarrassed.

"The whole was family erased, good people, too. Ahh, well... His mother survived, though."

Perso suddenly turned on him.

"Mother?! You're sure?"

The intensity of his reaction startled Vicinotta.

"Yeah. It's why nothing's been done with this lot." Up close, Perso's skin gleaned a sickly shade of pale, and the cuff of his coat couldn't hide that he wore only one glove, on his left hand. The pinky sleeve was unusually wide. Vicinotta took it for a prosthetic. "Valuable piece of land," he explained, "but she won't sell or rebuild. I take care of things for her, my wife and I. She lives over at Bu'urke now."

"I'm sorry," Perso gasped hesitantly, again looking everywhere at once. "I shouldn't keep you any longer."

His bad breath hit Vicinotta like a brick, like he hadn't eaten in a long time. Vicinotta turned a bit to reach into his pocket.

"There's a decent hotel a few blocks down. If you need a couple a ducats to get a room, I've got—"

When he picked his head up, Perso had vanished. Behind him, a black ground car with tinted windows approached. It slowed a bit, then accelerated and disappeared around a corner. Vicinotta looked curiously up and down the street, then shrugged. He put his money back in his pocket and continued onward to work.

The commercial district dominated the north side of Sophrire. Row upon row of densely packed stores and chain restaurants crowded the wide, congested thoroughfares. In contrast to all of the ads and neon signs stood the wrought iron gates that marked the entrance to the Bu'urke Rehabilitation Hospital.

Twelve buildings cut in the classic old style sprawled over sixty hectares of lush green lawns. Separately, the fine marble and brick buildings appeared as opulent residences. Elaborate gazebos pock marked the grounds, along with neatly trimmed bushes and clusters of grand willow trees. The idyllic calm appealed to those recovering from seriously debilitating illnesses or injuries. The main buildings housed the rehab facilities and rooms for those staying temporarily. Set off to the side, a separate dormitory for permanent residents idled on the shore of a still pond, surrounded by picturesque grottos and gardens.

Darkness fell.

Track lighting along the gravel roadways and paved sidewalks kept everything brightly lit. Pierce moved easily across the damp lawns, carefully keeping to the shadows between the buildings. During the day, a few rent-a-cops lounged in the lobbies and some rode around casually in electric buggies. There were even fewer of them after hours.

Pierce evaded the glow of the track lighting surrounding a gazebo and moved soundlessly behind the shrubbery near the entrance to the permanent resident domicile. He observed the comings and goings of the night staff. He took a moment to collect his thoughts. His encounter with Mr. Vicinotta earlier that day had left him shaken.

He had fond memories of the Vicinottas. They were good friends with his parents, and always available to baby-sit him at a moment's notice. Mr. Vicinotta seemed to be around whenever they were in a pinch, whether a large project needed to be done, or a machine to be fixed. He was very good with his hands. Pierce found it difficult to stand there and lie to him, but to reveal himself to Mr. Vicinotta would only have put him in danger. Even that brief exchange proved costly. The Abbies had come within a few seconds of catching him. Or maybe it was the Charlie Squares. Sometimes he got the feeling every stranger he passed on the street was out to get him. His need to go back to the house outweighed the risk. He knew that it would be the first place anyone would look for him, but he needed his things. And it paid an unexpected dividend.

His mother.

Clearly, none of his pursuers had any knowledge of her, or they would have already finished her off, or used her against him long ago. To this point, he had been lucky. He resolved to be more careful now. He had many debts to repay, obligations owed, the least of which was to Zoeicelli Galvin.

Pierce smiled at the memory of the wily Zoe and how they outsmarted the Abbies. Zoe told him that in the beginning, there had been a number of voices paraded through those dark boxes, all of which he assumed were ploys to get at the secret of his diamonds. Once Pierce used phrases exclusive to Canite War vets on The Rim, phrases that Pierce always heard his father use, only then did Zoe know that he was different.

Once together in the clear boxes, Zoe was taken aback by how strongly Pierce resembled Lorenzo de Abernathé. This didn't sit well with him at all. Zoe didn't know what to make of it, until Pierce started using the hand cant he learned from his father, who had learned it in the Marines while on The Rim, the same as Zoe, during the Canite War. Somehow, Zoe knew their captors were Navy and much too young to be Canite vets, so they could not have learned of the hand cant.

From that day forward, they communicated somatically. Sometimes one letter a day, one syllable, or just one word. Some days nothing at all. Zoe told him about the Abernathés, how they prevented him from vindicating his own name. Pierce learned that the Abbies kept them imprisoned because of these diamonds, these Ecks Stones. Zoe could never fully explain why they abducted Pierce in the first place. He simply didn't know.

Meanwhile, he rehabilitated Pierce physically, taught him discipline and, most importantly, demanded that he never show emotion, lest their captors inadvertently glean something of their communications. He taught him how to maintain control over his mind and body. He told him of his potential. Most of all, he taught him patience.

Revenge consumed Pierce, as it did Zoe, but the old commander demanded a disciplined approach. Zoe knew that he was never leaving that box alive and that Pierce would have to eventually carry on alone.

The Abbies didn't bother to gas Zoe, as they did Pierce, when they entered the cages. Zoe watched everything they did, memorized their routines, studied their every movement, their every gesture, and listened to their conversations. He learned their weaknesses. Most importantly, he knew how they got in and out. He figured at least three of the handlers weren't loyal to the Abbies and that the most logical time for them to make a move would be during a disruption of the status quo. He learned all of this without speaking or interacting with anyone. He told this all to Pierce, and then Zoe didn't say anything for a long time.

When he did speak again, Zoe described in detail how these insurgents would come for him and extract him from his cage. Once outside, he shouldn't underestimate his own superior physique and cunning, and would need to be absolutely lethal in order to overcome his new captors. Then he told Pierce how to find these diamonds and that he should guard their secret carefully and use their wealth wisely, because Abernathé would never stop coming after him to take them for himself. Zoe then warned him to trust no one, and that was it. A few days later, he was dead.

The status quo disrupted.

And Pierce was ready.

He was prepared.

He originally planned to get off Lethe by stowing away in the luggage modules of a passenger liner, or in the storage tank of a cargo freighter. While trolling the shipyards, he stumbled upon a recruiting agent for a questionable outfit that needed cheap, expendable labor, no questions asked. He was given counterfeit credentials with the name John Perso and shipped out as a bilge rat on a cargo ship transporting malcarno livestock. He worked along side a motley assortment of roughnecks and other bilge rats, tending to unbroken malcarnos flagged for selective breeding with other choice stock in Center Web.

The bilge rats undertook the most menial, and dangerous, tasks. Those that survived their shifts then had to deal with the greater threat posed by the roughnecks, their bosses and other predators. Pierce proved no easy mark and earned some measure of respect from the roughnecks, but as the number of bilge rats dwindled, he found himself at a numerical disadvantage. His contract called for him to work the return trip, but he bolted once the ship touched down on Gran Nexus. He waded into a transport pen of carnos and triggered a stampede. He ran with the hard charging mammoths as they thundered into waiting outdoor pens. After that, he hopped a few fences and disappeared into the familiar surroundings of MemStar.

He originally intended to ask the Vicinotta's for help, to ask them if they knew how to find Angelica. This intention evaporated once he saw the ruins of his house. He had held out some small hope that his house would still be there, that the fire wasn't really as bad as he remembered. Zoe had warned him about this, how ruthless the Abbies could be, but his arrogance overruled his better judgment. Did the Abbies know about Angelica? He had to assume they did.

His mother was another matter.

He had to get to her before the Abbies learned of her, too. There appeared to be no time to waste, judging by his encounter with Mr. Vicinotta.

Pierce waited until a group of three nurses exited the building together. He put his hand out and stuck two fingers in the door jamb at floor level to keep it from closing. He jumped up and went inside quickly.

Inside, the lobby was empty. The marble floors and walls were polished to perfection. A dark green carpet tracked in front of him, splitting off to the left and right, like a big 'T'. Light shone from the reception window directly in front of him, but he saw no one. The security desk, adjacent to the reception window, had been abandoned as well.

He marveled at his good fortune.

He took only a step forward, and then a security guard appeared and froze him mid-step. The guard appeared old and tired, and unarmed.

"Can I help you," he sighed, yawning.

Pierce considered just shoving his way past him, but he had no way of knowing in what room his mother resided, nor did he want to attract the attention of the authorities.

"Yes," Pierce said. "I'm here for Saffron Sicuro."

"It's a bit late for visiting hours, son. Come back in the morning."

"Please. My flight was late, I just landed at MemStar. I need—I just got out of the service, I promised my mother…I need to see my mother. Now. Please."

The guard looked him over, then noticed his bag.

"Navy man, huh?"

Pierce faked a wry smile.

"Yes. I've been touring the circuit between The Rim and Arietta's Star. I haven't been home in a few years. My mother…I was told she was burned?"

The old guard nodded sympathetically.

"Hang on." He pushed a few buttons in the glass on his desk, and a data scroll illuminated his face.

"Sandra, you there," he asked.

"Gerry?"

"I'm sending a young man upstairs to see Saffron Sicuro."

"*At this hour?* Tell Mr. Vicinotta to come back tomorrow."

"I said a young man! Her son! He's a *veteran*."

After a long silence, the voice said, "Okay. Send him up."

Pierce stepped off the elevator on the third floor. Quiet prevailed despite a great deal of hushed activity. Dull, pink music played softly somewhere. A dirty white stench permeated the air. He walked down the dimly lit hall to the nurse's station. A nurse in a crisp white uniform waited for him, her arms crossed over her chest.

"The man downstairs told me to ask for Sandra," he said quietly.

"I'm Sandra. And you are?"

"Perso."

"Just Perso?"

"Well, Petty Officer Perso until a month ago. I apologize for the hour, but my mother?"

She smiled at him reluctantly.

"How long have you been away?"

"Since…since before the fire."

"So you haven't seen her since she came here?"

"No."

She frowned.

"You really should come back in the morning."

"Please. I've come so far, it's been so long. Just a few minutes."

Pierce looked behind the desk at a large marker board that listed all of the room assignments. He saw his mother's name. He turned to his left toward the nearest door. She stepped in front of him.

"Mr. Perso, there's something you need to understand."

He looked at her inquisitively.

She hesitated.

"She was very badly burned. She…"

"I'm aware of that."

"Let me see if she's awake," the nurse said quickly.

She opened the door gently and went into the darkened room. She came back out a moment later.

"She's awake. But be quiet. She likes it quiet."

Pierce nodded and entered the room. He clutched the neck of his bag anxiously.

A single occupant lay in a soft bed, surrounded by machines. A respirator hissed rhythmically. The brackish white scent hung in the air here, an odor so terrible he pinched his nose against it. He moved closer and he felt the soft yellow again, oh, how he ached for that soft yellow, and his tension melted away. He was suddenly ten years old, his mother was here, and she would make everything okay.

Tears welled up in his eyes.

He knelt on the floor next to the bed.

He expected to see his mother, with her radiant golden hair and beautiful smile. What confronted him instead sent him recoiling in anguish.

Absent hair and eyebrows, her face was barren of expression. A taught sheen of alabaster white skin clung to her scarred head, like a wet sheet of wrinkled plastic. Red lines of scar tissue criss crossed her scalp like a road map. One ruined eye bobbed milky and lifeless, while the other twitched uncontrollably, a machine dripping fluid into it every thirty seconds. One side of her mouth sagged further down her chin than the other. The heavy covers hid everything below her chin, but they couldn't disguise the frail, emaciated shape underneath.

He covered his mouth with the back of his hand to hide his anger.

His disgust.

His grief.

His hand quivered, and for a moment, he lost all hope. If they could do this to his mother, what chance did he have?

She turned just tiny bit, which was all the hook ups would allow. She looked at him with her unblinking eye. The good half of her mouth smiled. He moved closer to her. With some effort, a thin, gnarled hand forced its way from under the covers. She reached up and touched his face. Her fingerstips traced the wicked scar on his cheek and over his thick, unkempt beard.

"Pierce? Pierce," she whispered. "I must be dreaming. Again."

He took her small hand in his and leaned in closer.

"It's no dream, Mommy. It's me."

"Such strong hands, so handsome, just like your father."

He swallowed hard.

"Are they treating you well here?"

"Oh, yes. The people here are so nice. Hello, Sandra."

Pierce looked over his shoulder. He had forgotten about the nurse.

"Please give us a moment," he said.

Sandra smiled sadly and left the room, softly shutting the door behind her.

Pierce turned back to his mother.

"Mom, what happened? How did you end up here?"

"Oh, Pierce! You know. Everyone died in the fire. You, too. What happened to your face? You should really be more careful."

"I didn't die in the fire, Mommy. I'm here. I'm alive."

The smile left her face.

"Oh, no. No. It was just an accident, a terrible accident. And you died. All my children. Gone."

"No, Mom. I'm real. And I'm going to take care of you."

"Oh, no need for that," she said wistfully. "The people here are so nice."

He took a deep, frustrated breath and held it for a long moment.

"Mom, what about Angelica?"

"Who?"

"Angelica Smart. My girlfriend."

"Oh, what a pretty girl. But she was so wrong for you, so ugly on the inside."

"We talked about this."

She smiled again and she looked at him, but didn't see him.

"Yes, the night of the fire. You kept a box in a hole in the floor, in your room, in the basement. You didn't think I knew about it, but I did. You were putting a ring into it. You had a fight with that girl, you were so upset. She had this way of making you feel so inadequate, so ugly. That ring, you wanted to marry her. Do you remember?"

He smiled weakly.

"You said that people thought you and Dad were a mismatch, and you got a hard time of it."

"That's right. Oh, there were plenty of boys who were more handsome, more polished, but they were just boys. Your father was a man. I could tell."

"He took good care of us."

"Yes, he did."

He trembled, unable to speak. He wiped at the tears in his eyes.

She said, "You were determined to see that girl in the morning, to make things right again. You didn't understand what I was trying to tell you, that she never saw how special you were. Never saw that. Never saw the real you, and then..."

"Then what?"

"You died. That night, in the fire."

"Do you know where I can find her?"

"Oh, no. I haven't seen her since you died."

"Mom, what do you know about my biological parents?"

"Oh, Pierce. Your father knew more than I did. You were born on The Rim. Father Sfiatatoio, remember? I don't really—"

"Mom. Am I an Abernathé?"

"Ab-Abber...? Who..."

She rambled incoherently. He turned his head and listened instead to their surroundings. He heard very little.

He came into his mother's room amidst the sounds of people moving about, soft music, discreet conversations. He still heard it, even with the door closed.

Now, he heard nothing. For how long?

"Mom, be quiet."

She obeyed him without comment and drifted off to sleep.

Pierce opened the door a crack.

No one at the nurse's station.

No one moved in the hallway.

He shut the door and checked the bed, to make sure it had wheels. He then disconnected her from all the machines and pushed them out of the way. He grabbed the foot of the bed and started pulling her toward the door.

Sandra burst into the room.

"Stop right there! What do you think you're doing? She'll die without those hook ups!"

He turned to her and spoke very calmly.

"There are people coming here to hurt my mother."

"Why would—"

"I need for you to call the police immediately."

Her face went white with fear and with a trembling hand, she held the door open for him. He wheeled his mother out into the hallway and then swiftly into the room across the hall. Sandra ran to the nurse's station and Pierce could hear her telling security downstairs to call the authorities. He yanked a curtain around the bed so they couldn't be seen. Before he could shut the door, he heard the sound of many muffled footsteps approaching. He hovered over his mother and clutched her hand, watching the hall through a break in the curtain.

Maybe a dozen humans in black suits appeared, half of them storming into the room they had just vacated, the others taking up positions in the hallway. A canite with jet black hair and a glinting nose ring gave silent instructions, then disappeared from view.

Saffron's breathing became raspy and more labored. Pierce gently rubbed her forehead and her breathing eased. The canite then reappeared and ordered his people away, and they disappeared as swiftly as they had appeared. Pierce didn't hear them pass through an exit, nor did Sandra reappear.

Confused and sweating profusely, he considered his options. How could they be here? How could they know about his mother?

Then her hand slipped out of his, her tiny, shriveled form now unmoving and lifeless. Panic stricken, he shook her gently, then rattled the bed.

Rattled the bed.

In the blink of an eye, Pierce snatched up his bag and disappeared out the window.

A fraction of an instant later, the men in black stormed the room, only to find it deserted, save for Saffron's body. The curtains billowed in the breeze, a breeze let in by the open window. Nothing moved in the darkened courtyard three stories below.

"Anything," a voice over a radio crackled.

"Negative," the canite responded.

In the distance, the sound of police sirens grew louder.

And then the canite cursed.

Chapter 12
Nostrova

Twelve planets orbited the yellow, main sequence star of Stelumiere. Three habitable worlds thrived within this star system, collectively known as Center Web. However, when one spoke of Center Web, only two worlds came to mind, and both had played a large part in giving rise to the human race.

The bright blue world of Gran Nexus, the fifth planet, had long ago eclipsed her neighbors as the true center of the Interstellar Web. The fourth planet was Nostrova, the acknowledged cradle of human civilization. This lush green world boasted the oldest and most august educational institutions in all The Web. These colleges and universities attracted the brightest and most talented The Web had to offer.

Elysian University dominated the society of the southern hemisphere as the oldest and most venerable college on the planet. Throughout history, EU had provided The Web with its most brilliant and revered leaders, from businessmen to politicians, to lawyers and scientists. It boasted quietly of its arcane traditions and customs, often lauded as a culture unto itself. The campus spread over 1200 hectares, the size of a small city, and comprised the largest urban area on the continent.

A college of this size and influence, with so many prominent students, alumnae and benefactors, required attorneys. Scores of them. Not only did they assist the administrators with overseeing the day to day operations of the college, but they managed its interests outside the narrow confines of academia. A maze of buildings on the western edge of the sprawling grounds housed the law offices of the Elysian legal team.

Angelica Smart sat at her desk in a modest office, oblivious to the setting sun outside her window. She sat in the darkening room and stared blankly at an oversized black and white monitor, the harsh light bleaching away her features. Every year, the University hired a few select graduates to work as interns in the law offices while they pursued their law degrees. As the shortest tenured tax attorney in the department, she had the unenviable task of ranking the hundreds of resumes for the highly coveted one or two jobs that would be made available at the close of the term. Angelica had followed this route herself to complete her education and to obtain her current position.

She sighed loudly, bored beyond reason, and more than a bit miffed at the menial assignment. That morning, she obediently followed tradition and dragged herself to commencement in order to introduce herself to some of the applicants. She considered not going. The thought of having to make small talk with mere students and their parents turned her stomach. But she went, however unhappily, as breaking with tradition wouldn't sit well with her bosses, her peers or the entire academic community.

Angelica had a reputation as an eager young lawyer, pretty enough, and with some talent for corporate law. What she lacked in versatility, she made up for with her connections. Her engagement to Vincent Scoreggia, a special agent for the Interstellar Bureau of Investigation, secured her current position with EU, even if she never achieved great things for herself or the University. She desperately aspired to the finer offices on the ninth floor, where the senior attorneys made policy, managed relationships with various regulatory agencies and courted contributors to the annual fund. She worked hard at her job, putting in twenty hour days when Vincent disappeared on assignment, which happened often. She firmly believed in the inevitability of her advancement, and she dreamed of that corner, glass walled office that waited for her on the ninth floor, complete with a team of secretaries and personal assistants.

For now, drudgery.

She scrolled through resume after resume, none particularly interesting. All brilliant, all impeccably credentialed, but none that stood out. Like a bunch of clones. She amused herself with the fleeting thought of recommending a canite. After perusing the last resume, she sighed in frustration. Only one applicant distinguished himself from the rest, but for no good reason.

Lorenzo de Abernathé IV.

She was intrigued by the possibilities. Filling the position wasn't about financial need, but about finding the best candidate, and sometimes the best candidate could do more for the University, rather than the other way around. Why an Abernathé would want an internship here confounded her. She vaguely remembered him from a few years ago, as one of the dozens of undergrad interns that floated in and out every semester. She found him vaguely familiar for some reason, but didn't know why.

The monitor next to her chirped loudly. She fumbled across the items on her desk, searching for the 'answer' key. She ran her finger along the fine print on the button, then depressed it firmly.

"Angelica Smart."

"Angelica, it's your mother."

She rolled her eyes.

"What do you want, Mom?"

"Audio only? You know I don't like that. You know I like to see you."

"I'm really busy, Mom."

"Too busy to turn on the video?"

"Yes."

There was a moment of frustrated silence.

"Well. I was thinking that the colors for the wedding should match the nursery—"

"Nursery?"

"Well of course! Right after the wedding, you'll stop working. I can help you set up the house—"

"I already told you, I'm not stopping work."

"Don't be ridiculous. You'll never keep that man if you're working. You don't know how lucky you are. Oh, the IBI," she sighed. "Now, about the nursery..."

Her mother rambled on, dismissing Angelica's half-hearted protests. Half an hour later, frustrated beyond reason, she left the building and walked out into the cool evening. She strolled leisurely across the campus grounds, the stress over her mother fading. She loved this school, this place, and basked in the good fortune to have a career that kept her here. This part of the campus was older than the rest, and many of the buildings were converted from their original purpose. One building had the look and feel of an old hospital, as over one hundred years ago it operated as a sanitorium for those with communicable diseases. Another used to be a library with actual paper books, people said. The observatory used to be a house for picture shows. She enjoyed the feel of the place, the atmosphere, even though she could barely see it.

It had been three years since the accident. An accidental blow to the temple that took most of her vision. She didn't blame Vincent for what happened. She had made her peace with it, but that day brought about a profound change in their relationship. He became less rogueish, less impetuous and more serious. She forgave him for being overprotective because he meant well, but as much as she loved him, she didn't want his pity.

She could still see dark shapes and distorted images, but nothing defined. As she strolled confidently down the cement path that wound its way through the well manicured lawns and fountains, she didn't notice the odd shadows that soundlessly moved behind her...and in front.

Her belt comp vibrated on her waist. Without breaking stride, she held it to her ear.

"Yes?"

"Where are you?"

"Well, hello to you too, Vincent."

"Are you okay? There was no answer in your office."

"I'm fine. I'm almost to crossroads."

"I'm on the other side of Rhonson Hall. Wait for me there, I'll be over in a minute."

The connection terminated abruptly.

She returned the comp to her waist, dismissing his abrupt manner. That's how IBI agents behaved, no nonsense and always direct to the point. She eagerly looked forward to their wedding day. She liked the idea of being the wife of an IBI agent and all the priveleges that would come with it.

Regular people suck, was the way Vincent put it, and she giggled to herself at the coarseness of his language. She knew better than to keep him waiting, so she picked up her pace, and arrived at crossroads a bit out of breath.

Flourescent lamp posts illuminated the intersection of cement pathways. The many stone benches alongside were unoccupied. She sat down to catch her breath, feeling for a seat. Then she sensed something move across from her.

Tree branches? There was no wind and no noise but chirping crickets. Then, under the lamp post, something definitely moved.

She wasn't alone.

This normally wouldn't have bothered her, but the bulk of the campus population had departed after commencement. There shouldn't be anyone else here.

She took some comfort in that Vincent was only minutes away. With that thought, the glass doors to Rhonson Hall flew open, and her fiancée, Vincent Scoreggia, bolted toward her with long, furious strides. He barked one profanity after another into his comm.

She stood up, relieved.

"Vincent! What's wrong?"

"Fucking lawyers," he said. "They've got enough evidence to convict The Messiah Himself, and still they want more. They just keep putting up one more impediment after another. Useless douche bags!"

"Vincent, maybe—"

"C'mon," he said, grabbing her roughly by the arm. "Let's go."

"Vincent, you're hurting me!"

"Then keep up, willya? You don't know what real pain is."

He stopped and grabbed her chin, examining her face.

"You're wearing too much make up. Again."

"I'm sorry, Vincent, sometimes it's hard to tell—"

"Make more of an effort. You look like a circus clown."

Scoreggia turned and the dark figure from the far bench stood only a centimeter from his face. It was a man, sweating profusely, and breathing hard.

"Take your hands off her," he whispered forcefully.

"Who in Blazes are you," Scoreggia demanded. "Get the fuck outta my face."

"You're hurting her," he rasped. "Let her go."

Scoreggia waved his badge.

"You're in way over your head, asshole. Get lost."

The man crushed Scoreggia's hand and the badge it held.

"AHHHHH, you son of a bitch," he screamed, reaching for his gun.

The man grabbed Scoreggia by the lapels of his coat and threw him into a stone bench.

Angelica screamed and made a futile attempt to restrain Scoreggia's attacker, but he moved away from her too quickly.

"Stop," she cried. "Somebody help!"

The man pulled Scoreggia's limp and bleeding body from the ground, clearly prepared to continue, when a crowd of thugs in muted colors melted out of the darkness.

The man discarded Scoreggia like a broken toy and backed away, slowly at first, then bolted into the night. Two of the mysterious figures chased after him, one of them a canite with nose ring, and the rest disappeared back into the shadows.

Angelica ran to Scoreggia, kneeling at his side.

"Help," she wailed. "Somebody, please help me!"

Lorenzo de Abernathé III sat quietly with his son at a table in Nostrova's most exclusive restaurant, Ammalato's of Pranzo. He again surveyed the dining room, hoping that his initial impressions of this place were inaccurate. Gaudy bell crystal chandaliers hung below a frameless skylight and reflected onto the fixtures of polished brass. *Brass.* The room was filled with an equal mix of all the races, including canites. He wrinkled his nose at this supposed cream of Nostrovan society. The menu was weak, the food merely adequate and the wait staff far less accommodating than he preferred. That his son would arrange for his graduation dinner in such a trough perplexed Lorenzo to no end. Young Lorenzo's continued willingness to compromise the standards expected of an Abernathé had to stop.

His son sat across from him, still wearing his graduation gown, unzippered down the front. His cap, adorned with multiple tassels, lay on the table. Young Lorenzo hadn't stopped talking since they sat down, and Lorenzo found his prattle annoying.

Lorenzo wiped his mouth with a linen napkin, his dinner untouched.

"All of these musings, all of these half considered plans. Where do you see yourself six months from now?"

Young Lorenzo seemed surprised by the question.

"Why, in an office next to yours in Elsasser, heading a stone procurement division for AbStone, of course."

"Really? A division head?"

Young Lorenzo hesitated.

"I earned my degrees in geology, economics and finance. I completed the requisite internships, graduated in the top third of—"

"*What* do you have to offer AbStone that it doesn't already have?"

"I-I can do the job—"

"So can a lot of others."

"I have my degrees—"

"Just another face in the crowd. *What* do you have that no one else does, that can make my company a profit?"

Young Lorenzo set his fork down, confused. He had done everything asked, even excelled. He stammered, searching for the response he thought his father wanted.

Lorenzo's comm beeped. He glanced at it, then got up and abruptly left the table. He walked out into the lobby where Siniscolchi waited. Siniscolchi looked haggard, like he hadn't slept in days.

"I'm sorry to interrupt your dinner, Mr. Abernathé."

"Unimportant, Max. What are you doing here? What do you want?"

"You asked to be updated regarding any new field developments. I happened to be nearby and felt I should speak to you in person."

"And?"

Siniscolchi measured his response.

"Sicuro is here on Nostrova. Only a few kilometers from this very spot."

"Then the Ecks Stones are here?"

Siniscolchi shook his head.

"No, sir. But the Cathedrals have escalated their involvement."

Siniscolchi found the Sicuro boy's behavior confounding. Sicuro believed that everyone thought he'd died trying to escape. With this freedom, he should have gone directly for the Ecks Stones. Instead, he returned home. Then he went to his mother. Then his girlfriend. All places where he could be immediately discovered, and was. It made no sense. Maybe he didn't know anything about the Ecks Stones after all.

"Escalated? I take that to mean they know the boy is still alive."

"Yes, sir."

"And how did they learn this so quickly?"

"Any number of ways, Mr. Abernathé. The Cathedrals are as determined to find the Ecks Stones as we are."

"Then why is the boy here if the stones are not?"

"He tried to reconnect with the Smart girl," Siniscolchi explained. "She works at EU. Before that, his mother and one of his father's old friends, both on Gran Nexus."

"You mean to tell me that this *thing* is freely running amok, leading you everywhere but to the Ecks Stones?"

Siniscolchi nodded.

"I know it appears that way, sir, but I wouldn't say 'freely'. The Cathedrals now seem bent on capturing Sicuro rather than being content to follow him. A few minutes ago, they nearly apprehended him." He cleared his throat. "For a third time."

"A third time," Lorenzo almost shouted.

Several people passing by turned to look at them. Lorenzo led Siniscolchi to the side.

"Clorox fucking the Messiah on a beach, Max! If the Cathedrals capture the boy they will undoubtedly figure out what he really is!

I want that subhuman monstrosity thrown back in The Tombs tonight! *Tonight!* Before this whole thing goes public! Then you grab his mother and beat the shit out of her in front of him until he talks, am I clear, Max?"

"His mother is dead, Lorenzo."

Lorenzo fumed.

"Then the Smart girl!"

"It's complicated. She's attached to an IBI agent."

Lorenzo looked away for a moment, his face burning red.

"The IBI? Are you sure?"

"Yes."

Lorenzo now understood why Max had come to him with this. He eyed Young Lorenzo in the dining room, his son chatting easily with the pretty young girl clearing the table.

He turned back to Siniscolchi.

"I want that thing back in The Tombs. Leave Smart alone."

Lorenzo tugged angrily at his cuffs as he sat back down at the dinner table.

"So, Dad, I was thinking about your last question. I—"

"Enough. You've convinced me. I do see a future for you with AbStone."

Young Lorenzo smiled.

"But not in stone procurement."

His smile faded.

"There's still work to be done here on Nostrova," his father said.

Young Lorenzo ate his dessert in silence.

Angelica Smart sat alone at the bedside of her fiancé. Scoreggia had been brought to the EU Hospital at Nostrova by the EMTs. A broken hand, a broken jaw and three broken ribs. The doctors said he would recover, and he slept soundly after a heavy dose of sedatives.

All of the drama had ended about an hour ago. She spoke to the police. She spoke to Vincent's bosses. She called his family, she called her family. She arranged for treatment with the doctors. She'd done everything expected of the wife of an IBI agent.

Now she worried about how this would change him. So far, she'd done all the right things, and if she continued, then perhaps he wouldn't turn his anger on her. Exhausted, she wanted nothing more than to go home, but if she wasn't here when he woke up, then all of her efforts would be for naught.

She dutifully sat next to him, dozing from time to time throughout the long night. In the half light, a shadow fell across her. A long, urgently silent minute passed before she awoke with a start. A hulking figure in a dark raincoat towered over her.

She gasped loudly and a large, rough hand slapped over her mouth.

"You will not make a sound," a gruff voice whispered. "I'm not here to hurt you."

As a silhouette, she couldn't make out his features. He smelled terribly. His voice, however, was unmistakable. This was the same man who had attacked Scoreggia earlier.

Her eyes widened in panic. She labored for breath.

"Listen to me carefully. You are in danger. You must leave with me now."

It took a moment for his words to register. She shook her head.

Yanking her out of the chair, he took his hand off her mouth and escorted her roughly out the door.

She was so afraid, afraid to even breathe. She couldn't believe this was happening.

"Utter a sound and you kill us both."

They walked quickly down the empty corridor and stopped at one of the large service elevators. Far down the corridor, coming out of the public elevators, stepped a plasmoid and a macropian.

"Angelica," the plasmoid called out. "Angelica Smart?"

Angelica recognized the voice. It was Bischero, Scoreggia's partner.

"Not a word," the man hissed. "Don't even look up."

Frightened beyond reason, she obeyed. The man inserted a keycard into the call panel and the large doors opened.

Bischero and the macropian only watched.

He pulled her inside and the doors shut. The elevator began a slow descent.

She squirmed away from him, cowering into a corner. She squinted to get a better look. Long dark hair, dark face, broad shoulders. It was hard because he wouldn't stand still. She needed to get closer.

"You knew those two?"

She looked away, then nodded.

"They're IBI agents."

He ran his hands over his face.

"Angelica, I'm sorry. After all this time, Angel, you've got to trust me. There is a reason for all this. You—" His demeanor, his inflection, suddenly changed. "You can't see me, can you?"

"I—"

"You don't know who I am, do you?"

"I-I…How am I in danger?"

He cursed under his breath. He seemed angry.

"From that man Scoreggia, for starters. But he's not your most immediate problem."

"You've got it wrong. He's my fiancé."

This gave the man pause.

"Really?" Then he turned on her. "When these doors open, we need to move quickly—"

She retreated further into the corner

"No!"

He grabbed her forcefully by the shoulders and pulled her close, then swept her up into his arms. She fought against him in vain, but despite his enormous strength, she sensed that he didn't want to hurt her.

The door opened to a blast of thick, humid heat. The hum of industrial machinery echoed off stark, damp concrete walls. He dashed down the corridor, passing laundry rooms, trash compactors and other alcoves that belched steam and weighed down the air with the stench of bleach.

He ran still faster with her in his arms and side stepped startled maintenance personnel, some pushing large carts and wagons. He kept running until they came to a loading dock where the fresh night air beckoned. He leapt out into the dark and suddenly stopped short.

A dozen flood lights hissed to life.

A semi-circle of police cars hemmed them in. An even mix of uniformed police officers and IBI wind breakers pointed guns at them. In the bright light, Angelica got a good look at his face. A mangy beard and a hideous scar from his mouth to his ear. This man seemed to know her in some way, but she found him completely unfamiliar.

"Put the woman down," a voice boomed from a bullhorn. "Put the woman down, and lay face down on the pavement. There's nowhere to go."

The man hesitated, and then his knees wobbled. He let Angelica go and she ran away from him, into the crowd of policemen. He fell on his hands and knees, his chest heaving in labored desperation. He vomited violently and his guts spilled all over the pavement. The plasmoid Bischero and a group of IBI agents casually formed a circle around him, twirling nightsticks.

And then the floodlights went out.

Cell number nine.

Behind the bars of cell number nine, Pierce sat alone on a hard metal bench. He hadn't slept all night. He nursed some bruises and a cut lip, dabbing at it from time to time with the back of his wrist. He felt pretty good, considering the last few hours, but there was a reason for that. What worried him more were these bouts of nausea. The last time he had felt that ill was with Angelica at MemStar years ago, right before the Abbies got him. As a kid, he always passed it off to his overall sensitivity to things, but now that somehow didn't feel right.

He felt gritty and mealy. A coating of dried sweat left him clammy, but not cold. Temperature extremes stopped bothering him as he got older, but the dank olive feel of this place made him uneasy.

Cell number nine.

It was painted in white up on the wall. It annoyed him because the number nine should be red, not white. Nobody ever got the colors right.

Then again, his being here wasn't right, either. He shouldn't have gone home and he shouldn't have gone after his mother. He certainly shouldn't have come for Angelica. At least not so soon.

He glanced at the iron bars and knew that he could bend them just enough to get out. He resisted the urge. His stomach churned violently at being confined, but his instincts told him he would not be here for very long. And he resolved to follow his instincts from now on.

After ruminating on everything that had happened since landing on Gran Nexus, he guessed that more than one interest pursued him. He had eluded the goons at his house, Bu'urke and then EU far too easily. The Abbies knew everything about him and should've been one step ahead of him at all times, instead of one step behind. Whoever else was out there, they knew nothing of him, but now he had given them everything, his house, his mother and his girl.

The night had not gone as planned. Helpless and sick, the IBI agents beat him with enthusiasm. They stuffed him into the back of a car and then deposited him here. He had not been read his rights, nor had he been charged with any crime. He knew from watching all those picture shows with his father that they couldn't keep him here indefinitely. He started to wonder about that as he had not seen anyone in about eleven hours.

Quiet, patient footsteps interrupted his sulking. Without looking up, he could feel the eyes on him, just out of his line of sight. Without thinking, he slowed his breathing and cleared his mind.

Whoever's watching, give them nothing.

A man in a black suit and sunglasses stepped into view. He stood with his hands in his pockets, his face inscrutable behind those lenses. He stared at Pierce for a long time. Finally, he took off the sunglasses and put them in his jacket pocket.

"You are one lucky man, John Perso," he said. "You look pretty good for someone on the wrong end of a night spent with a bunch of angry IBI agents. But then again, you're not the average person, are you?"

Pierce maintained his veil, his practiced calmness.

"You learned well from Ecks."

Pierce looked at him.

The man smiled.

"That's right. I know who and what you really are. I was with you every day for the last ten years, although you wouldn't know it." He stepped up to the bars. "I'm going to give you the same option that I gave to Mr. Ecks. Tell me where the diamonds are, and you'll go free."

Pierce looked away.

"You're in a lot of trouble, son. You unplugged the life support of an infirmed burn victim in a nursing home. You attacked an agent of interstellar law enforcement and put him in the hospital. Then you tried to abduct his fiancée. They can't prosecute you for killing your mother because the only eyewitness has mysteriously vanished. They can't charge you with assault and battery because Special Agent Scoreggia doesn't remember being attacked, and the only other eyewitness is legally blind. As far as the abduction goes, that very nice young lady is refusing to press any charges, despite being heavily pressured to do so. Imagine the IBI's surprise when they ran your picture through the face recognition databases, finding no matches other than…well, you couldn't possibly know. They dismissed it as a false positive, a common failing of that technology. My timely arrival has helped the locals sort out this confusing mess. Now that they know all about John Perso, they won't bother to run your fingerprints or retinas. I've seen to that. It's a shame they can't hold you, but they're not just going to let you walk out of here, either.

"There's an outstanding warrant for the arrest of John Perso on the planet Lethe. Skipped out on a labor contract. Imagine the value of that contract, because extradition warrants of this kind aren't cheap. Fortunately, I am authorized to take you into custody and escort you back to Lethe. The authorities here on Nostrova don't recognize Lethean warrants, not many planets do, but it was made very clear to me exactly which door they're going to shove you out of, and at exactly what time. Make no mistake I'll be waiting there for you. And then I'm going to put you back in your box for the rest of your life."

He knelt down and made eye contact with Pierce.

"Unless you tell me where Mr. Ecks got those diamonds."

After a long pause, the man said, "I consider solitary confinement to be cruel and unusual punishment." He stood up. "It would be a very simple matter to have Ms. Smart join you for the duration."

Pierce seethed.

The man smiled in a mean sort of way.

"I will see you on the outside."

Chapter 13
Menscher

A fresh blue breeze blew across the top of the wide open steps of the police station. Pierce stood at the edge of the steps, looking down. His oily hair danced in the air about his head. Way down at the the bottom of the steps, the man in black was coming toward him, followed closely by an albino macropian. A dozen others in identical black dress came up at him from all sides. His eyes were drawn to the shocking white fur of the macropian.

And he remembered.

The night of the fire.

His eyes burned into those of the macropian and he strained against the cuffs binding his wrists. Behind him stood two angry IBI agents, Bischero and an anthropod.

Pierce readied himself for a fight. He wasn't going anywhere with this guy. Zoe said to trust his superior physical skills and these guys didn't want to kill him. That gave him an advantage. They were also coming up the steps at him, another advantage. He wanted to get at the macropian, but he was too far away. He needed to escape first. Everything else later.

A sudden wave of nausea came over him. That vile, syrupy black stench roiled through his body from the bottom of his stomach and upward. It clogged his throat and nostrils. For a moment, he despaired. Then he caught himself. This time, he fought against it. He refused to let it incapacitate him. He kept his feet, but he didn't trust himself to move. Not yet. And the thugs in black, only a few steps away...

The anthropod clicked its pincers angrily, then took the cuffs from his wrists. It shoved him forward. He stumbled on the first step, but kept his feet. He couldn't control his gag reflex and he spewed vomit on the steps. Disgusted, the men in black took a step backward to avoid the splashing bile.

The pain in his gut intensified like never before and his legs turned to jelly, like he'd been stabbed. Before he hit the ground, an arm slid under his that stood him up straight. A man equal to his own height dressed in a dark blue cloak now held him steady. Looking at this man's face was like staring into a fun house mirror. His ears edged a distorted jawline, one side a bit bigger than the other. A very thin beard covered his jaw and mouth. A big head bobbed on the tiny shoulders of a stick-like body, which Pierce could feel through the billowing cloak. In his free hand, he carried Pierce's navy bag. Pierce didn't know whether to be relieved or frightened by this person. He looked out at the sea of angry, dark bespectacled faces. They all looked the same, but this man, he looked like him.

"Well, well, well," the man helping Pierce said, almost whimsically. "What seems to be going on here?"

The man in black who had spoken to Pierce inside stepped forward.

"Stand aside, sir. This is no concern of yours."

"Oh, but it is. I'm not going to allow you to abduct my cousin right off the street, in front of the police station, no less."

"I have a warrant for this man's extradition."

The cloaked man looked over his shoulder.

"Judging by the lack of enthusiasm from the locals, it must be a Lethean warrant. Stand aside, my cousin and I have people to see."

"You, sir, need to just walk away from here and mind your own business."

"This is my business. You don't think we're related? Take a close look at us."

The man in black's mouth flattened into a hard line.

"You wanna hash this out right here," the cloaked man asked. "In this very public space?"

The man in black pulled back his jacket to reveal a gun.

"Sir, I'm giving you one last opportunity to step aside."

The other man laughed.

"You're not gonna shoot us! You're not gonna do anything except let us walk outta here! How would your employer react to seeing you on the next Suetonia feed engaged in a gun battle on the steps of a police station? The IBI questioning us all? Me shouting your employer's name from the rooftops?" The man lowered his voice. "Me explaining what *we* are?"

The man in black backed down a few steps. The snow white macropian hovered nearby. Pierce stared at them quizzically, recalling half a memory. The bright fur stung his eyes. The man holding Pierce helped him down the steps and the men in black parted to give them just enough room to get by. The man half carried, half dragged Pierce to the sidewalk and propped him up against a waiting ground car.

"I'm not…I'm not going anywhere," Pierce gasped between dry heaves, "with you."

"Shut up, Pierce," the man said. "We've only got about thirty seconds before those guys change their minds and come after us."

Pierce startled at the use of his real name.

"I'm not a cop," the man said. "I'm not an Abbie or a Charlie Square. But I am the only friend you've got left in this entire galaxy. And I'm also the one making you sick."

He threw open the car door and shoved Pierce and his bag inside. The man got in, and peeled out into traffic.

"Put this on."

He handed Pierce a brown pad. It felt heavy, like it had magnets sewn into it. Pierce stared at it blankly, his head spinning from nausea.

"What…what is it?"

"On the back of your neck! C'mon!" The man did it for him, nearly colliding with another car. The pad stuck tightly to his skin, pulling at his hair. "You've got a homing device sewn just under your skin, at the base of your skull. It's how they're able to track you. That pad will block the signal, but only temporarily. We've got about twenty minutes to lose these guys and dig the thing out before they recalibrate."

They raced recklessly through the traffic.

"It was dumb of you to go to your mother. It was even dumber to go looking up old girlfriends. I don't know where you've been the last ten years, but it obviously wasn't college."

The car peeled around a corner and careened dangerously the wrong way up a one way street. He forced other cars onto the sidewalks before turning wildly down a ramp and through an exit for an underground parking garage. The car screeched to a halt in a parking spot.

"This'll buy us a few extra minutes. Those law and order types think one dimensionally and always use aircars." He grabbed Pierce's bag and got out of the car. He came around and dragged Pierce out and kept him on his feet. "Now we walk."

"I can't"

"Fight it," the man snapped. "Oddly, movement seems to help. Force yourself to walk, and you'll feel better."

Pierce did as he was told. He stumbled after the man to a dark corner of the garage. They got into an old elevator and went down.

Pierce clutched at the grimy hand railings. Panting, he used all of his strength to hold himself upright.

"Those were Abernathé's men?"

"Yes. And you are definitely an A-list problem. Unless memory fails me, that was Max Siniscolchi himself. Been awhile since I've seen him creeping around. That guy gives me the willies."

"And who are you?"

The man smiled. He held up a right hand that had six fingers.

"I'm you. Cloned from the DNA of Lorenzo de Abernathé II. I go by Menscher. Eiger Menscher."

Siniscolchi stood near the top of the steps and watched the ground car peel away from the curb. Sa'am stood next to him, one step down, his short, white fur rustling in the breeze.

"Way to go, meat bags," Bischero sneered. "Your hands need help finding your ass, or you just gonna stand there, all dumb an' shit?"

Siniscolchi ignored him.

"You morons," the anthropod shouted. "Bunch of clowns without a circus!"

"Hey," Sa'am shouted back. "You got a big mouth for a centipede. Keep it up, I got an extra big fly swatter with your name on it."

"Are you yelling at my badge," Bischero said. He turned to the anthropod. "Is that furry mutt yelling at my badge?"

Siniscolchi wasn't listening, still focused on the empty space that Menscher's ground car recently occupied.

Bischero flashed an obscene gesture, which Sa'am returned. More IBI agents came out of the police station and formed a line. They glared angrily down at them.

"Stumpy little fuck," Sa'am scowled. "Bunch of punks with badges." He adjusted his sunglasses. "Here comes Stick."

Breufogle climbed the steps and stopped even with Sa'am, giving orders into his wrist.

"We're tracking him, Max," he said. "They're headed west, air pursuit is already engaged. I've got cars on the ground in position to—"

Siniscolchi already knew this. He could hear it all in his own earpiece. Sa'am and Breufogle were already moving down the steps toward a waiting aircar.

"Call it off," he said.

The two stopped abruptly, heads snapping around. They looked up at him in disbelief.

"Max," Breufogle said heatedly. "We've got them!" He suddenly put his hand up to his earpiece. "What do you mean you lost them," he shouted.

Breufogle turned his back, screaming into wrist.

Sa'am looked up at Siniscolchi.

"How?"

Siniscolchi pulled the receiver from his ear. He couldn't listen to it anymore.

Breufogle turned around, his face flush with anger. He looked up at Sinicolchi.

"I'm sorry, Max. We lost them, but we can—"

Siniscolchi cut him off.

"Shut up, Stick. Just...*enough.* You two couldn't find a barn on a farm. You've fucked this up from the very start, outwitted by an old man, a child and now a retard. You can jackass all over this city and you might catch them, but captivity is not the answer. We had him for ten years, every word, every movement documented, and learned nothing. Locking him up again gets us nowhere. Let them think they got away. They'll be back."

Breufogle was incredulous.

"I'm sure Mr. Abernathé does not want them at large and unchecked. What if the Cathedrals—"

"Lower...your...*voice,*" Siniscolchi admonished severely, conscious of the prying ears only a few meters away. "I worry about what Mr. Abernathé wants. You worry about what *I* want."

Clearly irked, Breufogle adjusted his coat and stood up straighter.

"Alright, Max. What about the Charlie Squares, then?"

"If you do your job properly, they'll never get anywhere near him, will they?"

Breufogle nodded, bristling.

"Fine. So we'll go and pick up the Smart girl instead."

Siniscolchi cast a furtive glance over his shoulder. A row of IBI agents stared down at them with dozens of thumbs lounging on gun belts. Breufogle's eyes followed his.

"I gotta know, Stick. Does it hurt to be so stupid? Does it?" Frustrated, Siniscolchi continued. "You will not touch that girl. Just watch her. Am I clear?"

Breufogle nodded, simmering. Siniscolchi ambled down the steps, hands in his overcoat, his back to the IBI agents. Sa'am and Breufogle followed closely, walking quickly to keep up.

"Menscher and Sicuro are clones. Clones are not only drawn to one another, but also to their organic source. They are hardwired to keep coming back, and not in subtle ways."

"So we're going to wait," Sa'am said.

"Yes."

They all stopped in front of a waiting aircar.

"Mr. Abernathé's not going to like this," Breufogle warned.

Siniscolchi motioned for Sa'am to get in the back seat as he got in the front. He looked at Breufogle and said, "You get the next one."

Pierce sat calmly in a soft, plush chair, fingering the back of his neck. Menscher sat next to him on a couch and dropped a tiny microchip on the table in front of them. He crushed it under his thumb.

"Don't touch the incision," Menscher said. "Give it a chance to heal." He set a laser scalpel on the table and leaned back to relax.

"How are you feeling," he asked.

"The nausea?"

Menscher nodded.

"Your reaction is quite severe."

"It's getting better."

"We have this effect on each other, our fellow clones," he explained. "Or at least used to. We'll eventually become attuned to one another and we won't make each other so sick all the time."

"You feel it, too?"

"Yes."

"The laser scalpel," Pierce said. "My skin has gotten harder to cut as I've gotten older."

"I know," Menscher nodded. "You're not the first one."

"How many, um, others are there like us?"

"There were eight in your crèche. You're the only one left. I've got to give Abernathé credit. I really thought you'd died in that fire with the Sicuros."

"How did you find me?"

"This cloning business. It's an imperfect science. Some of us have, well, had, unusual characteristics. Hard skin. Brittle bones. Heightened relflexes. Stunted emotions. Intelligence, or lack thereof. Extra fingers." He smiled, looking at his hand. "In my case, a sixth sense. I have an affinity for our fellows."

"I'm really having a hard time with all this. Now that I'm thinking about it, it oddly makes sense. But I still don't believe it."

Menscher nodded.

"You mean you don't want to believe it. Again, a common reaction."

Pierce's thoughts were a jumble. Too much, too fast. He suddenly sat bolt upright.

"Aren't you worried they're going to find us here?"

"They won't. We lost them underground and we've been off their tracking devices since we left the police station. This building isn't open for occupancy yet, not for a few more weeks. Relax, I know what I'm doing."

Pierce settled back into the chair. Despite Menscher's cartoonish appearance, he seemed comforted by this man, his very presence somehow putting him at ease. He instinctively felt that he could be trusted, but Zoe warned him against trusting anyone.

This could be another trap to learn the location of the stones.

"Why are you helping me," Pierce asked.

"You're suspicious. Good. I'd expect no less. Here's your answer. For more than four decades, Lorenzo de Abernathé II has been dying."

"Just so I have this right," Pierce interjected. "We're talking about the jewelers?"

"Jewelers," Menscher exclaimed. "Jewlers?! Now there's an understatement! Yes, AbStone sells jewelry, but they've amassed enormous wealth and power as excavators of precious stones, metals and anything else they can pull out of the ground. They buy up their competitors and sell them off in pieces, or bury them in pieces. We are not talking about simple merchants, do you understand?"

Pierce nodded.

"Our benefactor," Menscher continued, "or whatever you want to call him, did not want to die. He started out small, cloning his own organs for transplanting. Nothing wrong with this, it's a legitimate medical practice. Prohibitively expensive, but legitimate. Then he started having trouble thinking and found himself stricken with progressive dementia, so tragic at such a relatively young age. So he moved into cloning brains. But he found that just the organ wasn't enough, it had to be active, thinking, functional. *Sentient.* So he moved into cloning entire people."

Pierce chuckled in spite of himself.

"Oh, I know it sounds ridiculous," Menscher said. "But look at us, Pierce, and it's suddenly not so funny anymore."

"Oh, I was thinking more of the idea of a brain transplant."

Menscher smiled wryly.

"Yeah. Well, necessity is the mother of invention. That, and a lot of money. Thirty-eight years ago, and I was the result of the experiment. Myself and some others. Our true natures were kept from us, but I was better made. I figured it out. The others died of natural causes, transcription errors. But I got away, impersonated Lorenzo II himself and just walked out. Since then, I've been waging a personal war against the Abernathés.

"Ten years after that, your crèche was 'born'. This time the idea was to create infants, let them grow up in natural circumstances, then grab them one by one, until a suitable brain was found. 'Harvesting', they called it. Well, I did all I could to rescue each of you, to hide you, protect you." He became visibly upset. Tears rolled down his face. "I failed each and every one of them."

Pierce waited until he collected himself.

"So what happened?"

"I'm not sure," Menscher said, wiping at his eyes. "The whole project was shut down right after I thought you'd died. Suddenly, no one was looking for me. I thought it had to do with the Cathedral Corporation. They suddenly moved into the same markets as AbStone. A conflict has been brewing for the last few years, now it's about to come to a head. I thought AbStone was restructuring for the coming fight with Cathedral. But now, you've reappeared."

Through his tears, he smiled at Pierce.

"You don't know how happy I am to see you," he said, slapping Pierce's knee. "I don't know what to make of things now, except that I'm committed to keeping you safe. Now, you have to tell me. Where were you? I can't imagine a place where you'd be that I wouldn't know."

Pierce still resisted his intuitive need to trust this man.

"You've been stalking me my whole life?"

"I wouldn't call it stalking. Hovering. In case I was needed."

"In case you were needed," Pierce shouted. "What about the night they burned my house down, killed my family?!"

"I tried to stop you from going back," Menscher said quietly, trembling. "You were at the starport with that girl. I was too late!"

Pierce fumed. Over the years, all that nausea was Menscher creeping around nearby? His flesh crawled at the thought.

"But look at you now," Menscher said, smiling weakly. "Your appearance is perfect. No physical defects, save for the extra finger. No...no other defects. You have only positive enhancements. Pierce, you are the culmination!"

"And according to you, all they want is my head."

Menscher calmed down.

"Yes," he said flatly. "But you must tell me, where have you been hiding?"

Pierce considered this. The Abernathés had his head in their grasp all this time, and they never took it. Then a dim memory from when he was first abducted. Outside the operating room. His head wasn't important anymore. No reason to tell Menscher that.

"I'm sorry, Mr. Menscher, but I'd rather not."

"I understand," he said. "You can tell me when you're ready. And it's Eiger. We are brothers. Of a sense."

Pierce took a hard look at Menscher. He wondered if he was staring at his future, at something more than just his likeness. How much of Menscher was a part of him?

"What color...," Pierce hesitated. "What color is the number six?"

Menscher looked at him quizzically.

"Any color you like, I guess. Why?"

Pierce nodded.

"No reason. Ahh, look, Menscher...I mean, Eiger. I want to thank you for your help," he said. "But I have to go now. Angelica is still in danger."

"In danger? From who?"

"That man. Siniscolchi, you called him. He threatened her if I didn't surrender myself to him. I need to fix this somehow."

"Understand this, Pierce. We are the dirty secret of the Abernathé family. They do not want it known what they've created. Kidnapping us is one thing, but abducting or overtly threatening the wife to be of an IBI agent is not something they will do, at least not now. They are not going to bring the weight of the interstellar government down on them, not with a war with Cathedral looming. That was an empty threat, my friend. Besides, stay with me and they will never find you, and if they can't find you, they can't threaten you. Also, if you leave her alone, if you cease to give her importance, they can't use her against you. You went after her because you thought she was in danger, but she really wasn't. Pierce, there's no room for her in our lives."

"Our lives?"

"Yes. We've only got one mission left in this life, and that's to avenge all the misery that Lorenzo de Abernathé II has caused. We will kill that man. It's all we live for. It's all I've ever planned for. He will suffer and die at our hands. It's the only way to make this all stop."

Pierce thought a moment.

"How far have you gotten with your plans?"

"Information. I've been gathering information. It's difficult with my limited resources. But one day, I will act. The two of us together? Hah! They'll be no match for us!"

Pierce weighed his next words carefully.

"I'm...not sure I agree."

Menscher was taken aback.

"W-we need a plan! We need to work together. Separately, we've accomplished nothing! With your extraordinary physical abilities, my information...we'll get to that man! We'll kill him! We'll kill him, we must!"

"And then what?"

"What? What? There is no what! We kill him. It's no more than he deserves!"

Pierce still felt drawn to Menscher, even as he unraveled before his eyes. The idea of killing this man, Abernathé, had a very strong appeal. Still, all he wanted was to be left alone, to be with Angelica again, the way it was...but first the debt.

He owed Zoe.

He owed his family.

And Angelica wasn't safe, no matter what Menscher believed. He had to get her away from that man, Scoreggia.

Pierce stood up and walked away from Menscher. He paused in front of a full length mirror. Still a bit light headed, he looked from himself to Menscher. He felt drawn to him. It wasn't affection, but an affinity. Brothers, maybe? Then a flash of memory, again, outside the operating room.

And take...this...to The Tombs.

This.

That man, Siniscolchi, he backed off. What was it that Menscher said?

Me explaining what we are?

The pounding in his temples ebbed. He studied his face, his jaw line carefully. The scar carved into his face. He clenched and unclenched his hands, feeling the size and power of his fists, the strength in his arms and legs. He looked at Menscher in the glass, now standing behind him, his lean frame and large head a pale image of his own.

Clone.

He shuddered violently and a ruddy pink weight yanked at the bottom of his stomach. He turned away from the mirror, away from the now repugnant twin images of himself and Menscher. He dizzily searched for an exit, staggered, then stumbled over a chair. He put the back of his hand over his mouth, but was unable to filter the odorless stench of himself from his mouth and throat.

Menscher tried to help Pierce to his feet, but he only pushed him away. His bony, pecking, poking fingers sent filthy yellow waves coursing through his body. This Menscher, this *thing*...this whole *thing*, was so utterly disgusting that he couldn't move.

"Pierce?"

Menscher's inflection, the sound of his voice, dripping that ruddy pink...

"Don't...don't you *ever* say my name," he gasped. "Oh, Peroxide, I can't breathe..."

The air coated his mouth and lungs like a soapy, syrupy teal.

"The nausea will pass," Menscher soothed, his eyes misting. "It will."

No.

Pierce knew it wouldn't.

He needed to get away. He needed to get control of himself, of his emotions. He needed time to think. This Menscher said they were the same, but Menscher didn't hear or smell the colors.

No one did.

He couldn't trust him. He wasn't a man like Zoe, like his father.

Dad.

And Zoe.

He needed to be more like them, to not fall into the trap of relying on other people. He found his legs and stood up.

"I want to thank you," Pierce said.

Menscher panicked.

"No! We must stay together!"

"For getting me past Siniscolchi. For what you've been able to tell me. But I have promises to keep."

"Promises?"

"I have my own money and a diamond ring I can still sell. It will get me where I need to go."

Menscher recoiled, crestfallen.

"N-no."

"Good-bye, Mr. Menscher."

Pierce picked up his bag and rushed for the door. He still felt that this was the wrong decision. He wanted to stay with Menscher, even though he couldn't think of anything more disgusting. All those years, so totally alone…but Menscher was not someone his father would trust. Neither would Zoe.

"Wait," Menscher exclaimed, darting between Pierce and the door. "I can protect you! W-we must stay together!"

"I don't think so, Eiger."

Pierce shoved Menscher easily to the side and yanked the door open. He exited the apartment and quickly dashed down the stairwell.

Alone.

Chapter 14
The Charlie Squares

The planet Nostrova offered much in terms of culture, education and fine places to live. The cities centered in the south eastern corner of this planet were less opulent than the rest of the world and appealed to the disenfranchised of Center Web, which now included Pierce Sicuro. In his desire to go unnoticed, Pierce very easily melted into the bustling crowds that pushed and shoved along the narrow streets and smaller buildings.

He immediately located a jeweler and sold the ring he had bought for Angelica all those years ago, and got back almost what he had paid for it. He then wandered from town to town, city to city, reveling in simple pleasures. Taking in picture shows, reading, eating ice cream, dining in restaurants, the wind and rain on his face—all of the things he despaired of ever doing again.

These seemingly random wanderings did have a purpose. He patronized many different kinds of retail establishments, sometimes making purchases, often not. What he did purchase he had discreetly delivered to a private storage container in the nearby town of Croton. He also visited libraries, where he learned everything he could about the Pan Slothe Observatory at Ursus.

He appeared outwardly calm, at peace with himself and his surroundings. Behind this mask of practiced patience, his mind burned. He found himself succumbing to increasingly intense moments of raw morbidity, a sickness brought about by a blasphemous pain, a pain so black and foul it forced him tear at his own flesh, as if tearing himself apart from the inside out would somehow ease his torment and stem the nausea and disgust that wracked him day and night. And then there was the voice in the back of his mind, which was at its loudest and most commanding in that twilight right before he fell to sleep each night, urging him to find and kill Lorenzo de Abernathé II.

While he battled himself for control over his mind and body, he never wavered in his attention to detail, his constant memorization of his surroundings. He had to be careful. Too much was at stake. There was no margin for error because even though he moved about by himself, he was not alone.

Pierce hadn't seen Menscher since he bolted from the vacant apartment on the other side of the planet a month ago, but every once in a while, he felt an extra tinge of a particular dark green, bilious nausea from when his fellow clone got too close. Pierce expected this and Menscher's presence alternately comforted or irritated him, depending on his mood.

In addition to Menscher, multiple entourages were in constant orbit about him. He noted the same faces, scents and sensations of many different people in disparate locations. For instance, two plasticky-yellow anthropods and a third green scented man seemed to be working together. The canite with the nose ring, the one from the hospital, was also with them. The anthropods made little effort to stay out of sight, probably relying on the general human inability to tell them apart. They also relied on their greater foot speed to follow ahead and behind. As fast as they were, Pierce was faster, and he could have eluded them at any moment he chose. Instead, he let them follow, so long as they kept their distance.

The other group worried him more than the anthropods. The man with the buzz cut and t-bar posture he remembered from the police station, the one who liked to talk into his wrist too much. And the two other guys with earpieces, one who smelled like pork and beans and the other who reminded him of rain. These three behaved professionally and he had a harder time keeping track of them.

All the while, he conducted himself as if he was unaware and completely at peace, as if he hadn't a care in the whole galaxy.

Tucked away ninety kilometers up river from the ocean, the small town of Croton occupied a thin slice of the eastern riverside. It boasted a lower to middle class population, most of whom worked in the local chip manufacturing plants for NYSAAC, or in the retail stores that employment supported. The lights of the Croton Aerodrome reached skyward from atop a flattened, custom configured plateau. Various buildings dotted the airfield. Small planes and starships lined the green fields in neat rows, parked to the side of the landing platforms and runways. Local ground traffic snaked around its base. The starport catered mostly to private enthusiasts or long distance private charters, but did handle small amounts of commercial traffic. Ship rental agencies located on the grounds did a brisk business for mostly within system travelers.

The Amerex rental agency maintained rows of private storage units and operated out of a small stand alone building half a kilometer from the flight tower. In the early hours before dawn, a lone man made his way down the darkened rows of locked steel doors. He moved stealthily, careful to avoid the alternating circles of light cast by the fixtures mounted high on the walls. He stopped at a particular unit and double checked the serial number. He disabled the unit's meager defenses and forced the magnetic lock. He lifted the perforated door upward. With a small flashlight, he surveyed the contents methodically, then stepped cautiously inside.

Stacks of corrugated boxes lined the walls. Precise block lettering labeled each box. He rifled through the boxes, moving quickly from one pile to the next, verifying their contents. The last box gave him pause. He removed an object and observed it curiously. He knelt on the floor, then used his flashlight to study it more closely. Distracted, he didn't notice the silhouette that appeared in the open doorway behind him, nor the weapon hidden in the shadows.

"Vic," a voice crackled faintly in the silence. "Vic, come back."

The man cupped his ear, then spoke into his wrist.

"Vic here. Go ahead, S'Roub."

"One Actual is en route to your location. Your window is closed. Repeat, your window is closed. Get out of there now."

Suddenly alert, Vic looked over his shoulder. The shadows enveloped him, and something hard, yet pliable struck his hand, forcing him to drop the object in his grasp. Before Vic could reach for his gun, he was flung with impossible ease against the back wall of the storage unit and bounced off the sheet metal with a loud clang. His flashlight clattered to the floor and went out.

Stunned, barely conscious, he was dragged to his feet and lifted half a meter off the ground. A calloused hand pinned his throat to the wall. First, the receiver disappeared from his ear, then the transmitter from his wrist and finally the gun from his waist.

A bearded face pressed close against his, so close he could taste the cinnamon on his attacker's breath.

"Who are you," a gruff voice whispered. "And what are you doing here?"

Vic tried to form words, but his voice died in his throat.

"You, that canite and those two anthropods have been following me all over this planet. Why?"

"There's no need for this," Vic rasped. "You know why."

"And just what am I supposed to know?"

"You can still make a deal."

"Who are you? NYSAAC or Cathedral?"

Vic smiled weakly.

"What's a guy like you need a secant monocle sensor for?"

Yellowed teeth grit in anger. The hand around Vic's throat constricted and crushed his windpipe like styrofoam. His lifeless body slumped to the floor in a tangled heap. Vic's killer stood immobile in the near darkness, staring at his hand, flexing and unflexing his fingers.

"Vic. *Vic.* Do you copy?"

The voice came from Vic's earpiece, now in his coat pocket.

"We have a confirmed visual on One Actual, approaching the Aerodrome from the northern gap. Hold your position, I'm sending Str'Assey."

In moments, the contents of the storage unit were swept onto an anti-grav sled and the space abandoned. Through the open door, Vic's mottled shape lay on the floor, his lifeless eyes transfixed on his earpiece.

"Vic," a voice crackled. "Vic, are you there?"

"Victor Pryce," the bleary eyed rental clerk said, reading the ID card. "This is you?"

"Yes," Pierce replied.

The canite woman raised a curious eyebrow and yawned, her hand slow to cover her mouth.

"Doesn't look much like you."

"Picture's old, before I grew all this fur." Pierce slid his last cash ducat across the counter, under his hand.

"Let me guess, you were sick that day."

Pierce smiled congenially.

The clerk squared her back to the security camera, then pocketed the ducat. She turned to a computer terminal and inserted the ID into a slot reader.

"According to your ID, you work for Cathedral. Is that still accurate?"

He nodded.

"You have a Nostrova address. Still accurate?"

Pierce nodded again.

"Occupation?"

"Security."

"And why do you need a hull size six vessel?"

"I've been transferred to Gran Nexus." He gestured over his shoulder at the plate glass window. "That's my stuff on the anti-grav tray outside."

"For that you need a sixer?" She shook her head. "A two would be more like it, and cheaper."

"That's only the first sled."

"Uh-huh. And you'll be departing when?"

"Now."

"Of course. Why else would you be here before the crack of dawn." She yawned again. "You have a system only license. If you plan on leaving the solar system, you'll need a pilot. We can provide one, if you like."

"That won't be necessary."

She nodded.

Pierce's eyes moved casually about the small rental office, noting the security camera above him and the empty maze of pole ropes behind him. He had come straight here after leaving the storage container, forced to move up his timetable for departure. He had planned to obtain forged credentials, but the Cathedrals had just changed all that. He did his best to appear outwardly calm, but he couldn't fathom how she couldn't hear his heart pounding in his chest. He didn't want to kill Victor Pryce. He only wanted to learn the name of his employer. This careless rental clerk had just confirmed for him that Victor was indeed a Charlie Square, which confirmed what he already suspected. His own strength and quickness still surprised him, especially when angry or scared, and he needed to get better control of his emotions and reflexes. Zoe had told him the key to survival was ruthlessness, plain and simple. He couldn't have let Pryce go, especially after he had seen the secant monocle sensor.

Killing Pryce wasn't what bothered him. It was the ease with which he'd done it.

"Okay," the clerk yawned, sliding the ID card back to him over the counter. "Here are the access codes to your ship, the *Amerex-Affito.* She's parked on the South Field in Lot 28. A sixer, like as you asked for, Noleggio class, of course. Have the tower confirm your flight plan and check for clearance. Should we bill you directly, or your employer?"

"My employer."

"You can turn the ship in at any of our 528 Amerex offices on Gran Nexus. The autopilot can be used to locate them."

"Okay."

"Any other questions?"

Pierce shook his head, took the ID card and left.

Pierce moved briskly along the paved path that led to the South Field, lifting his hood over his head. He pulled the tray behind him with two fingers, his eyes studying the dark shapes of the parked spacecraft on both sides. Light from the fluorescent lampposts glinted off the green grass, wet with dew. He held Pryce's gun nervously in his other hand, not sure what to do with it.

As he approached the intersect for Lot 28, he heard voices. He cautiously peered down the path to the small platform, where a modest hull size six freighter was parked underneath a humming spotlight. His stomach bottomed out, and a twinge of bile green lingered in his nostrils, which could only mean one thing.

Menscher.

Next to the freighter, down on the ground.

Two anthropods, a human and a canite stood over him. Very quietly, they were giving him quite a beating.

Between Pierce and the goons around Menscher stood a macropian who smelled of black rot, his stringy, knotted fur matted flat in the damp air. Macropians could see into the infrared spectrum and he should have spotted Pierce easily in the dark, but he was more interested in what his companions were doing to Menscher.

Without a sound, Pierce let go of the anti-grav tray and took a blackjack from his pocket. He had made this weapon himself, from the discarded spring of a screen door, a looped leather belt for a handle, and some electrical tape. It folded up neatly in his pocket when not in use and it proved a very practical instrument at close quarters, as Victor Pryce had already learned.

Pierce crept closer and then wielded the blackjack with all his strength. He shattered the macropian's skull at the base of the spine. Pierce eased the body to the ground, then stepped over it and approached the mob.

The human picked up Menscher and struck him hard at the bridge of the nose. Blood seeped from his nose and mouth. A thick gash swelled on his forehead.

"You didn't have to kill him, Pierce," one of the anthropods clicked. "We're not savages, like those damned Abbies. Them, they won't ask this nicely. We're businessmen. You could've just told Vic where to find the diamonds."

"W-what diamonds," Menscher gasped.

"I'm sick of this shit," the canite spat. His nose ring glinted in the light. He rammed his fist into Menscher's gut and he fell to the ground in a gagging heap. The canite leaned in close. "You see, Pierce, Vic was our friend. No one was going to hurt you, we just wanted information. Time for a little payback, asshole."

As the canite stood up straight, his throat exploded in a burst of red. His head flopped to the side as the rest of him fell over backward.

All eyes turned on Pierce, who stood at the edge of the platform, gun in hand. The two anthropods and the human meekly put their hands up, studying him warily.

"Back off," Pierce said, his face hidden in the shadow of his hood. "Step away from him."

Nobody moved.

"I suggest you move along," one of the anthropods said. "This doesn't concern you."

"It does now."

"This man is coming with us. This is your last chance—"

Pierce shot the anthropod through the head. Before it could hit the ground, the remaining two reached for their weapons. Pierce dropped the man first with a single shot through his chest.

The anthropod, much quicker than its fellow and with a spring draw up its sleeve, got off two panicked shots at Pierce, which he sidestepped with ease. He took careful aim and killed the remaining anthropod with two shots to its neck and head.

Pierce looked around cautiously and didn't move again until sure no one had observed the quick exchange of laser fire. He stepped over one of the anthropods to reach Menscher and knelt down next to him.

"Eiger. Are you okay?"

Menscher had taken quite a beating. His nose had been broken and dark circles ringed his eyes, eyes now swollen shut.

"Pierce! I'm sorry..."

"Why did you do this?"

"I had to lead them away...away from you. The Abbies had you trapped!"

"They weren't Abbies. They were Charlie Squares, and I wasn't in any real danger."

"They were going to kill you—"

"No," Pierce corrected. "No, they weren't. Nobody wants to kill me."

"The feeling isn't mutual."

"It gives me an advantage."

"Naturally."

Menscher put a hand to his chest and winced painfully.

"What's wrong," Pierce asked.

"My chest hurts. Hurts to breathe."

"You've just got the wind knocked out of you," Pierce said. "They weren't trying to seriously hurt you, just scare you."

"What's all this about diamonds? Now you've got CC's after you, too?"

"Apparently."

"But you killed them."

"Yes."

"And they didn't want to kill you?"

"That's right."

"What's all this about, then," Menscher asked.

Pierce ignored his question.

"C'mon," he said, helping Menscher to his feet. "I'm not going to leave you here like this."

"I can't see."

"I know."

"Where are you going in such a hurry?"

Pierce grunted.

"You mean *we*. Where are *we* going."

Menscher smiled broadly, allowing Pierce to help him toward the waiting ship.

Chapter 15
Aphelion

For the last sixty turbulent years, momentous events have taken place all around the Aphelion Binary System. Never in. Always around. Since the last inhabitants left this overlooked and isolated part of space eleven years ago, very little had changed. The only trace of their presence visible from space, the chlorid foam that once threatened to shroud the entire fourth planet, had long since burned away. The denizens of The Web continued to seek their destinies elsewhere, in other corners of the known galaxy, like The Rim and The Frontier.

Four planets orbited the larger star, unofficially known as Aphelion Alpha. Along with the dwarf star Aphelion Beta, they formed a unique a stellar construct unknown to modern physics. The four planets glided through space in strained, elongated elliptical orbits, always true to the soft, warmth of the yellow star, but never quite free from the influence of the red. Time after time, the red star failed to snare its prey, and for all eternity, they attracted and repulsed one another, unobserved, yet oblivious to all else, singularly focused on this gracefully elaborate dance.

Once every eon, all of the celestial bodies that comprised the Aphelion Binary System reached agreement and aligned themselves perfectly with one another. For this brief instant, the participants paused, reflected, and then launched into the dance anew. A non-descript freighter, Noleggio class, cruised at the edge of the solar system, an unwitting witness to this most sacred moment. This drab, box-like starship stood in stark contrast to the natural majesty it circled. It kept its distance, held at bay by the raw, listless power that could destroy it on an impersonal whim.

Pierce Sicuro set the auto pilot to keep a respectable distance from the star formation. He sat quietly for a few minutes and stared blankly at the darkened canopy. He watched the nav-computer slowly build a holo-map on the board in front of him. Pierce plugged the secant monocle sensor into the navigation computer and it chirped to life.

Pierce checked and double checked for any communications traffic and found none, not expecting to find any. The data showed no unnatural objects within range. He turned on the viewer so he could take in the picture of majesty that was the Aphelion Binary System.

Without a doubt, this place matched the coordinates Zoe had given him. So forbidding and utterly isolated, it seemed an unlikely place to find a fortune in diamonds. Over and over again, he rhythmically repeated Zoe's instructions, like a mantra. He could ill afford any missteps at this point, both literally and figuratively. It had cost him his every last ducat to get this far, only to be confronted with a practically unnavigatible obstacle.

The interference radiating from the two stars, and the heavy gravimetric distortions resulting from their close proximity to one another, played havoc with the standard navigation instruments. Now that the SMS unit had had a few minutes to work, the data it gathered filled in the gaps in the 3-D holo-image of the solar system, gaps that the standard scanners couldn't interpret. He sighed with relief as one, two, three then four planets appeared around the larger star.

Thunking footsteps preceded the arrival of a still weary Menscher. He yawned loudly and felt his way to the co-pilot's seat. He gingerly touched his swollen eyelids with his fingertips, still unable to see. Pierce had stitched his cuts and cleaned up the rest of his bruises, but purposefully did nothing for his eyes.

"Alright," Menscher said, rubbing the armrests of his chair. "Are you going to tell me where we are?"

"Far from the prying eyes of both the Charlies and Abbies," Pierce replied, annoyed.

"And where is that?"

"Will you be quiet," Pierce admonished, raising his voice. He continued to study the data in front of him.

"You could at least explain why we left Nostrova! How is running away going to get us closer to Lorenzo de Abernathé?"

Menscher continued his rant. Pierce did his best to ignore him, and tapped his fingers on the armrest of his chair, rapidly losing patience with his fellow clone.

Fellow clone.

How easily this truth now rolled around in his mind. He had come to accept it. It made sense.

All of it.

Somehow.

But it still did nothing to mitigate the blackness that clawed at his soul.

Menscher had this compulsive need to continually speak. It unnerved Pierce so much that over the last few days, he found himself missing the peaceful silence of his captivity.

...and to top it all off, now we've got no money! I—"

"We're in the right place, Eiger."

"Right place for what? Where?"

"I also need to be sure that no one followed us out here."

"You already said no one followed us."

"You said you trust me."

Menscher trembled a bit.

"Yes. But you said you had means."

"Be quiet, please."

Menscher did as he was told.

Back in that apartment with Menscher, forever ago, Pierce remembered something his father repeatedly told him about relationships. His father believed that he let Angelica lead him around by the nose too much, and that it was always better for people to need *you* more than you need *them*.

'Don't underestimate the importance of being your own man,' he would say. 'Do as much as you can by yourself, so you won't have to rely on anyone else. A man who stands alone will attract others like him and those are the people you should associate with, that you should trust.'

Pierce and his brothers got a lot of laughs out of this, whenever his father went on one of these monologues, because if it wasn't for their mother, he would've been naked and living in the streets, chasing ground cars.

He originally intended to leave Menscher behind on Nostrova, but the beating he took for him on the platform, his willingness to give up his own life, finally convinced Pierce of his sincerity. Menscher also had no knowledge of the Ecks Stones, which reassured him that he wasn't a tool of the Abbies. What Menscher had said about them becoming attuned to one another turned out to be true. They were sitting right next to each other, and though he still felt the gnawing in his gut, and the occasional whiff of black tar clogging his nostrils and throat, he could manage it.

Master it.

Suppress it.

This overwhelming compulsion to trust Menscher, to simply be near him, assailed him every waking moment, like storm waves pounding a beach head. This compulsion, this sense of unjustified closeness, this overwhelming *need,* had no rational basis. It wasn't familial, but something greater, as if he were reaching out to *himself.* Reflecting on it now, leaving Nostrova without Menscher would have been a serious mistake, but he had no sensible explanation as to *why,* only this intense feeling that it was *right.*

During the flight to Aphelion, Pierce had learned a lot about Menscher. For one thing, he liked to talk.

A lot.

From from his 'birth' in the lab, to how he tried to help the other clones, to how he managed to outwit the Abbies, gather information and live cheaply without attracting attention, ad nauseum. He told Pierce about it all. How he worked a lot of janitor jobs, hired himself out as unskilled labor in order to gain access to sensitive areas, how he 'mastered' the art of forceful confrontation, how he learned to hide in plain sight—all part of the less than vivid, less than intricate tapestry of the life and times of Eiger Menscher.

He led a solitary existence, which he lamented, but deemed necessary. Pierce didn't think it required that much effort. Menscher could pass for normal for a time, even with his unusual body shape, but random, innocuous triggers would propel him into fits of mania over the Abernathés. Pierce felt the same impulses and empathized to a degree, but had less and less patience for these outbursts.

Menscher did have a talent for quick and clever improvisation, and the guts of a burglar, but no aptitude to formulate long term goals, or at least one goal: killing Lorenzo de Abernathé II. Elude detection, yes, and also capture, but completely devoid of initiative. Fortunately, for the both of them, Pierce had a plan.

Space travel proved a significant obstacle, but not insurmountable. Pierce did not want to hire a ship, which necessitated that he obtain one for himself. He had removed the nodule that limited the rental ship to in-system travel. He wanted a ship at least a hull size of five, because anything that or larger had interstellar capability. He could fly just about anything this size in system, but interstellar navigation was a problem. To his good fortune, there had been a revolution in space travel in the Post-War Era.

Before The War, plotting space travel at faster than light speeds was a specialized skill. Even with computer assistance, it required extensive and complicated calculations. Astrogation was a noble profession, always in demand, and the best well compensated. During The War, necessity demanded improvements to the process. The software designed by Naval astrogators proved easily adaptable to civilian use. While expensive, it became far easier for the private citizen to travel between star systems. The astrogation profession went into a corresponding decline.

The bulk of Pierce's funds went to the purchase of navigation software and the rental of this Noleggio class freighter. As easy as it was to use this nav software, it could not chart a course through a binary star formation.

Pierce made no approach for several hours, hoping that the sensors would continue to add more detail to the holographic map of the star system. The holomap hadn't changed since painting the fourth planet. The instruments weren't equipped for the in depth analysis he required. He manually fed data into the database, based on his own theories and observations, and hoped the nav software would produce something he could work with.

He ruminated on the old adage, 'garbage in, garbage out'. He couldn't do anything about it now. There was no turning back.

While waiting on the holomap, he continuously monitored the other sensors for any trace of another man made object within or without the solar system. So far, nothing. He wanted to believe they were alone, but anything could be hiding out there.

Menscher grew impatient in the pointless silence. All kinds of body and facial ticks manifested themselves.

"Dammit" he pouted, "tell me where we are!"

"Eiger, I'm trying to concentrate," Pierce said patiently, as if speaking to a child.

"On what?"

"I'm trying to find a way to navigate to the fourth planet without getting us torn apart."

"Planet? What planet? What system are we in?"

"Eiger," Pierce sighed. "Please."

Menscher continued to mumble.

Binary star formations were akin to a planet and its moon, Pierce recollected. They appear to be in orbit around one another, but they're really circling a center point of gravity. The planet and moon circle this center point of gravity while orbiting another center point of gravity with the nearest star. Theoretically, it was possible for natural objects to exist in a binary system, but not for planets to form. And if they did form, the heat, radiation and whatever else generated by the close proximity of the two stars would prevent life. Plus, the gravimetric stresses are far greater than the planet/moon relationship, so any planet would be torn apart.

Yet he was looking at a binary star formation with four planets.

Was Zoe wrong? Did he misunderstand?

After a few more minutes, the nav software provided him with several options. Pierce decided to approach from around the dwarf star. He would use its gravity to propel his ship into the orbit of the fourth planet, which orbited the larger star, along with the other three planets. The nav software worked seamlessly with the SMS and displayed a safe course, with clearly defined gravity wells. He wasn't skilled enough to navigate through all this manually. He had no choice but to trust the machines, and ultimately his own guesswork.

Pierce fired the engines and the small ship eased forward.

"Buckle up, Eiger."

"We're moving." Menscher's head tilted upward, his puffy eyes straining to see. "Where are we going?"

Pierce didn't answer.

He kept one eye on the holo map and the other on the nav computer, watching their progress, afraid to breathe. The ship successfully completed one full orbit of the dwarf star. As the ship came around and into alignment with the orbital path of the fourth planet, Pierce fired the engines and sent the ship hurling away from the red star. The freighter shook violently and Menscher grabbed his arm fearfully.

"Pierce! What's going on? What's happening?"

"Relax, Eiger," he said easily, masking his own anxiety. "We're okay."

On the holo map, Pierce watched as the ship overshot the orbital path of the fourth planet. In the same moment he considered taking manual control, the software corrected itself, and now they shared the same orbital plane around the larger star as the fourth planet. Pierce pushed the throttle to max and they began their pursuit of this elusive, white world.

Pierce turned on a second viewer and filtered out the luminosity of both stars. Gradually, the planet peeked out behind the yellow star and grew larger as they approached. This white world took his breath away, its existence impossible, yet there it was, staring back at him, just as Zoe said it would. He shook his head at the improbability of it all, and wondered what could've brought his cell mate to a place like this, and how he discovered this world that frightened, yet captivated, at the same time.

As the world loomed larger, he could make out streaks of dark green, black mountaintops that interrupted the unrelenting white, and bright fields of blue water. He found no evidence of civilization, no radio traffic. The entire spectrum was silent. At the realization of just how isolated and alone they were here, and how forbidding this world seemed, it chilled him to the marrow.

Pierce took manual control of the ship and steered it into a standard orbit. He looked at Menscher, his eyes still swollen shut. Literally in the dark, he gripped and ungripped the armrests of his chair and alternately pulled fitfully at his shirt, his ear lobes and even his hair, on the verge of losing control.

Control.

Pierce reached over and buckled him into his seat.

"What are you doing," Menscher demanded. "What's happening?"

"Planetfall," Pierce responded, securing his own restraints.

"What planet?"

"Be—"

"I know, I know," Menscher shouted. "Be quiet! Dammit!"

Menscher folded his arms over his chest and sat in a huff.

Pierce retracted the slats from the canopy windows to take in the planet Aphelion Four with his own eyes. It struck him as a cold, hard place. He could find nothing inviting about it, but it still commanded his attention.

Unspoiled.

Pristine.

And so white...

He had never seen anything like it. No patterns of light to mark cities or highways. No navigational beacons. It scared him, yet he wanted to experience it.

He held his breath as he steered the ship into the atmosphere of the bright, clean planet. He guided the ship easily down into the lower stratosphere and cruised at fifteen kilometers above the frozen surface, in awe at the sun drenched snowscape that stretched unmarred between spectacular mountain ranges and dense forests. He streaked along the frozen coastline on the east side of the northern continent, decelerating once identifying a frozen, crescent shaped inlet in the shadow of a forbidding range of angular peaks. He checked his readouts and confirmed the coordinates he had memorized so long ago. He double checked the geographical features, mountains to the east, forest to the west, frozen bay in between. His magnetic compass spun crazily in front of him.

This was the place.

He deployed the landing struts and brought the ship to a gentle landing on the ice sheet. He shut down all of the systems and looked at Menscher.

"Time to do something about those eyes."

The hatch to the freighter closed with a hiss.

Menscher stood next to Pierce, scraping at the granite-like ice with a booted foot. The sun blinded Menscher and the wind howled in his ears, stinging his face and burning it red. He watched in utter disbelief at the rising of a second sun. Shadows muted, shifted, and the shade of the mountain range to the east raced at them and washed over them like a tidal wave. It got colder. Flecks of snow and ice stung his eyes.

Pierce pulled a neoprene mask over his face and put on sungoggles. Menscher did likewise.

"Where are we," Menscher asked breathlessly.

"This way," Pierce shouted over the wind, pointing toward the mountains.

The wind blew hard on their faces, pushing against them, like the elements themselves wanted to turn them in the other direction. Pierce held a compass that he glanced at every few minutes. The dial spun wildly, occasionally quivering oddly. He stopped every few hundred paces and looked about, his face taught with concentration.

The ship faded from view, now a few hundred meters behind them. No footprints trailed behind them in the ice. Menscher worried that if they lost sight of the ship, they would have trouble finding their way back to it.

"Can I help," Menscher asked, shouting over the wind. "I'd like to help."

Pierce just waved him off, shaking his head.

Snow gradually mixed with the ice. Menscher followed Pierce as he marched onward, now knee deep in the fine white powder. They criss-crossed between the peaks of the snow dunes.

With the wind pushing against him and the snow deepening, Menscher stopped in his tracks, exhausted. The stiff breeze nearly knocked him over. Pierce looked back at him, still holding the compass.

"What," he shouted.

Menscher waved his arms in resignation.

"I'm going back!"

Pierce shook his head.

"No! We're almost there!"

Menscher glanced at the erratic behavior of the compass.

"You can't know that! I don't think you even know what you're looking for!"

Pierce pulled at Menscher's sleeve.

"Stay with me, Eiger!"

Menscher sighed and nodded wearily.

They trudged onward.

After another half an hour, they reached the base of the summit. Menscher leaned against the rock and ice, panting heavily. Pierce walked around the snow in slow, deliberate circles.

"What are you looking for," Menscher shouted over the wind. "Let me help."

Pierce ignored him, slowing his pace. He stopped abruptly, the compass needle spinning wildly. He pocketed the device and then screwed together a metal pick axe. Again and again he hacked at the snow and ice in a wide circle. He finally motioned for Menscher to approach. Together, using their hands, they pulled away all of the broken chunks of snow and ice to reveal the tip of an enormous, polished black stone.

Before Menscher could form a question, Pierce got up and walked away. Confused, he followed Pierce to the ice and rock wall. Pierce used the pick axe to knock away a thin crust of ice and snow and uncovered what appeared to be hand holds. He went up the embankment, which looked at first to be a treacherous climb, but proved rather easy as if stairs had been carved into the rock.

Eventually, the embankment leveled off into a plateau, a shelf that looked out over the ice sheet below. They could see the running lights of their ship in the distance, now also in the shadow of the mountains. A broken T-shaped piece of wood stuck out of the snow. It had metal fasteners and riggings. The wood had split and cracked from prolonged exposure to the wind and cold.

Pierce turned and approached the solid wall of ice. He hacked at it with his pick axe until he heard a dull thunk. It took him only a few minutes to clear away enough of the ice to reveal a slatted wooden door.

Awestruck, Menscher grabbed his shoulder.

"How did you know?"

Pierce didn't answer.

He took a flat disc from a pocket in his sleeve and slid his fingers through a harness strap. The disc glowed with orange heat. He used it to melt away the rest of the thick layers of ice that covered the door. With some effort, he worked the frost covered latch and with a mighty heave, the door slid open.

Menscher reflexively threw up his arm for protection, but behind the door was only a dark space. Pierce pulled off his sungoggles, as did Menscher. They stepped closer. Inside was a cave. A small cave. A bunch of wooden sticks were tied up in neat bundles on one side, wrapped in animal skins. On the other side were two wooden barrels and a row of cups hanging on hooks above them. A spool of rope and an assortment of metal poles and tubes were next to them. Menscher puzzled over a rusty halogen lamp, a frosted over space heater and what looked like solar panels. An assortment of laser and ballistic weapons were tucked into a corner. A large, furry brown animal tapestry hung on the wall to his left, flapping in the breeze.

Pierce stepped inside, motioning for Menscher to follow. Hesitant, he reluctantly obeyed, and Pierce grunted as he slid the door shut behind them. Now out of the wind, they felt immediately warmer, although only thin shafts of light shone through the door slats and seams. Pierce turned on his wristlight and waved it about the small space, looking through everything.

"What is this place," Menscher breathed, steadying himself against the rock wall. "What's all this for?"

Pierce suddenly stopped, then aimed the light upward. A gray metal pipe ran along the rock ceiling, less than a meter above their heads. One end ran through a gap in the top of the wooden door. The other end disappeared into a hole in the inner rock wall.

"Pierce," Menscher demanded. "What are we doing here?!"

Pierce smiled.

"Following the pipe."

He brushed past Menscher and pulled the hanging animal skin aside. They found another wooden door, which Pierce slid open. Another furry tapestry hung over the door way, which Pierce also pulled aside. Menscher reluctantly followed.

This even smaller space contained an assortment of clothing and footwear all fashioned from animal pelts. Various hand made knives and spears, and other primitive weaponry, lined the walls. On a small table, pushed to the side, were a few pieces of jagged metal and glass. Another tapestry barred their path. Behind it, another wooden door. Again, Pierce opened it, as casually and confidently as if he lived here.

Stepping inside, Menscher turned on his own wristlight. Now sweating, he pulled off his face mask. Both men breathed deeply, their breath visible in the cool, dry air. They stealthily explored the large space, wristlights flitting this way and that, each afraid to make a sound.

Menscher viewed the stone fire pit in the center of the cave curiously. The wood stacked in it glistened with a syrupy accelerant. Two big pieces of flint were on a table next to it. A metal duct hovered above the fire pit, connected to the pipe that ran outside. A collection of weapons were spread out on a larger table, from pistols, rifles to hand made clubs and axes. A collection of smaller tables had other items laid out on them, including wooden flatware, utensils and cups. He made out a butcher block in the back, complete with a gruesome looking cleaver impaled in bloody wood. Three wood framed partitions marked off four distinct living spaces. Multiple wooden barrels, piled one upon another, with carved labels like 'beffer guts', 'ammonia', 'cones', 'dry stores', and more, lined the walls. A very neat line of red and blue plastic crates, stacked from the floor to ceiling like a checkerboard, lined a far wall. They had no labels. Everything was very neat, very organized and set up for an emergency entrance, as if things would be needed quickly.

Pierce, barely breathing, picked up the two pieces of flint, and held them reverently in his palm. He then closed his hand and pressed it to his forehead. He shut his eyes and inhaled deeply, trying to catch his breath.

Menscher put a hand on his shoulder.

"Are you okay," he whispered, his voice barely audible.

With a profound sadness, Pierce nodded. He returned the pieces of flint to where he found them. He ignited the fire with a cigarette lighter instead, and soon the room filled with the warm glow of the roaring flames, the air scented with a hint of mint.

Pierce and Menscher doused their wristlights and looked around in a revered silence. The layers of dust that coated everything spoke volumes. Clearly, no one had lived here in a very, very long time.

Menscher felt drawn to the partitioned living spaces. A few personal effects laid about, but nothing that indicated who lived here. Pierce sat down at a table to better examine an airtight box with a keycard still in its slot. He watched Pierce open the box. It contained a disc player which looked like it had been removed from a suitcomp. Pierce pressed the playback button, and the face of a cold, stern woman with gray hair filled the small screen. Transfixed, Menscher came up slowly behind him.

"My name is Lieutenant Rhonda Class," the image said. "Political Officer, late of the IWS *Solonova Pathfinder.* This message is intended for—"

"Who is she," Menscher asked. "Do you know her?"

Pierce quickly shut off the player and returned it to the box, slamming it shut. He put the keycard in his pocket. He jumped to his feet and glared icily at Menscher.

"No, Eiger. I don't."

"Then what—"

Pierce turned his back on him and moved slowly about the cave. He looked at everything very closely, but touched very little. By the time he reached the plastic crates, his face had hardened, his jaw set, his mouth a chiseled, thin line.

He nodded as if coming to some unspoken conclusion.

He touched the crates and found them heavy.

"Eiger," he said.

Menscher stepped forward and without a word, the two of them moved the containers, one at a time. Behind the line of crates were two more wooden doors, one labeled 'DRY', the other intricately carved with the image of a starship that visited several solar systems, including one with a binary star system that had four planets. Both had hinges sewn into the rock, and one was secured by a latch mechanism.

Menscher looked at the carved door.

"What is all this? It's time you explained—"

Pierce stepped forward and opened the door. An avalanche of diamonds of all sizes spilled out. Without blinking, he opened the second door, with identical results.

Slack jawed, Menscher fell to his knees. He scooped up handfuls of the precious gems and let them pass through his fingers like water.

"Impossible," he gasped.

After a moment, he laughed loudly, his shouts of exuberance echoing throughout the cave.

He picked up a large stone and held it up for Pierce to see. Octagonal rainbows sparkled in the firelight.

"We're rich," he exclaimed, jumping to his feet. "Rich!"

Pierce looked at him sternly.

"What do you mean we?"

Menscher reacted as if he'd been struck.

"I—"

"Put that back," Pierce demanded.

Any thought Menscher had of asserting himself wilted with Pierce's disapproving countenance. He put the gem gently back on top of the pile.

"These are *my* diamonds," Pierce said, pounding his finger into his own chest. "All of them. Is that clear?"

"I-I…O-of course," Menscher trembled. "I only meant—"

"Go sit over there," Pierce commanded, pointing to the other side of the cave. "Now."

Menscher obeyed and moped over to a table. He sat heavily, round shouldered.

Pierce opened a few of the plastic crates, each of them filled to the brim with the precious stones. He resealed the containers and then sat down on one of them. He didn't move for a long time. All the while, Menscher sulked like a scolded child, involuntarily twitching, barely able to contain himself. He shoved his hands under his armpits to try and still himself.

Finally, Pierce stood up.

"This has to be done right, Eiger."

"I don't understand," Menscher shouted, the words exploding from his mouth. "With all this wealth, killing Lorenzo de Abernathé should be easy! There's no limit to what we can accomplish!"

Pierce nodded, now sitting next to Menscher.

"Yes. But how?"

"I can hide you, protect you, until we can strike!"

"How do we strike?"

Menscher's mouth quivered. He struggled for words. Confusion contorted his face.

"We just kill him, that's how!"

Pierce put his arms on Menscher's shoulders. Menscher looked up at him, his eyes bulging and his mouth quivering.

Pierce put a hand on his counterpart's face until he calmed down.

"I need to know that I can trust you, Eiger."

"W-w-we are brothers, Pierce," Menscher stammered, aghast at even the suggestion. "More than brothers! We are the same!"

"No doubt," Pierce said. "And you made this possible."

"Yes! Or you'd be with Siniscolchi now!"

Pierce tipped his head toward the diamonds.

"The diamonds. This place. It remains our secret."

Menscher smiled conspiratorily.

"Of course! I—"

"And everything here belongs to me."

"I—"

Pierce again jabbed a finger into his own chest.

"*Me.*"

Menscher frowned, then smiled weakly.

"Y-yes. Of course."

"Then you and I are in complete agreement," Pierce said, pulling him close. "This place is our secret."

"Yes."

"The diamonds are our secret."

"Yes."

"And we are going to kill Lorenzo de Abernathé."

"*Yes.*"

"His whole family will suffer."

"*Yesss...*"

"You and I together, Eiger." He pulled Menscher's face close to his own. "My way."

"Yes." Menscher nodded eagerly. "Your way. Together."

Chapter 16
The Vestitian Job

A thick haze filled the air in Conference Room Nine of the Hotel Vestitia. The filtration system clicked on and off with a dull hum to keep the air circulating. The small group of canites sitting in the back puffed on one cigar afer another, muttering incessantly, and cared little if the odor and poor air quality disturbed anyone else. The plasmoids in the room found the foul air most unpleasant, unlike the macropians who found it quite refreshing.

An anthropod stood at the front of the room, dressed smartly in a torso business suit and leggings. It spoke into a small microphone curled around its pincers.

"In the Post War Era, the demand for starships, both military and commercial, will only increase. While The Enemy has been beaten, there is still a need to protect ourselves from future threats, to defend the newly organized cities on what was formerly known as The Rim, and to oversee our expansion further into The Frontier. The largest contractors such as Cathedral and NYSAAC will dominate this market, but the real fortunes will be made in supplying these larger operations with the raw materials they need, various aluminum alloys, titanium, plastic steel, to name only a few."

Colorful three dimensional pie charts materialized in the air behind the anthropod.

"We can use something familiar as an example. These holograms represent the cost of doing business on Malzao, in the Bostakar system, where I believe the gentlemen in the back are from."

The chatter amongst the canites suddenly stopped, and all eyes fell on the anthropod.

"Malzao has the most abundant and easily accessible stores of titanium in the Quad, and the cost of transport is negligible as the manufacturing facilities are located within the solar system. However, no smart businessman should go anywhere near this star system. Real estate taxes, licensing fees, access fees and multiple fee surtaxes are excessive. Collective bargaining statutes will require labor lawyers, union payoffs and political kickbacks. Environmental protection lawsuits are rampant—the complete list is much longer. The cost of doing business here is prohibitive. Again, no smart businessman should go anywhere near Malzao."

The canites exchanged angry glances, puffing testily on their cigars. The anthropod continued.

"This next series of images represent a more remote locale, in this case Ven Terre Three. In this Frontier solar system, strong local government has yet to develop, Web influence is far too removed, and military presence scant. On VT Three, the titanium is harder to find and even harder to extract. The shipping costs are considerable. However, with the absence of any strong civil authority, taxes, fees, labor and environmental concerns are non-existent, and consequently, the net profit is four times greater due to the absence of crushing overhead, as seen on Malzao.

"The absence of infrastructure and strong local law enforcement make securing these remote sights problematic, and this is where the T'Teleonoma Corporation can be of great use to small to mid-size companies, such as yourselves."

It was nearing midday, and the audience grew increasingly impatient. Restless, they fiddled with the workstations built into the tables and with their portable devices. The need for bipeds to eat at regularly appointed intervals annoyed it.

The anthropod signaled for the next series of images. A trio of holographic combat drones appeared behind it. It paused before speaking, irritated at the casual disinterest of the crowd now that it was moving into its sales pitch.

"TTC has been manufacturing CB drones for three generations. Our drones supercede the need to maintain large numbers of organic mercenaries and all the logistics that come with them. Mechanized defenses, both stationary and mobile, are more suitable to your needs. Our latest class of drones can perform in any terrain or environmental conditions, and can be fully integrated into existing defensive systems. Our prices are far more reasonable than our competitors, and include generous maintenance and service contracts."

One of the canites in the back sighed loudly and another threw his cigar onto the carpet, extinguishing it with a twist of his foot.

"I see that we've crossed over to midday," the anthropod observed testily. "Let's break for a meal and meet back here in fifty minutes."

The occupants of the conference room filed out in small groups, save for one man. He remained seated in the front row. He sat alone only for a moment. A macropian and a canite, both dressed in dark blue suits, came in and sat behind him.

"Are you Mr. Enn," the macropian asked.

"Yes. And you are?"

"We represent those who wish to purchase what you have to offer."

Enn turned in his chair. His thin neck barely supported his large head, like a lollipop on a stick. A beige suit hung on him like a tent.

"You mean the Cathedral Corporation?"

"You contacted us," the macropian whispered angrily.

"And what do I have to offer?"

The macropian smoothed his tie with a tiny hand and cleared his throat. He put a briefcase on the table and it opened with a click.

"Eight hundred million in Cornerstone Reserve green disc notes, just as you asked."

Enn looked over the discs and handled several of them with a casual indifference.

"All right," he finally said.

"The Ecks Stones," the macropian pressed. "The terms of the agreement are that you will provide three of them now, and that any future transactions involving these diamonds are to be conducted exclusively with the Cathedral Corporation or their designated representatives."

"Agreed," Enn nodded.

The macropian held out an e-pad. Enn's hands remained still. He shook his head.

"No documentation."

The macropian smirked a bit and leaned forward.

"A transaction of this magnitude requires a legally binding document."

"The conditions of the agreement will be honored."

"On a handshake," the macropian sneered. "Who are you people? How and where can you be reached?"

"We are a private, not a corporate interest. We prefer to remain anonymous."

"I am not handing over to you nearly a billion in discs solely on your word."

"Whenever more stones become available for sale, you will be contacted and have exclusive rights to their purchase."

The macropian shook his head.

"We want to know who you are."

"Then I can find another buyer. Representatives of AbStone will be back inside this room within fifty minutes."

The macropian leaned back and conferred with his partner in hushed tones. They stopped whispering and then they each cupped an ear, listening intently.

"All right, Mr. Enn," the macropian said, putting his hand down. "We agree to your conditions." He paused. "For now."

Enn reached out for the briefcase. The macropian pulled it back.

"Not so fast. The stones first."

"Once I have the discs, then you get the stones."

"No. We see the stones now."

Enn sighed.

"I can be on Lethe before the end of the month."

The two men frowned, then pushed the briefcase full of discs forward. Enn produced his own briefcase and transferred the discs with shaking hands. He put the briefcase inside a thin gauss sleeve, then sealed it.

"And now the stones," the macropian demanded.

Enn took a hotel key card from his pocket and slid it across the table. He stood up and started to walk away. His suit billowed like a sheet in the wind.

The two Cathedrals stood up, the canite holding a gun.

"Hey," the macropian shouted. "What the fuck is this?!"

Enn turned and spoke with deliberate impatience.

"Go to the front desk. Ask for the manager. Tell it that you want the items you have on deposit." He tipped an imaginary hat. "Gentlemen."

As Enn approached the exit, a very large plasmoid appeared and blocked his way.

"What is the meaning of this," Enn demanded. "Is this the way you Cathedrals do business?"

The macropian's mouth curled at the corners under his snout and he smiled with false congeniality.

"Surely you don't mind waiting with us until we confirm that the stones are safely in our possession?" He pulled out a chair and his companion gestured at it with his gun.

"It appears I have no other choice," Enn fussed, and tugged with one hand at his lapels. He took the seat offered.

The plasmoid at the door was given the key card and disappeared. The macropian and canite sat down on either side of Enn and pulled their chairs in very close. They stared at him severely, eyeing him all over, their faces only centimeters apart. For the first time, Enn seemed unsettled. He squirmed a bit and his hands trembled. One corner of his mouth repeatedly ticked upward.

The macropian abruptly leaned back, then stood up. The canite slowly did likewise, returning his weapon to his jacket. He looked at Enn, then gestured with his head toward the exit.

Enn stood up, nodded quickly, then left.

The plasmoid stood in the center of a windowless room, deep within the Hotel Vestitia. Taupe concrete walls surrounded a black marble countertop.

An anthropod dressed in the maroon and black uniform of the hotel entered through a pocket door and placed a white plastic box on the table.

"When you are finished, Mr. Enn, you can use the elevator reserved for VIP's down the hall, to your right."

The plasmoid nodded and the anthropod departed.

It removed the box lid and found it contained three glittering diamonds nestled in soft, green velvet fittings. The rough diamonds reflected the light brightly and cast a honeycomb of octagonal rainbows over their surface. Mesmerized, it paused to admire them, momentarily distracted from the urgency of the task at hand.

From inside its porous jacket, it unrolled a cloth lined with tools. Using the smaller instruments, it quickly verified the authenticity of the diamonds. It held an N-ray monocle against its eye ganglia to eliminate the possibility of any mistake. It handled one of them delicately and then replaced it in the box as if it were an egg.

"A-2," it said into a mouthpiece. "I have the diamonds. Whatever you're paying for these, it's not enough. Let him go before you get held up for more."

Very carefully, and one at at time, it transferred the diamonds from the white box into a smaller black box of its own. The pocket door slid aside and it stepped out into the hall, cradling the black box in its elbow. An escort waited, a trio of fellow plasmoids, all armed. It nodded and the four of them walked briskly to the elevator. They waited anxiously, eye ganglia darting this way and that. A score of hands gripped their weapons tightly.

The doors opened to an empty car and they went up without mishap to the parking garage on the first sub-level. Here an aircar waited, engine running, with four more thugs standing around it, also holding weapons. The quartet of plasmoids darted out of the elevator and into the car.

The car door slammed shut and an instant later, an explosion erupted from underneath the car, lifting it almost two meters off the ground. Shrapnel whistled through the air and the guards surrounding the car tumbled to the ground. Engulfed in flames, the car crashed to the pavement.

For a moment, nothing moved.

Emergency sirens wailed in the distance.

Out of the shadows, an ordinary looking man dressed in the maroon and black colors of the hotel valets appeared. A black shear covered his face and head. The man walked casually toward the flaming wreckage. Of the four guards standing around the car when the blast occurred, two stirred and reached for their guns. The valet shot them both dead with a penetrating laser, then tossed the gun into the fire.

A car door still hung by a hinge. He grabbed onto the hot metal with his bare hands and ripped it off, tossing it effortlessly aside. He bent inside the burning interior of the car, into the back seat, oblivious to the searing heat. He took the black box from the center of burning smear of jelly that had once been a plasmoid. Brushing embers, gel and ash from his clothes, he pried open the box lid with only his hands. He verified the contents of the box and replaced the lid.

With the black box tucked safely under his arm, he turned and skulked back into the shadows from whence he came. A moment later, emergency vehicles screamed into the garage and surrounded the burning car. The firemen worked quickly and efficiently to douse the flames, and no one noticed the gray metal door that was pulled shut from the other side, only thirty meters away.

Chapter 17
A Rumor of War

The sun burned thick and hot over the Metropolia dell'Elsasser. In a freshly refurbished part of the city, a very large crowd had gathered in an open plaza, a plaza constructed entirely of black marble blocks. The unrelenting heat weighed heavily on the thick midday air, and the sun seemed to be in the face of the crowd, no matter which way it turned. The cream of Lethean society weathered the heat, demurely elbowing one another in order to be seen. Atop a temporary steel platform, an anthropod stood behind a podium, pausing momentarily in its speech to the crowd. Behind the anthropod stood the Duro de Ferro Building, recently restored to its original glory by the Abernathé Family. It housed the Ricco Sfondato Hospital, today draped in festive bunting that bore the Abernathé Crest.

"The Abernathé Family spared no expense in the construction of this great hospital," the anthropod said into a microphone. It paused again to take a deep breath, clearly affected by the heat. "This site was chosen to maintain the glorious history of this iconic address. The Duro de Ferro Building housed the original offices of Abernathé Stoneworks, erected under the careful direction of Lorenzo the First himself, and both the interior and exterior still bear the distinctiveness of his own hand.

"The Abernathé family has always been a fervent patron of the medical sciences, and the Ricco Sfondato Hospital will mark the onset of a new chapter in the practice of medicine. Tomorrow morning, when these doors open for the first time, it will be remembered as the day that a new standard was set for the care of all webkind.

"The care to be offered here will be unavailable anywhere else in all The Web. Revolutionary advances in organ transplants, orthopedics, and genetic engineering, all readily available to anyone with means, without discrimination. The highest standards will be rigidly maintained, luxurious while nurturing, as any proud Lethean would expect no less."

Representatives of the media were on the stage to one side of the podium, with camera personnel placed at different vantage points in the crowd. On the other side of the podium sat the hospital board of directors and Lorenzo de Abernathé III himself. He sat calmly, clapping politely at the appropriate moments. He was the only biped in the plaza that day not sweating, despite his full business attire. Behind him stood Max Siniscolchi in his customary black suit, wearing dark sunglasses. Sweat rolled in beads down his forehead and face and stained his white collar.

Siniscolchi's face remained expressionless, but inwardly he beamed. He had planned this event personally, down to the last detail. He had spread enough disc notes around the city to ensure that the right people would attend, in spite of the heat. In the front rows, he spied the faces of all the most prominent Lethean politicians and celebutants, among others, all of whom competed for positions in front of the cameras.

He insisted that Alvese S'Gobbo, his head PR bug, give the address itself. This not only underlined the importance that the Abernathé family assigned to the event, but ensured that the delivery of the message would play out properly for the media. Other species had difficulty reading the emotions of anthropods from non-verbal cues, such as facial expressions, because they didn't have any. Bugs tended to be very well spoken and unflappable, even under duress, or when under public scrutiny. Most companies utilized them for PR for precisely this reason.

Running S'Gobbo out in front of the cameras today also leant itself to simple biology. Bugs didn't sweat. This event was not to be mistaken for anything else other than a gross display of Lethean narcissism, self-indulging, self-aggrandizing, nothing more than a rich man projecting a fake interest in the public welfare. This meant no sweating, as this feed would be seen all over The Web. He didn't care that bugs couldn't tolerate this kind of heat. Heat cannot be seen on a vid screen, and the image of flop sweat could not be associated with the Abernathé name.

Lately, the entire Web had its eyes on AbStone and the Cathedral Corporation. Sides were being chosen, and in light of that, this event had multiple purposes. The first was to build up public support for the Abernathés here on Lethe, where morals and scruples were at best questionable, and even the poorest residents had deep pockets. The Letheans to be treated at the Ricco Sfondato Hospital would be hand selected to strategically create the impression of a place where the miraculous occurred as a matter of course, except for pregnant women and children.

Absolutely no children.

Stories about genetic engineering in utero and in infancy had been circulating in the media with increasing frequency in recent years. The bigotry directed against perceived 'enhanced' children was rapidly becoming institutionalized, progressing toward violence.

This expensive exclusivity would keep AbStone far from that ugly controversy, and also hide the identities of the hospital's true patients: mercenaries. The mercenaries hired by AbStone for the coming conflict with Cathedral Corp would be sent here to convalesce, for the veiled purpose of being sent back into the fray. Not only would the hospital's availability serve as a powerful recruiting point, but projections estimated that it would be more cost effective than paying off the injured, and then vetting, hiring and training new recruits. For the benefit of the Abernathé name, this venture would forever hide the abominable research of James Cervello, hide it in plain sight, while putting it to good use.

Siniscolchi's belt comp vibrated and interrupted his musings. He glanced at the scroll. A public announcement of another deal between Cathedral and AbStone. He nodded assent.

Good.

If one believed the reports from the various Suetonia news outlets, a new, and very profitable, business relationship had developed between Abernathé Stoneworks and The Cathedral Corporation. Cathedral, with the multiple business concerns of a huge conglomerate, had allied with the small, but powerful, niche company of AbStone to expand its interests into the precious stone and metals markets. According to reports, this was just another story of Cathedral trying to get a leg up on its traditional rival, NYSAAC.

If one believed the reports.

The truth ran much deeper. The business community recognized the indicators of coming conflict. Business circles buzzed with the news that Cathedral wanted to absorb AbStone as a subsidiary, but that the latter had refused. Now, with Cathedral moving to isolate AbStone in the business world, in the same way a predator weakens its prey before striking, AbStone had been selling off its expendable assets to Cathedral as tribute. Both were reorganizing, plotting, eying each other warily and preparing for the inevitable conflagration.

While a much smaller entity than Cathedral, AbStone was no trifle. Cathedral could not simply come at them directly, and its movements resembled that of a lumbering giant. Siniscolchi proved adept at keeping one step ahead of the slow, deliberate movements of his adversary, literally buying time, until Breufogle could learn the secrets of the Ecks Stones.

Siniscolchi turned his attention back to S'Gobbo.

"Citizens of the planet Lethe, residents of the Metropolia dell'Elsasser, on the momentous occasion of the 140th anniversary of the founding of Abernathé Stoneworks, I give you the Ricco Sfondato Hospital."

Enthusiastic applause erupted throughout the plaza. S'Gobbo gestured at Lorenzo with an open palm and the applause intensified. Lorenzo stood, posed elegantly for the cameras, and waved with a broad smile. The applause waned and the lights on the news cameras dimmed. Siniscolchi pulled aside the chair behind Lorenzo, who promptly spun on a heel and walked briskly down a side street to a waiting aircar. Siniscolchi joined him the back seat, and then they were airborne.

"Well done, Max. Very well done."

"Thank you, Mr. Abernathé."

"Where are we on the Applrik deal?"

"I just received confirmation. It's done."

"So now they have access to a score of plastic steel forges, which means they can now manufacture an assortment of stealth class ships."

"Yes."

"And the arrangements?"

"AbStone is generously waiving all access fees." Siniscolchi paused. "For future considerations, of course."

Lorenzo nodded, then frowned. Future considerations, indeed. Now Cathedral could compete with NYSAAC in the next fiscal year for the new round of ship building contracts. All at the expense of AbStone.

"And our position," Lorenzo asked.

"Conventional forces are ready," Siniscolchi replied. "We have numerous operatives within Cathedral itself."

"Max, I don't want a conventional war."

"At the risk of sounding repetitive, Mr. Abernathé, Cathedral now *needs* us. If we turn off the tap to all of the raw materials we're providing them, they can't compete with NYSAAC."

"We're hemorrhaging revenue, Max. We can't keep this up forever. Once we run out of disc notes, they'll simply take everything. They keep undermining any business we try to conduct with other companies. We're slowly being strangled."

"Cathedral will be most vulnerable at the beginning of the next fiscal year. We can hit them and hit them hard, give them pause, and maybe NYSAAC will finish them off for us."

"And then you think NYSAAC will just leave us alone?"

"Yes. We have nothing to offer NYSAAC. They already possess everything that AbStone is."

Lorenzo simmered.

"I'm tired of having this conversation, Max."

"There's always the government."

"We're not at that point yet, Max."

"We need to consider—"

"I said no!"

Siniscolchi took a deep breath and nodded.

"Even though it appears that Cathedral is having some trouble with The Navy?"

"What kind of trouble?"

"There was an episode of corporate espionage at one of the new shipbuilding plants erected on the old TGS site in The Hub. It involved a company called Pollone Presa Outfitters. The company is a sub contractor for NYSAAC, customizing the interiors of many of the ships NYSAAC is building for The Navy. Nothing secretive going on there, but Pollone Presa's workshops were destroyed and their databases stolen. The IBI investigated, tracking the stolen data to an information broker, who then gave up the sellers. The sellers turned out to be the actual saboteurs themselves, who, when apprehended, confessed to having been hired by another party, a party with close ties to the Cathedrals."

"So?"

"The data theft is the key. They contained the schematics, the very designs, of the ships NYSAAC was building."

Lorenzo perked up.

"And?"

"And now Cathedral is being investigated, at a time when they'd like to avoid such a thing at all costs. Such a thing surely will escape the public eye, and Cathedral will use its influence to derail any investigation."

"Unless I come along and blackmail The Navy into going after them."

"Yes."

They locked eyes, then Lorenzo looked away, shaking his head to clear his vision. He leaned back in his seat.

"No. Not yet. What else?"

"I've got some new information on the Vestitian Job."

"You found the Ecks Stones," Lorenzo said sarcastically.

"No. The stories reported in the media agree with the official investigation that Cathedral was trying to sell an Ecks Stone to a private buyer. The private buyer double crossed them, keeping the disc notes and then stealing the Stone. This has prevented you from selling or even revealing your Ecks Stones as it would appear to make AbStone the perpetrators of the Vestitian Job."

"Yes, yes, yes," Lorenzo sighed irritably, resting his chin in his hand, staring out the window. "And the picture show won an award. Old news, Max. Old news."

"Breufogle was recently able to confirm that the circumstances were in fact the opposite."

Lorenzo picked his head up and looked at him.

"The opposite?"

"Yes. Cathedral was the buyer, not the seller."

"Who was the seller?"

"Unknown."

Lorenzo mulled the possibilities.

"The seller had actual Stones?"

"Yes."

"The Sicuro boy?"

Siniscolchi shook his head.

"I've been over the evidence myself. This was clearly the work of professionals."

"If not Sicuro, then who? Presumably, he's the only one with potential access to Ecks Stones."

"Unknown. Sicuro hasn't been seen or heard from in ten years, not since he murdered several Cathedral operatives while stealing a starship on Nostrova."

"Maybe the Cathedrals caught up to him and killed him."

"No. They haven't had any success in locating him, same as ourselves."

Lorenzo again leaned back in his seat.

"It doesn't matter anyway, Max. I still can't sell my Stones, even if I wanted to. Which I don't."

"This indicates that someone else is in possession of some of the Ecks Stones, or has access to the source."

"Is that all Mr. Breufogle could come up with?"

"He's working on it."

"I want to be notified daily of his progress."

"Of course."

Siniscolchi knew that there would be nothing new to report. The very subject of the Ecks Stones often threw Lorenzo into a rage and now with the knowledge that a third party had a stone, it would only get worse. Mr. Sa'am was really responsible for this information and it represented truly outstanding work. He gave credit to Breufogle instead so that when no new information materialized, Lorenzo wouldn't be angry at Sa'am. Breufogle's incompetence had served the interests of AbStone, until now. The inability of anyone to locate Sicuro or uncover the secret of the Ecks Stones was truly the only thing holding Cathedral at bay at this point. Everything else was simply excuses, but Lorenzo didn't see it that way. He couldn't see beyond the normal machinations of the business world.

Siniscolchi accepted that soon he would have to remove Breufogle, then replace him, which he could use as another reason for continuing to come up empty.

For awhile.

Another concern was the recent conduct of Mr. Sa'am. He'd gone out of his way to alienate himself from Breufogle's inner circle, probably chafing at having to work under him, or distancing himself from the stain of failure. Probably both. That whole Ecks project was a mess.

"On the subject of revenue," Siniscolchi continued, "a promising lead reached my desk regarding a mining consortium from Inner Haven. The—"

"The Hyyvonen Group?"

"Yes, the—"

"Poor revenue flow?"

"Yes, the—"

"They own the rights to a gigantic liquid and mineral strike on The Frontier?"

"Yes, the—"

"They're ripe for us to swoop in and take over?"

"Yes, the—"

"I thought I told you to stop coming to me with my SON'S CRAP!!"

"The—"

"And don't you defend him," Lorenzo shouted, pointing an angry finger.

"The—"

"What was found on Pianeta Three is superficial, not sustainable, and therefore useless to AbStone! I knew this a year ago! What in Blazes is he doing investigating stone business?!!"

"The—".

"Well," Lorenzo demanded. "Will you just shut up and talk to me, please?"

"The...," Siniscolchi paused deliberately. "The information was arrived at independently. He doesn't have geologists or anyone else working for him. He came to this data all on his own. He's good at this. He's being wasted on Nostrova, at EU. Anyone can recruit. He has a real talent for the stone business."

"Max, I value your intelligence and insight, but now you're straying into family, and more importantly, legitimate business matters. This is my only, and final, comment on this subject. My son has no true talent for the stone business. He doesn't have the stomach. His value to AbStone is as an evaluator of talent, and a procurer thereof. He is in an excellent position to recruit the most brilliant young minds in The Web. To be recruited personally by an Abernathé is a powerful incentive, especially to young and impressionable college students. He is also the only one I trust to properly vet new personnel, and to not hire Cathedral operatives for a bounty. I also need him to remain close to Mrs. Smart-Scoreggia, in the event that Sicuro should resurface and try to contact her."

"But he doesn't understand this."

"You don't think this is painful for me, Max? I'm nurturing an *idiot*. The Abernathé legacy is *an idiot*."

"Of course, Mr. Abernathé."

"You need to remain focused on out maneuvering the Cathedrals, not showing pity on my son."

Siniscolchi nodded.

"Of course."

Lorenzo activated the small console in the back of the car, and Young Lorenzo's image appeared on the screen.

"Hello, Dad," the smiling image said.

"What is it," he snapped.

"I wanted to know what your thoughts were on Hyyvonen Group. Max did mention it to you, didn't he?"

Inwardly, Siniscolchi winced

"He did," Lorenzo snapped. "It's a dead end."

"But—"

"But nothing! I don't need you wasting your time chasing the wind! What I need from you is very specific, Lorenzo. What about my geneticists? Chemists? Geologists? Software techs? My future executives?"

The young face on the screen trembled, trying to hide the hurt from his father's stinging barbs. Siniscolchi had a soft spot for the kid, which was why he agreed to advocate for him from time to time. He had told Young Lorenzo not to call. Pecking at his father like this was entirely the wrong way to gain approval.

"I-I've recruited enough to backfill the staff of the new hospital, some others to our offices on Lethe. Procurement will assign them to their posts."

"Excellent, Lorenzo. Surely it would have been better if you hadn't purposely divided your attention with garbage like the Hyyvonen Group. Concentrate on the one job that you have. I expect better."

"Yes, Dad."

He picked up an e-pad and perused its contents.

"What else is going on there?"

"Angelica is settling in as the new head attorney of the Tax Department. We now have separate offices, but she's still my supervisor, so I tagged her systems profile and portable comps, in addition to the other surveillance devices I have planted throughout the network."

He nodded, not really listening.

"Fine."

"Um," he paused. "Dad, what do you know about Salestus Havok?"

Lorenzo looked up, putting down the device.

"What about him?"

"The University is awash in surplus revenue. Every quarter, Mr. Havok makes huge endowments, millions upon millions, and there's a lot of debate about what to do with it all."

"How much influence do you have in this decision making process?"

"Angelica has to sort out the tax ramifications and all that, and she relies heavily on my counsel because he's from Lethe. Is there still a lot of excitement about him back home?"

"What have *you* learned on your own," Lorenzo asked, frustrated.

"Well, he's having a big coming out party."

Lorenzo glanced at Siniscolchi, who nodded. Siniscolchi had done his due diligence regarding Salestus Havok. He appeared on the Lethean scene eight years ago, a very wealthy man with diverse interests. No one has ever met him or even seen him, at least no one Siniscolchi could find. This most enigmatic man had a reputation as an aviator and an outdoorsman who enjoyed sport. Anthropod intermediaries handled all of his business, all tight lipped, all loyal, none susceptible to bribery or coercion.

Havok claimed to be from the former Rim system of Outer Segreta, the planet Nascosto, which had been razed during The War. In the Post War Era, those who wanted to recreate themselves often hailed from The Great Eight, as they were known in law enforcement circles. These were the eight star systems on The Rim and outer Web that suffered the most at the hands of the Vaengel. By itself, claiming to be of Nascoston descent proved nothing, as many millions legitimately comprised that particular diaspora.

This man with no past and no face had come to Lethe and brazenly built a palace at the north pole, in the backyard of the family that owned the planet. Many rich robber barons sought refuge in the anonymity and salutary autonomy of the planet Lethe, and Salestus Havok appeared no different from any of them. That he took up residence at the north pole, the most inhospitable and remote region on the planet, raised an eyebrow. This was a man who wanted to be noticed, but not approached.

"Something I don't know, Lorenzo," his father sighed impatiently.

"Angelica's been invited."

Both men leaned forward.

"Is she going?"

"She doesn't really want to, but the school is insisting."

"Lorenzo, I want you to make sure she goes, and you be sure to go with her."

"Dad—"

"If his wealth is truly as great as it appears, I want him investing in AbStone. Do you understand?"

"Yes," he sighed petulantly.

"Don't screw this up, Lorenzo."

"The assumption around here is that Havok has a connection to our family, because we're both from Lethe. I've cultivated this, because otherwise there's no way to explain his connection to the University. His big contributions make me, and by extension Angelica, look good. It's the reason for her promotion."

"And what is his true connection to the University?"

"I don't know," he admitted, blushing.

"Rather than chasing your tail over useless stone business, don't you think your time would be better served if you devoted the sum of your efforts to discovering this connection? Especially since this Havok is the source of your influence and standing? It was smart of you to take advantage of this Lorenzo, very smart, but equally dumb because eventually you're going to have to prove this relationship, and if exposed, it would destroy your reputation and diminish the family name. Do you understand me?"

"Yes," he replied softly.

"I don't want to hear from you again unless you've discovered something that is of use to *me*."

The image on the screen nodded. Lorenzo terminated the connection and the screen went dark. Lorenzo looked at Siniscolchi.

"Is it him, Max?"

He shrugged.

"The odds are unlikely that Havok is Sicuro. Havok isn't any different from thousands of other publicity shy people living on Lethe. Sicuro barely finished secondary school, and he wasn't especially bright. For him to have amassed such a significant fortune is inconceivable."

"Then why the endowments to the Elysian University? It could be Sicuro trying to reach out to the girl."

Siniscolchi frowned.

"All right. I'll have it looked into." It sounded like a job for Mr. Sa'am. "Also, Lorenzo, you were invited to Havok's gala as well. You and your father."

"So was the whole planet. I declined on both our behalves."

"And why was that?"

"A waste of time, Max. Let my son deal with it. I'm too busy trying to save my family."

Chapter 18
Atro Viscus

The Abernathé family owned most of the land on the planet Lethe. The rest they controlled through their vast holdings and influence. For centuries, the land mass above Lethe's arctic circle remained uninhabited, left unspoiled for the especially cunning and vicious wildlife that lived there. The rugged, angular mountains were black, the soil a brackish brown and the rivers ran rough and ice cold. Pine trees with razor needles hid flocks of carnivorous ravens, while bruins and mountain lions with skin like armor ruled the ground. A string of dormant volcanoes ringed the shorelines, ominously venting vapor in precarious silence. Everything about the region was cold, hard and unforgiving. It was the most inhospitable place on an inhospitable planet. Not a single person had ever attempted to establish a residence here. Even the Abernathés had chosen to reside in the more amenable climes of the antarctic. So when the representatives of Salestus Havok offered to buy this black and barren continent from the Abernathés for a ridiculous sum, a deal was easily agreed upon. The Abernathés needed the influx of cash and the additional licensing revenue that would be generated from the development of the land.

Little was known of this man, Havok, whom it seemed everyone knew, but had never laid eyes upon. The source of his wealth also remained a mystery, although rumors abounded. Defense contractor, scientist, information broker, venture capitalist, treasure hunter, soldier, fighter pilot, mobster, thief, gambler, bookmaker—all had been used in connection with his name at one time or another. His reputation as an outdoorsman had evolved into legend. Second and third hand accounts about those who had hunted or done business with him circulated widely. In truth, no one had ever met anyone who had actually met Salestus Havok.

The cost of building his estate was measured in lives, the lives or the well being of scores of mercenaries and laborers. Despite the danger, Havok's business managers had no trouble recruiting the best talent in all The Web as the salary differential offered more than offset the potential risks. Even when finished, constant vigilance and maintenance was required to protect those who resided within. Lethean tradition demanded a name for this place, and so it became Atro Viscus.

Like Summa Avarici, its larger counterpart on the opposite pole, Atro Viscus was also built from stone blocks cut from the surrounding mountains. Three magnificent blackstone structures, called the Tri-Towers, formed the heart of the estate, encircled in wide arcs by three rings of smaller, yet equally imposing buildings. A small village, erected separate from the tri-circles, housed the personnel who maintained the infrastructure and provided services for the entire estate. An immense wall, dwarfed by the dense forest that surrounded it, separated the whole community from the wilderness that threatened to devour it at the slightest moment of weakness.

Atro Viscus operated independent of the Lethean power grid. Those curious enough to investigate, and there were plenty, detected none of the traditional sources of power. Starstone power plants and fusion generators were conspicuously absent. They puzzled over belching steam vents and the gray and black smoke that swirled out of multiple chimneys and smokestacks.

The majestic spires of Atro Viscus sat on the top of a rock shelf that commanded a view for thousands of kilometers. This top shelf was ringed below by three lower shelves, each one separated from the next by cliffs hundreds of meters high. The powerful flood lights that surrounded the four rock shelves turned the night into perpetual day and could be seen by sea going ships on the horizon, and their space faring counterparts in orbit.

The waves of a frigid, blue ocean pounded the rock face of the lowest shelf. An air limousine hovered uncertainly over the coastline. Bright white clouds raced overhead, riding the stiff breeze. The sky alternated from leaden gray to bright sunshine, the sun fading in and out in powerful pulses. The aircar wavered in the severe wind, then accelerated and followed another car to a platform jutting out over the ocean. It landed precariously in the hard wind and parked next to half a dozen other air limos.

A canite driver hopped out to open the door, one hand holding a hat to his head. A trio of valets dressed in black trousers and white coats unloaded luggage from the trunk. The driver helped an elegant, beautiful blonde woman out of the car. Angelica Smart-Scoreggia took an akward step as her evening gown billowed in the wind.

"Easy ma'am," he said. "I've got you."

"Thank you," she replied. "My, the wind! Where are we?"

She looked out over the ocean, her eyes bright, but vacant.

"The carport, ma'am," the driver replied.

Her husband climbed out of the car next. He gripped the door frame with beefy hands and pulled himself to his feet. He was a stocky, square jawed man with a thick build and short, greased back hair. He looked uncomfortable in his tuxedo, like a child stuffed into hand me downs. He pulled nervously at his cuffs and rolled his shoulders under his jacket.

"Hands off, pal," he said, separating the driver from his wife. The wind picked up and she had trouble controlling her skirt.

"Are you alright, Babe," he asked, putting his arm around her to steady her.

"Yes, Vincent. Thank you. The wind here is very strong. Is that the ocean? How close are we?"

"I dunno, it's just over there," he said, gesturing.

"About a hundred meters into the wind, ma'am," the driver said.

Another man, much younger, gracefully stepped out of the car. He stood up straight and faced the wind, a broad smile on his face. His diamond cuff links sparkled and his custom made tuxedo complimented his lean and tall physique, his face clean shaven and very handsome. He wore his dark hair long, like his father, and had a perfectly cut red diamond broach pinned to his collar.

The canite driver smiled and tipped his cap.

"Mr. Abernathé, sir."

Young Lorenzo put on a pair of sunglasses and continued to smile. He discreetly passed a cash ducat to the driver, who responded with a genial smile of his own, and a polite nod.

An anthoropod wearing a headset, adorned in a red torso jacket and black leggings, approached the couple.

"Welcome," it said. "And who should I convey to Mr. Havok has arrived?"

"Vincent and Angelica Scoreggia," he said.

"That's Smart-Scoreggia," she corrected.

Scoreggia cleared his throat roughly and tugged at his shirt collar with a finger.

The anthropod looked beyond them and spoke to Young Lorenzo.

"And Mr. Abernathé. Of course."

He stepped forward easily and nodded.

"Lorenzo de Abernathé the Fourth. Wonderful to be home."

"Welcome back, sir. Mr. Havok is pleased to have you."

"Where to next," Scoreggia asked gruffly.

The anthropod stepped to the side and gestured toward a walkway that ran along the rockface.

"You can follow the others along the path that leads to the train station. It's only sixty meters."

Scoreggia turned Angelica gently in the right direction and started toward the path, trying to put some distance between themselves and Young Lorenzo. As he passed by, Socreggia looked at the valets handling their luggage.

"Easy on the bags, bozos. And don't lose any, got it?"

The valets paused and looked at him, dumbstruck.

After slipping a ducat to the anthropod, Young Lorenzo went over to the grumbling valets and doled out gratuities to each of them in turn.

"Don't worry about that guy," he said. "He's not one of us, see?"

"Yes, sir," they replied, doffing their caps with a thumb and forefinger, sharing a smile. "A pleasure to have you back, Mr. Abernathé."

Young Lorenzo dramatically took in a deep breath and looked around, nodding his approval.

"Good to be back. Thanks, guys."

He then strode casually along the path, trying to catch up to the Scoreggias without appearing to be in a hurry. The other couples in front recognized him and eagerly engaged him in conversation, slowing his progress.

The winding path led them into the mountains, through a smoothly carved rock cut that extended under a fine mesh that arced high over the rock walls. As the couples leisurely made their way toward the train station, they pointed with amused fascination at the black ravens perched on the upper outcroppings. Dozens of pairs of ravenous eyes stared back down at them as narrow white slits. Beaks latticed with sharp, yellow teeth glinted in the lamplights.

A mag-lev train idled at the station, its lines accentuated by sleek silver and blue streaks. A dull hum hinted at the power held temporarily in check. The small crowd here murmured its approval as they boarded the elaborately detailed cars.

Scoreggia steered Angelica to the nearest seat. After he saw to her comfort, he went back to the door, just in time to meet Young Lorenzo.

"Vincent," he exclaimed happily, clapping his hands. "This is all very impressive so far, wouldn't you say?"

"Yeah, a thin slice of Paradise."

"I can't wait to see the rest!"

"I'm all a tingle."

"I trust you saved me a seat?"

"Yeah, about that," he said, as the train powered up. "This one's full, Larry. Sorry."

Scoreggia took half a step back and the door closed between them. Incredulous, Young Lorenzo watched the train pull out of the station. The half empty car whizzed by in a blur of wind.

Three hundred meters above the tree line, the train sped along a magnetized track on an inclined plane. It ascended the cliffs at an ever escalating angle and seemed to fly through the air as it traversed arched track lines. The arches spanned the chasms that separated the rock shelves, chasms hundreds of meters wide and deep. The train moved ever upward, without losing momentum. The panorama on display ranged for a thousand kilometers. The rugged forest sprawled far below, dark and forbidding. A dense fog choked the lush landscape, the mists like tendrils snaking through the trees. Intermittent, muted conversations on the train continued, but most sat in awed silence, overwhelmed by the power of the train and the view from the large windows.

"What's going on, Vincent," Angelica whispered. "Why is everyone so quiet?"

"Nothing to see, Babe," he replied off handedly, looking across the empty seats at the other people in the car. "Just a train ride."

"But we're going up."

"Yeah, it's an elevated train," he explained dismissively. "Looks like we're in some very fine company."

"Really?"

"Two seats up, I see Bahn Yorke and Frem C'Zernack, for starters. A lot of people of interest to the Bureau in here."

"Vincent, you promised."

"Are you telling me what to do?"

"No, I—"

"I didn't think so."

He tugged at his cuffs angrily and exhaled sharply through his nose.

She frowned nervously and stayed quiet for a moment.

"Vincent, why are we on a train? Couldn't the aircar take us to the estate?"

He sighed, annoyed.

"Because," he said, still looking around the car, "the only space large enough to land an aircar near the main house is Havok's private platform, which is covered by a retractable dome."

"That seems inconvenient."

"Not if you want to discourage visitors."

"How do you know this?"

"I had it all checked out before hand."

"You promised you wouldn't be working tonight."

"Are you gonna be like this all night?"

"No, but—"

"Then shut up and enjoy the view."

After a very steep ascent, the train finally leveled off at the top of the fourth rock shelf and skimmed the top of the tree line. It then accelerated further, toward its final destination.

Atro Viscus came into view, a monolithic citadel of black stone and marble partially obscured by clouds. Like a missile, the train rocketed toward a tunnel barred by a portcullis. At first, it appeared that there was no way the barrier of plastic steel could be raised in time, but it did retract, and the train plunged into the dark, the interior lights flickering like a strobe. A gradual, yet lurching, deceleration finally brought the train to a stop at a platform identical to the one it departed from.

Scoreggia disembarked from the train, his wife on his arm, and strode proudly up the grand walkway toward the garden courtyard. Arranged as a large circle, the garden itself was surrounded by gothic stone buildings. Dark green hedges, sculpted meticulously to soft angles at waist height, lined gray gravel paths, which in turn were highlighted by sparkling white stones. Numerous guests strolled along the paths, champagne glasses in hand, admiring the multiple circular fountains and the elaborate stonework within. Flower beds, robust with color, graced the landscape, many comprised of flora not native to the region. A polished platinum railing ringed the edges of the rounded paths, their continuity unbroken, save for their beginning and end at the train station.

"You should see this place, Babe," he said, wiping his nose on the sleeve of his tux. "This guy's got it all goin' on."

"I'm sure it's wonderful," she replied.

Ushers, dressed identically in black trousers and royal blue coats, lined the entrance to the garden and each nodded and smiled in turn as the couple passed. A plasmoid stood at the entrance, its skin also dyed a matching royal blue.

"Mr. Scoreggia, Mrs. Smart-Scoreggia. If you need to freshen up, go to your left. Otherwise, please enter Mr. Havok's private garden. Dinner will be served in the main house within the hour."

They waded into the clusters of people already engaged in lively, but quiet, conversations. The only appetizers served in the garden were slices of sumptuous bread. Almost everyone had a big piece in one hand and a glass of champagne in the other. It quickly circulated that the bread was of Havok's own recipe, and that it had been prepared by his own hand. They walked in silence, Angelica with both hands on her husband's bent arm, Scoreggia less than subtle in his observations of the other guests, ogling everyone as they passed.

"Got a who's who of Lethian royalty here," he observed. "And more than a few Web heavyweights. I haven't seen this big a collection of creeps since the Ashpole Hearings."

Scoreggia didn't recognize anyone he knew personally, so he stepped to the side, near a black stone fountain with a ledge where Angelica could sit easily. He stood self consciously with his hands in his pockets, then glanced down at the gravel. His eyes grew wide as he bent down and picked up one of the white stones, which wasn't a stone at all.

"Holy CloPerox," he gasped. "Babe, you gotta see this. The white rocks are diamonds! He's sprinkled diamonds around like gravel!"

A couple walked passed him as he stood there in amazement and he held it up for them to see.

"Maybe I should put a handful in my pocket for safe keeping," he jested, then laughed.

The couple turned their nose up at him and kept walking. The smile left Scoreggia's face, and he glared at them with contempt as they continued along the path. He looked around suspiciously, to see if anyone else had their eye on him, then reluctantly dropped the diamond at his feet.

He turned as a plasmoid and a macropian came toward him. They paid him no mind, their full attention devoted to their quiet conversation. Scoreggia recognized the macropian as Sta'an Hossenfuss, one of the IBI's regional commissioners, who often prefaced their training pictures. He breathed easier, relieved to at last see a familiar face.

"Mr. Hossenfuss," he said, approaching the two.

They stopped and looked at him.

"Mr. Hossenfuss, my name is Vincent Scoreggia. I'm a special agent under the supervision of Mark Blackthorne."

Scoreggia extended his hand, which Hossenfuss did not take.

"I know Blackthorne," Hossenfuss replied coolly. "Something you want?"

"Well, sir, I only thought it appropriate that I should introduce myself, as I don't see any of our fellow agents here among the guests."

"I'm not a guest. Scoreggia, was it?"

"Yes, sir."

Hossenfuss took a cigar from his pocket with a tiny hand and lit it with a gold engraved lighter.

"I was invited, but I accepted under cause for official business, to learn about this Havok character. His defense contract is coming up for renewal."

"I wasn't aware of that, sir."

The plasmoid seemed impatient, and wandered away a few steps.

"Why in Blazes are you here," Hossenfuss demanded, his fur bristling.

"I'm here with my wife. She was invited. Work stuff."

Hossenfuss looked over his shoulder.

"That's your wife over there? *Angelica Smart?!*"

"You mean Angelica *Scoreggia.*"

The macropian grabbed him by the elbow with a tiny hand and with unexpected strength, pulled him aside.

"Scoreggia, right?"

"Yes, sir. What—"

"What is this? Some kind of kickback? Coming here could be construed as you accepting payment for the services you rendered his company, that he owns you."

"Yeah, I handled the Pollone case. So what? Never met the guy. Never even got a thank you."

"But you have now, right?"

"It's not like that."

"He throwing all those disc notes at your wife's university for nothing? You need to avoid the appearance of being bought, of an ethics violation, for accepting ritzy invites and steering business to your wife in exchange of the influence of your badge. We don't take rewards for doing our jobs."

"Wait a second! It's not like that at all!"

"The truth doesn't matter, only appearances. You should know that. It's going to appear that you are under his influence, no matter the sequence of events. It impugns the integrity of your office and the Bureau. You should know better than to have ever set foot on this planet without proper authorization from Blackthorne."

"Sir, I believe you're overreacting."

"Am I? Now every time we solve a crime that affects this man's interests, and he has many so it will undoubtedly happen again, will officers accept invites to his parties?"

"Sir, I wasn't invited! My wife was!"

"The Bureau is impartial in the administration of its authority. We cannot appear to have favorites. You need to leave here immediately."

Hossenfuss let go of his elbow and resumed walking along the path. The plasmoid rejoined him and they resumed their whispered conversation.

Scoreggia sneered at their backs. He grabbed a passing waitress by the arm and took two drinks off her tray. He handed one to Angelica.

"Who was that," she asked.

"No one."

"Oh. Well, he sounded mad at you."

"Never mind. Just drink your drink."

"What is this?"

"Whatever it is, it's not cheap, so just drink it."

She sipped at it and then gave it back to him.

"This is too strong."

"All of a sudden you don't like wine?"

"I lost my taste for it in college. Please see if you can get me a glass of champagne."

"Sure, Babe," he said. He stood there, alternately sipping from a glass in each hand, scanning the crowd as waitress after waitress passed in front of him.

"Where's Lorenzo," she asked.

"Uh, I thought he was sitting behind us on the train," he said, distracted. "Must've gotten separated on the way in."

She hadn't smelled his cologne since the aircar.

"Vincent," she sighed. "Did he even get on the train?"

"Babe, you should see who's here!"

"You can't be rude to him here, Vincent. His family owns this planet."

"There he is, over there," he lied. "Looks like he's talking to someone he knows."

"I can't hear him."

"Uh, he's too far away, Babe. Don't worry, he's good."

"Promise me you'll show him respect. At least while we're here."

"He should be showing me more respect," he demanded, "by staying as far away from me as possible."

"Vincent, please. His family's connections on this planet are vital to the University."

The glasses in his hands now empty, he set them on the fountain ledge.

"Sure, Babe. Sure."

"So who's here? Anyone we know?"

"No one *you* know," he said. "Senator Leccapiedi. Looks like he's talking to Senator Munny. Also got a good mix of rich guys and corporate weasels."

"Like who?"

"Some mid-level NYSAAC and Cathedral execs. Roscoe Skok, too. Lots of business people. Well, well. That looks like Sterling Hobson on the other side of the fountain, there. I'm pretty sure there's still a warrant or two out on him."

Scoreggia reached for his belt.

"Vincent, please. Not tonight."

He paused, then put his hand back in his pocket.

"I'm just saying, Babe. I think that's James Class over there. He's talking to Admiral Emmett."

"Should I know those people?"

"Class used to run the political officer corps some years back. He got his daughter into the club, then she disappeared on assignment. From what I hear, he went more than a little nuts searching for her. Ended up forced into an early retirement, abuse of authority stuff. It must've been spectacular because the mission statement for the PO's was to abuse authority. It was bad during The War, even worse since."

"I've never heard of them."

"Funny that he's talking to Emmett. He was hooked into the PO pipeline as well…and…and…Peroxide and Clorox, I don't believe it!"

"Really, Vincent," she said dryly. "Both of them? Right here in this park?"

"No, no—what? No—it's Sfero Colletore, the receiver for the Altopiani! And Black Jack Dornan, the field general for The Black Aces. And the other two must be—wait here, Babe, I'll be right back!"

"Vincent, please," she said. "You promised you wouldn't—"

And then he was gone.

"—abandon me."

She sat alone.

With her hands demurely in her lap, she listened for him intently, and instead picked up scatterings of other conversations. She strained to locate her husband's voice. She couldn't pinpoint him and began to worry that he went off somewhere where he couldn't see her.

Angelica heard two glasses clink together, then caught a whiff of perfume.

"Is someone there?"

"I'm sorry, I didn't mean to startle you. Nichelle, please take these glasses."

"Yes, ma'am."

"Please excuse me. You must be Angelica Smart-Scoreggia."

"Yes, I am."

"Are you and your husband, Vincent, enjoying yourselves?"

"Yes, yes we are. He saw someone, a striker or a feeder, I think."

"A ballplayer?"

"Yes! Please, do you see him?"

"He's on the other side of the courtyard, about twenty meters to your left, with a group of professional athletes. He seems rather excited."

Angelica paused.

"You know I can't see."

"I do. I'm sorry. I didn't intend to make you feel uncomfortable."

Angelica hesitated.

"But how," she asked akwardly. "I make an effort to be discreet."

"And you carry yourself exceptionally well. It's my job to know these things."

"I'm sorry. I didn't get your name."

"My name is Elisabéta Pascucci. I—"

"—work for Mr. Havok. You're his attorney."

"Mr. Havok has many attorneys."

"We've been trading correspondence for years."

"And now you have a voice for the name."

Angelica smiled. She turned her head as a waiter with a tray of bread passed by.

"Is that the bread that everyone is talking about?"

"Yes, it is. Nichelle!"

Suddenly, a piece of bread was placed in her hand.

"Please walk with me," Elisabéta invited. "We'll move closer to your husband."

"Thank you."

"When you stand, there is a railing within reach of your left hand. You can use the railing to guide yourself along the garden paths."

Angelica did as Elisabéta suggested, and her hand ran over a series of symbols engraved in the platinum.

"It's Ciechi Script!"

"Yes. What does it say?"

"It's a physical description of the fountain and the nearby flower bed arrangement."

"You'll find the placards at regular intervals."

"I'm impressed."

"Mr. Havok is very interested in the comfort of his guests."

They started walking, Angelica sliding one hand along the railing.

"Will we have the pleasure of Mr. Havok's company? I would like to personally thank him on behalf of the trustees for his enormous generosity."

"Of course. In the interim, he asked me to make sure you were comfortable."

"Me personally? What is Mr. Havok's connection to EU, if I may ask."

"Mr. Havok is very interested in the furtherance of formal education, especially for those who demonstrate extraordinary potential. Elysian University is a place that attracts and cultivates these rare individuals. Our society is a complex one and will need exceptional leadership going into the future."

"Many of the trustees are suspicious of his motives. They believe that his ideals are only as big as his bank account."

"You don't believe in ideals?"

"It's very easy for someone of Mr. Havok's worth to have lofty ideals. Without an obvious connection to the University, there is concern over what he may someday ask for, in return for his generosity. Our research has revealed that EU is the only recipient of his largesse. Why?"

"I've already explained."

"We're not the only school in The Web."

"He believes in EU."

Angelica nodded, conceding the point.

"Well, he's certainly an enigmatic figure."

"Mr. Havok is very jealous of his privacy."

"As are we all. Ms. Pascucci, there's a message that I'd like for you to convey to Mr. Havok. On the behalf of the trustees,

I'd like to extend an invitation for Mr. Havok to come and tour the University, at his convenience of course, to see for himself the results of his generosity."

"Of course," she smiled. "I would be very happy to bring your offer to his attention."

"Hey, Babe," Scoreggia called out. "Angelica, there's someone I want you to meet!"

He grabbed her by the arm and pulled her away from the railing.

"Over here," he said excitedly. "I'm talking to Sfero Colletore and Alix Dox."

"Vincent, what are you doing," Angelica said, flustered. "Ms. Pascucci, this is my husband, Vincent."

Scoreggia nodded briefly in her direction.

"C'mon, Babe, before they start talking to someone else."

"That's okay," Elisabéta said graciously. "It's a party. Enjoy yourselves."

Scoreggia hustled Angelica away and she stumbled a bit on the gravel.

"Vincent! You were very rude to her!"

"Aw, forget her. She's nobody."

"You can't know that! And she's not a nobody! She was very important to why I came here!"

"Like I said, she'll get over it. I want you to meet these guys. These two won the title almost single handedly last year!"

"Vincent, please don't pull me!"

He stopped her in her tracks and held her forearm firmly, squeezing until it hurt.

"Do *not* ruin this with your whining," he whispered harshly.

"You're hurting me," she complained, pulling her arm free.

He snatched the bread from her hand.

"What's this," he demanded.

"Ms. Pascucci got it for me. I guess I was too busy talking to try it."

"When you need something, when you need help, you ask me. Don't make me say it again."

"I'm sorry, Vincent. Can I please try the bread?"

"Forget the bread." He tossed it into the bushes. She sensed his intent and tried to stop him. There was a flurry of hands and then he had her by the arm again.

"Dox," he called out. "Dox! This is my wife. I want you to meet my wife! Is she something or what?"

Scoreggia spent the better part of the next hour trying to ingratiate himself to the pair of professional athletes. At first they found him amusing, but they quickly tired of him and were too polite to separate themselves from his company. His wife seemed far less annoying, but she couldn't get a word in edgewise. The coming night rescued them from this akward situation. The sky wasn't completely dark when a spectacular fireworks display abruptly commenced.

The sudden onset of thunder and light startled the guests milling about the circular paths of the garden. They watched with a sense of awe and a hush fell over the entire crowd as they watched in silence. As colorful as it was elaborate, the riveting display ended as suddenly as it began. At its conclusion, the onlookers erupted in startled, yet enthusiastic, applause.

Once the applause died down, a voice boomed from above.

"Now that I have everyone's attention..."

Standing behind a semi-circle of marble fencing with an ornately carved façade, stood an impressively tall man of almost two meters. He commanded the space he occupied, as well as the attention of everyone in the garden.

"...I wanted to thank you all for coming. Allow me to introduce myself, for those of you who are not familiar. I am Salestus Havok. As the Praetor de Atro Viscus, I welcome you to my home. Please enjoy yourselves, as if it were your own."

His voice echoed through the garden without the aid of electronic amplification. He stood close enough to his guests to be seen, but far enough away for any distinct features to remain muted.

A macropian usher stood in front of the entrance to the largest, and most impressive, of the main buildings.

"Ladies and gentleman and plasmoids," he announced. "Dinner is served."

A murmur of approval rippled through the crowd. When all eyes settled again on the marble fencing, Havok was already gone.

The guests marveled at the interior of the Havok's home, finding it as equally impressive as the grounds. Furnishings and adornments were sparse without leaving the rooms vacant. The expensive, yet refined, décor spoke to the simple elegance of the occupant. Circular track lighting in the floors, and an occasional table lamp, cast soft yellow hues that lent to each guest a sense of comfort, both warm and inviting. Mostly wide open spaces graced the interior. The large rooms had very few doors, and overlooked in all the excitement was that those few doors all had locks. Ushers guided the throng of guests through a grand foyer to a large and elaborately decorated dining room. Across the room, an open archway led to a series of comfortable smoking rooms with roaring fireplaces. The intimate, yet spacious size of these three rooms concealed the fact that the guests were confined to a relatively small space. In all, many of the guests regarded the whole residence as a masterpiece of interior decoration, deliberately dark, but not dreary.

Glass cases built into the black stone walls of the dining room displayed various items of substantial value. This collection of rare gems, crystal glassware, Lethean artifacts and exquisitely detailed sculptures of solid gold and platinum earned Havok the envy of every man in the room.

The dining room table had been set with crystal flatware and goblets, the kind of crystal that belonged behind the display cases. Havok's guests nodded their approval, impressed that his formal table settings were things that even the richest Letheans put in museums. The crystal on the tables reflected the light in prisms, and the whole table sparkled and crackled with energy.

Scoreggia guided Angelica to her seat and helped her sit down.

"Looks like everyone gets their own bread," he commented, sitting on her right side. Each place setting had a loaf of the sumptuous bread placed in front. The seat on her left remained empty.

"The yeast is outstanding, is it not?" An anthropod couple sat down across from them. "I understand our host prepared the loaves with his own hand."

Scoreggia half smiled.

"Yeah, it's great. Means you can drink twice as much!"

The anthropods nodded, their expressions inscrutable.

Once all of the guests were finally seated, hushed, yet lively conversations grew into an overall hum of excitement as the room came to life. The guests all shared similar exchanges, mostly concerning their host. They discussed what they knew about him, what their connection to him consisted of, and it all conflicted. Some knew him as an outdoorsman, others a socialite, then a businessman, a patron of the arts, a musician, a construction magnate. Some of the guests were business associates, some were employees, some celebrities, but most were very high profile and powerful politicians and bureaucrats. He seemed to be all things to all people, except no one called him a friend. No one claimed to have met him, but some did brag to know people who had.

As appetizers were served, an usher stepped in and rang a very loud bell.

"Ladies and gentlemen and plasmoids," he bellowed. "Lorenzo de Abernathé the Fourth!"

All conversation in the room instantly ceased. A standing ovation and a thunderous round of applause greeted the young Abernathé as he walked into the room. Even Vincent Scoreggia grudgingly got to his feet. Elisabéta Pascucci greeted Young Lorenzo graciously. They exchanged a few brief words and then he gave a quick wave to the room.

As Young Lorenzo made his way around the table, he acknowledged one enthusiastic greeting after another with a vigorous hand shake or a polite nod. By the time he reached his seat, the vacant one on Angelica's left, his face was flush with excitement.

"You're all far too kind," he said, making eye contact up and down the table. "Thank you. It's good to be home!"

Then his eyes fell on the brightly lit display case behind Angelica. His face went instantly pale and the smile left his face. Another round of applause erupted from the table and he reluctantly tore his eyes away from the glass. He nodded politely, forced a broad, distracted smile, and then sat down.

"Lorenzo! Where have you been," Angelica asked, nibbling demurely on a piece of bread.

"I'm sorry," he said, looking back at the display case again. He then leaned around her to look at Scoreggia. "I got held up on the train. I didn't want to be rude to anyone."

The anthropods sitting across from them clicked anxiously. They introduced themselves to Young Lorenzo akwardly.

"Please," he said. "Be yourselves. It's been very nice to meet everyone here."

One of the anthropods looked at Scoreggia.

"So what do you do for Mr. Abernathé?"

"I don't work for him," he snapped angrily. "He works for my wife!"

There was strained moment of silence.

"As a matter of fact," Scoreggia continued, "I'm an IBI agent and I worked a break in at one of Havok's properties. Solved the case, even got his stuff back."

The other anthropod looked around and gestured with its antennae across the room.

"Do any of you know who that striking woman is, in the black dress and long wavy hair? I noticed her walking alone around the gardens during the cocktail hour and now she's standing alone, almost in the corner! Isn't she going to be invited to sit down?"

Young Lorenzo smiled.

"That's our hostess. At a dinner party this size, it's her job to make sure that all of the needs of the guests are met, and she also functions as a sort of traffic manager, making sure all of the wait staff and ushers are positioned properly. See how she's discreetly communicating with the servers as they pass by, a slight hand gesture, brief eye contact, a slight nod?"

Both anthropods nodded.

"I see. That's why she greeted you when you came in."

"Well, yes. Only the highest ranking guests receive her direct attention. It's all part of Lethean tradition. I assume you're not from my wonderful planet?"

"We've visited before, but it's our first time attending an event this elaborate."

Scoreggia leaned in close to Angelica and whispered, "That's the woman you were speaking to outside!"

"Was it? I can't see from here."

"Don't play games with me! Funny how she speaks only to Larry and then *you*." He tugged at his lapels indignantly. "You did explain to her who I was, didn't you?"

Angelica set her bread down on her plate and sat ramrod straight, her face suddenly vacant.

"I'm sorry, Vincent. I tried."

Scoreggia scowled and leaned across her.

"Larry!"

Young Lorenzo didn't hear him. He was gazing into the display case behind Angelica, his face aglow from its contents.

"LARRY!"

Startled, Young Lorenzo leaned forward and looked at him, but made an effort not to intrude upon Angelica.

"So what was so important when you came in," Scoreggia demanded. "What did she say to you?"

He smiled coyly, and with a long pause, seemed to consider whether to answer or not.

"On the behalf of our host, she inquired as to the health of my grandfather and lamented the absence of my father, both of whom were invited, but unable to attend."

"Well, where in Blazes is this guy," Scoreggia grumbled, perhaps a bit too loudly. "Who throws a party and then doesn't show up?" He sat up straight and looked around at everyone who had heard him. "He could at least eat with his own guests, am I right?"

He seemed oblivious to the icy stares all around him.

Young Lorenzo cleared his throat.

"I must tell you, Vincent, that the custom on Lethe is that the host does not join his guests until after dinner. He will end the meal with a toast and then join his guests for after dinner drinks." He then turned his attention back to the display case.

"Then why bother at all? Most people bail after dinner, anyway."

Young Lorenzo sighed, annoyed.

"You don't understand, Vincent. All of the people invited here tonight have some connection to our host. Some business, some political, some personal. The occasion is to give these friends of our host a chance to develop relationships with each other, which can only further the interests of our host. It would be impolite for Mr. Havok to be here, distracting them with his presence, with competition for his attention, forcing them upon one another. And nobody *bails* after dinner."

Scoreggia leaned across Angelica again.

"Hey, you can at least look at me when you're talking to me. Don't you know how to sit? What in Blazes do you keep looking at?"

Scoreggia leaned back and looked into the display case behind Angelica. His eyes widened and he opened his mouth to say something, then thought better of it. He slowly turned back around. He made eye contact with Young Lorenzo, who returned the knowing gaze with one of his own. Young Lorenzo then enjoyed the company of the people around him, while Scoreggia didn't utter another word until well after the final course.

As the dessert dishes were cleared away, the dining room still hummed happily with lively conversations, punctuated by bursts of bright laughter from up and down the table. A quiet anticipation fell over the room as some started paying more attention to the entrances rather than to each other.

Angelica took the last piece of bread on the table and held it in her hand, then sighed softly and reluctantly ate it.

Scoreggia scowled at her.

"What now? You didn't eat or drink anything, except a few pieces of bread."

"It was all delicious."

"All you did was push your food around the plate with your fork. Your glass is still full. What's the matter?"

"You know I don't like wine and everything else was cezzanovan cuisine."

"You were born there, y'know."

"I was born in Sophrire. And that doesn't make the food appetizing."

"You're just determined to be unhappy, aren't you?"

She took a deep, frustrated breath and turned away from him, pretending to be interested in Young Lorenzo's ongoing conversation with the anthropods across the table.

With the air of expectation at a fever pitch, Salestus Havok finally entered the dining room from the foyer archway. He presented himself impeccably groomed, from his long, dark hair parted casually to one side, to the thick, dark beard that covered a lean, rugged face and strong mouth. As a very tall man, he loomed larger than life, with broad shoulders and big, strong hands. The perfect cut of his black tuxedo evinced the spirit of the oldest, and most subtle, of Lethean traditions. He broke his stride a few meters away from the table and his guests. A hush came over the room as all heads turned in his direction.

Scoreggia cleaned his teeth with his tongue. He sipped at a glass of wine and swished it around his mouth like mouthwash. He looked in Young Lorenzo's direction, who continued to steal glances at the display case behind him. He oddly had a hand on his midsection, clutching and unclutching his stomach.

Elisabéta Pascucci greeted Havok with only a welcoming smile and handed him a glass of champagne.

"Ladies and gentlemen and plasmoids," Havok said. "My dear friends and associates. I trust everything has been to your liking? I have always viewed dining with friends to be a time of solemn contentment, a time to be savored."

He smiled genially at the round of polite applause.

Young Lorenzo smirked and then winked in the direction of Scoreggia, who scowled in return.

Havok nodded approvingly in the direction of Elisabéta Pascucci, who responded with a barely perceptible nod of her own.

"You all honor me with your presence. Please stay and enjoy the hospitality of the sitting rooms. For those of you with pressing business, the absence of your company will, of course, be regrettable."

Young Lorenzo quickly stood up and raised his glass, his hand still clutching at his midsection.

"To the Praetor de Atro Viscus!"

"Hear, Hear," the table chanted in unison.

Havok returned the gesture and they all drank. He then handed his glass to Elisabéta and left the room.

The remaining guests gathered in the very elaborate, and very comfortable, sitting rooms. In groups of threes and fours, they sat in chairs or stood in tight circles. Warm, cozy fires took the edge off a chilly evening. Drinks were served more liberally here and the conversation became the liveliest of the evening. The plasmoids all reported favorably on the state of the art filtration system that prevented the air from becoming too thick with cigarette and cigar smoke.

Angelica remarked to her husband that she got a very cold feel from the place. All of the sound echoed, like there was nothing soft or comforting in their surroundings. She found it all unsettling and asked him if he could arrange for their departure at the earliest opportune moment. He promised her that he would.

Once stepping into one of the rooms, Scoreggia immediately drifted into a conversation with a group of men, while Angelica sat patiently in a large chair next to them. Only a few minutes elapsed before he had the group enthralled with embellished tales of his career in law enforcement. The group included the professional athletes Colletore and Dox, who found him interesting again, at least for the moment. The more Scoreggia drank, the louder he became and the coarser his language. He exercised less discretion in revealing the inner workings of the IBI. All the while, the macropian Hossenfuss stood to the side, puffing on a cigar with forced patience, speaking intermittently with the same plasmoid and carefully absorbing every word coming out of Scoreggia's mouth.

Young Lorenzo stood near one of the fire places, surrounded by a crowd of admirers. Numerous women, and men alike, vied for his attention. He renewed several acquaintances of his father's and found himself in the company of many old friends from primary school. Repeated toasts to his good health interspersed the laughter over shared memories of school and growing up on Lethe.

Elisabéta Pascucci drifted about the room, joining each individual conversation for a few minutes and then politely moving on to the next one. The men in the room were impressed with her beauty and simply awed by way she moved, and the ladies with her flawless manners and charm.

"Mrs. Smart-Scoreggia," she said, suddenly standing next to Angelica. "Is there anything I can get you?"

Angelica smiled at the sound of her voice and stood up.

"Thank you, no. My husband is nearby."

Elisabéta nodded.

"I understand. You should know that Mr. Havok is inviting selected guests to remain for a longer stay."

"That's very gracious of him."

"Yes. He is very interested in becoming a part of Lethean society, now that the construction of Atro Viscus has been completed." She paused. "To that end, Mr. Havok would also like to extend this invitation to the young Mr. Abernathé. I understand that he works for you?"

"You know that he does."

"That seems very odd, given his family situation."

"Yes, but his influence is a great benefit to the University."

"Mr. Havok would like to prevail upon you to allow Mr. Abernathé to be his guest for awhile."

Angelica considered this.

"Of course. You can have him for as long as you like."

"Mr. Havok will be pleased. If I could ask—"

They were interrupted by a burst of raucous laughter from Scoreggia's circle, Scoreggia the loudest.

"Hey, hey Dox! Get this! I heard Havok's so tough, he scratches his back with a hacksaw," he bellowed. "Man, I hear he's so tough, I'll bet he has sandpaper in his bathroom!"

Scoreggia roared with laughter, while the rest of the circle smiled weakly and glanced at each other uneasily.

From behind Scoreggia, a cold voice froze him to the marrow.

"Indulging in vicious rumors speaks more to the character of the one who spreads them, rather than the subject of them, don't you think?"

Scoreggia turned around, nearly spilling his drink. He found himself looking up into the face of Salestus Havok.

"The hacksaw," Havok said icily. "Simply not true."

A tense moment passed. Scoreggia shuffled his feet akwardly.

"But the sandpaper," Havok said matter of factly, "that's one hundred percent accurate. I use thirty-weight."

The group laughed politely, but the tension still hung in the air.

"Well, well," Scoreggia said with a boozy grin. "Look who finally decided to stop by his own party!"

"Vincent Scoreggia, thank you for coming," Havok said, shaking his hand firmly. He did the same for all the men in the small circle, addressing each by their full name. "I trust everyone is enjoying themselves."

"Hey, Salestus, right?" Scoreggia punched him playfully on the shoulder. "You can take a joke, right? I didn't mean nothin' by that sandpaper stuff."

"On the contrary," Havok said coolly, brushing at his shoulder, "I'm quite used to hearing all about myself. And like I just said, some of it is even true."

"Hey, what's with your hand," Scoreggia asked. "Is that a glove?"

A flesh colored glove covered Havok's left hand, which he quickly put in his pocket. Angelica moved to stand next to Scoreggia and put her hand first on his shoulder, and then held on to his elbow. This seemed to steady him and he stood up straighter. He started to speak again, but Havok looked past him, to the macropian, Alix Dox.

"Mr. Dox," he said. "I must confess to being a fan of yours. I admire your direct approach to the game. You play your position in the most sober, forthright method possible. A style of play that is now sadly lacking."

Dox nodded earnestly, his snout pressed tightly closed.

"Thanks, I guess. I didn't know rich guys like you cared about sports."

"Yes, that is the popular perception of my fellow Letheans, but I must confess, there are times when I think about nothing else."

Havok turned to Colletore next.

"And your most excellent teammate, Mr. Colletore. What Mr. Dox is to the more physical style of play, your are his equal in cunning and agility. Without your leadership, your team certainly would not have earned its latest title."

Colletore raised his glass in acknowledgement.

"Thanks, Mr. Havok. You got that right!"

Colletore smiled and winked at Dox, who snarled in return.

Havok looked over the small group with shrewd, dark eyes.

"Mr. Dox, Mr. Colletore. I would like to extend to you an invitation to prolong your stay here at Atro Viscus. Another aspect of my reputation that is accurate is that I am something of an outdoorsman. The forest that surrounds my home is a very dangerous place, but I hunt, and am sometimes hunted in return, throughout its confines on a regular basis. I would like you two gentlemen to hunt with me for a few weeks, to test your athleticism, your mettle, in a setting other than a playing field. Are you equal to the challenge?"

The eyes of both athletes lit up. Without looking at each other, they both agreed readily.

"Excellent," Havok said. "Elisabéta?"

She came forward.

"Yes, Mr. Havok?"

"Mr. Dox and Mr. Colletore will be my guests for the next few weeks. Please see to their accommodations."

"Of course."

Havok nodded.

"I will see you gentlemen tomorrow."

"Hey, hold on," Scoreggia said, grabbing Havok's shoulder. "Can any of you guys shoot?" He looked at all three of them. "These two guys are jocks. Either of you ever carry a gun?"

They all looked at him blankly.

"I mean, you know what's out there, right?"

Havok paused for an akward moment, then looked at Elisabéta.

She said, "Mr. Scoreggia, or rather Agent Scoreggia, is with the IBI. He recovered the property taken from Pollone Presa and saw to the prosecution of those responsible."

Scoreggia smiled in spite of himself and brushed at his lapel in an unflattering manner. Havok looked at him dully.

"And with him is his wife, Angelica Smart-Scoreggia, of Elysian University."

Havok's eyes turned to Angelica and his expression brightened.

"Ah! How pleased I am to finally meet you personally. I take it everything was to your satisfaction this evening?"

Angelica beamed, but she was quick to hide her smile.

"Yes, you've been a most gracious host and you have wonderful home."

He gave a polite nod.

"Perhaps your husband would like to join our hunting party?" Reluctantly, he added, "He would be a welcome addition."

Angelica hesitated.

"I would love to," Scoreggia said eagerly.

Havok looked him up and down.

"It will be dangerous."

"I can handle myself."

Havok raised a disbelieving eyebrow.

"Vincent," Angelica interjected. "We can't stay."

"Don't worry," he said. "I got some personal time I can use. You can take an early vacation."

"Vincent, can I speak to you alone for a moment?"

"Nothin' to discuss, Babe. We're stayin'."

She blushed with embarrassment.

"We're not prepared for this. We have a change of clothes for only a day or two. And I have to work."

"Please, Mrs. Smart-Scoreggia," Havok interrupted. "I will provide you with any amenity that you require. I'm sure I can convince your superiors to allow you to remain here as long as you like. Or, if you prefer, I will arrange for you to continue your work for the University from here."

Angelica stammered, flustered.

"T-That's very nice, but—"

"Babe, you're being ridiculous," Scoreggia said. "Don't insult the man."

"But it's dangerous."

"It'll be fine."

Angelica fumed in silent frustration.

"It's settled then," Havok said. "Elisabéta?"

She very gently placed Angelica's hand on her forearm.

"Come with me, Mrs. Smart-Scoreggia. I'll help you get situated."

"Vincent," Angelica said. "Are you coming?"

"Go on, you'll be fine," he said, turning away. "I'll see you in the morning."

She flushed in anger, then allowed Elisabéta to escort her out of the room.

Chapter 19
Havok

As the party drew to a close, the only guests who remained were that small number who had been personally invited for an extended stay by the Praetor himself. They continued to smoke and drink, and enjoyed each other's company late into the night.

Far below them on the lower floors, the staff was still very active. Servants, maids, valets and other staffers rushed to and fro, a hectic, yet controlled chaos that operated in quiet whispers. The Praetor had a general disdain for loud noises and commotion, and the principal method of communication amongst the household staff was non-verbal.

Elisabéta Pascucci walked briskly down the stone corridor that led to the staging area. Her heels clicked on the marble floor and the sound of quick taps always alerted the staffers to her approach. Now free of the formal evening gown she had worn earlier in the evening, she felt more relaxed. She now had on her familiar black business suit with a red blouse, complete with the red Havok family crest pinned to her lapel. A small earpiece carefully hidden behind her ear hummed with the conversations of the various departments that ran not only the main house, but the entire grounds. It was necessary for her to be in constant contact with all components as she supervised all of Mr. Havok's interests, from business transactions to the day to day operations of Atro Viscus.

Of all the people in Havok's employ, only she had access to the Praetor himself.

She entered the staging area and stood to the side as the valets busily organized the bags and other personal items of the overnight guests. Each guest had been assigned a personal valet, and each of them took turns placing items into an anti-gravity shaft that delivered them to the guest suites above. The supervisor of the valets, an anthropod named Da'Abonne, skittered about the room, watching over everything that transpired.

"Mr. Scoreggia," Elisabéta said, approaching a young man.

The valet turned and stood up straight.

"Yes, Ma'am?"

The anthropod moved quickly to join the conversation.

"The Scoreggias do not have sufficient personal items of their own. Be sure that they receive a full set of amenities directly from the Praetor's personal stores. In addition, you are to remain available around the clock to grant whatever item or service they require. Be aware that Mrs. Smart-Scoreggia is blind. The Praetor does not wish for her to be uncomfortable in any way. If you have any difficulties, you are to notify Mr. Da'Abonne, not the shift supervisor, immediately."

The young valet nodded.

"And Mr. Da'Abonne, I wish to be informed of any difficulties, no matter how trivial."

Da'Abonne nodded and the young valet returned to work.

Elisabéta then observed a young canite struggling to set some bags properly into the shaft. She gestured at him with her eyes and Da'Abonne nodded.

"Mr. Colletore," it said.

The canite did not respond, still fumbling with the machine.

"Mr. Colletore," Da'Abonne repeated impatiently.

Another valet tapped the canite on the shoulder and pointed at the anthropod. The canite sheepishly approached Da'Abonne and Elisabéta.

"Mr. Colletore," Da'Abonne said, "we do things here in the traditional manner. You have been assigned to Mr. Colletore, and as Mr. Colletore you shall be referred until his departure. Do you understand?"

The canite nodded.

"I'm sorry, Mr. Da'Abonne. My first couple of days down here. I just got promoted out of the parking att—"

"Please take greater care with Mr. Colletore's personal items," Da'Abonne interrupted. "While it is necessary to be efficient, keep in mind that this is not a race. One item at a time, and increase the setting to .001 standard."

The canite nodded curtly, then returned quickly to his work.

Elisabéta nodded at Da'Abonne, then continued on to the culinary rooms. The prep stations were quiet and clean inside the darkened kitchen. She walked past the pantry and the main stairs that went up to the dining room, and instead took the back stairs that led to Mr. Havok's private dining room. The track lighting that lined the edges of the room and the table had been dimmed and the table lamps doused. She paused for a moment, listening to the faint sound of a violin. She resumed walking, the crisp clacking of her heels muted by the thick area rugs that lined Mr. Havok's personal living space.

In keeping with The Praetor's particular tastes, there were no overhead light sources in all of Atro Viscus, nor any above eye level. Standing instructions in this part of the house called for very little light. While made of black stone and generally dimly lit, the place held its charm, a sense of warmth and comfort, which stood in stark contrast to the environment that surrounded the compound. The faint scent of roses filled the air. She liked this place, this job and her employer. However, like many enormously wealthy men, Salestus Havok had his peculiar wants and habits.

As a solitary man, Havok rarely interacted with anyone beyond her and when he did venture outside the confines of his home, he did so without anyone knowing his true identity. He seemed pleased that most of The Web thought he didn't really exist. He liked to work with his hands and spent many days working anonymously along side the laborers and craftsmen during the construction of Atro Viscus. He maintained workshops all over the grounds and outer circles, and spent a lot of time in them, alone. He often disappeared for days at a time in the very dangerous forests outside the perimeter walls of the Third Circle. He seldom smiled and carried with him a profound sadness that seemed to dictate his every action, some undefined, yet onerous obligation. He was generally kind and calm, but at times exhibited an irrational bitterness toward certain corporations and people, which she still failed to understand. It had something to do with his brother, Eiger, who lived in an isolated section of the house and who suffered from an undisclosed illness. Havok aggressively protected his sibling's privacy and severely curtailed the staff's interaction with him.

Elisabéta had first met Salestus Havok nine years ago, a few days after she had earned her degree in corporate law. She had offers from all of the big conglomerates, like Cathedral, NYSAAC and Malpercorso Partners. Of all the overtures for her services, only his was made in person. Curious, she entertained his offer in spite of all the advice and conventional wisdom that insisted she ignore it.

She listened patiently as he spoke of possessing significant assets that he needed to convert to true wealth, assets that he did not want to reveal or part with. He spoke of building his own company, of building this place, Atro Viscus. She found him to be alternately charming and then suddenly akward, not at all comfortable with the trappings of the enormously rich. For someone so young, he carried himself with the weary acceptance of an old soul. He said he needed someone exactly like her: someone very bright, very young and very beautiful to successfully represent his interests in the manner he required. His earnest sincerity resonated with her, and any ambivalence she felt was swept away after he offered her a ridiculous sum of money for her services. She had been in his employ ever since.

Elisabéta had the distinction of being Havok's first, and most trusted, employee. He conducted all of his business through her, never revealing himself to the rest of The Web. Through her, he selectively hired those in the most desperate of circumstances, mostly those who had been broken by their attempts to colonize The Rim and The Frontier. Without a compelling need to do so, he overpaid them all, from administrators to craftsmen to laborers. He arranged for state of the art working conditions. He took an interest in their personal lives and invested in them as people. He provided the materials for them to build their own homes. He paid for their educations and that of their children. When Elisabéta's own parents fell ill in their old age, Havok arranged for all of their care and paid for their funerals when they passed. Havok did not do such things just for her. He did them for everyone.

Havok's largesse was not without cost. He demanded honest, hard work from those he employed. He expected them to work together and to support one another in building a community for which they could all be proud to call their own. All who lived in Atro Viscus adored The Praetor, and in return for their loyalty, they received his full protection.

Elisabéta followed the rich scent of roses and the mournful violin music to the hall that led to Havok's private rooms. On the rounded staircase that led to the servants quarters sat the kitchen staff, arrayed in rows of twos and threes. They listened contentedly to the music. Elisabéta permitted this from time to time, so long as they remained quiet. As an accomplished musician, Mr. Havok played numerous instruments, but she knew he didn't like having an audience, regardless of how appreciative. She smiled and nodded at the kitchen manager, who did the same. She then waved her hand across her throat and the kitchen staff obediently departed without a sound.

She walked into Mr. Havok's favorite sitting room and took five more steps, then stopped and waited to be acknowledged. The Praetor himself played a violin on the far side of the room. The fireplace roared and cast flickering shadows on the chairs and sofa. Scented candles burned on a table and the heavy drapes had been drawn over the windows. Again, as with all of Atro Viscus, track lighting along the floor provided most of the illumination.

Havok still wore his dinner clothes, although he had removed his tie and jacket. His eyes were closed, but she knew that he was aware of her presence, although he gave no sign. She stood primly with her hands clasped together in front of her waist. At moments like this she pondered him the most. Sometimes she thought that he continued playing just for her.

She knew his moods well as they often dictated his actions. When angry, he disappeared for weeks in the forest. When inspired, he could be found in the industrial shops.

But alone.

Always alone.

At these moments, when she imagined he played just for her, she wondered if he had ever truly loved anyone, or if anyone loved him. After all this time, she felt close to Havok, but knew little about him or even if that was his real name. His background had all the classic earmarks of someone running from something, and she knew better than to inquire of someone so intensely private.

So cold.

And for long stretches, so emotionless.

She wondered if he realized that she would be more than willing to curl onto his lap, become a part of his personal life, if only he would ask.

After a minute or so, he serenely removed the bow from the strings and set the instrument carefully on top of a piano. He walked over to a table and picked up an open bottle of Hestian rum. He put some ice in a half-filled glass and then topped it off. He sat down on the sofa and put his feet up on the table.

"Good evening, Elisabéta."

"Mr. Havok."

She sat on the edge of the couch across from him, her back straight.

"Your long term guests are still conversing in the guest sitting room. Apparently, your invitation inspired a second wind."

A sardonic smile crossed his face.

"And Ms. Smart?"

"She prefers Mrs. Smart-Scoreggia. I've made her as comfortable as possible. She's not happy. She doesn't want to be here."

He seemed saddened by this and sipped at his drink.

"You're sure?"

"Yes. This bothers you?"

"It does."

"Yet you went out of your way to deliberately upset her by inviting her husband to stay."

He shifted uneasily and sipped again at his drink.

"And the railings in the garden?"

"She appreciated that very much."

He smiled, but it faded quickly.

"You're sure about how she lost her vision? And when?"

"Yes, Mr. Havok."

"I want her to be happy while she's here. I want her to like it here."

She nodded.

"Yes. Of course, Mr. Havok."

"You just hesitated. Why?"

She looked at him, but wilted under the intensity of his gaze.

"You don't like her. Why," he demanded.

Clearly uncomfortable, she responded, "It's more her husband, Mr. Havok."

He eased back into the couch and gulped the rest of his drink.

"Yes. Vincent Scoreggia." He rubbed his chin thoughtfully. "He is quite a boor."

"It's not my place to comment on the character of your guests."

He looked at her oddly.

"You're right, as always."

"For how long will you be in the pinefields this time? I need to know in order to see to the happiness of Mrs. Smart-Scoreggia."

Again, he looked at her, this time crossly, she thought.

Finally, he said, "Three days, maybe four at most."

She raised her eyebrows in surprise.

"I know what you're thinking," he said. "I won't let anything happen to them." He smiled wickedly. "At least nothing serious."

Havok tugged absent mindedly on the flesh colored glove that covered his left hand. Elisabéta had never seen him without it. She wondered about it often, but had never asked about it.

Without warning, Havok suddenly sat up straight.

"Mr. Havok? Is something wrong?"

He frowned, and put his hands over his ears.

"WHERE THE BLAZES ARE YOU??!!"

The voice came from nowhere and echoed up and down the halls, like nails on a chalk board. Startled, Elisabéta jumped to her feet.

"THERE YOU ARE!!"

In the doorway appeared a stick figure of a man. His emaciated form made his head seem bigger than normal, which bobbed precariously on a thin neck over small shoulders. His long, dark hair fell like oily strings over his face and ears, and his wrinkled clothing hung on him like a scarecrow.

Eiger.

He pointed an angry, bony finger at Havok.

"She's here, isn't she? I heard the maids talking about preparing a room for her! Don't lie to me! She's here! I know it!"

Havok stood up.

"Eiger, please don't raise your voice."

"OR WHAT?!! You'll run off and hide in the woods until your puke breath fades, until that knot in your belly unravels?!"

"Eiger, please—"

"I'LL SHOUT ALL I DAMN WANT!"

Havok, clearly flustered, said, "Elisabéta, you'll have to excuse us, please. My brother and I need to talk."

"Of course, Mr. Havok."

Menscher mimicked her derisively and glared at her as she walked out.

They stared at each other for a long moment.

"Eiger, what have I told you about controlling these outbursts? Especially in front of the staff?"

"DON'T YOU MAKE THIS ABOUT ME!"

"You will not speak to me in this manner, Eiger."

"SHE'S HERE!"

"I will not converse with you until you get control of your emotions."

Menscher stood in the doorway, fists clenched at his sides, panting loudly. Havok walked around to the table and refilled his drink.

"What do you want, Eiger?"

"She's here," he shouted indignantly, pointing at him again as he walked forward. "She's got nothing to do with this, and she's here!"

"Eiger, Young Lorenzo works for her. It is necessary. We discussed this."

"We did not discuss her staying here!"

"A subtle change in plans."

"Subtle?! No, no. You planned this all along, didn't you? Didn't you?!"

"Eiger—"

"And you're wearing the glove! You take that damned thing off when you talk to me! Are you so ashamed of what you are?!"

Reluctantly, Havok set his drink down, then pulled the five-fingered glove off, one finger at a time. He held up his hand, displaying all six fingers.

"Better?"

"You put that on because of her, didn't you? There's no room in our lives for this woman! There's one thing and one thing only that matters! Your infatuation with, with…*her* is a distraction! You see, we have the Abernathé child here, at our mercy! Yet we do nothing! Why? Because you're blinded, fixated on this woman!"

"Eiger, please. We get nowhere by harming the young Abernathé."

"Why?! Why let him go? Killing him will get his attention! Oh, yes it will!"

"You know why."

Menscher trembled, still simmering.

"I NEARLY DIED FOR YOU!! BECAUSE OF YOU!!"

Havok sighed.

"And you remind me every day. I haven't forgotten."

Menscher pulled at his hair in frustration.

"You're sure he saw the diamond?"

"Yes."

"You're absolutely sure?"

"It was in the display case behind his seat at the dinner table. He couldn't take his eyes off it."

Menscher crossed his arms over his chest. His head wobbled from side to side as his eyes welled up with tears.

"And he will tell his father?"

Havok put his hands on Menscher's shoulders.

"Yes."

Menscher wept uncontrollably. Havok took him in his arms and held him until he lifted his head.

"You promise," Menscher asked, sniffling.

Havok put a hand tenderly on his face.

"I promise."

Menscher buried his head in Havok's shoulder. Havok held him tightly, trying to muffle the sound of his sobbing.

Chapter 20
The Razorneck Pinefields

Young Lorenzo hesitated in the dark. His chest heaved violently with each frantic, desperate gasp for breath. His tattered camos fluttered in the fierce wind, a wind that chilled him to the marrow.

His face burned.

His body ached.

He had never been more scared in his entire life.

So he ran.

His legs now warm and damp.

He ran faster.

Across the soft mossy ground, he ran as fast as he could.

His whole body screamed from the effort, especially his shoulder. He had fallen the day before, dislocated it, and at that moment he didn't think anything worse could happen. That is, until Havok roughly forced it back into place.

And now this.

The needles of these dense, coniferous trees were as sharp as knives. They punished him as he ran, slicing and dicing the thick cotton twill of his coat and coveralls as easily as his flesh. He could barely see with his goggles so badly scratched, but he didn't dare remove them.

Not for a second.

The stygian darkness stuck to him like ink. He could only see every few moments, when the lighting flashed and permitted intermittent snapshots of his surroundings. The rain hadn't come yet, but the deafening thunder and the shocks of lightning battered his senses and left his ears ringing. He was familiar with these air storms. They were also common around Summa Avarici, where the dense hot air that permeated most of Lethe met with the bitter cold of the poles.

Young Lorenzo had made a serious mistake in coming here. He mistook Havok for a true Lethean Gentleman. He expected this to be a proper excursion with footmen and guides, and basic amenities to make their stay in the wild more 'civilized'. They weren't in these woods for a day when a flock of those vicious, man-eating ravens descended upon them with a vengeance. Havok incomprehensibly threw all of their food stores out into the open, ostensibly to draw them away. They were all nearly killed.

Havok explained that these birds had become more visible over the last few weeks, appearing in larger groups rather than the customary pairs. He said the birds were now overpopulated after feasting on easy game for years. Now that game is gone, either eaten or retreated into the denser forest center. The others readily accepted this explanation, even thanked him for his quick thinking. Young Lorenzo felt differently. Something about Havok, he couldn't quite put his finger on it, but he believed Havok knew this would happen, and that he was counting on it.

Depsite being out of provisions, no one suggested returning to Atro Viscus. At Haovk's direction they ate pine nuts and berries, and cooked small game over a covered fire.

Like savages.

This terrible diet did nothing to ease the flu-like illness in his stomach, which had already been bothering him for days. It afflicted him most in the mornings and evenings, and encumbered him with horrible bouts of dysentery. The onset of this terrible condition always struck him at the most inopportune moments, like every time he tried to demonstrate some ability to contribute to Havok. He first felt the twinge in his gut at the table during the dinner party and believed that he had eaten something that still disagreed with him.

He remembered feeling like this all the time growing up, before his father sent him away to school in Elsasser. All the taunting from his grandfather, the constant visits to those creepy doctors. Going away to school put an end to all of it. Maybe the illness was all in his head. Just a bad case of nerves.

All he wanted was to earn Havok's good favor, to speak to him for a few quick minutes about that diamond. A brief excrusion into the forest seemed ideal, but he never expected anything like *this*. It was simply un-Lethean. Still, he put on a brave face and reacted with forced good humor to the repeated jokes made by Scoreggia about being 'scared shitless'.

He tried to stay focused on his surroundings, but his disorientation only increased. A flash of lightening and he saw someone running along side of him, several meters to his right. Probably Scoreggia or Dox. Already anxious, his stomach twisted into a tighter knot and his legs turned to rubber. A booming roll of thunder knocked him to his knees. Another flash of lightning and he saw it.

The bruin.

Or something bruin-like.

On its massive hind legs, clawing at a tree.

It was hairless, save for a mat of fur around its head and a goatee and mutton chops. Its black leathery skin made it hard to see in the dark. They had been chasing this beast for most of the day, trying to corner it, trap it, but it was too smart. It kept eluding them. Havok insisted on forcing the beast into this section of the woods, what he called the Razorneck Pinefields, a narrow outcropping of land that jutted out over an enormous lake. The dense pines that occupied this peninsula had deadly sharp needles, hence the name for this place. Havok warned them about what they would find here and that the bruin's skin was tough enough to resist the needles, but that it would be afraid of the water and have nowhere to run, trapped against the cliff edges.

Of course, Scoreggia readily agreed to enter this place. Colletore and Dox went along, but were less than enthusiastic. This was the pattern over the last few days, Havok suggesting something ridiculously dangerous and Scoreggia going right along with him. Scoreggia was so desperate to impress Havok with his machismo that Young Lorenzo believed if their host suggested cutting off a limb, he would, or at the very least run through a field of razor blades. Havok kept pressing Scoreggia into greater and greater danger, apparently unsatisfied until either one of them got seriously injured or worse.

Young Lorenzo did owe a debt to the athletes. Dox and Colletore subtley did their best to help him along. Without their kindness, he would've quit this excursion at the beginning, and then would never have forgiven himself. He desperately needed to gain Havok's favor, to discuss a business deal for that diamond.

That incredible, beautiful diamond.

He had never seen anything like it and was sure his father hadn't either. If he could obtain that gem stone and present it to his father, surely he would reconsider letting him leave the University and take up a more prominent role in Abernathé Stoneworks. To this point, he had been unable to engage Havok in any meaningful conversation. He seemed fixated on Scoreggia and virtually ignored the rest of the party.

More deafening thunder, another flash of lightning. The animal sat back on its haunches and looked right at him. From his knees, with trembling hands, he raised his rifle. He had a clear shot, no way he could miss. Thunder exploded in his ears, which muffled the roar of the second bruin that struck him on his right side, knocking him to the ground. This other bruin jumped on him in an instant and he feebly blocked its long, sharp claws with the rifle, which then slipped from his weak grip. Another flash of lightening and it reared up on its hind legs, joined by the first one. Together, in a nightmare blur, they set to work on him, showing no mercy.

Suddenly, the weight of the animals was gone and he felt very cold and wet. Another flash of lightening and he could have sworn he saw Havok holding one bruin by the throat while tossing the other one aside. He knew that he had been cut very badly and stayed very still, afraid to move. His hands and feet twitched uncontrollably. He felt Havok's warm breath on his face and the next thunderclap concussed him into unconsciousness.

Young Lorenzo awoke in bed, in the guest room lent to him at Atro Viscus. He felt dry and clean, and sighed in relief at the quiet sunshine that streamed through the windows. Soft, white bandages covered his hands and forearms, as well as his legs. His right arm hung useless at his side, his shoulder heavily taped. His stomach rumbled angrily, but not nearly as crossly as out in the woods. He slowly became aware of Havok standing next to the bed, holding his hand. Young Lorenzo looked up into the Praetor's face and thought he was looking into a mirror. For the first time he noticed a thin, white scar that ran between Havok's mouth and ear that his thick, dark beard could not fully conceal. Havok pinched the edge of Young Lorenzo's palm with a thumb and forefinger, from the base of the wrist to the top of the pinky. He dropped Young Lorenzo's hand and stepped back, hands now in his pockets. Havok didn't have a mark on him. His hair was neatly combed and not a wrinkle marred his clothing.

"Mr. Havok," Young Lorenzo groaned. "I—"

"Dinner is in one hour," he said, then turned and left the room.

Young Lorenzo gasped incredulously, then lay back down. He felt for his neck and chest and detected nothing. No cuts, no scars. He sat up and his whole body ached, especially his hips. He thought he had been hurt much worse. He remembered feeling the bruin claws scrape his rib cage. He shook uncontrollably at the memory and a chill went through him. He lay quietly, replaying the attack in his head over and over again, realizing how lucky he was to be alive.

The pain in his gut faded, the sweating stopped and he suddenly felt much better. Then he got angry. Everything with this Havok needed to be a contest of strength. This was not the way Lethean Gentlemen conducted business. He considered abandoning his purpose here, overwhelmed by the prospect of rejoining this sick competition. He wanted nothing more than to leave Atro Viscus forever. He renewed his resolve to have a direct conversation with this man about the gem stone before the next dawn.

He grit his teeth and got out of bed. He looked in the mirror and saw that his face had only a few knicks and scratches and again considered himself fortunate, considering what it felt like. He washed his face, brushed his teeth and got dressed. A knock at the door interrupted his struggle with his dinner jacket.

"Who is it?"

"Angelica."

He opened the door.

"It's not right for you to be here without Vincent."

"It's okay," she said. "I'm not alone."

He looked behind her at Elisabéta Pascucci.

"I asked to accompany her," Angelica explained. "She was coming to see how you were feeling."

"That's very kind of you both."

"Unlike her, I didn't come here to ask after your health."

"No," he asked, puzzled.

"No."

She reached out and felt for his chest, then his shoulder and then up to his chin. Then she slapped him hard across the face.

"You let him fall into a nest of hornets! He—"

"*I* let him? Who? Vincent?"

"A nest of poisonous hornets! He could have died, Lorenzo!"

"There were hornet nests everywhere! They were easily disturbed! Wha—I don't remember him getting stung by any hornets!"

"And you! What happened to you?! This was all so damned foolish! Are you happy now?"

"Happy? I—"

"Why shouldn't I fire you for this?"

"*Fire me?* For what?"

She turned in a huff, felt her way along the open door, and left.

Elisabéta turned her nose up at him and said, "Mr. Havok said you'll be joining everyone for dinner?"

"Wouldn't miss it," he sighed, still struggling with his jacket.

When Young Lorenzo entered the dining room, he found only Scoreggia, Colletore and Dox at the table. The athletes greeted him warmly as he gingerly made his way to his seat.

"Where's Angelica," he inquired.

"Working," Scoreggia said abruptly. "Some report that had to get done."

"I see. How long—"

"It's been seven days since we left," Scoreggia interrupted, gulping his drink. "You were out cold for two."

"And so were you," Dox added, winking at Young Lorenzo.

Scoreggia grunted.

Young Lorenzo looked at Colletore, who nodded confirmation.

At that moment, appetizers were brought out and the conversation drifted into recollections of their adventure. They talked about how they braved the elements, fought off the carnivorous birds, frogs, and the like, all while hunting the bruin that ultimately took down Young Lorenzo. He found out that he had been so badly injured that the excursion had to be cut short. Havok called for an aircar that brought only Young Lorenzo back to Atro Viscus, where Havok's personal physician saw to his injuries.

Everyone else returned on foot. Havok challenged the group to traverse a narrow land bridge dangerously close to a large honeycombed nest of poisonous hornets. This shortcut would shave a day off their return trip. Havok traversed the land bridge successfully, doing a cartwheel as he went, to show how easily it could be done. The athletes told Scoreggia not to do it. They were all tired and nursing various aches and bruises. It wasn't something that should be attempted in a weakened state. When Scoreggia insisted and then tried to goad them into it with mocking insults, they decided they'd had enough and opted to take the longer route. From a safe distance, the atheletes watched as Scoreggia took two steps, lost his footing, and fell into the nest. He scrambled out, the honeycomb crunching under his feet as he went. Havok helped him out as a cloud of hornets swarmed all around them, as dense as smoke. Scoreggia took the worst of it as the hornets mysteriously had no interest in Havok.

The athletes had a great many laughs this night at the expense of Young Lorenzo and Scoreggia. Young Lorenzo laughed easily right along with them, finding the humor in his own akwardness and inexperience. The athletes admired his refusal to quit, and they complimented him on the courage he displayed in refusing to back down from not only one bruin, but standing up to two.

"He didn't stand up for long," Scoreggia remarked.

"Said the fool who took a nose dive into a pit of hornets," Colletore said, laughing loudly. Young Lorenzo and Dox joined in and laughed harder as Colletore pantomimed Scoreggia's fall.

Scoreggia scowled and buried his chin in his chest, sipping at his drink angrily.

"I almost made it."

"Two steps is not 'almost'!"

Scoreggia did a slow burn, but said nothing else until the gibes at his expense subsided.

"So, fellas," Scoreggia said. "Not many people have had this experience, to spend so much time with the mysterious Salestus Havok. What do you guys think of our host?"

They exchanged nervous glances. Young Lorenzo wiped his mouth with a napkin very slowly, very deliberately.

"Vincent," he said, shaking his head. "Not at his table. Not in his house."

"What? C'mon! Don't you think the guy is just a little bit psycho?"

"No more than you," Dox said.

"Look, you guys know that I'm an interstellar agent."

"Yeah, you never get tired of reminding us," Colletore said, rolling his eyes.

Scoreggia flushed in anger.

"Look, my wife was here the whole time we were gone and she couldn't learn a thing. The staff around here doesn't gossip, the place is huge, but she was steered to remain in a small area. We've been with Havok more than a week and we still don't know a thing about him. Strange the guy's so tight lipped, don't you think?"

Colletore and Dox looked at each other, then stood up.

"See you guys in the morning," Dox said.

They paused at the rapid approach of quick taps. Elisabéta stepped into the dining room, followed by Havok, and smiled broadly at the group of men.

"Leaving so soon," she said to the athletes. "I trust everything was to your liking."

"Very much so," Colletore said. "But we're a bit tired, you know how it is."

"I'm sorry to hear that, Sfero," Havok said. "I was going to invite you all to take advantage of the larger sitting room. The bar has been fully stocked, the fire has been started. I find it an excellent way to relax after a week in the forest. It would also provide me with an opportunity to privately discuss some business with Mr. Scoreggia."

Scoreggia perked up at this, as did Young Lorenzo.

"Mr. Havok," Young Lorenzo interjected. He stood up and held a bandaged fist over his mouth, as if he might throw up. "I also have some business that I would like to discuss with you." He paused, suddenly out of breath. "At your earliest convenience."

"Yes. Make an appointment to meet with Ms. Pascucci before you leave."

"Mr. Havok, I must protest—"

"Did I misspeak, Mr. Abernathé?"

"No," Young Lorenzo said, completely cowed. He leaned on the table for support. "You did not."

"Say, Mr. Havok," Colletore said. "A room like that, it wouldn't be right without a beautiful lady present." He looked at Elisabéta. "Would it?"

"Ms. Pascucci is free to do as she pleases," Havok said, indifferent. "Now, Vincent? If you wouldn't mind joining me for a private conversation?"

"Don't mind if I do," he replied. "I was thinking along the same lines." He got up from the table and bumped Young Lorenzo with his shoulder as he went, then left with Havok. Elisabéta's disapproving eyes followed their exit.

"Now how about that drink," Colletore asked Elisabéta, holding out his arm. "I love a woman in black nylons."

With a subtle glance, she looked him over. A quick frown rolled over face, but it just as easily turned to a smile.

She took his arm and said, "I'd like that very much. You gentlemen are coming?"

Dox looked at Young Lorenzo with some concern, but Young Lorenzo waved at him congenially.

"Thanks, Alix, I'm okay," Young Lorenzo said. "Still got a bit of that bug. Not so bad this time. It passed. I could use a drink. Or two."

Dox smiled at him and patted him roughly on his good shoulder with tiny hands.

"Y'know, Larry, I've seen plenty of cowards in my day, but you, you got heart. You can play on my team anytime. Let me tell you about this rookie we had a few years ago..."

Chapter 21
Smart-Scoreggia

"Please, sit," Havok said, offering a drink to Scoreggia. They sat in black leather chairs in front of a roaring fireplace.

"Thanks, Sal. So what is it you wanna talk about?"

"I couldn't help but notice how happy you and your wife are."

"Thanks. We do okay."

"I couldn't…" Havok started, then stopped. He took a deep breath. "I couldn't help but notice the limitations on her vision."

"What? That she's blind? Well, almost blind anyway."

"I also couldn't help noticing that it has affected her stay here."

"Nah. She has a hard time in new places, that's all. She'll get used to it. Why all the questions about Angelica?"

"I like to get to know my guests. I have so few of them. If I may know, how did she lose her vision? Was she born this way?"

Scoreggia took a big gulp from his glass.

"No," he said, clearing his throat a bit. "No. When we were young, before we got married. She, uh, had an accident."

"What kind of accident?"

His eyes fell out of his head.

"A bed post...she hit her head on a bed post. I, uh, we...had just come back from a party with friends, *her* friends, and..." His eyes suddenly darted at Havok. "Why all the questions, Sal?"

"I must confess that I've taken quite a liking to you, Vincent. Our excursion into the forest. The athletes, while personable, were far too catious. Far too soft. Remove them from the playing field, take them out of their element, and they become weak. You, on the other hand, have true courage. Shrewd. Decisive. Unafraid. All qualities that I admire."

"Look, Sal, I'm an IBI agent. That forest out there? That's my every day."

"Of course, Vincent. I meant no offense. I spend so little time socializing, I apologize if I misspoke. I meant it as a compliment."

"Hey, it's all right, Sal. I understand. You're direct and to the point. No bullshit. Those are qualities *I* admire."

Havok smiled.

"You should know, Vincent, that I've spoken to my business managers. Your actions in pursuing the burglary at Pollone Presa Outfitters saved me millions, possibly more. However, the money wasn't my real concern, a trifle, really. My real concern was that several employees who were not loyal to me and my interests were discovered and excised. I value loyalty above all else. Money cannot buy trust, honesty or true friendship."

Scoreggia put his hand on his chest.

"Look, Sal, I was just doing my job."

"Of course. But your dedication deserves some kind of acknowledgment. I want to put some my resources at your disposal."

"Hang on, Sal. This is way above my pay grade. You need to talk to the bean counters, not me."

"You misunderstand. I was thinking on a smaller scale. Would you, and most importantly Angelica, be receptive to the restoration of her vision?"

Scoreggia emptied his glass and shook his head.

"No. No. I'm sorry, Sal. We've been down that road. Cloned eyes won't help because it's brain damage that's causing the problem."

"I see. When was the last time you looked into the matter?"

He shrugged.

"Right after we got married. Why?"

"A new hospital has been opened, right here on Lethe, that purports to be at the forefront of all types of medicine. I've made some inquiries and I believe they can help her."

"Yeah, the Ricco Sfondato Hospital. We can't afford that. We even had Larry try and talk to his old man about it, but no freebies. Not even a discount."

"I'm astonished! And what about Young Lorenzo himself?"

Scoreggia laughed.

"Larry doesn't have that kind of money! He has no access to the family fortunes. He trades on his name, that's all."

"But I do have that kind of money *and* that kind of influence. I've arranged for everything. She can be seen tomorrow morning."

"Thanks, Sal, that's very generous but—"

"I won't take no for an answer. You need to understand, Vincent, that good things should happen to good people. If you refuse to go, I will have the physicans brought here. If you leave, I will have them brought to wherever you are."

Scoreggia considered this and squirmed a bit in his chair. Havok refilled his glass, which Scoreggia downed in one gulp.

"Okay," Scoreggia said, wiping his mouth with the back of his hand. "I'll talk to her."

"Very good." Havok refilled his glass. "And now I must continue to commend you on the way that you conducted yourself in the forest, especially the Razorneck Pinefields. Most impressive."

They clinked glasses and Scoreggia again downed his in one gulp. Havok put his drink to the side, untouched.

Havok leaned back in his chair.

"You hinted that there was a matter you wished to discuss?"

Scoreggia grabbed the bottle and refilled his own glass.

"Y'know Sal, I really admire this house you built here. Especially the dining rooms. The display cases."

"Ah, yes. I would be remiss if I didn't give the credit for much of the design and décor to the team of architects and engineers involved."

Scoreggia emptied his glass again and continued to drink, while Havok entered into a long discourse on all of the planning that went into the construction of Atro Viscus. The bottle was long empty by the time their conversation ended and the subject of the display cases in the dining room never came up again.

With the help of his personal valet, Scoreggia made his way back to the guest quarters he shared with Angelica. He staggered through the door and into the darkened room. He slammed the door behind him, startling Angelica, who was working in the dark.

"Dammit," Scoreggia exclaimed, fumbling to turn on the lights. "How many times do I have to tell you to turn on the damn lights when you enter a room?"

"Vincent! You gave me such a fright! I'm sorry. I forgot."

"Forget it. Listen, Babe, I got great news!"

"You're drunk."

"Yeah, yeah, but I'm gonna fix your eyes!"

"What?"

"That Ricco Hospital place. I got you in."

She seemed crestfallen.

"How?"

"Havok, Babe! He's gonna pay for it all!"

She stood up and put her hands on his arm.

"Vincent! You can't! It will look like a payoff!"

"What payoff? What're you worried about? He's our friend now!"

"Vincent—"

"We're good people, Babe! Good things should happen to us!"

"But *what* is he going to ask for in return, in the future? It's the same thing I've been trying to get the University to understand!"

"Look, Babe, you got it all wrong, as usual. None of that matters, cuz nobody's gonna find out anyway!"

"No. It's because it's not going to happen."

"Wha? What did you say?"

She backed away and crossed her arms defiantly over her chest. "I've made peace with my eyes a long time ago. I can't go through the testing, the whole thing, all over again. I—"

"What in Blazes is wrong with you," he exploded. "This is it! The fix! One more time and you'll be all better! Don't you want that?!"

"You don't have to go through all the pain and prodding!"

"*You* are not *listening*—"

"You want this for you, not me!"

"What did you just say to me? Hm?" He closed in on her and she sensed the turn in his mood. *"It wasn't my fault,"* he shouted. He slapped her with the back of his hand and then flung her roughly against the stone wall.

She slid to the floor. Tears rolled down her face, mouth agape, unable to scream for the pain radiating throughout her body.

"You'll go, dammit," he screamed, standing over her, pointing down at her. "You'll go because you have no idea what's good for you and what isn't!"

He stormed into the bathroom and shut off the lights as he went, leaving her in the dark.

Chapter 22
Revelation

All of the rooms in the Ricco Sfondato Hospital were spacious and luxurious. They smelled heavily of disinfectants and cleansers. Angelica didn't mind it. It was the smell of clean. What she did mind was being there at all.

She reluctantly agreed to have the surgery on her eyes, but she refused to convalesce at Atro Viscus. Of course, Havok arranged for both her and her husband to stay in an apartment he owned here in the plaza. Havok visited them almost daily, to check on her progress and to further ingragiate himself with the both of them. On the days he didn't come, he sent Elisabéta Pascucci. Her dislike for Havok intensified with each passing day, while her husband's infatuation with him only grew. She knew better than to make it an issue, so she retired to her bedroom, feigning fatigue or a headache, each time he appeared. At first, she looked forward to when Elisabéta came alone, but Elisabéta's demeanor grew colder and more distant with each visit.

A few days after the surgery, Scoreggia received a message from The Bureau, not his superiors, but a lawyer, and he often disappeared for hours at a time. Although he denied it, she recognized the signs that he was working. He went about things with an intensity that bordered on panic. He denied any problems with his bosses, but, from half overheard conversations, Angelica suspected that he was in trouble with ethics violations and scheming to get out of it.

Angelica had sent Young Lorenzo back to Nostrova and had been continuing her work through him, which posed many complications because she didn't trust him. He arranged his contacts with her for when Havok would be present, despite her repeated instructions not to, and persistently tried to speak to him.

She'd had enough of Salestus Havok and wanted him out of their lives forever. Only a few more days. Today, she would get the bandages off her eyes. She would say what she needed to, true or not, and then they could leave this place and get back to their normal lives.

She sat on the bed and gripped the bed rails nervously. Scoreggia stood next to her, shifting his weight impatiently from one foot to the other.

"Vincent, please stand still. You're not making this any easier."

"I am standing still!"

She sighed.

"I can hear your shoes on the floor, the rustle of your pants."

He mumbled something to himself and sat in a chair across from her.

Quick taps approached. Scoreggia jumped to his feet. Angelica closed her mouth and steeled her nerve.

Havok and Elisabéta Pascucci entered the room. Havok was speaking with Angelica's doctor.

"Yes, Mr. Havok," the doctor said. "The procedure was a total success. The synapses are responding as they should and her body has not rejected the new tissue."

"Good morning, Doc," Scoreggia said.

Scoreggia exchanged greetings with them all. Angelica remained silent.

The doctor approached her.

"How are you this morning, Mrs. Scoreggia?"

"Smart-Scoreggia," she snapped.

"Of course. As I was just telling the good Mr. Havok here, the procedure—"

"I heard you," she interrupted.

"I'm going to take the bandages off. And you should be able to see."

"Perhaps. Get on with it."

"Babe," Scoreggia whispered, leaning close to her. "What's wrong with you?"

"Do *they* really need to be here," she whispered back.

Scoreggia looked at Havok and Elisabéta.

"Don't you want them to share in this big moment?"

"It's *our* moment. Please."

Scoreggia shook his head and stood up.

"Go ahead, Doc."

Using a pair of scissors, the doctor cut into the white gauze and then slowly unwrapped the bandages from around her head, exposing her closed eye lids and a band of red, irritated skin.

"That's it," the doctor said. "Now, Mrs. Scoreggia, all you need to do is open your eyes."

"*Smart-*Scoreggia," she corrected again.

The doctor sighed.

"Of course."

She opened her eyes slowly, then blinked furiously. She held her head perfectly still. Her eyes were dull with a blank, straight forward stare. The slants of her eyes trembled and her hands, set in her lap, raised and then crossed over her lap again. She turned her head about the room, her eyes still immobile and dull, and squinted.

"Well, Babe," Scoreggia said eargerly. "How do I look?"

"There's no change," she said matter of factly. "Nothing is different."

Scoreggia frowned angrily.

"What in Blazes, Doc," he shouted, advancing on the physician.

"Now, wait, wait," the doctor said, holding up his hands. "This—this—this is not unheard of! It could take a few hours, a few days, for the normal range of vision to be restored. It's improbable, but there are documented cases—"

"You never mentioned any of this before," Scoreggia yelled. "What kind of bullshit are you people selling around here anyway?!"

Havok stepped between Scoreggia and the doctor.

"Vincent, get control of your emotions. This is not the doctor's fault."

Scoreggia walked away, his back to them all, silently fuming.

Havok turned to the doctor.

"I take it we're finished here, then?"

"Yes," the doctor said nervously. "There—there are some after care items that need to be covered. And the final accounting."

"Let's go, Babe," Scoreggia said, pulling on Angelica's arm.

She yanked her arm away.

"I wish to remain here."

"Okay," Scoreggia said. He looked at Havok and Elisabéta. "You two go—"

"Alone."

Havok put his hand on Scoreggia's shoulder.

"Vincent. There are other matters that require your attention."

Scoreggia nodded reluctantly and they all filed out, leaving Angelica alone with her thoughts.

Angelica sat with her eyes closed. She barely had a minute to collect herself before Havok came back into the room. It didn't surprise her, she heard him coming. He stood there for a long moment and stared at her in silence.

"What do you want, Mr. Havok," she snapped.

"I know you can see."

"You don't know anything."

"Really?"

"Yes."

"You tried to act like the light wasn't affecting you. You couldn't fight the urge to blink, but you fought off squinting for as long as you could. You wanted to rub your eyes, but stopped yourself just in time. Even Elisabéta noticed. Your husband may be a detective, but he's not a good one."

She shifted her weight uncomfortably.

"Please leave. Thank you for all this, you've been very generous, but we don't want or need anything else from you."

"You don't like me, do you?"

"What's to like, Mr. Havok? You goaded my husband into danger, seduced him with your wealth, taken over our lives. Please leave us alone."

He nodded.

"I can change your mind."

"No, you can't."

"For how long are you going to keep up this pretense with your vision?"

"I'm done speaking with you."

He pulled up a chair and sat down across from her.

"Do you recognize the sound of my voice?"

She sighed through her nose and sat up straighter.

He cleared his throat and when he spoke next, his accent changed.

"Do you remember the first time we ate at Costoso Merde? How excited you were? How hard we laughed after I asked the waiter how much the main course was, because there were no prices on the menu?"

She searched her memory, then all of the color drained from her face.

He smiled matter of factly.

"Do I sound familiar to you now, Angel?"

Her eyes suddenly opened, opened very wide.

"*Look* at me," he demanded. "Am I familiar to you?" He ran a hand over his face. "Imagine me without the beard and mustache, shorter hair, and much thinner."

She peered at him as if looking through a long tunnel.

Her mouth quivered.

"You remember, Angel," he nodded, smiling. "You remember the time we skipped school and I rowed us out to the woods, across the lake?"

She put a hand over her open mouth.

"P-Pierce? Pierce Sicuro? How in the name of Clorox and Peroxide..."

He smiled at her sadly.

"Yes, Angel."

Overwhelemed with shock and confusion, she stood up and backed away from him.

"I-I don't understand how..."

"This must be a complete shock to you. I know you thought I was dead."

"Dead? I never thought you were dead! The last time I saw you was the night before I left for college, when I broke it off!"

"Broke it off?" He seemed confused. He stood up and paced a bit, a flesh colored glove stroking his beard. He realized this, then put it back into his coat pocket. "You must return with me to Atro Viscus, so I can explain all of this to you."

"I'm not going anywhere with you. I barely even remember you. The only place I'm going is back to my own home."

"Angel, please. That last night we were together, my family was killed and I was held prisoner by the Abernathé's—"

She put her hands up over her ears.

"Stop! Stop! Stop! I can't listen to anymore of this! The Abernathés may be a powerful and rich family, but they're not thugs or mobsters! They're jewelers, for Clorox's sake!"

"I can prove it all to you." He hesitated. "Listen to me carefully. You are in grave danger. You must leave with me now."

He moved closer to her and she backed away. He grabbed her arm and held her fast.

"It was you," she gasped. "The hospital on Nostrova! You—"

"Yes," he said quickly. "I'm sorry for that, it was a mistake, but the Abbies and Charlie Squares were both searching for me, and you were in danger because of it."

"Take your hands off me," she shouted.

"Angel, please..."

"You stay away from me! Vincent!"

A look of desperation crossed his face.

"Angel. I am a Lethean Praetor. I have limitless wealth and power. I can protect you."

"Vincent!"

"You don't want to believe me, but now that you can see, now that your eyes are open, you go back to your life."

"Vincent!"

"And the next time you see Young Lorenzo, you look at him, and look at him closely. If he reminds you of me in *any* possible way, in a brief gesture, an odd facial expression, his posture, I want you to contact me. Promise me that, and I will leave you now."

"The only person I'm in danger from is *you*," she shouted, breaking his grip. Her hands curled into angry fists at her side. "VINCENT!"

"But you musn't tell anyone who I really am," he begged her. "Especially Young Lorenzo!"

"VINCENT!"

Scoreggia burst into the room, out of breath.

"What in Blazes is going on in here?"

He looked from Havok to Angelica and back again.

Havok averted his eyes as he adjusted his coat on his shoulders.

"Angelica has some very good news for you." He glared at her. "Her vision has returned. She could not contain her excitement."

Scoreggia looked at her and his expression lightened.

"Really?"

She looked at Havok crossly, then at Scoreggia and forced a weak smile.

"Yes."

He moved past Havok and took her in his arms.

"See, Babe? I told you it'd be okay! Hey, Sal—"

Scoreggia turned around and Havok was gone.

"What the—? What was he doing here, anyway, Babe? He excused himself to make a call."

"Nothing, Vincent. Everything's fine."

His brow furrowed in anger and suspicion as he stared at the empty doorway.

"Sure, Babe. Whatever you say.

Elisabéta sat across from Havok in his private study, a very large desk between them. She had never been in this room before, which meant that no one else had either, but she wasn't focused on her surroundings. Since their return from the hospital, Havok had been behaving very oddly, as if angry, but unfocused. He liberally sampled a bottle of his favorite Hestian rum, refilling an ice encrusted glass to the very top. He couldn't sit still, turning anxiously in his chair or his arms moving this way and that. She had never seen him so agitated.

Her presence here spoke volumes about her place in the pecking order, yet it still fell far short of the place she longed to occupy in his life. She admired him for his simplistic, yet resolute belief in right and wrong. He had started from nothing and built this place, Atro Viscus, with his own two hands. The opportunities he provided for the disenfranchised earned him the respect and admiration of everyone who worked for him. Surrounded by all this success and affection, he seemed unsatisfied.

Restless.

His brow furrowed in anger.

He slammed his glass on the desk, rum sloshing over the sides, as if coming to some sort of conclusion. Only then did she have his undivided attention.

"I'm sorry, Elisabéta. It's been a difficult day."

"I understand, Mr. Havok."

"The Scoreggias?"

"They booked passage back to Nostrova, refusing the first class arrangements you made for them."

"What about Hossenfuss?"

"He has recommended the renewal of your license, with the concurrence of Admiral Emmett. Official confirmation is pending."

"And Class?"

"Mr. Class has made a cryptic inquiry about a separate transaction. I did not authorize any additional transactions."

Havok nodded knowingly.

"It was something I initiated personally, Elisabéta."

She started involuntarily.

"You need to let me know these things, Mr. Havok! I wouldn't want to inadvertantly interfere with your concerns."

"No need to worry, Elisabéta. Is that it?"

"No. We need to discuss Mr. Abernathé."

"Young Lorenzo, yes?"

Elisabéta nodded.

Havok sighed, his cheeks red.

"Did he keep his appointment with you?"

"He did, only to insist that he meet with you personally. Since then, he's been contacting me daily, being forceful in his own polite way, to set up a meeting with you."

"And your opinion of him?"

"Personally or professionally?"

"Both."

She hesitated.

"Young Lorenzo is not yet his father."

"Very perceptive," he said ruefully. "And accurate."

"He still wants to meet with you."

Havok considered the glass of rum, then emptied it.

"Hmm. Has he said about what?"

"Yes. He's interested in the precious stones on display in the main dining room. You said to expect this. You also said to keep stalling him."

"Is he interested for himself? Or for his damned father?"

"He said himself. He was very clear that he does not represent his father."

"And how does he expect to pay for these precious stones he covets so, so greatly?"

"Nothing has been said about a purchase. When I pressed him further, he finally confessed that he would discuss that subject only with you."

"Of course."

Elisabéta's ear pierce beeped, very softly.

"Yes?"

She listened for a moment. He refilled his glass and drank some more.

"Vincent Scoreggia has landed at the carport on the coast."

"Really? You just said he'd left for Nostrova."

"A deception, apparently. He's demanding to see you. In an official capacity."

Havok seemed unfazed.

"Well, then I guess I better see him then," he said off handedly. "Have him escorted up."

He slammed the empty glass on the desk top.

"I want you to greet him," he said. "Be difficult."

She turned to leave, then paused. She glanced over her shoulder apprehensively. He sat completely still, his chin buried in his chest.

He spoke to her without looking up.

"You can leave now, Elisabéta. Thank you."

She nodded and left.

Scoreggia slouched angrily in the grand foyer, his badge gleaming from the front pocket of his jacket. He refused the seat offered to him by the usher. He thumbed the sidearm at his waist heavily, unintimidated by the armed rent-a-cops just outside the door behind him. He knew he was being watched. Just because he couldn't spot the cameras didn't mean they weren't there. It had taken almost an hour to get up here and he had stood like this for another hour, waiting for Havok. It didn't make him any less angry. He heard the approach of quick taps. His whole head flushed a deep red as he stood up straight.

Elisabéta Pascucci entered, dressed smartly in a dark blue business suit. He met her congenial smile with a scowl.

"Hello, Mr. Scoreggia. How nice to see you again so soon."

"Where's Havok? Bring him out here. I'm here in an official capacity conducting the business of the IBI."

"You can speak to me as Mr. Havok's attorney."

"Not you. *Him*."

"For what purpose?"

"He's a person of interest in an open investigation."

"What sort of investigation?"

"Again, this only concerns him. Produce him, *now*, or I will return with a warrant and an army of agents, and we'll pick this place clean."

She allowed herself a bit of a smirk.

"An empty threat, Agent Scoreggia. You do know that this is Lethe? No warrants will be served on Atro Viscus."

"No, no. No local bullshit. I'm talking about a Web warrant. I'm not leaving until I speak with that son of a bitch."

"I don't like your tone, Agent," she said crossly. "Mr. Havok gives his regrets."

"I'm not leaving."

"Agent Scoreggia," she said patiently. "You are now trespassing on private property. I will have you forcibly removed."

"Go ahead and try it."

Elisabéta touched her earpiece and was about to speak. Then Havok entered from the dining room.

"There will be none of that," Havok said, waving off Elisabéta. She retreated a few steps and clasped her hands in front at the waistline.

"What is the meaning of this, Vincent," Havok demanded. "What do you want?"

"Not in front of her," he said.

"Ms. Pascucci is my attorney. What you say to me, you say to her."

"Gonna hide behind the skirts of a woman, Sal?"

"Speak. Or leave."

"Fine. If it wasn't for her, I wouldn't be here, anyway."

"Excuse me?"

Scoreggia smiled nastily.

"Thought you could do whatever you wanted, because you're rich? Didn't count on the help telling me that Angelica was calling for me?"

Havok glanced at Elisabéta, who stood impassive.

Scoreggia advanced on Havok.

"At the hospital, you thought you could just have your way with her, right there? Hm? Was that the idea? Get yourself off, taking what you want, with me just down the hall?" Scoreggia pointed an angry finger to his chest. "You stay away from my wife, do you understand?"

"Do not yell at me, Vincent."

"I know what you're up to," he shouted. "This whole thing with inviting us here, fixing her eyes, the donations to the University! It all makes sense now! You coming on to my wife, making a fool out of me in front of everybody? Gonna force yourself on her, right under my nose?! You think you can get away with that?"

"Vincent—"

"You shut your damn mouth," he screamed, his face purple. "You stay away from her, or so help me Clorox you will regret it!"

"You'd best lower your voice, Vincent."

"Or what, huh?! You gonna make me? You're talkin' to the 'I' now, pal. The 'I'! Lay a finger on me and I'll have your ass in custody before nightfall."

"And if I do, you'll only go home and take it out on her. If you already haven't."

"What did you say?!"

"You beat Angelica. You banged her head on a bedpost until you blinded her. Do you deny it?"

Scoreggia fumed silently.

"Could your reputation survive such an allegation," Havok pressed. "Come now, Vincent, it's no secret. The same as it is no secret that she would be better off with me."

Scoreggia sputtered, then screamed, "I'll fucking kill you!"

He took a swing at Havok and Elisabéta let out a startled yelp. Havok caught his fist with an open hand, then crushed it.

Scoreggia grimaced terribly and reached for his gun.

Havok grabbed him roughly by the lapels and casually threw him into the stone wall. He rebounded to the floor with a loud crack.

Havok stood over him.

"Anything else, Vincent?"

Scoreggia collected himself, clutching his hand, and unsteadily got to his feet.

"Yeah, Sal, yeah. One more thing. Your dining room was decorated with diamonds. Not just any kind of rocks, but rocks casting octagonal rainbows. Just like the kind that were lifted from the Hotel Vestitia ten years ago. Know anything about it?"

"Don't answer him, Mr. Havok," Elisabéta called out from behind him.

Havok nodded and backed away.

Scoreggia smiled, wiping spittle from his chin.

"I bet you know all about it."

Havok turned and left the room.

Armed security entered the foyer.

"Please show this man the way back to the coast," Elisabéta ordered. "His return is not permitted under any circumstances."

"I'll be back," Scoreggia said.

Elisabéta walked away.

"I'll be back," he shouted.

Havok retreated to his private study and took three discs from one of the desk drawers. He held them in his hands and shuffled them absent mindedly as he gazed out the window. A line of red stormclouds approached. He watched until the clouds eclipsed the sunlight and the sound of thunder rolled across the heavens. In the premature darkness, he considered the shredder, then placed the three discs in a line on the desk top.

He depressed a button to call for Elisabéta. He was interrupted before he could speak.

"THERE YOU ARE!!"

Havok looked up and there stood Menscher, arms spread wide, clinging to the door frame in his black cloak, his head bobbing low, like a vulture.

"WHAT IN BLAZES WAS THAT ALL ABOUT??!!"

Havok put a hand to his temple.

"Eiger, please stop yelling."

"That was her husband, wasn't it? You're still consumed by that woman!! What about Abernathé?!"

"Eiger—"

Menscher pointed an angry finger at him.

"That damned woman doesn't love you! She never has and you can't make her!"

Havok bolted around the desk and grabbed Menscher by the front of his cloak.

"You will not speak of her like that," he shouted back. "You have no idea! I have wealth! I have an estate! I have a grand home! I am a Lethean Praetor! All the things she covets! *I* am *better* THAN HIM!"

Menscher, wide eyed in shock at the outburst, tried to back away, but Havok only pulled him closer.

"I invited Abernathé and his son," he shouted into his face. "And they didn't come! How dare you question my motives?! They killed my family! They let my girl fall into the clutches of that monster! They killed my only friend in this whole galaxy! They took ten years of my life! The only thing I can get back is Angelica and who in Blazes are you to tell me how to make that happen?! Of course she loves me! I will make her see that!"

Menscher tried to wriggle free from Havok's grasp, arms flailing.

"This—this was always about revenge," Menscher rasped. "To kill the Abernathés! That was enough to balance the scales! You promised—the youngest of them has been after you for weeks, we have him in our clutches, and you hesitate? This loyalty to your false lineage makes no sense! *I* am your family!"

Havok screamed in anger and hurled Menscher across the room, knocking him into a display case. Glass shattered and the precious items within clattered to the floor. Menscher fell on his hands and knees, gasping for breath.

"You listen to me, Eiger! She loves me—"

"No," he gasped. "She doesn't."

"SHE DOES!"

"Not then, not now."

"I AM BETTER THAN HIM!"

"But she doesn't love you, no matter what you give her."

Havok turned away in a boiling rage and slammed his fist on the desk, cracking the finish in a spider web pattern.

"She just doesn't understand! But I can convince her! What do you know of love, Eiger? In any form? Your sole reason for revenge is just some genetic short circuit! My reasons are true. I will get them! I will get them all! I have a plan. And I've never broken a promise to you, Eiger."

Silence fell between them, neither of them moving. Outside the window, thunder rolled and lightening crashed. Rain began to fall, spitting at the window like bullets.

A voice called out of the semi-darkness.

"Mr. Havok!"

Elisabéta clacked into the room, flush and flustered.

"Mr. Havok, is everything okay? I heard a commotion."

She looked at Menscher, still sitting on the floor in the remains of the display case.

Menscher picked himself up and brushed some broken glass from his cloak.

"I can't stay here as long as you're fixated on that woman. I'm leaving. Leaving here forever."

Havok snorted.

"Do whatever you feel is necessary, Eiger. I will miss you."

Menscher turned his nose up and swept from the room.

"Your brother is leaving again," Elisabéta asked.

"Yes," Havok confirmed. "Have him followed until he returns. The ususal."

"Yes, Mr. Havok."

Menscher threatening to leave was a regular event and every once in awhile, he followed through. He never left the grounds of Atro Viscus and usually sulked about in the outer buildings and machine shops at the edge of the Third Circle, then returned after a day or two.

"And Scoreggia?"

"Personal issues aside, he believes you to be the perpetrator of what is known in the popular vernacular as the Vestitian Job. The diamonds on display in the dining room do indeed fit the profile of the stones described. Based on that alone, he could get a Web warrant, but it will take time."

"Have his train delayed on the rail line. Block any communications devices he may be carrying. I don't want him contacting anyone for the next twenty five hours."

"Yes, Mr. Havok."

"There are three discs here on my desk. I want the data on them transmitted immediately." He handed them to her one at a time. "This one to James Class. This one to Sta'an Hossenfuss. This last one to the Board of Directors of Elysian University. Are my instructions clear?"

"They are, Mr. Havok."

"Are you sure?"

She pursed her lips.

"Yes."

"I don't want any misunderstandings, like at the hospital. I told you to keep Scoreggia away and yet you directed him back into my presence."

"Yes, I did."

"Do not presume to interfere in my affairs. Ever. Do you understand?"

Elisabéta took a tiny step forward and took a deep breath.

"Mr. Havok, I've worked for you for a long time. I am loyal to you and only you. But your infatuation with Angelica Smart-Scoreggia is incomprehensible. No good can come of it."

His expression darkened. His eyes narrowed into thin white slits, his face taught. She wilted under the severity of his gaze.

"I'm sorry if I overstepped, Mr. Havok. I have only your best interests at heart."

"I will say this only one more time. You will never again interefere in my personal affairs. Do you understand?"

A chill ran up and down her spine.

"Yes, Mr. Havok."

He waved her out and then sat heavily in his chair, looking out into the storm.

Chapter 23
Fear and Loathing

Max Siniscolchi stood on the car port platform, very near the edge, and looked out over the ocean. His customary black suit puffed and flapped in the breeze, and his polarized sunglasses reflected the intensity of the sun. He breathed in this brief moment of calm. There were so few of them these days.

He ignored the extra security that buzzed around him, faceless drones that flitted about, irritating and omni-present in this time of war. It was a necessary evil. Summa Avarici and Castel Mons had to be protected at all costs.

The aircar he had been waiting for appeared in the distance and rapidly approached. The non-descript black limosine first circled high over the entire compound before landing in the center of the platform.

Siniscolchi waited impatiently.

The attendants opened the door and out stepped Lorenzo de Abernathé IV, smiling broadly from ear to ear. He struck a pose, as if there were photographers present, and smoothed his jacket and tie. As his things were unloaded from the trunk of the car, he gave quick instructions to the valets, and then walked over to Siniscolchi.

"Hello, Max!"

The two men shook hands.

"Hello, Lorenzo. How was the trip from Nostrova?"

"All very good. I'm so glad to be home!"

"Good to have you back. Did you instruct the driver to circle the compound?"

"He said he wasn't allowed, but I told him it was okay. It's been a long while, I wanted to see if everything was as I remembered."

"Don't ever do that again," Siniscolchi admonished. "AbStone is at war. There's no reason to give the driver a good look at the place."

"Hasn't he been vetted?"

"*Everyone* has been vetted, but there's still no reason to take any chances. Also, it was dumb to announce your return and then to pose outside the car like that, like it was a photo op. That was twice inside of five minutes that you gave someone a clear shot at you."

"Max, c'mon, what could happen here? We're safe!"

Siniscolchi only looked at him.

"Okay, Max," Young Lorenzo said sheepishly. "If you say so."

"Now that you work for the company, you've gone from being a tertiary target to a primary one. No more grandstanding for the media. You will lower your profile. You will conduct yourself accordingly. Do you understand?"

Young Lorenzo grinned smarmily.

"Yes, it means you work for me."

"Rather the opposite. I work for your father, which means *you* work for *me*. You're here at my insistence, over your father's objections. I can have you removed in an instant. You will conduct yourself accordingly."

Young Lorenzo stiffened a bit, then smoothed his hair.

"Okay, Max. I get it."

"Let's go. We shouldn't spend so much time out in the open."

They walked inside and were escorted by security to the elevator. Once in the elevator, they were alone.

"How akward was it leaving the University," Siniscolchi asked.

Young Lorenzo grimaced a bit.

"Well, they perp walked Angelica Scoreggia out of the place. It was unnecessary, but it looked good on Suetonia. For the last few weeks leading up to it, her mind was elsewhere. Made it easier for me to maneuver."

"Undoubtedly she was distracted by her husand's disappearance."

"Yes. The charges brought against him by the IBI, bribery, abuse of authority, influence peddling, racketeering, and the rest. Once they added spousal abuse, he vanished without a trace."

Siniscolchi nodded.

"So what is the truth in all this, Lorenzo?"

"As far as I can tell, it was the result of an internal investigation by the IBI into Scoreggia that spilled over to EU. Apparently, Scoreggia investigated this break in at one of Havok's companies, Pollone Presa Outfitters. Over the span of a year or so, Scoreggia demanded bribes from Havok to continue the investigation. These bribes were paid out as larger and larger donations to EU, where Havok was already a significant contributor, so Mrs. Scoreggia could take credit and increase her standing. As part of the pay off, they were both invited to the party at Atro Viscus, but only Angelica received an official invitation, so as not to arouse suspicion. While at the party, Scoreggia threatened Havok with preventing his defense contractor license renewal if he didn't pay to restore Angelica's eyesight. After that, Scoreggia returned to Atro Viscus to extort more favors in return for his protection, and that's when Havok finally had enough and reported him. Scoreggia was suspended pending an investigation."

"Yes. That's what was reported by Suetonia. Now the truth, Lorenzo."

"The truth?"

"A man like Havok, bullied over such trivial nonsense?"

Young Lorenzo nodded in agreement.

"Over the years, Angelica was never comfortable with the huge sums of money donated by Havok, nor his demands through Pascucci—always through Pascucci—that no one else handle the transaction but her. The Board ignored her requests to look into things further and promoted her up the line."

"And?"

"Part of the evidence against Scoreggia is that the criminals who perpetrated the break-in at Pollone are now all telling the same story from prison."

"And that is...?"

"That they were hired by Scoreggia to stage the break-in, and that Scoreggia double crossed them by arresting them and then sending them to prison."

"This Vincent Scoreggia presents himself as quite the mastermind, so easily setting up and controlling such an influential and powerful man as Salestus Havok." Siniscolchi sighed. "Is any of it true?"

"No."

"You're sure?"

"Yes. I've seen most of this unfold with my own two eyes and the official version makes no sense. And the rest of it, I just don't believe. Well, except for the spousal battery part. That I believe."

"Evidence?"

"Plenty of it, from what I hear. That's why Scoreggia bolted. I don't like the guy. He's the biggest jerk in this galaxy, but I think he's being framed. He probably fell out of favor with his bosses and they're just using this as an excuse to get rid of him."

"Possibly. And Havok?"

"Media shy, as ever. Although he did submit an affidavit through his attorneys, essentially confirming all the charges."

The elevator came to a stop, the doors opened and they stepped out. More security greeted them.

"Max, you should meet this man, Havok! His estate at Atro Viscus is breath taking! It doesn't compare to Summa, but is still excellent in all respects!"

"So it's true that you've actually met this ghost?"

"Met him? I spent two weeks in his company. A fascinating man. He aspires to be a true Lethean gentleman."

"Aspires?"

"There are times when he prefers things to be harder than necessary. He has a scar on his face to prove it."

"What else?"

"We share a vague resemblance, it was the subject of some humor while I was there, while we..." A shiver went down Young Lorenzo's spine and he paled a bit, his hand impulsively going to his neck and running down his chest. "While we, um, hunted game, in the woods around his home."

"And? Was it as dangerous as they say?"

Young Lorenzo smiled weakly at first, then beamed.

"Mr. Havok not only proved a true gentlman, but an exceptional outdoorsman. With his guidance, nothing I couldn't handle."

"Good. I must commend you, Lorenzo. Your father was impressed that you managed to keep the family name from being associated with any of this."

"I'm afraid it's only temporary. For the last three months, since Angelica got fired, I've been covering my tracks while securing the services of three seniors, pending graduation, to fill the quota for the two geologists and chemist my father wanted."

"Your resignation was accepted without question?"

"In fact, with enthusiasm. In their next feed, Suetonia is going to break the story that EU was operating as a recruiter for AbStone. They're glad to be rid of me."

"We know about the story and it won't run."

They paused outside the doors to the elder Lorenzo's office.

"I didn't think anyone could get to Suetonia."

Siniscolchi smiled, pocketing his sunglasses.

"We couldn't risk you becoming the face of this story."

Siniscolchi opened the door and Young Lorenzo walked in first. Lorenzo de Abernathé III sat behind his desk, but stopped working and stood up when they entered. He shook his son's hand firmly.

"Welcome home, Lorenzo."

"Thanks, Dad."

They all sat down, and the young man could scarcely contain his excitement at being in the presence of his father, in his business office, and conducting business. He marveled at this room, a room he had never seen.

"Lorenzo," his father said, "as I'm sure Max has already told you, your work at Elysian University is finished. Even if it weren't for the scandal there, I was already prepared to call you back home.

"You will be working for AbStone under the direct supervision of Max here. You will do what he tells you to do. You've already had all of the necessary formal education. Now it's time to apply that knowledge. You will learn the size and scope of our operations, how everything works. There's the right way, the wrong way, and then the way it's actually done. And I still don't think you have the stomach for the way it's actually done."

The excitement vanished from Young Lorenzo's eyes. He sat up straighter.

"I can do the job, Dad."

"Lorenzo, we are at war with the Cathedrals. It was bad for AbStone in the beginning, but now that Max is running things, the tide has slowly turned. We have fought them to a stalemate, taking advantage of espionage and other extra legal tactics, but mostly by avoiding traditional battlefield encounters. However, we do not have the resources for an open ended conflict. With great reluctance, and as distasteful as it was, we recently resorted to blackmailing the government and have gained a bit of an advantage.

"We are still engaged in scattered armed conflicts over new mineral deposits on a dozen worlds. We are still raiding the Cathedral supply lines and shipping lanes, or having them seized, or at the very least delayed, by our new allies in the government. With the government on our side, we have the Cathedrals on their heels, however briefly."

"But not beaten."

"No, far from beaten. Our forced alliance with the government will not last forever and then we will lose the upper hand. Blackmail is never a long term solution and there can be a terrible backlash if exposed."

"What information could we possibly have that could intimidate the government?"

"*Your* concern," Siniscolchi interjected, "is generating long term revenue streams for AbStone. We need to be better prepared for when the conflict with Cathedral resumes in earnest."

Young Lorenzo nodded.

"I can handle that."

His father turned to the side in his chair, his face hidden by tented fingers, not looking at either of them.

"Our sources of revenue are strained," Siniscolchi explained. "We need new ones. And quickly."

"Perhaps we should consider—"

"Not now," his father snapped. "Get settled. Get your staff organized. Do your research. Come up with a plan. Only *then* do you talk to Max. This isn't complicated, Lorenzo."

"Okay, Dad. Sure."

"It's either 'sir' or Mr. Abernathé. You work for AbStone now."

"Yes, sir."

"You can leave now."

Siniscolchi nodded at Young Lorenzo reassuringly, and he got up and left. It was quiet until the door clicked shut.

"Dammit, Max," Lorenzo exploded, still without turning. "You better keep him out of my way!"

"I will."

"What else?"

"Havok is Pierce Sicuro."

Lorenzo turned the back of his chair to Siniscolchi.

"New information, Max. *New* information. Not speculation."

"It's for certain, Mr. Abernathé."

Lorenzo spun around.

"How do you know?"

"You shouldn't be so quick to dismiss your son. He's actually met Salestus Havok, which, as you know, is not easy. He not only met him, but spent some time in his company."

Lorenzo made a fist and gnashed his thumb and finger together.

"Go on."

"Young Lorenzo told me that he and Mr. Havok share a 'slight resemblance', that Havok bears a significant facial scar, and that the rumors of him spending time in those woods are accurate."

"Superior level of athleticism?"

"Yes. Havok even took Young Lorenzo into those woods. Judging by his recollections, I believe that your son was seriously injured in the process."

Unfazed, Lorenzo leaned back in his chair, still grinding his fingers.

"Also," Siniscolchi continued, "Havok, in a roundabout way, is responsible for Young Lorenzo's return. He's the one who provided the authorities with the evidence against the husband of Lorenzo's boss, Vincent Scoreggia."

"He's still fixated on the girl, then?"

"Apparently so."

"And he tried to hurt me by exposing Lorenzo's recruiting efforts at EU."

"Apparently so."

"All these years," Lorenzo sighed. "Laying in the weeds. And now he's taking the offensive." He thought for a moment. "We need to relay this information to Breufogle."

Siniscolchi shook his head.

"We shouldn't. Let the Cathedrals remain focused on him. He's been virtually useless to us for a long time and this makes him useful again, now as a decoy."

"You're right. His usefulness is almost at an end. Now we know where the Ecks Stones are."

Siniscolchi shrugged.

"We don't know that for certain, but this Atro Viscus that he's built is a good hunch. It's one of the securest places in all of Lethe. Tough place to sneak into, tough nut to crack with conventional forces. I'd only recommend something that crass as a last resort."

"Because we have an in."

Siniscolchi smiled broadly.

"Yes, we do."

The three majestic blackstone buildings that comprised the home of The Praetor de Atro Viscus, the Tri-Towers, dominated the skyline of the Lethean arctic. In the shadows of the pre-dawn, the other residents of Atro Viscus stirred and came to life.

In the Viscian vernacular, the Tri-Towers were known as the First Circle. The smaller structures that surrouned the Tri-Towers housed the business offices that ran the interests of Salestus Havok, and was referred to as the Second Circle. Outside this business district was the Third Circle, an industrial zone made up of underground power stations connected by maintenance tunnels to the above ground manufacturing plants. On the fringes were a farm and some machine shops, which included a car garage and an airfield. The Third Circle also included the barrier walls and supporting outstations.

Those who worked in the Second and Third Circles lived in a cluster of homes set to the side, along the cliff line, in a small town known simply as The Village. From The Village, an electric tram called The Light Rail ran in a never ending loop along the outer edge of the Second Circle. All residents of The Village made the same short commute on The Light Rail every day. Denim clad workers, suited businessmen and the polo shirts of the scientists all traveled together.

John Perso, the personal tech for The Praetor himself, was no different. He boarded The Light Rail at Village Station. Wearing a weathered leather jacket and faded overalls, he appeared the same as any other craftsman in the rail car. He found a seat next to Donn Scientia, a plasmoid he knew, who worked as an engineer in the Second Circle. He set his canvas tool bag on the floor.

"Hey, there, John. I haven't seen you in over a month."

"Hello, Donn. Been busy, alotta work orders lately."

"Since I haven't seen you, I surmise the Tri-Towers?"

Perso nodded.

"First Circle stuff." He shrugged. "You know how it is."

Scientia's face morphed into a smile.

"Are those buildings so poorly kept?"

"They're just like anyplace else, I guess. Stuff breaks. Got to be fixed."

"It's good to be The Praetor's personal tech."

"Sometimes."

"Still haven't met him, have you?"

Perso smiled.

"There's always hope."

"Listen, we were talking around the office the other day. Is it true that the foundations of the Tri-Towers are reinforced with plastic steel? None of us were here when the foundations were dug and framed, but you were here, part of the original crews that built this place. I got quite a bit riding on your answer."

"How much did you bet?"

"Enough that I need to know the answer."

"And what answer did you bet on?"

"C'mon, John! Do you know?"

Perso smiled coyly.

"Of course I know."

"Well?!"

"Look, I shouldn't tell you," Perso whispered, looking over his shoulder. "But for you, I will."

"And?"

Perso hesitated.

"Questionite," he finally said. "We poured liquid questionite into the foundation."

Scientia laughed uproariously.

"Let me guess. And then a layer of unobtanium?"

"And adamantium and then vibranium."

Scientia continued laughing as the trained hummed along.

They cruised quietly along side the small buildings of the Second Circle. Street lights doused with the dawn and the interior lights of the buildings came on. Red shirted maintenance crews walked in small groups toward the nearest Light Rail station, smoking and talking with one another as they went. The red shirts worked overnight and made minor repairs to the infrastructure of the Second Circle. It was a very rare sight to see them so visible during prime hours. Both Perso and Scientia got off at the next stop as the red shirts got on. Yellow tape blocked off a section of the walk to allow a cement patch to cure, in order to repair a crack in the concrete. Further down the street, a lamppost glistened in the morning light with a fresh coat of paint.

"Reds are getting sloppy," Scientia observed. "You don't usually see this kind of stuff in the morning. Used to be that they'd have everything cleaned up long before."

"I'm sure it's not from lack of effort," Perso said. "Those guys work hard."

"C'mon, level with me John. I'll bet Havok's really got an army of Viscian trolls that swarm this place by night, buffing out every scratch and emptying all the trash cans, and by day has them in an underground dungeon running on treadmills and pedaling stationary bikes to generate power. You've been everywhere around here, from the top of the Tri-Towers to the bottom of the geothermal plant. Tell me you've seen them."

"You mean you haven't," Perso asked in disbelief. "You've been down into the injection wells, right?"

"Nah, I inspect the cooling towers and condenser units monthly, but spend most of my time in my office. But you, you've been everywhere, seen everything. You've been here since the beginning."

"If I tell all The Praetor's secrets, I'll be out of a job!"

"So then you do know!"

Perso winked at him.

"No, not really."

Perso had the distinction of being one of the very few who could claim to be part of the original work crews that built Atro Viscus. He was very casual about this, at times self-deprecating, but Scientia knew that he was heavily relied upon by The Praetor as he possessed detailed knowledge of the entire Viscian continent.

They reached an intersection and shook hands.

"See you later, John."

"Keep looking for those trolls, Donn," Perso said with a smile. "They're not as invisible as you might think."

They parted, walking in opposite directions. Perso continued onward for another kilometer, pausing periodically to examine the conditions of fireplugs, storm drains and building fronts.

He arrived at the front gate to the airfield and presented his credentials at the security check point. Upon entering, he put his tools in the back seat of an electric cart, put on a pair of sunglasses and drove off toward the hangar buildings in the distance. It took him almost half an hour to reach the hangars. Despite the unseasonably hot morning sun, he stopped to talk with everyone and assisted one of the sanitation crews in clearing a jam from their front end loader. In front of AV Hangar Number Four, he endured a final search of his person and his vehicle before being allowed to approach the personal hangar of The Praetor. He put on his gloves and pushed open the enormous doors to let the sunlight stream into building. The hangar was mostly empty, save for a collection of classic ground cars that lined one side and an equally impressive collection of aircars that lined the other. A vintage Viper class starship, a fiver, was off to the side, painted a sleek dark blue. A huge canvas partition hung from the ceiling that blocked the back third of the hangar from view.

He checked in with the building manager, M'Olto Polynice, a plasmoid.

"Good morning, Em."

"Hello, John! I didn't expect you today. The schedule has you returning next week."

"I serve at the pleasure of The Praetor," Perso said. "Sometimes schedules are just outlines."

"Aren't they all. Everything here is as you left it. No changes. No one has been in or out of here since you last checked in, except for R.B."

"Reeber was here?"

Polynice pointed to a stack of boxes on a wooden palette, wrapped in cellophane.

"You ordered those parts from the metalworks on your way out. He delivered them the day before yesterday."

Perso nodded, remembering.

"Yes, yes. Perfect timing, as always. What's on your agenda for today?"

Polynice looked at its e-pad.

"Not much. Crews are coming in to service the aircars in the morning and *The Strongest* in the afternoon. Another delivery from..." It glanced up at him. *"Bruin hides?"*

"Leather, Em. Leather. Looks like The Praetor's been hunting again."

"And how would you know that?"

Perso only smiled.

"Oh, come on, tell me, John," Polynice begged. "Tell me you weren't out in the woods with Havok!"

"I never said that."

"C'mon, you can tell me!"

"Let me know when the hides get here," Perso said. He waved over his shoulder, and ducked behind the canvas.

It was late afternoon before John Perso noticed his timepiece. He didn't remember Porbeagle class ships being this difficult. It had been one mistake after another from the start with this ship and his own fault for deciding to work from memory. He had spent the entire day hammering, banging and sawing at the frame in order to get the interior done just right. So often he found his work unsatisfactory, that he had ripped it all out and started over a dozen times already.

The engineers did a first rate job preparing the hull, engines and all the other hardware. The ship's outer skin was smooth and seamless, and just the right color to accentuate its smooth racing lines, with absolutely no imperfections. It handled easily and provided a soft, sweet ride in both the air and the void. The only problem was the interior.

The interior confounded him.

He couldn't get it right. Six months he had been working on this ship and nothing matched his memory. He thought today would be easy. After measuring, cutting and preparing the fresh leather, he hand stitched the fabric over the seat frames. Installing them proved more difficult, one frustrating false start after another. It didn't help that he was in even more of a hurry to finish.

Irritated, he wiped at the sweat on his face and neck, and cleaned his hands with a filthy rag. He glanced at the cockpit viewer and saw Polynice talking to Elisabéta Pascucci. They stood in the wide open entrance to the hanger and cast long shadows in the early evening sun. Polynice pointed at the hanging canvas and Elisabéta waved at the camera. He resumed working. After a few minutes, he couldn't help looking at the viewer again. She was still there. He cursed. He knew that if he continued to ignore her she'd just wait for him, all night if necessary. Perso reluctantly exited the small ship and was met by Polynice.

"John."

"Em."

"That pretty lawyer is here to see you again. The one Reeber calls a hot box of rocks."

"I know. Thanks."

Perso turned off the light over his neatly organized tool bench. He tossed the rag into a red disposal container, then locked it, along with the green one next to it. He picked up a clean rag and took it with him. All of the boxes from the wooden palette had been opened and the empty cartons were in a pile, surrounded by white packing peanuts and shredded cellophane. He gently kicked a stray box back into the pile as he pulled the canvas partition closed.

Perso approached Elisabéta with a slow, reluctant stride. He crossed the dark line of shadow and stepped out into the sun.

"Hello, Elisabéta."

"I'm sorry to interrupt, but I tried to reach you directly."

He reached into his pocket and thrust an e-pad at her.

"This is a list of repairs that need to be effectuated. I want them addressed this evening."

She looked over the list.

"Scratched fireplug at Third and D, tarnished standpipe at chem labs building, fading signage at—"

"And the overnight crews are getting careless," he interrupted. "Remind them that no trace of their work is to be visible during prime hours."

"I will see to it imm—"

"And that they should not be wearing their red uniforms on The Light Rail. Am I clear?"

She nodded warily.

"Now," he sniffed. "Why are you here?"

"As I said, I tried to reach you remotely."

"And?"

She cleared her throat.

"It's Eiger. He's—"

"—left Atro Viscus," he finished.

"How could you possibly know this?

He sucked air through gritted teeth.

"Has he reached out to Scoreggia yet?"

She frowned. He knew she hated it when he anticipated her news.

"Yes. Apparently, I came out here for nothing."

He nodded, still cleaning his hands.

"Apparently."

"You also wanted to be informed the next time I heard from young Lorenzo de Abernathé."

"Have you?"

"Not directly, but from his representative."

"And?"

"Mrs. Smart-Scoreggia has asked me to arrange a meeting for next week."

Perso stopped cleaning his hands and the color drained from his face. He took a few steps away from her, hands on his hips, and stared with gaping eyes at a blank point on the horizon.

"Mr. Perso?"

When he turned around, he was angry.

"Set up the meeting. Here. He comes alone. You are to have no contact with him upon his arrival. On the day of the meeting, you will instruct security at the carport to remain out of sight and only observe, no matter what they see. Is that clear?"

She was taken aback at the ferocity of his response.

"Y-yes, c-certainly. I-I'll—"

He closed in on her.

"Is there a problem, Elisabéta," he asked, through angry, pressed lips.

She looked around nervously. She couldn't see into the hangar and had no idea if anyone was within earshot. She continued to stammer.

He sighed impatiently.

"*I asked you a question.*"

"Mr. um, Perso," she whispered quickly, finding her courage. "Remember where we are."

"*I know where we are!*"

"Y-your vindictiveness toward the Scoreggias, EU and Young Lorenzo makes no business sense. I work for you, but I also care about what happens to you. Your recent pattern of behavior can only be described as self destructive. You've so alienated your only brother that he's finally left for good and you don't care. You act like you expected it."

"You are well compensated to carry out my instructions," he whispered angrily. "Or you can leave."

"You clearly covet Mrs. Smart-Scoreggia, at the expense of everything else. Did you have a prior relationship?"

"What have you learned," he hissed, suddenly alarmed.

She flinched.

"Nothing," she said innocently. "Your instructions regarding her are so matter of fact, as if you already know her likes and dislikes, her tendencies. Yet you seem surprised that she's now working for the Abernathés."

He looked around uncomfortably, his mouth pressed flat in anger.

"My personal life is no concern of yours."

She put her hands on her hips and looked up into his face.

"It is when it affects business and the running of this estate. I can't do my job properly if you completely ignore my counsel, and my counsel is to leave this woman alone, especially now that she's mixed up in both a government scandal and a corporate war. At least you're showing some sense in finally seeing Young Lorenzo. Cultivating a positive relationship with his family can only further your interests."

He looked down at her and put his finger in her face.

"Set up that meeting," he growled.

Then he turned and disappeared back into the dark shadow of the hangar.

Chapter 24
Young Lorenzo

Lorenzo de Abernathé IV walked with a quiet confidence through the wide halls of Atro Viscus. Accustomed to the trappings of obvious wealth, he was pleased to once again be working in his natural environment, rather than the bland offices of Elysian University. On his last visit here, he found the entertainment and guest rooms impressive, but even more so the private rooms that he now eased his way through.

Mr. Havok clearly had excellent taste. The understated décor and carefully controlled climate spoke to the obvious wealth of the owner, and his power. The track lighting along the floor and perfectly spaced table lamps offered a unique method of illumination, both warm and comforting, which offset the cold appearance of the blackstone.

Everything he had seen of Atro Viscus thus far spoke of a man who liked things quiet and calm, who preferred nighttime to day, and most of all privacy. Even after spending extended time in the company of Salestus Havok, this represented the sum of his knowledge about the man. He still didn't understand Havok's former preoccupation with EU, nor his enormous generosity in restoring Angelica Scoreggia's eyesight. How Havok got her into his father's clinic when he couldn't still baffled him. Angelica refused to speak of it, her only comment on the subject being that Havok was just trying to be nice.

It took little convincing to get Angelica to come work for him. Scoreggia left her shortly after his indictment and disappeared into the ether with all of their savings and whatever valuables he could carry. This, combined with her leaving EU in disgrace, left her with no options. She liked the life she had on Nostrova, but, with her reputation in ruins, she left as a pariah. Now she worked as his personal attorney and comprised the entirety of his procurement staff. Young Lorenzo had come to Atro Viscus today to make a deal for those diamonds that he saw last year at the dinner table. He needed this badly. He needed this to prove to his father that he mattered.

Young Lorenzo felt strangely comfortable here in Havok's home. The anxiety he felt upon landing at the carport on the coast had faded. He still had nightmares about the bruins, and at times wicked flashbacks when he fingered the faint scars on his chest. Still, he wasn't scared, at least not at this moment. He pushed to the back of his mind the lingering apprehension that Havok might insist on a hunting excursion, back to those Razorneck Pinefields, before agreeing to a deal for the stones.

The anthropod usher that met him at the door showed him through an archway which led to a modest sized room, clear of any affectations. A dark, dormant fireplace dominated the wall to one side. The stone floor stood shockingly bare, with a luxurious red carpet rolled up against the far wall. A wooden credenza adorned another wall from floor to ceiling and a thick layer of dust coated the empty shelves. The wall mounted candelabras lacked candlesticks. The sun shone brightly through large glass windows and dust particles sparkled in the shafts of light. Dust encrusted plastic sheets covered the few pieces of furniture, save for a clean desk and two chairs on the far side of the room. They appeared brand new, the only items in the room not choked with dust.

"Mr. Havok will be with you shortly, Mr. Abernathé," the anthropod clicked. "Make yourself comfortable."

Young Lorenzo was incredulous. This is where Havok wanted to meet?

Here?

"Of course," he replied politely. "Thank you."

The anthropod skittered away and Young Lorenzo approached the desk. It acted as more of a display case than a stationary. It had a glass top and a cavity below lined with crimson felt. Light filtered in from the sides and illuminated a single item, an item which instantly took his breath away.

Nestled snugly into the dark red felt sparkled a diamond bathed in brilliant octagonal rainbows. This diamond was identical to the one he had seen in the dining room, only bigger.

Much bigger.

He put his hand on the glass, transfixed with awe. The lines, the angles, were so perfect. He marveled at how such a thing could possibly exist.

As he gaped in wonder, an odd tinge poked at his gut. He gripped his stomach and resisted the wave of nausea that sent a chill through his entire body. He took several deep breaths and the feeling passed, but not entirely. He couldn't shake the chills.

Havok abruptly entered from a door in front of him. His hair was pulled back tightly into a ponytail. He wore the weathered overalls and heavy gloves of a common laborer. His head and shoulders were covered with flecks of wood and metal. He used a clean white towel to wipe sweat and saw dust from his face and beard. He dropped the now filthy towel on the display case and without a word, sat down across from Young Lorenzo.

Upon seeing Havok, Young Lorenzo forgot all about his stomach.

"Good morning, Mr. Havok," he said. He hesitantly extended his hand, not sure what to make of this entrance. "I'm very pleased to see you again."

Havok did not accept his outstretched hand. He acknowledged him with only the slightest nod of his head.

Young Lorenzo slowly withdrew his hand and for a moment, the smile faded from his face. Sitting akwardly, he regained his composure and smiled at Havok's very unfriendly scowl.

"I can't tell you how excited I am to be back here at Atro Viscus. I so enjoyed my last visit here."

"As I recall, the last time you were here you were mauled by a bruin."

"Yes, well, I like to think of it as a learning experience."

"A smart man knows his limitations."

"Ah, yes. Yes he does." Young Lorenzo's eyes flitted from the diamond in the table top to Havok's face. "My family is very interested in fostering a positive relationship with yours. You are clearly a man of immense means and also someone who wishes to become part of Lethean society. I believe that we can help each other to mutual advantage."

"I've seen how your father operates. He doesn't have too many happy business partners."

"Propaganda, Mr. Havok. A family as powerful as mine has many enemies, but even more allies."

"I've no interest in helping fund your conflict with Cathedral."

Young Lorenzo put his hand on the glass table top, right over the diamond. He glanced at it, then said, "Conflict? There's no conflict. They are a competitor, but there's no—"

"*Why* are you here?"

"I'm sorry, Mr. Havok, did I catch you at an akward moment? You seem unprepared for visitors. You did know I was coming?"

"I did."

Clearing his throat, Young Lorenzo continued.

"Mr. Havok, as you already know, I am no longer affiliated with Elysian University, as I was the last time we were acquainted. I now represent the interests of Abernathé Stoneworks."

Young Lorenzo put a briefcase on the table and opened it. Havok looked out the window, disinterested.

"Also, as you already know, Angelica Smart-Scoreggia now works for me. There are some legal matters that need to be resolved regarding the transactions she handled for you at Elysian University before I can—"

With one finger, Havok pushed the lid of the briefcase back down onto Young Lorenzo's hands. His finger left a black smudge of grease on the fine leather.

"What is it you want," Havok demanded, his finger still on the briefcase.

"I need to clear up these legal matters regarding—"

"I have no interest in that sordid mess." He sighed impatiently. "Is this what you've been houding my business manager about?"

"No, Mr. Havok. I'm here to offer you an exclusive, lucrative opportunity to conduct business with Abernathé Stoneworks."

"I have no interest in entering into any kind of business arrangement with your father."

"Mr. Havok I think it wise that you to reconsider."

"*You* think it wise? Are you threatening me?"

"You should at least listen to my offer."

"I am not in the habit of repeating myself," Havok said irritably.

"Mr. Havok," Lorenzo pressed, "you profess to want nothing to do with my father. Yet you did invite him to your dinner party, did you not? Your actions suggest otherwise."

"And he didn't come."

"But I did."

"But not as a representative of AbStone."

"Mr. Havok, no offense was intended. My father is a busy man with many demands on his time..." Young Lorenzo paused, involuntarily glancing down at the diamond again.

"I—"

Havok sighed angrily and opened a panel on his side of the desk. He reached into the display case and picked up the diamond, then set it down roughly with a gloved thumb and forefinger on top of the glass.

"Is that what you're here for," he asked. "Then just come out and ask for it."

"It is a beautiful diamond. But what I'm proposing is not simply an exchange of goods."

Havok paused for a moment, looking beyond Young Lorenzo, over his shoulder.

"I'll tell you what," Havok said, annoyed. "Go back and tell your father that the only way I'll do business with Abernathé Stoneworks is if he brings himself down here and talks to me personally." He stood up and leaned over the desk. He took Young Lorenzo's hand and put the diamond in it. "Take this back to your father, as a gesture of respect, a token of my good will."

"Mr. Havok, this is very generous of you. I'm sure my father will be pleased."

"Generous? Can you really be swayed by a pretty rock? How about a whole box? I could have a fleet of starships filled with these diamonds delivered to your front door."

Young Lorenzo smiled.

"Surely, that's mere hyperbole."

"You question my sincerity? Do I strike you as someone who engages in trifles?"

"Mr. Havok, I meant no offense. I only—"

"Get out. Take your tribute and get out. Eb'by will show you the door."

"Tribute? Mr. Havok, you misunderstand—"

"*I said to get out.*"

Young Lorenzo looked over his shoulder and the anthropod usher stood waiting in the archway. He hefted the diamond in his hand and then looked at Havok's angry face. He put the diamond in his briefcase and left.

It was dark when Young Lorenzo almost danced off the mag-lev. Ebullient, he hummed happily to himself as he made his way through the rock cut back to the carport. He smiled up at the fanged ravens that cawed loudly and pecked at the metal grills. He couldn't wait to show his father this diamond. He tried to calculate its worth and amused himself at how much it would command at private auction.

And this was only the first.

Of many.

As soon as he reached the car and cleared Atro Viscus, he would contact Angelica and have her start drawing up a contract to give Abernathé Stoneworks an exclusive distributorship with Havok, a deal that would be worth zillions.

Zillions upon zillions.

This kind of wealth signaled the end of AbStone as a regional power. Cathedral could be bought and sold, brought to its knees, with NYSAAC soon to follow.

All because of me.

The greatest prize of all would be finally earning the respect of his father. No more snide remarks, no more being treated as an afterthought, no more banishments. Not only had he saved the company, but had also cracked the veneer of the enigmatic Salestus Havok. So what that he thought this was all a shakedown.

Screw him.

Save for a light pole next to his aircar, the carport was dark and barren. He stood at the end of the walk and waited for the valet. After a few impatient moments, he didn't see or hear anyone around. He waved for his driver to bring the car over. The limo hummed to life and hovered over the gravel, but remained idle. Because of the reflection of the light on the car windows, and the glare of the headlights, he couldn't see inside the vehicle.

No more of this nonsense, either, he mused. He sighed wistfully and strolled across the lot, humming a bit louder now. He could see the hands of his driver behind the controls. Why didn't he get out to open the door?

Whatever, Young Lorenzo thought. After today, no more second rate help. His first gift to himself would be to hire a beautiful girl to wash his dick every morning. His second would be a tricked out car and a new driver.

A girl driver.

As he approached the car his stomach knotted again, so he slowed his pace. These random stomach pangs were a rapidly escalating nuisance. He started to wonder if he had an ulcer or something worse. He decided to have a doctor look him over when he got back to Summa Avarici.

A girl doctor.

He opened the door himself and tried to remember the last time he had to do that, if ever. He sat down in the back seat and pulled the door shut.

"You're slacking off, Rahm," Young Lorenzo said, adjusting his overcoat. "You and the rest of the lot attendants. I need an extra smooth ride back to Summa. I've got a nasty bellyache."

Without a word, Rahm's head turned, only it wasn't Rahm. At first glance, it looked like Havok, then more like a cartoon version of the man.

"I'll bet you do," he said.

"Who in Blazes are you," Young Lorenzo exclaimed, alarmed.

He felt the cold metal of a gun press up against the back of his ear, then slide forward against his cheek.

"Hello, Larry," a familiar voice said.

He looked over his shoulder.

"Vincent?"

"That's right."

A black bag came down over Young Lorenzo's head and then cinched tightly around his throat. He struggled at the cord around his neck.

"Vincent! What are you doing?!"

"Shut up," Scoreggia barked, "and I won't kill you right here and now."

Young Lorenzo felt the barrel of the gun press into the back of his neck. He ceased his struggle.

"Just sit quietly, Larry. We're going for a little ride."

Chapter 25
Ab'baton's Furnace

Young Lorenzo gagged and sputtered desperately, gasping for breath. He couldn't see. Sweat burned his eyes and the cord chafed his neck. Panic churned up gallons of stomach acid and he rode the waves of nausea poorly, dry heaving with every slight bump of the aircar.

A single question screamed in his mind.

Why?!

Why was this happening?!

After only a few minutes, the car made a hard landing. A pair of hands pulled him roughly from the car, then dragged him across coarse, graveled pavement. After the creaky opening and thunderous closing of a thick door, he was lashed to a cold, metal chair. A few minutes went by that he didn't hear anything other than the sound of someone else's rapid breathing, and his own coughing and spitting.

He'd heard stories about things like this during wartime. Executives kidnapped and held for ransom or some other kind of leverage, sometimes by mercs, sometimes by double crossing employees. Is that what this was? A simple cash grab?

How could Vincent do this to him?

Without warning, the bag was yanked from his head and he gasped deeply, taking in as much fresh air as possible. He shook his head to clear his face and hair of perspiration and bile.

Young Lorenzo took in his surroundings.

He was in some kind of machine shop or monitoring station. They had to be somewhere near Atro Viscus, certainly still in the arctic. The car ride was too brief to be anywhere else and the air was cold. Metal consoles with exposed wiring ringed a cold furnace. Several boilers, and some other bulky machines that he didn't recognize, were all connected by oversized pipes that disappeared into the earth. The place had a damp, dank smell. Dust and cobwebs choked the air. A kerosene lamp on a thick metal table staved off the darkness.

And near that table stood his two abductors.

A thin, gaunt man in a dirty black cloak that resembled Salestus Havok. This man stared at him, his bloodshot eyes wide and mouth agape. He panted loudly like an animal in heat. Scoreggia lounged against the table, his arms crossed with a gun in one hand.

"What in Blazes is going on," Young Lorenzo shouted. "Vincent, untie me right now!"

Scoreggia rolled his tongue over his teeth.

"Mmmmmm. I don't think so, Larry."

"Gone to work for the Cathedrals? Now that the government won't have you?"

"I ain't no merc, you little douche bag."

"Where are we? And who is that?"

"I didn't bring you here to answer any of *your* questions."

"I *demand* that you let me out of here!"

"Scream and carry on all you want, Larry. No one's going to hear you out here."

Frustrated, Young Lorenzo struggled against his restraints. He felt weak, that pit in his stomach sapping all his strength. A thought flashed through his mind and he looked around the room feverishly for a moment, then strained to look over his shoulder.

"What're you looking for, Larry? This?"

Scoreggia held up the briefcase. Young Lorenzo stopped struggling and glared at him. Scoreggia chuckled and threw the briefcase aside.

"Or was it really this," he asked, taking the diamond from his pocket and holding it in a cupped hand.

"That diamond is the property of Abernathé Stoneworks," Young Lorenzo rasped, still sweating. "You will return it to me at once."

Scoreggia laughed.

"Sorry, Larry. This has been impounded as evidence."

"Impounded? You were dismissed from government service."

"You only wish," he sneered. "I've been suspended, pending an investigation, put on leave without pay. That's a long way from fired." He leaned over Young Lorenzo and held the diamond close to his face. "And this, you little pissant, this gorgeous gemstone is going to get me reinstated and then promoted, and your buddy Salestus Havok will be the one going to jail."

"You're crazy, Vincent. You'll be the one going to jail for this. Or worse. Angelica knows I'm here. She will tell my father and then it will be all over for you."

Scoreggia laughed.

"Angelica? *Angelica?!*" He became serious. "Yes, Angelica. Truth is, Larry, she was getting awfully mouthy since she got her vision back. Took care of that, though."

"By running away?"

Scoreggia's eyes narrowed.

"Good try, Larry. She'll keep her mouth shut, and at least for now, she still looks good standing next to me." He shook his head and stood back. He hefted the diamond in his palm. "This baby is my ticket out. Do you recognize it? It's stolen merchandise. From the infamous Hotel Vestitia. And your buddy, Havok, is going down for it."

For the first time, the other man's facial expression changed and he looked at Scoreggia with an odd curiosity.

"You think that's one of the diamonds from the Vestitian Job," Young Lorenzo burst out, incredulous.

Scoreggia tapped his temple with his gun.

"Not think. *Know.* I've done my homework. The diamonds taken in that heist had numerous but distinct characteristics, the least of which was casting octagonal rainbows, just like this one. There's no mistake."

"So what are you and your accomplice going to do next?"

The lower half of the other man's face sagged like molasses, and his lips curled with sinister glee.

"I'm going to kill you," the man said, his lips parting like silk. He took a long knife from under his cloak. He ogled Scoreggia for long moment, then stepped forward.

"Not so fast," Scoreggia said, clearly not intimidated. He looked at Young Lorenzo. "Why did Havok give this to you?"

"That's company business," he replied, his chest heaving.

"Always with the damned diamonds," the other man screamed. "Or it's the girl! It's always something! Delays, delays delays!" He tossed the knife into his other hand, which had six fingers. He pointed the knife at Scoreggia. "You promised me that if I got you in, you could get me him! I knew he'd invite him here sooner or later! And like always, I follow through on my promises and no one else does! All of that's over! Get out of the way, Scoreggia. I've waited a long time for thissssss..."

"Now wait just a second," Scoreggia said, arming his laser. "You stay right where you are. He's not going to get you his grandfather if he's dead. You kill him now and his father just sends a goon squad to shred your ass."

"LIAR," the man shrieked. "LIAR! I'LL KILL YOU, TOO!"

Scoreggia gave a slight nod toward his pistol.

"Think again, pal."

The other man only stood there, trembling with rage. An odd facial tick crossed the man's face and he dared not advance.

"You've no idea what you're dealing with," the man seethed.

Scoreggia seemed amused by him.

"Really? I think I do. The retarded brother of Salestus Havok is tired of being locked in the attic and wants a bigger piece of the pie. How far off am I?"

The man put a hand on his stomach and shook his head as if to clear his vision. Young Lorenzo winced as well and gasped harder for breath.

"We're running out of time," the man shouted, slamming his hand on the metal table, gripping the knife even tighter.

Scoreggia looked from one to the other.

"What in Blazes is wrong with the two of you?"

"He's here," the man growled.

Scoreggia shook his head.

"Ain't nobody getting in here. And nobody knows where we are." He turned his attention back to Young Lorenzo. "I got an urgent appointment back on Nostrova. Got a date to make myself a hero. I'm gonna leave you in the trusting hands of my new friend, here."

The man's sweaty face smiled.

"Truth is," Scoreggia said, "I don't care what he does to you, although it would be foolish of him to kill you now." He glared at the man out of the corner of his eye. "I don't even know what he has against you, although I imagine it's some kind of business dispute. You Letheans really know how to kill each other over a disc note. What I need to know, Larry, before I go, is *why* did Havok give this diamond to you? Today, of all days?"

"W-why don't you ask him yourself," Young Lorenzo gasped, sweat dripping from his nose.

Scoreggia spun around and held his weapon at the ready. His eyes scanned the dark, shadowy room and saw no one. There was only one way in and out, and it was a noisy one.

The other man wimpered and his shoulders rounded. His knife hand sagged, then his chin, and finally his eyes fell to the floor.

Scoreggia turned in time to see a shape melt out of the shadows, to see it glide toward him. A towering, monstrous shape clad in a black cloak. He instinctively backed away.

"So what kind of deal did you make with my brother, Vincent?"

Scoreggia tensed as Salestus Havok appeared at the edge of the light. He moved with a frightening calm, a calm that went beyond anger. Scoreggia's first impulse was to shoot him, but as the light shone on Havok's face it glistened over a sheen of sweat. Scoreggia looked at the three of them and first his face twisted, then his jaw went slack.

"What the fuck," he exclaimed. "Were the three of you separated at birth or something?" He looked at Young Lorenzo. "These two bastards looking to cut into the family loot, Larry? Horn in on your action?"

"My father and my, and my...my...," Young Lorenzo's voice trailed off, as if he couldn't say the word.

"I'll say you all got the same sweat glands." Scoreggia pointed his laser at Havok. "How in Blazes did you get in here?"

"It's my powerplant, Vincent."

"Yeah, funny thing about that. I've had a good look around. A really good look. Your brother tells me that this is where it all started. The Legend of Salestus Havok. That you started your business from here, laid the foundation for Atro Viscus here, all with your own two hands."

Havok said nothing, his face impassive.

"Truth is, this place has barely been used, Sal. That furnace can't generate enough heat to smelt metal, you got none of the proper tools or machines for mason work. This building isn't even hooked into the power grid. It doesn't even have its own power source. Looks like the Legend of Salestus Havok is all bullshit. You came from money. You didn't have to earn a single ducat, did you?" He turned and looked at the other man. "I get it all, now. The two of you. You're Abernathés. Cast offs. And now you're pissed."

The other man twitched a bit and looked anxiously from Havok to Young Lorenzo, and then back again.

"This is the last time I ask, Vincent," Havok said icily. "What kind of arrangement did you make with my brother?"

Scoreggia nodded, smiling.

"Oh, he told me all about you."

Havok's eyes turned on his brother, who wilted even further.

"And what did he say?"

"Told me all of your secrets. Told me he wanted Larry, but you kept getting in his way. I wanted the diamond. Even before my current legal troubles, I recognized this diamond as being from the Vestitian Job. I dented your security enough that we could abduct Larry, here. In return, your brother was to give me one of your diamonds. Larry having the diamond on him saved us some time."

Havok's face remained inscrutable. He didn't even blink.

Scoreggia raised his pistol.

"So, now, if you'll all just excuse me, I'll be leaving."

Havok advanced on him suddenly, his cloak billowing. Scoreggia expected this and got off three shots. Two of the red bolts passed right through Havok and scarred the stone wall behind him.

Havok grabbed Scoreggia by the throat with one hand and took the gun with the other.

"What in Blazes are you," Scoreggia cried out.

Havok took Scoreggia's hand in his own and crushed it. He took a fistful of the smaller man's coat and threw him with all his strength into the nearest stone wall. As Scoreggia writhed in pain on the grimey floor, Havok reached down and took the diamond from his pocket. He then wrapped some twine around Scoreggia's wrists.

Havok stood up unsteadily and turned on his brother.

"I'm very disappointed in you, Eiger," he whispered.

Havok's brother slumped even further, like a child caught with his hand in a cookie jar.

"I told Scoreggia nothing," he pleaded, near tears. "Please, he knows nothing."

"Now is not the time," Havok said gently, taking the knife away from him.

Young Lorenzo watched with relief as Havok's brother dragged himself into a dark corner.

"Mr. Havok, your intervention was very timely. And appreciated."

The entrance to the building opened slowly, with a loud groaning creak. Three canites entered, wearing the colors of Viscian security personnel.

Havok removed Young Lorenzo's restraints.

"Captain, please escort Mr. Abernathé to hospice. See that he gets whatever care he needs and please see that he is returned to Summa Avarici in perfect health and comfort."

The canite nodded.

"Yes, Mr. Havok."

Young Lorenzo's legs wobbled and the canite caught him before he fell.

"I seem to be a bit...light headed."

"You're in shock," Havok said. "You've been through a terrible ordeal. It will pass."

"I am in your debt."

"You owe me nothing," Havok responded, handing Young Lorenzo's briefcase to one of the canites. "I owe you an apology for my brother's behavior. Allow me to make this up to you in part by turning Mr. Scoreggia over to the Web authorities."

"That's not the Lethean way."

"True. But it's my way."

Young Lorenzo nodded, wiping sweat from his face with a dirty white sleeve.

"And your brother?"

"I will deal with him personally. Have Mrs. Smart-Scoreggia contact Ms. Pascucci. I'm sure a lucrative deal can be arranged regarding the diamonds that AbStone covets so earnestly."

Lorenzo smiled weakly.

"Of course."

"And I think it also in your best interest," Havok warned, "that you omit Agent Scoreggia's part in all this. For the sake of business."

Young Lorenzo seemed confused for a moment, then understood.

"Very good, then."

The three canites led Young Lorenzo out and shut the creaky, heavy door behind them.

The silence pounded in Havok's ears. The ever tightening knot in his stomach finally relented. He took deep cleansing breaths, but grimaced at the new pain in his side and leaned heavily on the table. He pulled his cloak aside and peered at the blackened wound just above his hip. His face contorted in terrible pain. He struggled to stand. Gradually, his breathing eased and he felt his considerable strength returning. He barely noticed Menscher charging out of the corner shadows.

"It's still all about that DAMNED GIRL," he shrieked, delirious with rage. "Even now you're still protecting her!"

Havok spoke with a distracted, vicious calmness.

"What did you tell Scoreggia about me?"

Menscher, his eyes rolling in hysteria, suddenly fixated on Havok. Then he melted, simpering.

"N-nothing, I—I did this for us. I had the child here. *Here.* Killing him would be one for us, yes? Make those bastards come to us, yes?"

"Eiger," Havok said, softening a bit. "You know that killing Young Lorenzo is wrong, don't you? The animosity you feel toward him is not genuine."

"DON'T YOU TELL ME HOW I FEEL!"

With difficulty, Havok came around the table and put both his hands on Menscher's shoulders. "It's not instinctual, but emotional. I know you feel it. Concentrate!"

Menscher tried to wriggle away, but Havok clenched the fabric of his cloak. Menscher's expression gradually changed. He stared in shock back at Havok.

Havok nodded knowingly.

"You feel it now."

Menscher nodded in return.

"H-how? I don't understand."

"There is still much more that we need to learn."

"Then we need to learn it! You can enter Summa Avaraci any time you want, yet you don't! And you let him leave here with one of the diamonds!"

Havok shook his head. He held up the diamond in his hand.

"I will enter Summa Avarici when the time is right."

Menscher was crestfallen.

"And you're done with the girl? At last?"

"Eiger…"

He broke free of Havok's grasp.

"You created this identity for yourself, *for her.* You got rich, *for her.* You built this place, *for her.* Well, what about me, *Praetor*? What have you ever done for me?"

"Eiger, don't start this again."

"You even fixed her eyes, with the same blasphemous science that created us, *and she still doesn't love you!* Yet you persist, you ruin her husband, strip away everything that's valuable to her, and you expect her to come crawling back to you? To say thank you? And you think *I'm* crazy?"

Havok turned away from him, clutching at the sides of his head in rage.

"Eiger! You don't understand!"

"I understand," Scoreggia coughed from the floor. "I should've... realized it sooner. That was you, Sal, on Nostrova. Who abducted Angelica."

Havok turned on him.

Scoreggia smiled and spit some blood from his mouth.

"Beat me up three times, now. The same way. Should've realized."

"How does it feel," Havok hissed. "To be consistently on the wrong end of a one way beating?"

"Who *are* you, Sal," he asked, squinting at him with one good eye. "And why?"

Havok picked up the knife from the work table.

"WHY," Scoreggia shouted.

Havok threw the knife. It buried itself to the hilt in Scoreggia's forehead and impaled his head to the wall. Scoreggia's head quivered for a moment, then his eyes went lifeless as blood spread across the floor.

Havok looked at Menscher.

"That," he said, "was for you."

Menscher shook his head.

"No, no it wasn't," he shouted, pointing a finger. "You did that for yourself! You were afraid of what he might know! I'm no fool!"

Havok moved closer to him, but Menscher backed away toward the exit.

"That was for the girl again," he screamed, still pointing his finger. "I'm through with you! I can't trust you anymore!"

"Eiger," Havok pleaded. "Eiger, listen to me."

"No! No! NO!! I'm done listening. You LIE! LIE! LIE! Lie all the time! I'm going to the Cathedrals! I'm telling them everything! They'll take those damned diamonds and kill Abernathé for me!"

"They won't."

"Yes, they will!"

"Eiger, you don't know enough. They'll kill you instead."

"A snow covered planet in a binary star system twenty-one days out of Nostrova!"

Havok became angry.

"What," Menscher shouted, still moving toward the door. "You think I didn't know? Just because I couldn't see?"

Havok screamed with rage and pounced on Menscher. They flailed at each other, their thick, black cloaks encompassing them both. Menscher punched and kicked at Havok, but was too weak. Even injured, Havok easily overpowered him. Havok fumbled with Menscher's hands, trying to restrain him without hurting him. Menscher worked his hands free and grabbed hold of Havok's throat. Blind with rage, Havok placed both hands around Menscher's throat in return and squeezed with all his strength. Havok felt Menscher's finger nails digging into his neck, even as Menscher's body contorted wildly. Havok stared deep into those bulging and crazed and desperate eyes, stared into them until the life faded from them, as the grip on his throat eased, as Menscher croaked his last breath. Even then, he didn't relinguish his grip until he crushed Menscher's windpipe and felt the snap of his neck in his hands.

Exhausted, Havok dropped Menscher's lifeless body to the floor and stood up, soaked in sweat. His blood pounded in his ears. For the first time in over ten years, his stomach wasn't in knots and there wasn't a twinge of nausea at the back of his throat. His bones didn't ache.

And it felt good.

Chapter 26
Memstar Redux

The Abernathés and Abernathé Stoneworks maintained lawyers all across the Metropolia dell'Elsasser. In one of these non-descript buildings, in an ordinary conference room, an extraordinary event was poised to take place.

A team of lawyers representing AbStone sat on one side of a long conference table, and an equal number of lawyers representing Salestus Havok sat on the other. Heavy security blanketed the room, inside and out, which included the entire building and the whole city block.

Multiple holographic images hovered over the table. Representations of graphs, charts and several documents rotated about the room, each discussed, revised and then finally filed. And after Angelica Smart-Scoreggia and Elisabéta Pascucci came to an agreement regarding the final language regarding remuneration, the images all coalesced into a final contract. AbStone would finally have its diamonds. The weeks of negotiating were now at an end and the only remaining requirements were the electronic signatures of Lorenzo de Abernathé IV and Salestus Havok.

The lawyers gave themselves a round of applause and then came around the table to shake hands and talk. After a few minutes of polite chatter and the exchange of business credentials, the lower ranking attorneys filed out, leaving Angelica and Elisabéta standing across from one another, each with their own security people standing behind them. They regarded one another silently and gathered their belongings.

"Well," Angelica said, breaking the ice. "I must compliment you, Ms. Pascucci. You are a far better attorney than I initially gave you credit for. I didn't think your expertise extended beyond transferring disc notes from one bank account to another."

Elisabéta smiled politely.

"And look at you. No longer the cheap ornament standing next to a money drop."

Angelica smiled wryly.

"Here I was all this time thinking you were the most overqualified caterer in all The Web."

"I see your new eyes haven't helped you find your husband. Seen him lately?"

Before Angelica could respond, Salestus Havok entered the room followed by two security guards. The conversation halted and both ladies turned. Havok wore an impeccably tailored dark suit and tie. He held a walking stick in a flesh colored gloved hand. He surveyed the room with his black eyes, first looking at the document that hovered over the table, then at Elisabéta, and finally at Angelica. His two bodyguards took up positions outside the door.

Her face creased with worry, Angelica looked away from him and busily finished packing her briefcase. Elisabéta acknowledged him with curt nod of her head.

"Good afternoon, Mr. Havok. We didn't expect you here today."

"I decided to check on the progress of the negotiations personally," he said. "I am very interested in their resolution." He glanced at the hologram. "Judging by the state of things here, I assume the deal is done?"

"Yes, Mr. Havok," Angelica said stiffly, looking at him as her face burned red. "All it requires is your signature and that of Mr. Abernathé."

Havok smiled sardonically.

"Young Lorenzo has risen far in the business world in a very short time, yes?"

Angelica emphatically clicked her briefcase shut.

"It was very nice to see you again, Mr. Havok. If you'll excuse me, I have a car waiting for me."

Havok nodded.

"Of course. But first I need a moment of your time. If you'll all excuse us? Elisabéta?"

Elisabéta nodded politely, then took her things and strode angrily out of the room. The security personnel followed, shutting the door behind them.

Now alone, neither one of them said anything. Havok stared at her intently with his dark, piercing eyes. She grew nervous in the akward silence.

"What is it you want, Mr. Havok?"

His lips curled at the question, as if fighting some internal struggle.

"I wanted to know," he finally said. "How is your vision?"

"It's taken some getting used to. I get headaches now and again, but the doctors have said that will pass."

"And your husband? How long has it been?"

Her face soured.

"Nine months. Still no word."

"A pity." He paused. "Have you given any thought to our last conversation?"

She sighed.

"As a matter of fact, I have. I even did some research. Pierce Sicuro died in a fire. With the rest of his family, 21 years ago. I checked with the authorities. There were no mistakes. You couldn't possibly be him. So who are you really?"

"You don't believe me?"

"I don't. And I also don't believe your real name is Salestus Havok. There's no record of you before eleven years ago. Tertiary vital statistics documents have your place of birth as Nascosto, which was conveniently destroyed during The War. Again, I ask, who are you really?"

"I already told you. I am Pierce Sicuro."

"What you are is a jewel thief."

"You call me a jewel thief," he mocked. "Look who you're working for."

She rolled her eyes.

"I don't think it a coincidence that the first public records of you date back to just after the Vestitian Job."

"These diamonds," he scoffed. "These diamonds are inconsequential to what's really important to me. *You* are the most important thing to me."

"Mr. Havok," she said uneasily. "This is not appropriate. I—"

He sat down and took a deep breath.

"I see I must convince you. Again, I must swear you to secrecy. Did you relate the details of our last conversation to anyone?"

She shook her head.

"How could I?"

He nodded.

"What if I could prove to you that I'm not a jewel thief?"

"Oh, I'm dying to hear this."

"All right," he said. "I want to preface this by saying that I'm not a bad man."

He paused for a moment, then swallowed hard.

"I learned of these diamonds while I was in prison."

Once he finished, he was afraid to look at her. He stole a quick glance. At least she was now sitting. She stared back at him with an elbow bent on the table and her chin in an open palm, a bemused smile on her face.

"So you expect me to believe you're a clone."

"Yes."

"Of an entire person."

"Yes."

"And not just any person, but Lorezno de Abernathé II, the Finest Lethean Gentleman."

"It's true. My mother was a petri dish and my father was a syringe."

"I'll admit you look like him and Young Lorenzo. It's either coincidence or you're a long lost cousin. No one has ever cloned an entire person."

"There were eight of us, I'm told."

"Were?"

"Yes."

"You don't remember?"

"I was a baby."

"I don't believe you."

He nodded.

"What about your eyes? The successful cloning of your eyes."

Her brow furrowed.

"From you?"

"No, not from me, but from the same science that created me."

She shook her head.

"This is all ridiculous. I don't believe a word of it. Pierce had six fingers on his left hand. You don't."

He pulled off the flesh colored glove, one finger at a time, and laid his left hand on the table. He spread all six fingers wide.

"We met at the end of junior year when your friend Fenchurch called me boring. A few months later, you were stranded on the side of the road, I fixed your aircar. We hit it off the next day while waiting in line to have our senior portraits taken. We used to sneak into the park at the old aqueduct in Doloret to drink with your friends, we used to have sex in the summer in those woods, you had a sheer white tank that you used to wear just for me. We got caught together sneaking out of school early by that anthropod hall monitor, L'Insetto. We used to call her Buggy-Bug Eyes. Remember I bought a bigger stuffed animal for you on your birthday than your father? How it angered him off so much that he threw me out of your house? How you used to sneak into my bedroom through the window in the basement of my house? I built a starship for you, so I could visit you on Nostrova once you went away to school."

"How could you know all this?"

"Because I was Pierce Sicuro!"

"No, no," she said over and over, holding her hands to her head and shaking it from side to side. "It can't be."

He stood up and sat down in the chair next to her.

"You once asked me why I loved you so much. Do you remember what I said?"

She stopped and looked at him.

"What?"

"I said because you're a rosey, vivacious red."

"I remember that. I never told anyone that, it was so stupid."

"You need to believe this, understand this. You are still in grave danger. You need to come and leave with me, be with me, at Atro Viscus. There I can protect you."

"What I need is protection *from* you."

"If you go back to Summa Avarici, they will put you in a cage just like they did to me and I won't be able to help you then. Because if you don't come with me, this deal might not go through and I don't think you quite understand how desperately your new employer wants this deal to happen. You don't realize what kind of monsters you work for. If you fail at this it will be very, very bad for you."

Indignant, she stood up.

"You're threatening me? Assuming I believe any of this, which I don't, why—"

"It was not a threat," he said sternly, "but a warning. I am offering you everything I have, including my protection. Forget all of this. Come with me, be with me again. I still love you. You will come to love me again. I can give you everything you ever dreamed of when we were young."

"I don't even know you! I barely remember you! We dated for a few months in high school—"

"It was a year," he corrected. "The thought of finally returning to you kept me alive for all those long, black years. Regardless of how you felt back then, I never forgot about you. What we had was real. We had a chance to build a life together!"

"No we didn't! You wanted to stay on Gran Nexus fixing furniture! I never had any intention of staying on that planet! After I broke it off with you and left for school, I never heard from you again. I assumed you moved on. You haunt me all this time, then tell me this sob story? Am I supposed to just swoon with pity? Is that what you expected?"

The corners of his eyes watered and his face collapsed.

"I'd always assumed you thought I was dead, killed when my house burned down. N-now you've made it clear that you were completely unaware of that event. You're right. This...this is not what I expected."

"This whole conversation is pointless, Mr. Havok," she admonished. "I don't believe any of this."

"I think you do. Can you honestly deny that Young Lorenzo doesn't remind you of me from when we were that age?"

"I was blind for a long time," she said. "And I still don't see things the same way from before I lost my vision, at least it's not how I remembered it."

"You're still blind to the truth."

"No, I understand everything now. You made the lavish donations to the University because of me."

"Yes. I did my best for you from afar."

"And you tried to separate me from Vincent..." She paused, remembering. "*...twice.* First on Nostrova, and then *now.*"

"Angelica, I love you. I would never do anything to hurt you. Unlike him."

She looked at him.

"And then you took it all away, after the hospital. That party at your estate. It was all a set up."

"Your life with Scoreggia was all wrong. He was a crooked law man. He was cruel to you physically and emotionally. Not like me. Not like I was. Not like I would be."

"Was cruel? Was a crooked law man? What's happened to him?"

"I can't answer that," he said quickly. "I don't know."

"Vincent has his shortcomings, but he is my husband and I love him. Not you! You've ruined my life! What's happened to my husband? Where is Vincent?"

"Angelica," he pleaded. "I'm not the villain in all this."

"You didn't understand then," she shouted, "and you still don't understand now! Always guessing at what I wanted! But what I didn't want, and still don't, is you!"

He stood up, near tears. He pulled the flesh colored glove back onto his left hand.

"So much has happened. We need to forget the past. Let's start anew. Now. I love you. Come and be with me. Vincent is gone. Your work for Young Lorenzo is done. You have no more excuses."

"I will not. Whoever you are, whatever you are…is *grotesque*."

He nodded matter of factly, stung to the core by her final rebuke. He gripped his walking stick tightly as he headed for the door. He stopped and turned.

"Go and tell Young Lorenzo that I will not proceed with this contract. I find it entirely unacceptable. I will only negotiate directly with his father." He paused. "When the whim strikes me."

She frowned in anger, her fists clenched at her sides, as he left the room.

Chapter 27
Congress

The Viscian Gentlemen's Club.

The most exclusive establishment on a planet full of exclusive establishments. The cost of membership was prohibitive, even by Lethean standards. The few members openly boasted of how they indulged in the beautiful hostesses, the fine menu, the fully stocked bars, the extensive gambling parlors, elaborate gymnasiums—no amenity was overlooked. But its appeal stemmed not from the rumors of the extravagances available inside, but rather for the ultimate experience that members craved, but never had the pleasure, for the opportunity it availed to possibly meet its owner, the most interesting man on the planet, Salestus Havok.

This most unusual day saw all members of the club turned away as the entire resort had been reserved for a private function. An aircar landed in front of the club and half a dozen canites in dark suits disembarked. The aircar then lifted off the ground and loomed over the street.

An equal number of the club's security personnel met the canites on the front steps. A ground car with tinted windows pulled up and Mr. Sa'am, the albino macropian, got out and opened the back door.

Max Siniscolchi emerged, followed by Lorenzo de Abernathé III. Siniscolchi and Sa'am escorted Lorenzo to the club entrance. A well groomed man in a black tuxedo met them at the door.

"Salestus Havok extends his welcome, Mr. Abernathé," the doorman said. "However, your pets will have to wait outside."

"I think not," Siniscolchi said. "These are Mr. Abernathé's personal bodyguards. He goes nowhere without them."

"Nothing with so much hair and fur shall ever cross this threshold," the doorman responded, looking down his nose at Sa'am. "We maintain a certain standard here."

Sa'am's fur bristled, but said nothing.

"Mr. Abernathé is entitled to protection," Siniscolchi persisted. "Now stand aside and let us enter."

"Mr. Havok guarantees the safety of everyone on the premesis. As you can see, we have adequate security of our own."

"Need I remind you that Mr. Abernathé owns this planet," Siniscolchi said. "Which includes this building. He goes where he wishes. With protection."

"And he shall have it. But your pets will have to wait here."

"It's all right, Max," Lorenzo said, impatient.

"Fine. Then just us," Siniscolchi snapped.

"But not this," the doorman said with disdain, indicating Sa'am.

Siniscolchi reluctantly turned to the macropian.

"Listen, Sa'am," he said quietly. "The rest of you wait here."

Sa'am's snout quivered and his eyes burned.

"We'll be fine," Siniscolchi reassured him.

Sa'am snorted angrily and took a step back.

The doorman nodded his approval and Lorenzo and Siniscolchi went inside. As they crossed the grand foyer, Siniscolchi could see Sa'am through the window shears speaking with the doorman rather earnestly. He worried that Sa'am would forget their purpose here and provoke an incident, except that the macropian kept a nervous eye on the windows.

They traversed a long, thinly carpeted hall. Their footsteps echoed on the fine marble. Even Lorenzo grudgingly marveled at the fine neo-Lethean stone work. They were shown into an empty conference room. Large windows overlooked a wide river. The bright sun sparkled on the rippling water. Ferry boats steamed lazily across its width. Restaurants and small designer shops lined the near shore and trees partially obscured the view of the rail line on the opposite shore.

Lorenzo sat in one of the plush, business chairs that ringed the black marble table. His own reflection stared back at him on its perfectly polished surface. Siniscolchi stood behind him and looked all about. He carefully studied the only exit and observed every other detail of the room.

"Relax, Max," Lorenzo said, gazing out the window at the placid river. "Havok didn't bring us here to murder us. Take a moment to appreciate our surroundings. His decorators are outstanding."

"I'm sorry, Mr. Abernathé," he replied. "But that's the just what he wants us to do. It's meant to be a distraction."

"I know that. But there's also something to be said for playing the game."

"Again, I must protest, Mr. Abernathé. I'm the only one who can protect you here."

"We've nothing to fear."

Siniscolchi reconsidered. He took a step forward and placed himself between Lorenzo and the open doorway.

At that moment, Havok appeared.

His long black hair was tied tightly behind his head, which melted into his jet black suit and tie, and was offset by a fine indigo shirt. His eyes, his cold black eyes, drank in the sight of the two of them, and the color drained from his face.

"You should heed the advice of your retainer," Havok said. "In times like these, none of us is safe."

Siniscolchi unclasped his hands.

"Salestus Havok."

"Yes," he replied.

Havok entered and with a graceful, yet casual elegance and sat down in the seat next to Lorenzo. He studied them resolutely, his face impassive. He took a palm sized diamond from his pocket and absentmindedly spun it like top on the table. It projected dazzling octagonal rainbows in the sunlight. Lorenzo's eyes widened and fell on the spinning stone, mesmerized.

"I suggest you gentlemen state your business," Havok finally said. "I have other matters that require my attention."

"This meeting was requested at your direction," Siniscolchi said. "An agreement was reached three months ago regarding the diamonds in your possession, like the one in your hand. You backed out. Why?"

"Because I don't trust you."

"The feeling is mutual. But you should seriously reconsider your position."

"And if I refuse?"

"I'm sure we can convice you to cooperate."

"I really don't think you can."

Lorenzo looked away from the spinning diamond and up at Havok.

Havok leaned in close to him.

"That's right, Lorenzo. Take a good look." He ran a finger over his own face. "The scar is hard to see underneath the beard, but it's there. It's right there."

Havok looked at Siniscolchi.

"I know you see it, too."

Havok slapped his hand on the spinning diamond and put it back in his pocket.

Lorenzo snapped back into the moment.

"I'm through fooling around with you! You exist here only with my permission."

"This is my planet."

"No, this is *my* planet," Lorenzo shouted. "I know where you are and who you are, Pierce Sicuro!"

"Always one step behind, Lorenzo," he shouted back. Havok smiled through slitted eyes. "Always one step." He shook his head. "There is no Pierce Sicuro. There is only me. And I've never been more disappointed in my own son."

Stunned, Lorenzo sat up straight.

"You're not my father!"

"No more than you are the father of Young Lorenzo." Havok stood up and towered over him. Siniscolchi quickly got between them. "Take a good look, Lorenzo! I never wore a beard in my previous life, but I should have. You were always *weak*. You will always be *weaker* than *I*."

"Please step back, Mr. Havok," Siniscolchi said.

Havok stood nose to nose with him, close enough to taste the spearmint on his breath.

"I remember you." Havok lingered a moment, then took a step back. "I remember." He hesitated, then nodded to himself, coming to a decision. "Yes. I'm going to kill you."

Siniscolchi's face hardened.

"I'm standing right here."

Havok shook his head.

"Not today. But soon."

"Stand aside, Max," Lorenzo ordered. "We didn't come here to fight. We came to make a deal."

Havok chuckled derisively.

"My son, my son. Making deals when you should be fighting. Fighting when you should be making deals. You have no business skills. This war you've gotten yourself into with Cathedral. You're running my company into the ground. You just continue to pile one embarrassment upon another."

A bead of sweat rolled down Lorenzo's temple.

"What's the matter, Lorenzo," Havok said derisively. "Nothing else to say? As I always thought, as I always knew. *You* are a *coward.*"

Lorenzo trembled. First his face turned red, then purple.

"And what about you, Pop," he exploded. "What about you?!"

Siniscolchi's head snapped around.

"You can't make that Scoreggia woman love you anymore than my own mother," Lorenzo shouted.

"You poor little bastard," Havok sneered. "I bet that ache in your belly is nothing compared to your inability to get at these." He again took the diamond from his pocket and spun it far out into the middle of the table.

Lorenzo stared at it, the sunlight defracting in octagonal rainbows, so close, yet so far. Siniscolchi took a step toward it.

"Take another step," Havok warned, "and I'll kill him, then you."

Siniscolchi eyed him warily while Lorenzo stared longingly at the diamond. It finally tumbled to a stop in the middle of the table, out of reach.

"Why can't you just cooperate, Pop," Lorenzo whined. "Why do you always have to be like this?"

Siniscolchi placed his hands on Lorenzo's shoulders and tried to get him to sit down. Instead, he shrugged him off and remained fixated on the sparkling diamond.

"Let's not lose sight of why we're here," Siniscolchi said. "This deal will be consummated."

Havok snorted.

"And if it isn't?"

"No good will come of it."

"No good for whom? The Cathedrals are wearing you down. Why shouldn't I make a deal with them so they can finish you off for good?"

Siniscolchi shook his head.

"Because you won't. You'd have done so long ago if that's what you really wanted. Your revenge is to make Mr. Abernathé squirm, to suffer slowly, to mirror your own experience."

"Know me so well, do you?"

"We've spent a lot of time together, you and I, although you don't realize it." He paused. "You're still fixated on the girl. But we have her and we will protect her from you."

Havok's jaw quivered.

Siniscolchi smiled.

"Surely you don't think you're the good guy in all this? You tried to abduct her, discredited her husband and destroyed her reputation when she refused to love you. She's surprisingly a very good lawyer and that makes her a very valuable asset. She will remain safely ensconced in her offices with Young Lorenzo. With us."

"If anything happens to me or my interests," Havok said, "Cathedral will get the secret of these diamonds."

"If Cathedral gets the secret of these diamonds, then bad things will happen to Mrs. Smart-Scoreggia."

Havok flushed in anger.

"You can't keep her from me."

"On the contrary, Mr. Havok, we can. We're willing to negotiate with you as Lethean gentlemen, to make a legitimate business deal lucrative to both your interests and ours. A deal that would keep the Cathedrals forever at bay. If AbStone were to come under the control of Cathedral, they would learn all we know. And they will *not* make a deal with you."

"The time for deals has passed," Lorenzo said, in a fog. He reluctantly turned away from the diamond and looked at Havok. "There will be no more deals."

Havok nodded.

"For once, I'm in agreement with my sniveling offspring. Leave here, while you still can."

Siniscolchi guided Lorenzo to the door, but then Lorenzo stopped.

"I run AbStone, Pop," he shouted back at Havok, pointing an outstretched finger. "Not you! Not for twenty years! I know what I'm doing, damn you!"

"Keep telling yourself that, son," Havok said. "Repeat the lie often enough, and soon it will sound like the truth. *But it's still just a lie.*"

Before Lorenzo could reply, Siniscolchi rushed him from the room.

Elisabéta Pascucci clacked her way through the narrow, winding servant corridors of the Viscian Gentlemen's Club. She came and went through the back stairs and corridors of the hired help, always mindful to stay out of sight, even though no members were in the club today. She maintained an office here for times when Mr. Havok visited the premesis and required her services. Today was one of those days.

She walked casually, conversing with each of the different department heads who were largely idle due to the lack of guests for the day. She lounged in the doorway of the building manager, Enn'Tomon. The anthropod clicked busily behind a desk.

"Hello, Enn'Tomon," she said, crossing her arms and leaning on the doorframe.

"Ms. Pascucci," it replied, still working. "I surmise Mr. Havok is in the building today."

"You surmise correctly."

"Is there something you want? I'm very busy."

"No, not really. Just hovering until I'm needed."

"And what makes you think you'll be needed?"

"Just a hunch."

It sighed.

"And your plan is to just stand there, annoying me?"

"All right. What is the status of the club, then? See how I just made this a meeting?"

"Yes," it replied dryly. "The membership is unhappy. Clearing out the building has a good number clamoring for compensation."

She nodded.

"Nobody cheaper than rich people. They all agreed to the same contract. No restitution. When Mr. Havok wants his privacy, he gets his privacy."

"Why are you really here," it sighed wearily.

"Like I said, just killing time until something happens."

"Annoying me amuses you?"

"Immensely."

Truthfully, Enn'Tomon bored her.

"And again, how do you know there will be an incident requiring your attention?"

She smiled coyly. Before she could respond, the tuxedoed front doorman came down the hall.

"Excuse me, Mr. Enn'Tomon," he said. "Ms. Pascucci, there's a...*macropian* asking to see you. He says he has information vital to Mr. Havok's well being."

"Did he ask for me by name?"

"No, madam. But this is the sort of thing you should know about."

"Who is this person?"

"His name is Sa'am, and he's part of Mr. Abernathé's security detail."

"Young Lorenzo?"

"No, madam. Lorenzo III."

She exchanged a knowing glance with Enn'Tomon.

"I see. Why now?"

"Opportunity."

"And what information does he posess?"

"He wouldn't say, but he appears to be on the edge of desperation. He said it had to do with why Mr. Abernathé's here today."

"That it?"

"He offered me a bribe," he sneered, shrugging. "I told him he didn't need to be so crass, but the furries are like that. I thought you might want to talk to him, so I made an exception and admitted him via a side entrance."

She shrugged.

"Well, I am in the middle of a meeting..."

"By all means," Enn'Tomon said. "Don't let me hold you up."

"What luck, my schedule just cleared," Elisabéta smiled. "I'll talk with this person."

She winked at Enn'Tomon.

"And no refunds," she called to it over her shoulder as she walked away.

Elisabéta stepped into a side room from the servant's entrance, off the main foyer. The albino macropian named Sa'am was already there, waiting for her. She stood with her arms folded.

"Who are you," he asked.

"I'm Mr. Havok's attorney. Your name is Mr. Sa'am. And macropians are not allowed in here, so be careful how you speak to me. You work for Abernathé, is that correct?"

"Yes, but I'm not here representing him."

"Who are you representing, then?"

"Myself."

"What do you want?"

"I know who Mr. Havok really is and where he got those fancy diamonds that everyone is so concerned about."

"Excuse me?"

"Look, Abernathé is here today to cut a deal with Havok to get at those diamonds. All I need to do is give Abernathé this information and your boss is as good as dead."

"So why haven't you already?"

"Alotta money involved in this deal. I want some of it."

"If you know where to get these diamonds, go get them yourself and stop wasting my time."

"That may not be so easy. See, my job at AbStone is to find these diamonds. It took awhile, but I found them. Me alone. Along the way, I also found out that your boss is desperate to keep Abernathé from figuring out his real name."

"Mr. Havok is not in the habit of suborning to blackmail. Feel free to take your information to NYSAAC or the Cathedrals, if you need money that badly."

"I'm making the offer to you first."

"With a gesture, I can prevent you from ever leaving this building."

"You can try. But if I don't leave here, I've arranged for the information to leak anyway."

"Of course you have. How much will your silence cost?"

"250 million. Two hundred and fifty one million green disc notes."

She didn't reply.

"Will you take my offer to Havok?"

"I have no way of validating what you allege."

"His real name is Pierce Sicuro."

"So?"

"I'm telling you, it matters a great deal to Abernathé. And the other thing, all I'm gonna say is binary stars."

She nodded curtly and stepped toward the exit.

"Will you take my offer to Havok?"

"No."

The macropian nodded.

"I'll give you twenty-five hours to change your mind."

Elisabéta calmly made her way through the back rooms of the club. She was in a hurry, although she didn't show it. The eyes of all the human males followed her as she walked by. This macropian had piqued her curiosity and knowing that Mr. Havok had no intention of following through on any deals with AbStone, she believed he would want to know about this Mr. Sa'am.

As she stepped off the staff elevator, she met a young canite in Mr. Havok's personal changing rooms. He was furiously cleaning the place, although it already positively sparkled.

She greeted the boy with a smile.

"Hello, Joseef."

The boy smiled shyly, barely able to look at her.

"Hello, Ms. Pascucci."

"Is Mr. Havok still in the gymnasium?"

A loud crash delayed his answer, only to be followed by more banging and the metallic clang of rolling pipes.

"Yes, ma'am," he answered nervously. "Some real awful noises coming from in there. I-I've been afraid to look."

Joseef took a lot of pride in maintaining Mr. Havok's personal equipment and changing rooms. What was happening in the gymnasium had to be upsetting him.

"I'm sure it has nothing to do with you, Joseef. Don't worry."

He twisted a dust towel anxiously in his hands.

"Yes, ma'am. But we put in the new bags today, just like Mr. Havok asked."

"Has he said anything?"

"No ma'am. He just came in and changed, then I could hear him hitting the bags, and then the noise started right after."

She nodded.

"All right, Joseef. You can leave now."

"Yes, ma'am. But what if Mr. Havok needs something? I-I don't want to lose my job."

She understood his apprehension. His employment here was a secret Havok carefully guarded.

"It's okay. You have my permission."

He nodded hesitantly, then put the towel in a nearby hamper. He reluctantly left through a side door.

Elisabéta took a deep breath and tugged at the waistline of her business suit. She walked out into the gymnasium and halted mid-stride at what she saw.

The weights from the bench pressing table were strewn about the room, apparently thrown against the concrete walls, judging by the cracks and chips in the cement. The rows of different boxing bags had been blown off their moorings and the various support rods and pipes lay scattered about the wooden floor.

Other bent and broken pieces of exercise equipment littered the room.

She spied Havok in the midst of it all, shirtless and drenched in sweat. His bare hands mercilessly pounded a full length bag and powerful muscles rippled across his back. What started out as a disciplined, rhythmic staccato of blows devolved into one haymaker after another. The bag's stuffing exploded in puffs at the seams. He mercilessly pounded the bag until he blew it off its moorings with a loud pop and it flew across the room, skidding across the floor.

When he turned, his eyes were laden with anger, flitting this way and that, desperately looking for something else to hit. Then he spied Elisabéta standing calmly amidst the debris. He was breathing hard, so angry he could barely speak.

"What do you want," he grunted.

"I trust your meeting with Mr. Abernathé did not go well."

He glared at her.

"And why would you think that?"

She merely raised an eyebrow.

He snatched up a white towel and wiped the sweat from his face.

"No, it did not go well."

"Are we proceeding with the business arrangement for the diamonds?"

"No," he said, his face still covered by the towel. "*We* are not."

"I have some information in that regard."

"What," he asked, his voice muffled.

"While you were meeting with Mr. Abernathé, I was contacted by a Mr. Sa'am, a detective of sorts in the employ of Lorenzo III. Acting independent of Mr. Abernathé, he wanted me to convey an offer to you. He said that he possessed information damaging to your interests, and for a price would remain silent. I declined his offer."

He rubbed his face with the towel.

"And?"

"He claimed that your real name is Pierce Sicuro and that you're desperate to keep this fact from Mr. Abernathé."

His continued rubbing his face with the towel.

"Abernathé already knows. He's known for a long time. Does this disturb you?"

"I don't understand."

He took the towel from his face and dropped it on the floor. He picked up a clean one.

"That I used to go by another name."

"Names are only labels, Mr. Havok," she replied. "Everyone has to come from somewhere. I always believed you were related to the Abernathés in some way. If you put a beard on Young Lorenzo, you'd appear separated at birth."

"You're not the first one to say that."

"I always thought it unfair that you know everything about everyone who works for you, but we know nothing of you."

"There are plenty of other employers in this galaxy."

"True. But I've always been curious about you, Mr. Havok. Your motivations. What creates a man like you."

He smiled sadly, sweat still running down his face.

"I can trust you to not share this information? About my true name?"

"Yes."

He rubbed his face again with the towel.

"Was there anything else?"

"Yes. He said he knows the undisclosed location of the diamonds you wanted the Abernathés to distribute. He only mentioned a binary star formation."

The towel fell from Havok's face.

"Did he say which one?"

"He only said—"

"DID HE SAY WHICH ONE??!!"

Her mouth suddenly turned to mush.

He thrust his head at her and spread his arms wide.

"DID HE *SAY* WHICH *ONE??!!*"

She flinched and stumbled backward, tripping over a barbell. She fell roughly to the floor. Instead of helping her up, he turned his back on her and pulled at the sides of his long wet hair.

"No, Mr. Havok," she said from the floor, annoyed. "He didn't."

She stood up, brushing dust from her suit.

"He offered twenty-five hours to reconsider, or he would either go directly to Abernathé or the Cathedrals with this information."

Havok turned back around and looked at Elisabéta angrily, hungrily. He wagged a finger at her.

"No, no, no. This is far too clever for Lorenzo."

Elisabéta found this highly unusual. She had never seen him this agitated nor inclined to think outloud. She watched in puzzlement.

"A macropian sniffing about at the same moment I confront Abernathé. Coincidence?"

She wasn't sure he really wanted an answer.

"How should we respond to this, Mr. Havok," she asked. "It appears that AbStone has no intention of consummating the distributorship contract, either."

"No, they still want it. Of that, I'm certain."

"How can you be sure? Everything indicates that they're just stringing us along."

"You've got it wrong. It is I who have been pulling the strings. This overture by the mysterious Mr. Sa'am is unrelated."

"Again, how can you be sure?"

"I have some insight into how Abernathé thinks. He wouldn't be pursuing this business arrangement so earnestly if he already knew the location of the diamonds. The involvement of this Mr. Sa'am is a trifle, but it will necessitate acting faster than I planned. All along, I never expected it to take this long for the location of the diamonds to be discovered, but it was inevitable that someone would learn of them sooner or later. And I didn't expect it to be this Mr. Sa'am."

"Who did you expect then?"

"How much time did he give," he asked, ignoring her question.

"Twenty-five hours."

He nodded.

"That's more than enough time, if we move quickly. I want Atro Viscus evacuated, all Circles, no exceptions, but not immediately. Do not give the order for another fifteen hours."

"Evacuated," she asked, confused.

He glared at her.

"Yes, Mr. Havok," she whispered.

"I want as many airtrucks as you can gather within the next hour. I also want an aircar brought around. I have specific instructions for the drivers."

"Of course."

He strode off toward the door.

"Do you have any plans for the next fifty hours, Elisabéta?"

"Never, Mr. Havok."

"Good."

Chapter 28
The Line

The late afternoon sun cast long shadows across The Village. The row of houses that ran along the cliff edge was known as The Line. The wide avenue was made from polished blackstone bricks, the same as all of the houses and other buildings in Atro Viscus. A gentle breeze blew in from the ocean, unusually warm for this time of year. A solitary church bell rang in the distance.

A young boy, a canite, ran along the curving avenue as fast as he could. His cheeks huffed and puffed, and flushed a dark brown from the effort.

"Father," he shouted, gasping for breath. "Father, he's coming!"

No one answered him. He ran even faster.

"He's coming! He's coming!" He gasped desperately for breath. "The Praetor is coming!"

Some people were about, sweeping walkways or sitting on their front steps, relaxing after the day's work. The small shop owners and patrons looked on with amusement as the boy went running by.

The boy threw his arms wide and jumped with excitement as he ran.

"The Praetor is coming!"

He reached the front door of his house, fumbled with the handle, then pounded on the wood.

"Father! The Praetor is coming! I saw him!"

His human father opened the door.

"What's all the noise about? White Clorox, look at you, Remmie. Take a moment to catch your breath!"

"I-I saw him," Remmie gasped, gulping for air. "The Praetor! He…He's coming!"

His father smiled.

"Calm down, calm down. I know."

"How…how could you know?"

His father continued smiling and tousled the boy's mane of dark hair.

"Everybody up and down The Line knows, you were yelling so loud!"

The Praetor appeared around the bend. In stark contrast to the blackstone, he wore a white three piece suit and scarf. He walked casually, looking from side to side, from his left down the mountainside, then to his right, admiring the small village carved from the rock. He seemed completely at ease, touching the brim of his white fedora politely to those he passed and stopping to shake hands and talk to those who offered. Some of the women who took his hands appeared to be thanking him in earnest. He shared a quick shot with some of the working men at the bar, graciously accepted a cookie from the bakery, and stopped to converse while he ate. As The Praetor got closer to Remmie and his father, it became clear to the boy that he was walking directly toward them. Remmie darted behind his father and peered around his waist.

"Good morning, Foreman," The Praetor said, offering his hand.

They exchanged a strong handshake.

"Good evening, Praetor Havok. And please, outside the shop, I prefer Forte."

The Praetor smiled. The white scar on his clean shaven face remained straight.

"Forte it is, then. And who is that, the one so shy?"

"My son, Remmie."

The Praetor seemed surprised.

"Your son?"

Forte nodded with proud sadness.

"We lost our children near the Greater Morass. Remmie lost his parents just the same."

"But there are other canite families here—"

Forte became defensive.

"And they're our friends."

"Forgive me. You misunderstand. I was being complimentary. There are many who would not have done as you have."

Forte relaxed and smiled again.

"Well, thank you, Praetor Havok, but it wasn't done for show. It was done because it was right."

The Praetor nodded knowingly, a tinge of sadness in his eyes.

"You're a fine man, Forte."

Forte beamed.

"But not finer than you, Praetor."

The Praetor paused at those words and his face became a mask.

Remmie shifted behind his father, peering around the other side of his waist.

"I'm sorry, Praetor. He's not normally this shy."

"Certainly not, judging by the way he just charged up the street." The Praetor forced a smile. "He's a fine looking boy. And if I say, this is a fine house you've built here, a fine town. You've much to be proud of."

"All thanks to you, Praetor."

The Praetor seemed impatient to hear that.

"Yes, everyone I've met has expressed that same sentiment."

"We owe everything we have to you."

"No. Not everything. Only the opportunity."

Forte amiably conceded the point with a slight nod.

"John Perso was in touch with you," The Praetor said, "about this time last year, about some very particular relay switches I required."

"Yes, Praetor. Please, come inside."

They went in and Forte offered him a seat in the small kitchen. Remmie bolted from his father's side and disappeared into the small house. His footsteps pounded up the stairs.

The Praetor sat comfortably and set his hat on his lap. Forte tensed a bit, his face apprehensive.

"Is there a problem, Forte?"

Forte's calloused hands placed a small, black canvas bag on the table. He locked eyes with The Praetor.

"There's only one possible purpose for these items."

"And you're worried about what I might do with them."

"More like what you *will* do with them."

"That's not your concern."

"Praetor, please don't misunderstand me—"

A woman, clearly Forte's wife, appeared in the doorway, holding a large pillow in her hands.

"Forte, Remmie's upstairs, babbling some nonsense about The Praetor being in—"

She stopped mid-sentence and set the pillow down on an empty chair. Both men stood up.

"Praetor Havok, this is my wife, Anna."

"Ma'am," the Praetor said. "A fine, fine house you have here."

"Why thank you," she said, fixing her hair. "Forte, did you offer him anything to drink? Praetor Havok, can I get you anything?"

"No, thank you," he replied, picking up the bag from the table with a hand in a flesh colored glove. "Your husband was just showing me out."

The two men stepped back out onto the blackstone street. Anna lingered in the doorway.

"I envy you, Forte," the Praetor said. A bit forlorn, he looked back at Anna, now joined by Remmie, hiding behind her apron. "Are you happy here?"

"Absolutely, Praetor. Considering the alternative, and the options I had ten years ago."

"And where did my agents find you?"

"Being deported back to the Morass, on *Gateway*, along with just about everyone else here along The Line."

"You've got a lot to lose here, Forte. All of you. You would do well to protect it in any way that you can."

"Praetor—"

"Now, just so you don't misunderstand *me*, what you have done here today has gone a long way to doing just that."

"Yes, Praetor. But it's not just about surviving. It's about *deserving* to survive."

"And did that offer any comfort, to any of you, while you were all waiting those long months on *Gateway* to be deported back to the Greater Morass? After the loss of your children?"

Forte stiffened.

"My father gave me one thing in this life and that was a good last name. I protect it vigorously."

"Even if that is to be your epitaph?"

"*Especially* if it to be my epitaph."

The Praetor's mouth curled as if he smelled something he didn't like. Forte turned and went back into his home, closing the door gently behind him.

With that, The Praetor nodded and continued his slow walk on down The Line.

Chapter 29
Magna Armarium

"Good evening, Lethe. Suetonia's coverage of the Great Lethean Banking Crisis continues, with commentary from leading financial experts within the next half hour. The entire quadrant is still reeling from one bank failure after another, and the collapse of several venerable brokerage houses and other lenders. As bad as the last fifty hours have been, experts are predicting that this is only the start of massive cascade of financial havoc that will be felt throughout the entire Web. The cause of all this can be traced back to the actions of one man, but his motivations to this moment remain a mystery.

"Lorenzo de Abernathé II, the patriarch of Lethe's oldest and most prominent family, made his first public appearance in almost 25 years, putting an end to rumors of his frail health. But his actions have caused many to question his faculties.

"Fifty hours ago, The Finest Lethean Gentleman strode into the main branch of the Bank of the Armarium in the Metropolia dell'Elsasser and demanded the withdrawal of all of his assets, including safe deposit boxes. This request extended not only to his personal accounts, but to those of Abernathé Stoneworks as well. One might have considered this a peculiar request were it for the purposes of transferring accounts to another financial institution. This was hardly the case. He demanded conversion into basic green disc notes, in denominations of 500 and 750 million. The discs were loaded into a procession of over 300 airtrucks and flown out of the city. A palette of an estimated one trillion in discs was left on the sidewalk, apparently due to space limitations. As our cameras show, it disappeared in a matter of minutes as passersby helped themselves to the unattended casings.

"Government offcials that represent our quadrant have asked for help from the other three quads of The Web, only to be answered with stinging rebukes and utter exasperation at how something like this could be allowed to happen. Lethean banking laws are very strict concerning withdrawals: all requests for access to funds must be met within 200 minutes. Given the magnitude of the withdrawal, BOA was forced to call in all of its loans and draw on other institutions to cover the full amounts of the deposits on record. All Lethean financial institutions are required by law to assist any other institution in honoring this kind of request. The magnitude of the Abernathé family's personal wealth is dwarfed by that of AbStone. This has triggered a cascade of bank failures and crippled many other financial instutions. The removal of this amount of wealth from circulation can only have a disastrous effect on the overall economy. With lenders all across the quadrant now calling in loans in an effort to maintain liquidity, it is only a matter of time before private citizens feel the impact as well."

Another man's face filled the screen.

"This is the reason why each individual, each corporation, is vetted and issued a license to bank on this planet, to keep out those who would use our free economic system to inflict deliberate injury not just on one person, but to the whole society. The spirit of our laws on this world is to make it as easy as possible for one to accumulate wealth, and to remove government interference and unnecessary taxes. This is our chosen way of life. There's nothing evil about wanting to earn money, to make your circumstances as comfortable as possible. The people of Lethe understand this. Lorenzo de Abernathé II understands this—his father invented the way we do business here. To abuse this great economic system we have only hurts us all. Lorenzo de Abernathé I was one of the founding fathers of this way of life, this culture, and Lorenzo II brought it to a full, robust life, which is why we affectionately refer to him as The Finest Lethean Gentleman. This is what makes what he's done today both incomprehensible and reprehensible at the same time. The Abernathé name, once revered, will now live in infamy."

The anchor's face returned.

"The search for explanations has revealed no answers. Lorenzo de Abernathé III has personally refused comment. Spokesmen for AbStone have issued assurances that there are 'no concerns for a widespread panic and that the company is, and will remain, healthy and profitable.' Many pundits have openly speculated that circumstances are in fact the exact opposite, pointing to AbStone's ongoing rivalry with the Cathedral Corporation. AbStone, the dominant corporate entity in this quadrant, has rapidly been losing stature in the marketplace over the last ten years to the massive Webwide conglomerate. In light of AbStone's rumored instability, many fear that Lorenzo de Abernathé's recent behavior is not so incomprehensible after all."

An angry fist pounded the desk top controls for the video screen and it muted with a squawking chirp. The Suetonia broadcast continued in silence. Behind the desk in his grand office, Lorenzo III's well manicured fist continued to pound at the screen controls. The veins pulsed in his neck and a single, purple line throbbed down the center of his forehead.

"Now, one more time, I want you to FUCKING EXPLAIN all this to me! How FUCKING Salestus Havok just walked into a bank and stole ALL of my money!"

Siniscolchi sat in a chair on the other side of Lorenzo's desk, his tie loose about his neck. His face taught with stress, he rested his elbows on his knees and rubbed his forehead.

"Technically, your money is still there. He only took your father's, and the company's."

"Fucking SEMANTICS, Max," he bellowed, smacking a glass off the top of his desk.

"I suspected he might try something like this at some point."

"SUSPECTED?! *SUSPECTED?!* YOU FUCKING IDIOT!!"

"Because Havok is an exact copy of your father, he had no trouble clearing the retina scan, finger prints and DNA test. Notice how he used his right hand there and not the left? Very clever."

"Clorox DAMN that son of a bitch!!"

"My guess is he dyed his hair gray to throw everyone off. A wig'd be too obvious. He shaved, too. Leaned on the cane a lot, played the old man gag to the hilt. Your father has basically been a recluse for over a decade. Hardly anyone's seen him, all of the press releases and pictures described him as the picture of health. Outside of his immediate caretakers, no one knows how sick he really is. What we should have done was revoke his fiscal authority years ago. It would have prevented something like this."

Siniscolchi noticed the 'call' light flickering on Lorenzo's desk, but Lorenzo was so enraged he didn't see it.

"It would've been a sign of WEAKNESS!! I'm also fighting a PR war, DAMMIT!! And now I can't do a DAMNED THING ABOUT IT without revealing my father's condition or the rest of this SORDID FUCKING MESS!! A mess you were supposed to have under control, DAMN YOU!!"

"It can't be worse than what's already happening, Mr. Abernathé."

"Really, Max? Oh, really? 'RUINED BY MY CRAZY FATHER'S CLONE' *is better* THAN 'RUINED BY MY CRAZY FATHER'?!"

"Mr. Abernathé," Siniscolchi said, standing up. "Now is not the time to lose control of your emotions. This obviously gives the Cathedrals an opening to escalate things. We are vulnerable and we need to decide what to do about that."

"Do, Max? What else am I to do but bend over and grab MY DAMNED ANKLES!! I'm ruined, Max! BEATEN!! There's no way I can recover from this!"

They were interrupted by a loud pounding on the door, as if a scuffle were taking place on the other side. The door flew open and Siniscolchi jumped to his feet, pulling a laser from under his suit coat. In the doorway stood Mr. Sa'am, stiff arming Lorenzo's anthropod administrative assistant with a stubby arm, who was doing its best to try and keep him out.

"Mr. Abernathé," the anthropod started, "I'm sor—"

"WHAT THE BLAZES IS THIS?! GET OUT OF HERE!!"

Mr. Sa'am appeared confused. He ignored Abernathé, his eyes settling for a long moment on Siniscolchi.

"What is it, Sa'am," Siniscolchi asked.

"Mr. Abernathé," Sa'am said quickly, "I know—"

"I SAID TO GET THE FUCK OUT!! OUT!! OUT!! OUT!!"

Siniscolchi put his weapon away and held up a hand.

"Wait, wait wait. Say that again, Sa'am?"

"I said, I know where to find the Ecks Stones."

"It's all right," Siniscolchi said, waving off the anthropod. "Close the door on your way out."

Siniscolchi eyed the young macropian severely. Beads of sweat formed on Sa'am's furry brow and matted down some of his longer fur. Lorenzo came around his desk and stood on one side of the macropian, Siniscolchi on the other.

"This had better be good," Lorenzo said softly into the macropian's pointed ear. "It hasn't been a good day."

Sa'am swallowed hard.

"I was able to confirm that this Salestus Havok is indeed Pierce Sicuro."

"I ALREADY KNOW THAT," Lorenzo shouted into Sa'am's ear. "WHERE ARE THE FUCKING ECKS STONES?!"

Sa'am winced.

"The Aphelion Binary System, sir."

"The Aph—? The what?!"

"A binary star system. Aphelion. On The Frontier, about 80 light years beyond The Rim."

Lorenzo threw his hands up in the air and walked away, his back to Sa'am. He rubbed his face in his hands, then stared out the window at the roiling ocean, hands on hips.

Siniscolchi paced around Sa'am in a tight circle, eyes riveted.

"And where does one find a diamond strike on a pair of stars?"

"I-I don't know that, Max. Must be asteroids out there."

"And how do you know this?"

"Hand signals, Max. From the picture data. The excercises concealed a cant Marines used on The Rim during The Canite War. I can show you."

"Good work, Sa'am. Now, how long have you known?"

"A few hours ago, Max. I had to make sure before I came up here. Your orders were to go directly to you with any new information."

"Hmmm. Now, who else have you told?"

Sa'am appeared offended by the insinuation.

"No one, Max," he gasped. "I owe you, Mr. Abernathé, everything! What have I ever done to make you question my loyalty?"

Siniscolchi looked over at Lorenzo, who leered at them in their reflection on the glass.

"It makes sense," Siniscolchi said. "Ecks was a Marine CW vet on The Rim, so was Sicuro's father. It's possible that Sicuro's father taught the cant to his children. Our personnel would've missed it because we have no ex-Marines on the payroll, on principle. But what about the language software?"

"The cant is based on one of the proto-human dialects that no one speaks or writes anymore. An extinct form of oral communication. I checked it out, and the tradition dates back to—"

"Whatever," Siniscolchi said, cutting him off. "It appears we have another solution, Mr. Abernathé."

"Another?" He turned toward the two men. "Another?"

"We can still threaten him with the girl."

"The girl?! What *good* is the girl now?!"

"Or we can go to Aphelion and get the Ecks Stones, and forget all about Salestus Havok."

"I seem to remember a little excursion you took out to Argulski's Star," Lorenzo recalled. "Also at the direction of Ecks. Remember that ship of fools, Max? What's your plan this time? To let Havok run amok and eventually he'll lead us to some random asteroid in the middle of *fucking* nowhere? Holy Clorox on a crutch, you damned damn idiot! AND WHO IN THE RED FUCK are you to tell me to forget Salestus Havok?! I'm supposed to JUST FORGET what he's done to me?! MY BUSINESS?! MY FAMILY?!"

"Mr. Abernathé," Siniscolchi said carefully. "Give me a chance to verify this information. This is the best lead we've had in—"

"YOU SHUT UP, MAX!"

Lorenzo paused, drawing deep breaths, his face a dark red. He turned and stared back out at the restless ocean, shoulders slumped, his face a sheen of perspiration.

"I'll tell you two fucktards what we're going to do." He pointed an angry finger. "You. Sa'am or whover in Blazes you are. Get your fucking people together and whatever else you need, and you go to Atro Viscus and you kill that son of a bitch Havok. You kill him and you get my money back. Do you understand me? Is that plain enough for you?"

"Yes, Mr. Abernathé."

"And if you fail, you'd better run. Run as far away as you can because you will never be dead enough, do you understand?"

The young macropian flinched at the threat.

"Yes, Mr. Abernathé."

"And you, Max."

Siniscolchi looked at him.

"You go with him. But first find Breufogle. Find Breufogle and get him the fuck back here. Now!"

Chapter 30
Sa'am

Two armored fortresses whistled through the frigid night air. Under a black moon high over the ocean, the arctic wind pushed against the pair of behemoths, and they groaned under their own weight as the dim outline of Atro Viscus loomed. Laser cannons on the lead ship clicked into position and then rotated in confused semi-circles.

"What's with the cannons," Siniscolchi asked the pilot.

"Nothing for them to lock onto. They're rigged to hone in on starstone energy signatures and power sources. Nothing of the sort down there."

"Anything else of note?"

"We've only got natural barriers to contend with. No mechanized defenses have been activated. Nothing moving in the infra-red or N-ray. Very little heat coming from the buildings and zero communications traffic. Looks like nobody's home."

Siniscolchi only nodded.

"No energy signatures from the power station," the pilot said. "No emergency lights, either."

"Probably a trap. Luring us in."

"What do we do, Mr. Siniscolchi?"

"No longer a need for us to be subtle. Change our landing site to right outside his front door, the tallest of those three spires.

Have the other fortress land here, to protect our backs. Call in the gun ships now, have them circle our position."

"You got it."

The pilot relayed the orders over his headset and Siniscolchi buckled himself in, across from Sa'am. Fifty other mercs lined the walls of the cargo cabin, twenty five on each side.

Siniscolchi glared across the way at Sa'am. At times Sa'am couldn't even look at him, other times he met his gaze hard on. Siniscolchi didn't try to hide his disappointment.

Siniscolchi had recalled Breufogle to Summa Avarici and put him in charge of securing the place, as Lorenzo requested. He purposefully kept Breufogle in the dark regarding Sa'am's breakthrough because he didn't know who to trust anymore. Years ago, he would have killed both Sa'am and Breufogle outright, the former for his dishonesty and the second for his incompetence.

So much was different now.

He kicked himself for tolerating Sa'am's poor attitude for so long and Breufogle's inability to recognize it. He checked with the techs who ran the picture room and neither Sa'am nor Breufogle had been there in weeks. He wondered who else Sa'am had been talking to.

He would deal with them both later.

First, he had to deal with this. Then he would convince Lorenzo to search the Aphelion Binary System.

"Touchdown in fifty seconds," the pilot announced.

"Listen up," Sa'am said into his headset. "Our landing coordinates have changed. We'll be in the garden outside the main entrance. We'll have air support and Beta Unit covering our backs. Conditions are totally dark and no sign of the opposition, but that doesn't mean they aren't there. Orders are to kill anyone we find and to recover what was stolen from Mr. Abernathé. The one who kills Salestus Havok gets the standard bounty. Lock and load!"

Fifty guns clicked in unison and were brought to the ready.

"Touchdown in five, four, three, two…ONE!"

Siniscolchi stood in the open doorway to the main dining room in the tallest of the Tri-Towers. He looked around warily, listening to the chatter of his men in his earpiece. Two dozen rifle lights circled and bobbed about the dark room. Sa'am's own light wandered into the middle.

Elegant place settings lined the main table. Sumptuous loaves of white bread filled each plate, accentuated by bottle after bottle of rare, and very valuable, wine. What had everyone's attention was not the table, but the stacks of green disc notes in denominations of 500 and 750 million piled neatly from floor to ceiling, and the other piles that snaked into the adjacent smoking rooms, smaller dining rooms and halls.

Sa'am approached him.

"We've secured this side of the main house," he said. "All chiefs are reporting the same: the whole place is deserted, and the whole place is stuffed with greenies. We've scanned all points of the spectrum. No indications of any weapons, explosives, booby traps, nothing. The place is clean. Looks like Havok came here with the money, then split when he saw us coming."

"You really believe that, Sa'am?"

"No other explanation, Max."

"Nothing with this man has been as it seems. Order your men not to touch anything. We need to get another team in here to clear out the traps you missed."

"I didn't miss any traps, Max."

"That's yet to be determined. Order your men to do as I said."

"So where do you think Havok's gone?"

"I don't know."

"So what do we do in the meantime?"

"We wait."

Sa'am sighed impatiently.

"You heard Mr. Abernathé. We got to keep moving, find Havok! We got the money back!"

"We stay here. And we don't have the money back until it's all safely ensconced in Summa Avarici."

"And while we wait, Havok gets further away!"

Out of patience, Siniscolchi pulled Sa'am to the side. He spoke to him quietly.

"So what happened with Breufogle?"

"He's a damned fool! You yourself told me that the only way I was going to get anywhere with this company is to produce results. Be successful. I can't work for that guy, he doesn't know what he's doing, he wouldn't listen to me. Guy's a bigot, too. So I did some independent research. What's wrong with that?"

"You put your interests before the interests of the company, of Mr. Abernathé. Then you lied about it."

"I lied about nothing!"

"Sa'am, you haven't been to the picture room in weeks. You begged to be on Mr. Abernathé's security detail to the club, a detail that you once complained was beneath you. Then you tried to blackmail Havok."

"I only spoke to his lawyer! How did you know?"

"I didn't until now."

Sa'am cursed.

"You have no idea what it's like, Max, having fur on this planet."

"Don't give me that crap, Sa'am. There's no telling how badly you've hurt our dealings with Havok."

"You're overreacting, Max!"

"Am I?"

"Look, I tried to get some of the gravy, I admit it. It's the Lethean Way, you taught me that. I thought I could get a nice pay off from Havok, then get in good with Mr. Abernathé! It was win-win, don't you see? As powerful as Mr. Abernathé is, I never thought Havok wouldn't pay! What's the big deal, anyway?"

"The big deal, Sa'am, is that you undermined your boss and tried to blackmail a man with no soul, no shame. A man who would sooner kill you and your whole family than pay tribute."

"Look, I gave myself an out—and about that. I was never serious about going to the Charlie Squares."

"The Charlie Squares?" Siniscolchi shook his head bitterly. "Who else have you told about Aphelion?"

"No one!"

"I don't believe you, Sa'am."

"I promise you, Max! No one!

"There was no need for any of this, Sa'am. If you had come to me or Mr. Abernathé immediately, a simple demonstration of loyalty, you'd have been set for life."

"With the bounties you guys give out? No way."

"Are you really that dumb, Sa'am? You could've made Mr. Abernathé the richest man in The Web, given him the power to crush his enemies and he would've had you to thank for it. The gratitude of a man like that is worth more than anything you could've taken off Salestus Havok. Instead, you've made enemies of them both."

"Max—"

"And what was your plan for after you got your payout from Havok? What makes you think Mr. Abernathé would be so understanding or forgiving? Do you think either of them would just let you walk away? That they would ever stop looking for you until they found you and killed you?"

Sa'am stood there speechless, stunned at the rebuke.

Siniscolchi's headset crackled.

"Commander Alpha, this is Chief Alpha-Five."

He stepped away from Sa'am and partially into the hall. Sa'am growled softly and wandered back into the dining room. He surveyed the table with his rifle light.

"Go ahead, Alpha-Five," Siniscolchi said.

"Nothing of note to report, sir."

Siniscolchi continued to watch Sa'am. He felt angry and embarrassed at the same time. He recruited Sa'am, brought him into the organization, had high hopes for him. While he didn't truly betray Mr. Abernathé, he did put his own interests first. And that is what couldn't be tolerated. He couldn't let him leave here alive.

"All we've got lining all the rooms and halls are money and bread."

"Bread?"

"Yeah. At regular intervals. On tables, on the floor."

"Don't touch any of it, understood?"

"No problem there, sir. This whole place creeps me out."

"Stand by."

Siniscolchi walked back into the dining room. He'd have to deal with Sa'am first, then get a team out here to find a way to extract the green disc notes safely. He watched Sa'am's silhouette standing at the dining table.

Something about the bread gnawed at him. Why line the place with bread? He'd heard Young Lorenzo remark about a social event he attended here awhile ago. He claimed that Havok made some of the food himself.

"Sa'am," Siniscolchi called. "You and I outside. Now."

The macropian's silhouette paused, then Siniscolchi saw the glint of a knife in the light.

"Mr. Sa'am, do not cut that—"

Sa'am brought the knife down and cut into a thick loaf of bread.

The ensuing explosion ignited all the other loaves in the room. Jets of searing, orange flame swept through the halls of the main house. Wireless relay switches clicked as one concussive blast after another blew out all of the windows in succession, and fueled the expanding fireball that soon engulfed the entire building. Fire burned through room after room and flames licked hungrily at the shattered doorways and window frames. The intense heat collapsed the ceilings and walls, and reduced the Abernathé mercs and the Abernathé fortune to seared ash and dust.

Chapter 31
Aegis

A white aircar sped across the ocean and skimmed the waves at a dangerously low altitude. The car traveled at an unsafe speed, yawling dangerously at times, as the wind pushed the waves against the undercarriage. Only the expert hand of its driver prevented it from crashing into the hard water.

Salestus Havok sat in the driver's seat of his private car and his strong hands gripped the controls tightly. He resisted and overcame the natural forces that buffeted the vehicle, natural forces that would have killed any other operator. Today, he traveled alone. He steered the large car with a grim determination, his knuckles white, his hands slowly crushing the handles of the steering column. A fire burned in his belly and an unspeakable hatred darkened his eyes. Once he saw the rocks that marked the shores of the Barrier Peaks, he yanked violently on the steering column and sent the car screaming high into the air. His body strained against an ascent that would have driven a weaker man into unconsciousness. Spying Summa Avarici and then Castel Mons, he forced the car down and the engine screeched and shuddered from the effort. Noxious, acrid smoke trailed behind the car as it sped like a black laser toward the landing pad.

The aircar careened to a landing at an unsafe speed. The reckless approach sent personnel scrambling and diving for safety. The whine of the engines reached a fever pitch before fading. A cloud of black smoke engulfed the white vehicle. The tinted windows of the car hid any trace of movement inside.

Dozens of security personnel surrounded the car, pointing weapons. Stick Breufogle approached the car and looked it over suspiciously. After the wind cleared out the black smoke, everything remained completely still.

"Stand ready," he said.

Breufogle didn't like this situation at all. First, he received orders directly from Mr. Abernathé III telling him to kill whoever or whatever approached Castel Mons. Then, as this car approached, he received a panicked communication from Young Lorenzo informing him that he had invited Salestus Havok onto the premesis for business reasons and to treat him with every possible courtesy. He was even supposed to escort him personally down to the conference room. At first, a thrill went through Breufogle at the opportunity to meet the most mysterious of all Lethean Gentlemen. Now more than a bit apprehensive, he tightly gripped the pistol in the holster at his waist.

He released the safety.

The door to the car abruptly flew open and out stepped a very distinguished looking gentleman. He sported a finely tailored white suit and hat, complimented by spotless white shoes and gloves. He carried a white walking stick in one hand, topped with a gemstone cut into the unmistakable shape of the Abernathé family crest. Dark menacing eyes, shark like, stared out from under his white fedora, the brim pulled way down low. The intensity of his expression was accentuated by an iconic clean shaven jawline and the trademark long gray hair that billowed in the breeze. The ranks of armed men hesitated and confusion spread around the circle like a wave. Oblivious to all the guns pointed at him, Lorenzo de Abernathé II strode with a grim determination right up to Breufogle.

"Get the Blazes out of my way," the Finest Lethean Gentleman barked. "The lot of you get back to work! I'm not inclined to pay people to stand about and gawk!"

Breufogle stood resolute, but confused.

"I-I was not aware that you were out, today, uh, sir. I need to confirm this with Mr. Abernathé, I mean—"

"You mean my son? The one who's run my business into the ground? This is my home!" He pounded his walking stick on the ground. "This is my planet!" He turned and pointed the short end of his walking stick at the men standing all around him. The diamond sparkled in the sunlight. "You all work for me, or have you all forgotten that?"

The guards looked at each other in confusion, some lowering their weapons, some not. The FRO units each guard carried confirmed the identity of the man in front of them. No prosthetics, no make up and N-ray optics verified the absence of a holo mask.

Breufogle held up his hand.

"Just give me one minute to verify—"

"You," Abernathé seethed. He approached one of the guards and pointed at Breufogle. "Get him the Blazes out of my way!"

Hesitantly, the guard moved on Breufogle.

Flabbergasted, Breufogle screamed, "Get back to your post!"

"I can't do that, Mr. Breufogle. Mr. Abernathé gave me a direct order."

Abernathé glared with disgust at the circle of guards.

"What are the rest of you standing around for?!"

The guards slowly broke their circle and converged on Breufogle, taking his weapon. After pressing Breufogle's hands to the back of his head, they shoved him to the side. Abernathé tugged at his lapels. Self-satisfied, he strode briskly toward the elevator.

"You damned idiots," Breufogle shouted. "There's no way that can be Abernathé! Does he look 120 years old to you?"

"I'm sorry, Mr. Breufogle," one of the guards said. "I saw him on Suetonia the other day and he looked just like that."

"It's all over the news," another said. "The Deuce is back and running AbStone."

Abernathé stopped and pointed with his walking stick.

"You're damned right about that!" He put his right thumb into the elevator call slot. After the door opened obediently, all doubt left the guards. "You there! Put him on the elevator with me! It's all right, I can handle the likes of him."

"Sir, it's not safe."

"Don't you tell me what to do, you witless bastard!" He pointed at the empty elevator car with his walking stick. "Put him in there! Now!"

"You're making a mistake," Breufogle shouted as three men threw him into elevator. "This man is not who he says he is!"

"If he wasn't, Mr. Breufogle, then he wouldn't have gotten past the face recognition opticals or been able to call the elevator."

Abernathé stepped into the elevator with Breufogle and the doors closed.

Breufogle took a second weapon from his ankle.

"I don't know what this is all about, but it ends here," he said.

In a blur, Abernathé seized him by the throat with a gloved left hand and lifted him off the floor, pinning him against the wall. Breufogle struggled in vain.

"I know you," Abernathé said. He leaned in close, close enough for Breufogle to see into his pores. Abernathé peered at him curiously. "Yes." He nodded knowingly. "From Nostrova."

Then he flung Breufogle violently against the opposite wall, shaking the whole elevator car. Then he picked him up with both hands, by the head, and rammed his face repeatedly against the wall with all his considerable strength.

Angelica Smart-Scoreggia stood in the elevator lobby and waited patiently for Salestus Havok to arrive. Determined to finish this deal for the diamonds, which had morphed after recent events into a literal life and death transaction, Young Lorenzo had spared no expense, nor overlooked any minor detail, in anticipation of Mr. Havok's arrival. This included a familiar face greeting him off the elevator.

Angelica kept her personal reservations to herself, given the magnitude of what was at stake. Her last conversation with Havok still resonated in her mind, but she believed in what Young Lorenzo wanted to accomplish. Then, after today, she hoped to never see Salestus Havok ever again.

She still hadn't decided how she felt about Havok's declaration that he was really Pierce Sicuro. Her memory of Pierce had faded and she didn't have any holos of him. Even some of the things he said they'd done together, she had no clear recollection. Something about Havok had a dim familiarity, but this nonsense about being a clone was just ridiculous. At odd moments, she took long glances at Young Lorenzo and aside from bearing a striking resemblance to his grandfather, he did not remind her of Pierce. Obviously deranged, even delusional in some ways, she found Havok's fixation on her frightening. At times like this, she longed for Vincent. Vincent had his faults, many of them, but he loved her. Vincent would always protect her.

She was still getting used to seeing again. She found herself continuing to do things habitually as if she were still blind. The headaches from eye strain and bright lights could be crippling, but the doctors said it wouldn't last. She hid her disappointment over a lot of what she saw. She remembered colors being more vibrant, faces of familiar people in different ways, the way people moved, the shape of clothing…all different.

Her own travails aside, it had been a terrible few days for AbStone. Young Lorenzo believed that an imposter somehow fooled the bank and got away with all that money. She believed that as well, since she had been personally introduced to Young Lorenzo's grandfather and that man clearly did not have the mental capacity to orcheastrate such a financial transaction, much less his own lunch. All that lost money would amount to a drop in the bucket if this diamond distributorship deal could be consummated.

In spite of the integral role she played in these negotiations, she knew that she was rapidly approaching her expiration date with AbStone. Young Lorenzo worked hard at creating a false impression of her importance, which started with the rare privilege of meeting his grandfather. He needed her, but she needed him more, and they both knew it. She had attained some level of notoriety in the media for how everything ended at EU, which she still didn't understand. The story refused to die, like someone at Suetonia had a personal vendetta against her. Until this media firestorm died down, if it ever did, she needed this job. However, as soon as this deal with Havok was closed, she expected to be shown the door.

The elevator chimed and the display showed it coming down. Only a few more hours, she sighed. Only a few more hours on her best behavior and this whole thing would be over.

She heard the most curious thumping sound coming from the elevator. She put on her most vibrant smile as the elevator doors opened. She took a step forward and then recoiled in utter and abject horror.

Havok stood in the elevator, covered in blood. He wore a white suit and hat, and the insides of his arms and his chest down to his knees were soaked with blood. Streaks of red criss crossed his face and hat. In his gloved hands, he held the headless body of a man in a black suit. Blood dripped from the walls and ceiling like rain.

Too terrified to scream, she threw her arms up in the air and turned to run. Havok dropped the body in his grasp and pounced. His bloody hands fell on her in an instant.

"Now, all of a sudden, you can see perfectly," he hissed. He held onto her with one hand and while he tossed his white hat back into the elevator.

"Where are we meeting with Young Lorenzo," he seethed.

Her mouth agape, her eyes wide with terror, she couldn't find any words. She could only feebly shake her head.

His bloody gloves smeared her crisp business suit and his grip tightened. He inhaled gutterally and grabbed her by the lapels, and shook her violently.

"*Where* is Young Lorenzo," he growled.

She weakly pointed in the direction of the conference room. He sneered at her in a sinister, yet satisfied way and then tossed her aside like a bag of dirt. She skidded across the carpet and cried into her hands as he stormed off down the hall.

Young Lorenzo looked around the conference table and smiled in satisfaction. Everything was going to be perfect. Mr. Havok knew and trusted him. Angelica, the pretty face that he seemed smitten with. And all of his best anthropods, to expedite the business side of things as quickly and efficiently as possible. Then, after it was all done, he would take Havok upstairs to surprise his father with the news, and maybe even a visit to his grandfather. What a great day this would be, in the light of recent events.

He paced anxiously, eager to get started. He couldn't imagine a single thing that could derail his plan. Then he felt a sweltering pain in his gut, a twinge at first, but then like a twisting knife. As he steadied himself against the table, cold sweat beaded on his forehead and dripped down his face.

He tried to get control of himself. He forced himself to stand on his own two wobbly feet. He fixed his tie. What bad timing, to come down with an illness, and right at this moment! *Why did this always happen?* He hadn't felt this bad since he last visited Havok at Atro Viscus. He had no time to contemplate the irony. His belt comp vibrated at his waist. It was his father.

He wiped at the beaded sweat on his upper lip.

"Yes, Dad?"

"Lorenzo! You're in danger! You need to get out of there, now! There's been multiple security breaches. Come to my study, we're leaving here immediately!"

"A-all right," he said, stunned at the news. "As soon as Mr. Havok arrives, we'll both be—"

He looked up and Salestus Havok stood in the doorway, covered in blood. His wild eyes darted about the room and the anthropods skittered to the other side of the conference table.

"…be…"

"Forget Havok," his father's voice shouted over the comm. "He's the threat!" His father then clicked off.

Havok entered the room, his dark and angry eyes drinking in the occupants.

"Get out," he shouted.

He pointed at Young Lorenzo.

"Everyone out but him!"

The anthropods skittered and clicked out of the room in a frightened, but orderly fashion. The pain in Young Lorenzo's gut intensified. His trembling fingers dropped the belt comp and it clattered noisily on the marble table. He gaped at Havok as if seeing him for the first time.

"It was you," Young Lorenzo breathed. "At the Armarium. *It was you.*"

Havok nodded, his chest heaving.

"What have you—" Young Lorenzo paused and clutched at his stomach, grimacing.

"What have I done," Havok rasped. "What I should have done a long time ago."

"You won't leave here alive," Young Lorenzo gasped, sweating profusely. "I'll have… security…here in seconds."

Havok gestured at the belt comp on the table.

"Go ahead. Pick it up and call them."

Young Lorenzo stared at it, wide eyed. He didn't dare to move. He stood transfixed, trembling.

"Feeling sick, Lorenzo? The brackish claws tearing at your gut, the bile in your throat, the jelly in your legs?"

"I feel no—no such…thing!"

"Don't lie to me," Havok said, coming toward him. "That muddy brown stench? I feel it, too."

Young Lorenzo raised an enfeebled, quivering arm. As Havok got closer, he could see that his face also glistened with perspiration and that his movements were also a bit hesitant.

"Unlike you," Havok said, now standing face to face, "I'm used to it. At least I used to be."

"You—you look like me," he gasped, wincing, fighting his gag reflex.

"You mean *we* look like Lorenzo de Abernathé II."

Young Lorenzo looked at him, confused.

"What?"

"You need to get control of yourself," Havok breathed through clenched teeth. "Master the illness."

"Wh-What is this illness?"

He smiled ruefully.

"It's what we are."

"You keep saying 'we'. You—"

Havok peeled off his bloody gloves and tossed them aside. He held up his left hand.

"I have six fingers on my left hand. So do you."

Lorenzo glanced at his own hand.

"I do not! Five fingers. Five fingers, see?"

"Feel for the sixth knuckle on your left hand. Feel it?"

Lorenzo did as he insisted and his face paled even further.

Havok roughly pulled him upright.

"You and I need to go and see your...*father*," he demanded.

The elevator continued to ascend.

Young Lorenzo leaned against the wall, crestfallen. He felt a bit stronger, but not better.

"You mean you feel like this all the time," he asked.

"You get accustomed to it. You learn to live with it."

"You said if I took you to see my grandfather, you could prove all this?"

"Yes."

"Probably all a trick, to get close enough to kill him."

Havok sighed impatiently.

"You still doubt?"

"I think it more plausible that we are brothers, not...*clones*. I have a mother."

"Do you? What do you know of her?"

Young Lorenzo shrugged.

"Nothing, really. Just someone my father hired."

"And you accept that explanation?"

"And you want to be a Lethean Gentleman?"

"I thought I made myself clear."

"Yes," Young Lorenzo said, raising his voice. "My grandfather is trying to cheat death. My father held you prisoner. The clinic. Our fingers. This illness."

"And what memories do you have of your...*grandfather?* Fond ones? Or does the thought of him make you sick to your stomach?"

Young Lorenzo stood up straight and turned to Havok.

"I'll not have you talking about my grandfather, my family, in that manner."

"Or what?"

The blood still dripped from Havok's sleeves.

For a moment, Young Lorenzo stood firm, then his knees buckled. He grabbed the wall for support.

"So you feel like this all the time," he gasped.

"*All* the time."

The elevator doors opened. Security personnel lined the grand stone hall in pairs. The four nearest the elevator, two burly canites and two macropians, produced weapons but lowered them once they saw Young Lorenzo.

"Mr. Abernathé," one of the macropians said hurriedly, coming forward. "Your father is requesting—"

Then they saw Havok.

Weapons clicked all up and down the hall.

"Stop," Young Lorenzo shouted, holding up his arms. "It's alright, it's alright! Don't shoot!"

"My orders are to let no one but you pass, Mr. Abernathé."

Confusion spread all up and down the hall as the guards all got a better look at Havok.

"All of you get the Blazes out of my way," Havok shouted. "I'll not be treated like a criminal in my own house!" He charged out of the elevator and crossed the marble floored hall. "First it was a bunch of damned fools outside my car, and now this? I have business to attend to! I can't be disturbed by these barbarians storming my walls. My grandson and I have work to do and I want no distractions."

He brushed passed the stunned security people, Young Lorenzo following quickly. At the end of the hall, a plasmoid with three arms came out of a door, talking feverishly on his belt comp. As he looked up, his ganglia widened and darkened in surprise.

"What the—"

Havok picked up his pace, bearing down on the plasmoid.

"Kill him," the plasmoid shouted.

It dropped its belt comp and produced three lasers.

Havok grabbed the outstretched arm of the nearest guard and used the guard's own weapon to gun down the three other men nearest him. Then he flipped the guard over his back, over the railing, and his screams echoed as he plummeted down to the marble floor below.

The remaining guards tried to line up a shot on Havok, but Young Lorenzo stood in the way, lost in a daze in the middle of the hall, amidst the chaos. The plasmoid got off a couple of shots before Havok pinned it against the wall. Havok calmly took a hunting knife from under his suit coat and gutted the plasmoid. He let it slide to the floor in a pool of gel.

Havok turned, gelatinous syrup still dripping from his hands. A guard tackled the stunned Young Lorenzo to the floor and the others laced the hall with laser fire. Several bolts cut into Havok and he crumpled to his knees. After a slight wobble, he stood up again, holding a sawed off mag-shotgun. He lowered the barrel and discharged round after round. The concussive blasts from the magnetized shells shook the walls and floor. When the dust settled, the one remaining guard turned his back and shoved Young Lorenzo toward the wall. Without hesitation, Havok hefted his hunting knife again, then threw it. The twirling blade whizzed past Young Lorenzo's head and buried itself to the hilt between the guard's shoulder blades. The guard fell to the floor, his arms akwardly trying to reach the middle of his back, until he no longer had the strength.

Young Lorenzo stood shaking, his mouth agape at the horror that surrounded him.

"How? How...you haven't got a scratch on you."

Havok grabbed him by his jacket, shotgun still in one hand.

"Simple science. I'm wearing an omnisuit underneath."

"But nothing could withstand that!"

Havok looked at him matter of factly.

"My skin is like brick."

"Did it hurt?"

"Yes."

"How—?"

Havok pulled him to the door at the end of the hall.

"Because I'm a clone of Lorenzo de Abernathé II, just like you."

"But I don't have skin like brick."

"Then I guess I'm just lucky."

Sirens sounded in the distance and red lights flickered in the ceiling corners.

Havok smiled wickedly.

"Right on time."

Young Lorenzo gasped and looked around, alarmed.

"I've got to find my father!"

Havok shook him.

"You'll stay with me."

"Evacuation," he said quickly. "That light means evacuation!"

"No more running."

Havok leaned back and kicked the thick wooden door off its hinges. Chunks of wood thundered to the marble floor. Inside the room, the infirmed Lorenzo de Abernathé II lay in his bed, surrounded by the machines that kept him alive. Two caretakers, a doctor and a nurse, stood immobilized with fear. Next to them ranted an exasperated and angry Lorenzo de Abernathé III, who paused in mid-gesture at Havok's entrance. They were clearly involved in removing the elder Abernathé from the room.

A macropian guard jumped forward from the side and stood between Lorenzo and Havok, pointing a gun. The macropian's eyes flit from one identical face to the next and his brow furrowed in confusion.

"KILL HIM," Lorenzo shrieked. "KILL HIM!"

"Which one," the macropian shouted, "your fath—son, or—"

Havok lifted his weapon with one hand and pulled the trigger. The deafening report of the shotgun sent everyone scrambling and the macropian fell backwards, a five centimeter hole gaping in his chest.

Lorenzo screamed with fear and ran for the exit behind him.

"No, no, no, NO NO NO," he wailed, almost crying.

"Don't you move, Lorenzo," Havok shouted, calmly reloading the shotgun. "You stand where you are!"

Lorenzo froze, then ever so slowly turned around.

"Please," he begged. "*Please* don't kill me."

The lights went out and a moment later, the emergency lights clicked on. The distant siren quieted.

"You two," Havok said to the doctor and nurse. "Get out. Now."

Without hesitation they scurried from the room, not looking back.

Havok eyed Lorenzo closely as he clicked the shotgun barrels back into place. He then held the gun casually up against the front of his shoulder and paced patiently around Lorenzo.

"Please," Lorenzo pleaded. "We have to get out of here. There isn't much time."

"What are you talking about," Young Lorenzo asked. "Why?"

"Main power and the back ups are down," Lorenzo said quickly. He watched as Havok's shrewd, piercing eyes moved from him then to his father. "This room has an independent power source. We have to leave *now*."

"Why? Who are we running from," Young Lorenzo asked. "Surely it was Mr. Havok who triggered the alarms."

"He's talking about the Charlie Squares," Havok interrupted, now standing over Lorenzo's father.

Young Lorenzo didn't understand.

"Dad, how—"

"It seems," Havok answered, his voice distant, "that someone tipped them off to a weakness in Summa Avarici's defenses at the base of the Barrier Peaks."

Lorenzo squirmed a bit, then stepped toward Havok.

"You get away from my father!"

Havok froze him with a glance, his face glistening with sweat. He looked at Young Lorenzo.

"How are you feeling?"

"You know how I'm feeling," Young Lorenzo whispered.

"It helps not to fight it."

Young Lorenzo nodded hesitantly.

"What are you two talking about," Lorenzo demanded, his eyes darting back and forth. "Havok, you will answer me!"

"I'm talking about this," Havok shouted, shaking the bed violently. "Wake up, old man!"

The Old Man stirred, his eyes opening dully.

"W-what? Lorenzo?"

Havok grabbed him by his nightshirt with one hand and pulled him up, the old man's head lulling from side to side.

"Wake up," Havok shouted again, shaking him even harder.

Lorenzo started in again.

"You get away from—"

Havok froze him again with the shotgun.

"I've waited a lifetime for this moment, my son. None—"

"I am not your son!"

"NONE," Havok shouted over him, "NONE of your guards or retainers can help you now! It's just you and your three fathers! Time we had a father to father to father to son chat."

Lorenzo's jaw quivered.

"What is it you want?"

"Just to talk."

"But the Charlie Squares—"

"I'm not worried about the damned Charlie Squares! Or haven't you figured that out yet?"

Havok ripped the shoulder of the Old Man's nightshirt, revealing a square shaped birthmark.

"Can you see that," Havok asked Young Lorenzo.

He nodded.

"Yes. I have one just like it."

"Me, too." Havok glared at Lorenzo. "Do you?"

"There's no need for this," Lorenzo said quickly.

"No need," Havok exploded. "NO NEED?! You've been raising a clone of your father as your own son! Not man enough to produce your own offspring, Lorenzo?"

Lorenzo wilted a bit.

"You don't know what you're talking about."

"He's impotent," the Old Man said distantly. "My own son. Flaccid."

A smile forced its way through Havok's sneer.

"So that's it. Farmed out the rest, but kept one for yourself, was that it, Lorenzo?"

"Dad," Young Lorenzo whispered. "Is...is this all true? I—"

"You are my son," Lorenzo said emphatically. "That's all that matters!"

"No," Havok said, dropping the Old Man to the mattress. "That's not *all* that matters. You hated the old man, but wanted a son. And instead, your son is the old man. The irony is almost comical. You couldn't top the old man on your own, but you would get revenge by deliberately keeping his clone down, belittling it, dominating it, in the way you never could the original. You sent Young Lorenzo as far away from you as you could, and now that I forced him back on you, he threatens to eclipse you again by making a deal with me that you never could. All of your fathers conspiring against you. Such conflict, such frustration. It's why you kept undermining Young Lorenzo's efforts. And now, it's all for nothing. Neither of you will ever learn where the Ecks Stones came from, or will ever see one again."

Lorenzo flushed a dark red.

"You don't know anything. How dare you make such presumptions about my family."

"You mean *my* family, Lorenzo," Havok shouted, then pointed at Young Lorenzo. "*Our* family!"

"I don't understand why you harbor such anger," Lorenzo shouted back. "It was me who stopped them from cutting your head open! I shut down the cloning project and turned the science into something positive! I saved your life, you ungrateful bastard! And this is the thanks I get?"

"What kind of life," Havok screamed, coming at him and grabbing him roughly. "You destroyed my life! You killed the Sicuros! My parents, my brothers! Locked me in cage for ten years like an animal!"

Lorenzo cowered.

"T-that wasn't me! My father, James..." He recovered his courage. "Galvin only had to tell us where the Ecks Stones were! Then we would have left you alone!"

"And what about him? What about Galvin? You would have let him go, too?"

"Galvin was not the man you think he was."

Havok threw him to the floor.

"*I* am not the *man* you think I am!"

"Pierce, you have to understand that—"

Havok picked him up by the throat and pinned him against the wall.

"Don't you ever use that name! Do you understand *that*, my *son?!*"

Young Lorenzo stepped forward, finding strength in his legs. A normal color had returned to his face.

"So it's all true then," he breathed in disbelief.

Havok paused and both he and Lorenzo stared at him.

Young Lorenzo pulled at his hair and ran his hands over his face, then looked down at his whole body.

"Am I even real? I can't...I don't..." He leaned on a chair with both hands and vomited violently, his bile tinged with red.

Young Lorenzo wiped his mouth with the back of his hand.

"This whole thing is disgusting." He looked at Lorenzo. "I find you, this whole house, *disgusting*."

The Old Man cackled from his bed, a cackle that morphed into a raspy cough.

"These two, Lorenzo, are my true heirs. The real Abernathés. And you said I could never live forever!"

Havok dropped Lorenzo and walked over to the Old Man.

The Old Man smiled up at him.

"You look like me. You remind me of me. Of course you do. Come closer, let me look at you."

Havok stood transfixed. He ran his left hand, his six fingered hand, gently down the side of the Old Man's face, feeling the shape of it, intoxicated by the sensation. Then he wrapped that powerful hand around the Old Man's throat and crushed it. A wave of such blood red satisfaction washed over him and he savored the feel of the bone and tissue collapsing into gelly in his hand.

Young Lorenzo grabbed him from behind and pulled Havok away.

"What kind of monster are you," Young Lorenzo shouted. "Was that really necessary?"

Havok staggered a bit as the red darkened into black.

"*I* am necessary! Remember how you said this was all just a trick, for me to get close enough to kill him?"

"Clorox damn you to Blazes."

"You should trust your instincts."

"Clorox damn you!"

"No more talk of Clorox," Havok shouted. "Clorox is dead! And your grandfather killed him!"

"Damn you, Havok!"

"We can't deny what we are."

"I am not him!"

Young Lorenzo looked Havok up and down and turned away with contempt.

"Nor am I you," he said, dismissing him with a wave of his hand. He headed for the open doorway.

"Wait," Lorenzo called out. "It's not safe! We have to stay together. You're still my son."

Young Lorenzo paused, then turned.

"You used me to try and get to the Ecks Stones, to claim their wealth as your own, and yours alone. I undertand that. It's the Lethean Way. But that you kept me down on purpose? All the petty humiliations…that I was just some doll to torture because you couldn't live up to your own father? Couldn't live up to me? That's why you kept me away from Lethe all these years?"

"Lorenzo, no, that's not how it was, you were sickly, it's not…"

Young Lorenzo shook his head and slumped into a chair, his face buried in his hands.

A series of rapid explosions shook the building. Pieces of medical equipment clattered to the floor and dust poured from cracks in the ceiling. Gunfire and muffled shouts echoed up and down the halls.

Lorenzo got to his knees and pounded his fists on the marble floor.

"Clorox damn you to Blazes, Pierce Sicuro," he growled. "To Blazes!"

Havok surveyed all of the wreckage in the room and nodded. His mouth curled inward for a moment.

"Probably," he finally said. Then he turned to leave.

"That's it," Lorenzo screamed, standing up. "That's it?! Now you're just going to walk away?!"

Havok paused and reflected for a moment, then came back.

"You're right."

He took the shotgun and shot Lorenzo through the face. His head exploded and the headless torso fell to the floor with a sticky smack.

Havok looked at Young Lorenzo.

"You should leave. You don't want to be here when the Charlie Squares arrive."

Then, without a sound, he was gone. The broad shoulders of his white suit disappeared into the dark.

Chapter 32
End of Days

For the first time since before Havok, darkenss claimed the Lethean arctic. The aircar lot at the base of the train station stood abandoned. Some cars remained there, a few overturned and others with doors and trunks open. The protective barrier over the walkway to the train had been compromised and the carnivorous ravens now controlled it, cawing aggressively. The mag-lev train rested in the station, dark and tired. With no power coursing through the line, it laid half off the track, slumped at an angle. Blood stained the open doorways and platform, and the picked over skeletons of various animals occupied the shredded seats.

At the edge of the Third Circle, nature attacked the containement wall with a passive fury. Vines and grass had already penetrated the cracks and gaps in the artificial structure, determined to bring it down.

The empty buildings in the Second Circle were still sealed and unscathed, in exactly the same condition as they were upon evacuation. The wildlife that wandered the open streets patrolled the wide avenues cautiously, aggressively, and probed for ways to enter the protected structures.

In the center of the First Circle, the Tri-Towers, including the main residence, had partially crumbled. Black vapor swirled from the charred rock, ever upward, into a murky, leaden sky.

While many of the walls had collapsed into piles of rubble, the foundation remained intact. The clear outlines of the rooms and walls were easily recognizable. The once magnificent gardens had been trampled and scorched by fire, and chunks of scarred, broken stone marred the elegant design. Animals moved in and out of the towers, and prowled freely through the smoldering shells of two armored air fortresses. Scavengers fought over the cooked carrion of scores of decaying corpses.

The wind whistled through the empty spaces. Singed green disc notes fluttered and danced along the ground, caught on the hard breeze.

One of the few places to escape complete destruction in the First Circle were the private rooms of The Praetor. Deep cracks snaked through the stone walls and into the foundation. That the whole structure hadn't collapsed offered testament to its builders. Everything within had been damaged by smoke and fire, and the broken and tattered remnants of furniture only hinted at its former grace.

The Praetor was here.

Still clean shaven, he wore blue jeans and a brown leather jacket lacerated with a clean tear along the back. Across the room, the carcass of an enormous brown bruin lay on the floor, its head twisted and neck elongated. Flecks of brown leather were still in its claws.

Havok knelt on the floor behind a desk. He dug his fingers into a seam in the stones and removed a loose block. He reached into the hidden hole and removed a black fireproof box.

He stood to leave.

He didn't wish to remain here one moment longer. He wanted to be as far away from Atro Viscus as possible before he gave the order to allow everyone to return.

Then he considered the box.

It felt electric in his hands.

He stood absolutely still, listening and looking, straining his senses. Once certain that he was alone, he eagerly grabbed a chair and set it upright. With a sweep of an arm, he cleared all of the dust and debris from the desktop. He sat down, grinning like a child, and placed the black box in front of him. He took a silver canister from his jacket pocket and set it next to the box. He sat and stared at the box for a long time, running his hands over it, marveling at its touch. Anxious, bumbling fingers tripped the magnetic combination locks and removed the lid.

He looked around again, then put his hand into the box, like a mischevious child who had stolen a cookie jar. He removed the contents one item at a time and lined them up carefully in neat rows. He smiled in amazement at each object, fingering each one carefully and astonished at how they all still felt the same, as if savoring someone else's distant memory.

A small stuffed animal. An embroidered patch. A lopsided ceramic mug. A watch. A Moon laser. An engraved keychain. A toy car. A shining silver holo projector. One holodisc, and then another.

He stopped smiling when he came to the last item. A black knot settled in his stomach. He had forgotten about the disc. He held the disc in his left hand and thought for a moment about how easily he could snap it in half between his thumb and forefinger. Instead, he broke open the side of the desk and pulled out some of the wiring. He rummaged through a drawer, took out a laser clip and rigged a power source to charge the holo projector.

He thought again about the disc.

He couldn't recall the specific images on it and his curiosity was overwhelming. He put the disc in the projector. His left hand trembled a bit and the device squirted from his hand. He trapped it with his right, then turned it on.

After a brief hum, the first image exploded to life. His eyes grew wide in delight. It was an image of him at nine years old, after he'd been stuffed into warm clothes by his mother. How he hated that thermal shirt. He wanted to look cool, like Dante, not like a puffy dork.

The next two images had degraded and he couldn't make them out. Then a clear shot of his brothers, him hanging upside down on Dante's forearm, laughing giddily as his brothers laughed with him. He laughed out loud, remembering how it would make his mother crazy that they would always turn every picture into a circus act.

He flipped through a series of degraded images, just smatterings of color. Then, there he was, himself as a teenager, right after his brothers had returned from The War. He was in front, standing tall, smiling brightly. His brothers stood behind him, also smiling, but oddly, weakly. They looked tired. They looked old, their vitality drained, while he, in contrast, displayed such vigor. The image struck him to the marrow and he covered his frowning mouth with his right hand.

The next image was of his parents, his father holding his mother, laughing, trying to give her a kiss. She was smiling too, but playfully trying to get away. He remembered this day. It was a barbecue, a block party, celebrating the end of The War. He had captured this image. He smiled sadly through moistening eyes.

Then his reverie was rudely interrupted.

The track lights suddenly came on in the hall. A moment later, the graceful shape of Elisabéta Pascucci filled the doorway. The lights then came on in the room, dim at first, then brightening as she approached. She smiled in that soft, warm yellow way that she always did and spread her arms wide.

"Mr. Havok," she exclaimed, obviously both happy and relieved. "What a relief! I really thought we'd lost you this time!"

In the blink of an eye, he swept the desk clear of his personal items, sweeping them into the box. He fumbled with the holo projector, dropping it in last.

"What are you doing here," he snapped, embarrassed, wiping at his face and eyes. "It's not safe."

She smiled wryly and showed him a small gun.

"Safe enough, I think."

He shook his head and pointed behind her. She glanced uneasily at the bruin carcass, then nodded. She put her weapon away.

He sniffled a bit.

"You didn't answer my question."

"I landed with the advanced recovery team. I wanted to seal your personal rooms until you could be located or contacted. I was just doing a walk through."

"What team? I gave no such instructions."

She noted his red rimmed eyes and became serious. Her eyes settled on the black box, so he flipped the lid shut, but it wouldn't close. The silver canister didn't fit. He moved it to the side, out of her line of sight.

Distracted, she said, "I assumed—"

"I ordered this place evacuated."

"And it was."

"I gave no instruction for anyone to return. *Yet.*"

"I apologize, Mr. Havok. I assumed—"

His expression darkened.

"YOU ASSUMED TOO MUCH," he shouted, annoyed.

She was startled by his reaction. He rarely, if ever, shouted. She found his normal calm insistence intimidating by itself. He terrified her when he yelled.

Her face paled.

"I-I acted on precedent—"

"I don't care about the past," he whispered.

Flustered, she continued.

"*—given* your inclination to disappear for weeks or months at a time. With the reports coming out of Summa Avarici, I wasn't optimistic about your reappearance, with all the innuendo about Cathedral corporate assassins. I only sought your best interests."

"Best interests?" He seemed amused at the words. He sniffed and wiped at his nose, indifferent. "No matter. You're free to leave." He shrugged. "Everyone is free to leave. Or return. I won't be coming back here. Ever."

He stood up and swept the box up off the table.

His meaning suddenly became clear.

"A-am I *fired?*"

He paused.

"Yes. You and everyone else. The circumstances that required your employment no longer exist."

A chill went through her.

"Mr. Havok, you don't understand," she pleaded.

Incredulous, he shouted, "I don't understand?! *I* don't understand?!"

She backed away from him.

"Please listen to me," she said quickly. "The workers, the staff, the villagers, they only heard that you were in some kind of trouble. Without equivocation, everyone immediately volunteered to come back and help. *Everyone.*"

"It's too dangerous for them to be here."

"They were willing to bear the risk. They *begged* me to let them come."

"So?"

She sighed, flustered.

"They didn't build this place *for* you, Mr. Havok, they built it *with* you!"

"But I didn't build it for *them.* It's my city. I own it. I can do with it as I please."

"Mr. Havok—"

"I ordered it emptied. End of story."

"But Mr. Havok—"

"Stop," he shouted, already weary of the exchange.

She hesitated.

He finally relented.

"All right, then," he said. "The threat has passed. They can return now, if they choose to do so. And they can have Atro Viscus as their own. I don't need it anymore."

"Why are you running away," she sputtered, confused beyond exasperation. "This is your home!"

He swelled with anger.

"Home," he screamed. "This is not my home! There is nothing within these walls that is worth having!" He yelled at her so loudly, so forcefully, that she recoiled from the power of his voice. The curls of her hair blew about her forehead.

She thought things would be different now, now that all this business with AbStone was finally over. Indignant, she found her courage and pointed an angry finger back at him.

"Just because Angelica Scoreggia won't have you?! That woman loved a man who beat and blinded her! You would give a woman that weak and pathetic that much power over you?"

Flustered, he shouted, "Where do you get the gall to speak to me like this?! This is *my* planet!"

"*Your* planet? Do you hear yourself?"

He paused for a moment, his head ticking to the side akwardly.

"You've no idea what you're talking about, Elisabéta."

"I have *every* idea! There are people out there who have invested more than money, indeed their very lives, in Atro Viscus. Invested in your vision of this continent!"

"Then they should have looked to themselves rather than to me."

Exasperated, she searched her mind frantically for words that would give him pause, force him to stay.

"But *I* need you," she blurted akwardly. Her lower lip trembled. "A-And I-I want you to need *me*."

He rolled his eyes at her outburst. He sat down heavily, as if struck, the box on his lap.

She had been holding that in for a long time and it felt good to finally let it out. She didn't intend for it to be under these circumstances, but she was desperate to keep him from leaving.

"I'm sorry, Mr. Havok! I—"

He waved her silent. He pinched the bridge of his nose, then set his fist over his mouth.

"I just want to be left alone. I can't—I don't want to be needed by anyone."

She took a deep breath.

"When these people had nowhere else to go, you *gave* them someplace to go. When they had nothing else to believe in, you gave them something to believe in. You helped them when no one else would. Now all they want to do is return the favor."

"Don't you mean 'you'? All this talk of 'they'?"

"Me? It's not just about me. This is so much larger than me."

He shook his head.

"You couldn't be more wrong." He paused. "You'll find a generous severance in your expense account. You've been well taken care of."

She flushed a dark red. Literally shaking in her shoes, she put her hands on her hips and defiantly leaned in, standing nose to nose with him, the box on his lap between them.

"You think this is about money?! I've stayed loyally by your side all this time, *indulged* you, *protected* you from yourself, *ignored* your mercurial peculiarities, all because I thought you cared about me and everyone else you brought to this place! And I developed an affection for you in return. Everyone did. But not for money! Even when it became clear to me what your real purpose was in coming here! It hasn't been easy working for you, Mr. Havok. I'd like to say that it's been equally difficult being your friend, but I can't. I can't because you won't let me."

"Elisabéta—"

"I would still gladly become mistress of all this," she said, softening her tone. "Even though it's a monument to another woman. If only you'll let me."

He shook his head, again rubbing his temples.

"I—," he started, then shook his head. "You don't understand."

She nodded, angry again.

"Really?! I think it's all very clear! You failed to win Angelica Scoreggia! So now you're done with us! All of us, this place, a means to a useless end!" Each word struck him like a bullet, and he flinched painfully with each syllable.

He said nothing, staring blankly at a far off point. She paused for breath, still furious. She looked at the black box, furrowing her brow, then at the hole in the stone floor behind him.

He started to say something, then stopped.

"Please," he begged, almost quivering. "Stop shouting."

She stood aggressively over him, panting, her face flushed. She shook her head and blew a lock of hair from her face. For the first time ever, she felt strong in his presence.

Without looking at her, he asked, "Do you know why I sleep on the floor?"

"What has that got to do with—"

"Please." He took a deep breath, rubbing his temple with a thumb and forefinger. "Do you know?!"

She crossed her arms.

"No. How could I? You never explain anything."

Her weight rested on one leg.

He paused. He grappled with himself, his mind changing from moment to moment about whether to speak.

"My...*affinity*...for the indoors. It was destroyed when I was a young man."

She shook her head.

"Mr. Havok..."

"Indulge me, Elisabéta, please."

His eyes rounded and sagged. He opened the box and took an object in his right hand and gripped it tightly, as if drawing strength from it. His chest tightened. He seemed overwrought.

She relaxed her stance and her color slowly returned to normal.

"I'm listening."

"I'm not comfortable with this ongoing reverence, as someone who merely stumbled upon some valuable rocks."

"But it's what you've done since then. You are a finer gentleman than any Abernathé. *You* are the true measure of the Lethean Gentleman. Why can't you see that?"

He cringed, wounded.

"Man. Gentleman." He said the words as if he didn't like their taste. "An imitation of one, maybe." He was silent for a long moment. "I hesitate to agree."

She pushed a frustrated tongue into her cheek and raised her eyebrows, urging him to continue.

He placed the object in his right hand on the desk. It was a holo projector. He turned it on. An image of himself and Angelica appeared. He stared hard at the holo. He studied the shape of his own face, the curls in her hair, the rounded edges of her nose, his neck and chin. He found the faces unrecognizable.

"Where did you get that image," Elisabéta asked, amazed. "They're both so young!"

He started involuntarily.

"They?"

"Angelica Scoreggia, and even with the bad haircut, that's clearly Young Lorenzo."

"No," he corrected. "That's me."

She gasped.

"You look just like him!"

His expression darkened.

"I know." He fingered the base of the projector with his right hand, then leaned back, letting it go. "Images of strangers," he said ruefully. "No matter. It wasn't long after this image was taken that I got this scar on my face."

His eyes were vacant, as if remembering something that happened long ago. His eyes suddenly darted up at her, the penetrating gaze taking her in. His eyes grew wide and manic.

"I was locked away in a cage. For ten years. Did you know that?! For ten years, I was never in the dark! They *never* turned off the lights!"

"Why—"

"The Abernathés," he hissed. "For those diamonds! And for my…Because I was, I was…" He stood up shaking his head and waved his arms about. He tucked the box back under his arm. He walked briskly past her.

"Mr. Havok?"

He kept walking.

"Salestus!"

He marched for the door. She instinctively knew that if he reached the door, she would never see him again.

"Pierce!"

He stopped and turned on her.

Pointing an angry finger at her, he shouted, "Don't you ever speak that name!"

Inexplicably, he fell silent and didn't move.

Astonished, she gained more courage from his inaction.

"What you're doing is wrong, Pierce!"

"Wrong?" He screamed, infuriated. "What do you know about wrong?!"

"I know your leaving is wrong!"

"This!" He shouted, hefting the box. He threw it at her with his left hand. She ducked and tumbled to the floor, squealing in fright. The box exploded against the wall. "*This* is a box full of wrongs!"

The items scattered all over the floor. He scanned the debris, then picked up the holo projector with his left hand. He shoved her face into an image of Angelica.

"She was taken from me! WRONG!"

He banged the projector on the floor to change the images.

"My mother, killed! WRONG!"

"Mr. Havok, stop!"

"My father, shot and burned to death! My brothers—all murdered! WRONG! But I killed their killers! I killed them back! RIGHT! You see how simple it is?"

Elisabéta cowered on the floor at his rage. He knelt over her and continued to shout.

"They took away everything I loved, so I did the same to them. RIGHT! And then I killed them! RIGHT! They made an orphan out of me, I made an orphan of him! RIGHT! No one knows more about right and wrong than *I*." He grabbed her roughly by the shoulder, another image of Angelica appearing. "Get a good look at her! She married and stayed loyal to a disgusting, vile man! What was right about that? I was better! I was better than him! Her being with me, that was RIGHT!"

He dragged her in a circle across the floor by her elbow.

"Get a look at all these things," he shouted. "Relics from an unfinished life! A good life!"

"Please stop," she begged, sobbing. "Why are you doing this?"

"Because you wanted to know!"

"It doesn't have to be this way."

"BUT IT IS," he shrieked into her face.

She held one hand up to protect her face from the force of his anger and leaned back on the other.

"Are you still so desperate," he shouted, waving his arms all around, "still so desperate to be the *mistress* of all this wreckage?!"

She sobbed, out of breath.

"I just wanted you to love me. I did everything I could. I thought I could make you happy."

"How could you even begin to know about my happiness?!"

"I know enough that Angelica Scoreggia was not for you, the same way you knew her husband was not for her."

He started and stopped, then his anger popped like a balloon.

"But she was mine," he sobbed, tears welling up in his eyes. "She...*they* took her from me."

"You talk about her like she's a thing, to be possessed out of spite."

"You don't understand. He was hurting her. I had to get her away from him."

"Yes, someone did. But that was an excuse. You coveted the idea of her." She pointed to the image. "That idea."

"All this..." He cast his eyes about in despair. "It's all gone, then. All for nothing."

"No. Not for nothing. There are over five hundred people who would disagree. Let us, let me, be with you. We're your family now."

"If only you truly knew what I am."

"Tell me. *Show me.*"

He looked at her severely, his face taut. A long moment passed.

"All right."

He got on the floor next to her. He displayed the picture of Rocco and Saffron.

"Who are they," she asked, tucking her hair behind her ears. She put a hand on his shoulder.

He wriggled free of her hand.

"Don't touch me," he snapped. "I don't like to be touched."

She took her hand back and nodded quickly.

He took a deep breath, then gave his attention back to the image.

"Rocco and Saffron Sicuro. The people who raised me."

"They're not your parents?"

"I think of them that way, but..."

"Then who...?"

"My mother was a petri dish and my father a syringe."

"You underwent a cloning procedure when you were young?"

He didn't answer.

"Some kind of enhancement," she asked.

All of the stories about bio-engineering. Designer children. Some of this started making sense to her, but he would have been too young by her own estimates of his age.

"Something like that," he replied.

"Were you sick as a child?"

"Sick?" He pondered the word. "No, not as a child."

She didn't know what he meant by that. She turned her attention back to the image.

"Your mother. She's beautiful."

"Yes, she was."

Then a picture of Saffron holding him as a baby. Rocco held them both in his arms, Dante, Alex and Nino, all around them, smiling.

She smiled brightly, wiping at her eyes.

"What nice people! Which one was Eiger?"

"Eiger?!" He raged. "Eiger?!" His eyes welled up with tears. "Don't...don't ever...*Eiger* was me. He was like me."

"Like what?"

"A...A..." He paused, tongue tied, then spat a single word. "*Monster.*"

Elisabéta, guardedly confused, asked, "What happened to them?"

"They're dead. They were all murdered. Burned to death. In a fire so hot, it cooked their skin, charred their bones. Burned to death! Can you conceive of such heat? Such pain? Can you imagine surviving? Living with that pain, that memory, every day?"

She fumbled for words, her mouth agape.

"I-I'm sorry. How—"

"*Abernathé,*" he hissed, transfixed on the image.

"Which one? II or III?"

He looked at her with an intense anger.

"*Both.* Then they locked me in a box."

Horrified, she kept perfectly still, afraid to react.

"After what they did, how could I not kill them?" He nodded at her. "That's right. I killed them. I killed them with these two hands." He sat quietly for a moment. "Corporate assassins? You really believed that?"

She warily backed away from him, still on the floor, unsure of what to say.

"I...killed...them," he said slowly, emphatically. *"I killed them all."*

She sat up on her knees, biting her lower lip.

"Does that frighten you, Elisabéta?"

She nodded nervously.

"And if I cross you, will you kill me, too?"

"You're not listening," he said, pounding his fist into his knee, transfixed on the image. "I killed them because they killed my family. Because they killed me."

She inhaled sharply and covered her mouth with her hand, coming to a sudden realization.

"Lorenzo II! That's why no one at the bank stopped you!" She looked at him as if seeing him for the first time. "You *and* Eiger!"

He glanced at her darkly.

"Yes. And Young Lorenzo. And the Sfondato Hospital—"

"It was a cover for the science that created you!"

He nodded.

Her perception of him instantly changed. She was now more afraid of him than ever before.

"I thought if I killed them, I thought if I made them suffer, it would be better. My father, my brothers, they would understand. But my mother, she wouldn't. She believed so strongly in forgiveness." He rubbed his face, clearly tormented. "But my mother, Peroxide bless her, was wrong. I built this place, tamed this continent, like I tamed the opposite pole, not for her, but for Angelica. For Angelica! Everything was built to her liking, and still...she loved that son of a bitch *instead!*"

Her hand still over her mouth, she whispered, "You killed Scoreggia too?"

"You're damn right I did," he shrieked gutterally. "And Eiger, Eiger who, who—" Tears welled up in his eyes, rolling down his

face. "Poor Eiger, he just couldn't understand what it meant, what *I* meant, what *she* meant…*He just didn't understand.*"

She stood up and wiped at the dust on her clothes, wiping at her mascara with her sleeves. She nodded, sniffling.

"Eiger, too, then."

"Yes," he shouted from his knees. "Eiger, too! You have no idea what it was like, having a madman constantly at your throat!"

He picked up a purple, diecast metal car that said 'Pierce's Collectibles' in cursive on the doors. He pushed it a few centimeters along the floor with his right hand.

Sobbing, through teary eyes, he said, "We…we used to have a carpet in our living room, it had a red and black pattern. I used to drive my cars on it. My Dad would get so mad at me when he'd step on them with his bare feet…" He wept bitter tears, then unwittingly crushed the toy in his left hand.

On his knees, he wept uncontrollably in great heaving moans. She stood over him, her arms folded, two words flip flopping in her mind.

Monster. Inhuman.

A dozen reasons immediately occurred to her to run from here, to run as far away as possible, but for his pain. There was nothing inhuman about his pain. She sensed that she no longer had anything to fear from him. She put her hands on his shoulders, tentatively at first. When he didn't object, she let them rest firmly.

"I still won't leave," she said. "This can all be repaired. Rebuilt."

He grabbed her hand with his left and her touch somehow stayed his torment. He wiped at both of his eyes with the crook of his elbow.

She sat down on her knees next to him and put her hand over the scarred side of his face.

"And you're right. I don't work for you anymore."

She looked deep into his eyes and saw only a man, not a monster.

He nodded, smiling weakly through his grief, wiping his nose.

He cast his eyes down and surveyed the objects all around them on the floor. He spied the canister and in an instant, he became sad again. He picked up the other silver disc.

"What's that," she asked.

"It's…it belonged to someone else," he said distantly. He looked at her and his face again became hard. He broke free of her embrace and headed for the door.

"Where are you going," she said, chasing after him.

"It's still not right. This is not how it's supposed to be."

"Stay here and—"

"No. I've been remiss. Careless." He shook his head ruefully. "This isn't over. I still have another debt to repay."

"How," she shouted desperately. "From what you told me, there's no one left to hurt you!"

He stopped and quickly turned on her.

"It's still not finished."

Exasperated, she said, "So when does this all end?"

"End?" He grit his teeth. *"Nothing ever just ends."*

"It will if you let it."

His eyes bulged in rage.

"I will persist, *I will live*, for as long as I need to. It is my *right.*"

"Please stay here with me."

He frowned angrily.

"I can't ignore this."

"Promise me you'll come back."

"Elisabéta—"

"Promise me."

He fingered his left hand with his right, then held it up for her to see. He flexed his six fingers and smiled sadly.

And then he was gone.

She stood alone, her eyes cast down upon the floor, now suddenly cold. She looked over the scattered remains of Pierce Sicuro for a long time, trying to make some sense of the odd collection of keepsakes.

She picked up the dented box and gathered the items one at a time. She placed them carefully back into the box, all save the silver canister, which she put to the side as it didn't fit. As best she could, she put the pieces of the lid back into place.

For when he came back.

He always came back.

She shivered in the stillness and wept angry, bitter tears.

Epilogue

Max Siniscolchi made his way across the Annaraka'raka'rakis Omni Station, the transit hub at the center of the Metropolia dell'Elsasser. The crowds of finely dressed Letheans parted with overt disgust to let him pass. He limped along, leaning heavily on a metal cane. The right side of his body had been badly burned and it had not been treated nor bandaged properly. The long concourses and grand staircases proved a great challenge to traverse, and not a single person acknowledged him or offered to help.

Not that he expected any. It wasn't the Lethean Way.

Siniscolchi had a simple goal this day. It amounted to nothing more complicated than to get off this planet. Once someplace else, anyplace else, he could seek proper medical care. He had only a few green disc notes and couldn't afford to see a doctor here on Lethe. He had spent the bulk of his resources on securing off world passage. He didn't dare access any of his accounts ever again. He would get off this planet, get fixed up, then get rich with a quick trip to the Aphelion Binary System.

So far, he had managed to elude the Cathedrals. He admired his own ingenuity at making it this far. Of course, it helped that they were searching for an uninjured man, and that his face had been so badly mutilated that he was unrecognizable.

He limped through the gate and gave his boarding pass to a repulsed clerk. He walked by a Web soldier, soldiers who seemed to be everywhere in their navy blue uniforms these days. Blue

Balls, the locals called them. A black visor obscured the soldier's eyes as his head moved from side to side, scanning anyone within his line of sight with face recognition optics. The Web insisted on additional security during The War and had continued the practice in many places well after. Letheans openly resented their presence and avoided commercial transport whenever possible.

The soldier looked right at him and then looked away. Emboldened at his success, Siniscolchi limped into the waiting area and sat down. Everyone else quickly got up and moved to the other side of the room. He stared eagerly out the window as his car, a bi-pi'into, landed and pulled up to the gate. It was hardly glamorous transportation, but it served its purpose. He had spent too much time with the Abernathés of this galaxy. He let himself get soft and overly consumed with pretense and aesthetics.

His escape from the fire at Atro Viscus he ascribed to either dumb luck or divine intervention. Without a doubt, the place was loaded with traps, but he never suspected the bread as the trigger. He should have evacuated the area immediately. Everything Havok did was old school and it kept him one step ahead the whole time. Not anymore. He knew all of the secrets of Salestus Havok now. He would have his revenge, but not for Abernathé. For himself. Nobody did this to Max Siniscolchi and got away with it.

The boarding sign turned from red to green. Everyone in the room stood up and gathered their things. No sign of the Charlie Squares.

Good.

Siniscolchi stood up, then was pulled back down by a strong hand.

A distinguished old man sat down next to him, dressed in a gray suit and trenchcoat. He took off his hat and put in on his lap. Siniscolchi regcognized James Class, former Web Administrator for Intelligence, spymaster, and creator of the political officer ranks.

"I see you got your eye on that bi-pi'into, Max. You don't mind if I call you Max, do you? I didn't think so. I wouldn't get on one of those things, Max. Suicide sleds are what they are. Military used them back in The War, but decommissioned all of them because of the vulnerability of the fuel tanks. You ever see one of those things blow? It'd take out this entire platform."

Siniscolchi stood up.

"You'll have to excuse me. I have a flight to board."

"Yes, you certainly do, but not that one." He pointed out the far window. "You're getting on that one." A ship with official Web markings idled ominously. "Besides, Max, you look like you've had a rough couple of days. I can't let you get into a bi-pi'into in your condition. Must be tough times for your boss if the great Max Siniscolchi is slumming it on commercial transportation."

Max sat back down.

"Who are you, exactly?"

"My name is James Class. I'm a special advisor to the Executive Officer."

"You have no jurisdiction here."

"Are you guilty of something?"

"I'm leaving now."

Dark figures in suits blocked the exits, badges shining on their lapels.

"Yes, but with me."

"You can't do this."

"Who's going to stop me?" He looked around and his face hardened. "Maxwell Siniscolchi, you're under arrest. You blackmailed the government with knowledge of a hoax and suborned a serious breach of Web security. Failure to cooperate at this time can and will be construed as tacit verification of your guilt in this matter. You are entitled to counsel. You have the right to stand silent against self-incrimination. Do you understand what I've just said to you?"

"Yes. And you can't prove any of it."

"Really? The government has seized all of the assets of Abernathé Stoneworks and the Abnerathe family. We have a number of people in custody who are more than willing to tell everything they know, and to show us a number of things that I'm sure you'd like to keep hidden, like transparent, plastic steel cages."

"You have no evidence."

"The government has plenty of evidence and witnesses to make their case against AbStone. The Cathedrals proved very helpful in pointing out a lot of these things, too. AbStone's not the first company to take on the Cathedral Corporation and then get shredded into dogfood. It won't be the last, either. You see, the government likes the Cathedrals. They cooperate."

"So what do you want with me, then?"

"We need someone to tie all of this together in a nice, neat bow. You're going to be the government's star witness."

"I'm not going to tell you anything."

"Too bad. Then you'll never see the light of day again."

"I have rights."

"No one's going to be missing you, Max. And I have the authority to detain you for as long as I like. You and my interrogators are going to spend some quality time together."

The PO's guarding the door allowed a single man to enter. He was clean shaven and long dark hair puffed out under his fedora, the brim pulled down over his face. He looked up and those icey, soulless eyes, those black shark eyes, chilled Siniscolchi to the marrow. The edges of a deep scar in the side of his face burned a dark red.

He sat down on the other side of Siniscolchi.

"You know Salestus Havok, don't you, Max?" Class asked.

"Of course he does," Havok said. "We were in each other's company for a great number of years."

"I'm at my wit's end with this one, Mr. Havok," Class sighed. "He simply refuses to cooperate, and for the life of me, I can't convince him to change his mind."

"Hmm. Perhaps I can be of service to the government. I have some knowledge of burn victims, just how painful it is to be cooked alive. Leave him in my care and I'm confidant that I can rehabilitate him, and in the process extract the information you require."

"Mr. Havok, I couldn't impose on you like that."

"It would be no imposition at all." He put a strong hand on Siniscolchi's shoulder and squeezed until it hurt. "I would consider it an honor."

At a signal from Class, additional officers entered the room.

"Allow my people to escort him to your ship. It's the least I can do."

"By all means."

Siniscolchi was yanked to his feet.

"You can't do this," Siniscolchi shouted. "Mr. Class, this man has threatened my life in the past! He's also a killer and a thief!"

"Mr. Havok is a licensed and vetted defense contractor," Class replied. "He has my respect and confidence."

Huffing and puffing, Siniscolchi was dragged out.

Class and Havok sat quietly in the empty room, neither man speaking. They watched through the windows as Siniscolchi was forcibly put on Havok's private ship.

Havok sighed deeply.

"You're sure you don't need him?"

"I meant what I said," Class responded. "The government's case is solid without him. In fact, he would hurt it. Nobody really wants all of this mess exposed."

"I understand."

Class looked at him.

"You have the disc?"

Havok nodded. He took a silver disc from his coat and held it up with two fingers.

"And Rhonda's on this," Class asked.

Havok nodded again.

"Yes. I firmly believe you will find it very enlightening."

Class took the disc and put it in his coat pocket.

"Then I guess we're done."

They both stood up and shook hands.

"I could lose my pension for this," Class said uneasily. "Go to prison." He paused. "Do I want to know what's going to happen to him?"

"No need to worry."

"Right," Class said sarcastically. He shifted his weight akwardly. "I can't thank you enough for giving me my daughter back."

"I'm not the one you should be thanking for that."

"Still..."

"And I expect you to hold up your end. You will see to it that Zoeicelli K Galvin's reputation, and that of his associates, is fully restored."

"And why would I want to do that?"

"Rhonda will explain it to you. Do I have your word?"

"You do."

"Or Siniscolchi will magically reappear."

"No need to worry."

Havok nodded. He pulled down the brim of his hat and left the waiting area.

Class watched him go.

END